THE WIFE IN THE *Attic*

ROSE LERNER

THE WIFE IN THE ATTIC
Copyright © 2021 by Susan Roth
ISBN: 9798510174953

Cover by Kanaxa

This book is a work of fiction. The names, characters, places, and incidents are products of the writer's imagination or have been used fictitiously. Any resemblance to actual persons, living or dead, or actual events is entirely coincidental.

All rights reserved. This book or any portion thereof may not be reproduced in any form or by any electronic or mechanical means, including information storage and retrieval systems, without written permission from the author, except for the use of brief quotations in a book review.

RoseLerner.com

Table of Contents

Acknowledgments 6
Chapter 1 9
Chapter 2 17
Chapter 3 23
Chapter 4 31
Chapter 5 36
Chapter 6 43
Chapter 7 51
Chapter 8 70
Chapter 9 80
Chapter 10 90
Chapter 11 97
Chapter 12 111
Chapter 13 119
Chapter 14 132
Chapter 15 138
Chapter 16 145
Chapter 17 160

Chapter 18 171
Chapter 19 179
Chapter 20 189
Chapter 21 194
Chapter 22 205
Chapter 23 216
Chapter 24 230
Chapter 25 240
Chapter 26 248
Chapter 27 257
Chapter 28 264
Chapter 29 276
Chapter 30 286
Chapter 31 292
Chapter 32 298
Chapter 33 306
Chapter 34 317
Chapter 35 334
Chapter 36 339
Chapter 37 351
Chapter 38 358
Chapter 39 368

Author's Note 379

EXCERPT: *Sweet Disorder* 381

for
Brites Coutinho ז״ל
and
Fernando de Medina הי״ד

Acknowledgments

I know I will forget to thank at least one very important person. You know who you are: thank you. I am grateful for your help. I am grateful to have more wonderful people in my life than I can easily hold in my head all at once.

The people I do remember:

Allison Carroll, my editor at Audible. You are brilliant, and I'm glad this was the project we finally got to work on together. Everyone at Audible who contributed to the audiobook at every stage: casting, production, design, editing, merchandising, music, and more. My narrator, Elsa Lepecki Bean, who brought my story to life. What we all created together is beyond my wildest dreams.

Erica Ridley, the virtual coworker I never knew I needed. Theresa Romain, Tiffany Ruzicki, Dr. Angela Toscano, Aleksei Valentín, and Olivia Waite, all of whom gave very helpful feedback; Aleksei also fixed the Portuguese. Keith Tinkler, who kindly shared his meteorological knowledge and historical weather data with me.

My esteemed Patreon patrons: I can never thank you obsequiously enough.

Katherine Locke, who helped with my pitch. Kim Runciman, the best copyeditor in the world, and Matt Youngmark, the best formatter. My fabulous cover artists, Kanaxa (ebook and paperback cover) and Sarah Brody (Audible and hardback cover).

Jellybones Jones (if that *is* your real name)—you were just a baby when I started writing this novel, and you're already writing novels of your own!

My aunt Bev Richard, a child psychologist who was beyond generous with her professional expertise. You are the realest doctor I know. My uncle

David, who answered endless questions about houses, house construction, and other, more spoiler-y subjects.

My mom, who read me *Jane Eyre* when I was ten and taught me most of the really important things I know (including about the mental health care system's history of injustices and misogyny). You've been gone for fifteen years, and I'm still learning from you.

All the queer and Jewish scholars, who help us remember the truth.

And finally: all the survivors, and all the people who didn't make it.

Thank you.

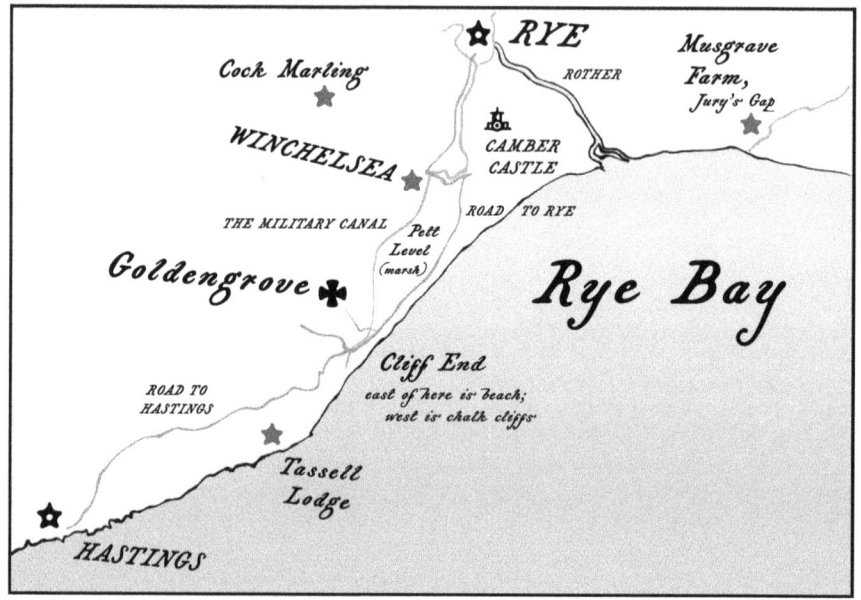

For detailed floor plans of Goldengrove, see smarturl.it/wife-maps

1

April 16, 1813 (Good Friday)
Lively St. Lemeston, West Sussex

Already I couldn't get any air. I knew it would be better to breathe in the smoke and suffocate before the fire reached my toes, but I couldn't. I lacked the strength even to turn my head away as heat kissed my face and the flames licked closer, closer…

I bolted upright, drenched in sweat, my heart pounding and the sheets tangled around my legs. I checked the bedside table and the hearth, but no candle burned, no coal smoldered. Only a few rays of pale moonlight lit my drab little room; no shade of red or yellow intruded.

It was barely three o'clock, with no chance of breakfast until half past eight, but I knew from long experience I wouldn't sleep again. I would be bone-tired all day, and it served me right for putting the extra blanket on the bed. I knew better, but I'd been so sick of shivering through the night, feeling the cold seep through my skin to the core of me.

It was too early to practice my guitar without waking Mrs. Humphrey's other boarders, and any other employment would require light. I couldn't bring myself to use my tinderbox. A candle would be all right once it was lit, a small friendly flame safely housed in Papa's old mica sea lantern, but striking the uncontrolled sparks…

In an hour, I promised myself. In an hour I would forget the nightmare, light the damn candle, and read *The Miseries of an Heiress*.

It would be a relief to immerse myself in miseries so entirely removed from mine. My own father, though his pension had supported us while he lived, had left me barely enough to pay for his funeral and a few new words on my mother's old stone. That out of the way, my inheritance came to:

the lantern; Papa's second-best wooden leg, currently serving as a hatstand; mãe's guitar, a plain but sturdy instrument I kept for my students to learn upon; and a handful of odds and ends.

I never lit the candle. I had bought foul-smelling lard candles that week, anyway, not having the extra penny for the tallow we had always used at home. I lay in my bed watching dawn creep across the warped boards in the ceiling, and at a quarter past eight dressed in a hurry and went down to the dining-room. I could immediately smell that the porridge was burnt.

Breakfast at Mrs. Humphrey's had never been plentiful or well-seasoned, but these last few months were a new nadir. We'd lost our maid-of-all-work, Sukey, just before Christmas, and I missed her heartily. Since then we'd been through six servants, and I felt certain the newest one would burn the house to the ground one fine day.

Of course Mrs. Humphrey didn't mind. When the porridge was scorched, we ate less of it.

Iphigenia Lemmon pushed her spice-box towards me. I took as much of her salt as conscience would allow, and together we choked the oatmeal down. Some days, this ritual amused me. Today, I saw a thousand such mornings stretched out ahead of me, thin and gray and unappetizing.

The maid-of-all-work in question brought in a folded note. Beside me, Miss Starling's fingers tightened on her spoon as though she might leap up from the table and stab the girl with it.

The note was held out to *me*. "What answer shall I give Lady Tassell's footman, ma'am? He's waiting."

I was so surprised I did not at once take it. Miss Starling set down her spoon to snatch and open the paper, for it was unsealed.

Iphigenia, reaching across my place at the table, read it next. "Ooh, lucky!"

She passed it to me. In a hastily elegant scrawl, it read:

Miss Oliver,
I shall be at the Lost Bell all morning. If you will be so good as to attend me there, I hope to be the means of doing you a service—
Yrs. v. sincerely, &c.,
Diana Tassell

"What do you think the service is?" Miss Starling asked, eyes bright.

"Maybe she has a husband for you," Iffy suggested. "Why not? She tried it with Phoebe Dymond."

"She must know of a child in town who wants to learn the guitar," I said tiredly, too out of sorts this morning to enjoy the game.

Smiles fading, my friends shrugged and turned back to their burnt breakfasts. A hollowness in my chest joined the hollowness in my stomach.

The Earl and Countess of Tassell were the Whig patrons of Lively St. Lemeston, here during Parliament's brief Easter recess to glad-hand, scatter largesse, and celebrate Holy Week. Even in their absence (which encompassed much of the year), their agent in the borough was kept very busy paying for funerals and finding apprenticeships for supporters of the local Whig party.

"Maybe her ladyship will have a collation laid out," Iphigenia said dreamily.

My spoon hovered over my bowl. Bad porridge was sure, a collation a faint hope. "Do you think she'll be in a generous mood? Last autumn's election was expensive *and* a failure."

Her eyes crinkled. "She's probably throwing good money after bad. People do."

I laughed. Iphigenia had always been an optimist, after her own cynical fashion. I was not, but if I was offered breakfast at the Lost Bell and was too full of oats to eat it, I would kick myself all week.

I pushed back my bowl—and poor Iphigenia pulled it towards herself. "It wouldn't do to keep her ladyship waiting," I said. "Please tell her footman I'll come straightaway."

Despite the early hour, the sidewalks and streets were thronged. Lent was the Sussex marbles season, and today's noon church bells would stop it short. Holding my skirts out of the mud—I wore every petticoat I owned against the cold, and washing-day was days away—I skirted chalked circles ringed with men and boys, competing with raucous good cheer and the occasional heated dispute.

Meanwhile, the local women skipped rope, a whole group on one long line swung by two people. They chanted and sang and laughed, cheeks rosy and eyes bright in the damp morning.

Lord Tassell and some of the other borough patrons joined in the marbles, heedless of muddy knees. But no ladies of equal rank joined the skipping, as they had when I was a girl. Lydia Cahill merely watched her husband's game, arms swallowed by her enormous muff; she would not even blow on his taw for luck until she had demurred for long moments, blushing. It seemed that spring grew chillier and the town's ladies more decorous with each year that went by.

I glanced down to be sure I was not lifting my petticoats too far out of the mud, and showing too much ankle.

At last I reached the Lost Bell. With so many people out-of-doors I had expected to find the coaching inn empty, but petitioners of every age and sex loitered in the corridor outside the countess's private parlor—some bored, some eager, and some desperate.

I hoped I was not one of the latter.

Yes, I was undeniably shabby-genteel in my faded pelisse and yellowing gloves. Yes, the soles of my boots were cracking. Yes, guitar pupils were in short supply. But I had paid my rent on Lady Day.

Barely, a scrupulous voice inside me amended. If I lost two pupils more, I might not manage it at Midsummer. And Mrs. Humphrey accepted nothing but cash in hand.

I pushed the thought away and stood straighter, hoping no one heard my stomach rumble at the smell of food wafting from the taproom.

At last a woman with ink-stained fingers asked me my business with Lady Tassell. I could not help evaluating her as she checked my note against her memorandum book and ushered me into the august presence: unruly hair, but blonde; not English, but her accent was refined—Scottish at the worst; not beautiful, but her features pale and delicate; not young, but likely no older than my own thirty-four. I would have thought her a nobody if I passed her on the street. What had recommended her for her good position, and guaranteed her hearty meals and new clothes?

Quickly averting my gaze from the groaning sideboard, I sank into the deep curtsy due a countess.

Clinging to gentility by your fingernails! the voice said, scornful now. At boarding school, we had been led to imagine adorning ballrooms with our accomplishments, not trading upon them in rented offices. Alas, it developed that balancing a book on one's head was a profitable talent for a trained bear, not a woman.

Lady Tassell smiled, gesturing at the food. "Please, help yourself."

Magic words! Probably she had seen my eyes fly greedily to the spread, but shame could not overshadow my pleasure. I filled my plate with hot buttered toast, smoked herring, marmalade—

"The ham is particularly fine," she said.

I pretended I hadn't heard, cutting myself two generous slices of hard local cheese and hurrying to take the hard chair placed opposite Lady Tassell's writing table. Balancing my plate awkwardly on my knees, I bit into my toast with exquisite joy. When had I last eaten white bread?

Lady Tassell poured a cup of chocolate from a pot at her elbow. I did not dare hope. I did not dare look at the cup.

She slid it towards me.

My fingers shook with eagerness as I picked it up. I hoped she thought it nerves.

Ohhh... Bittersweet chocolate and rich cream caressed my tongue, whispering of lemon, cinnamon, and cloves. It lingered in my throat like Romeo in Juliet's bed. I inhaled the steam, despising Mrs. Humphrey's weak tea with all my heart.

"You have a lovely smile," Lady Tassell said.

I wiped it from my face at once. Did the countess know that was the secret hope of every plain woman—that some Midas touch in her smile would transform her narrow face, long nose, and limp, mousy hair? But no change of expression could render me lovely. When I was solemn my lips were too full for English fashion, and my smile bared horsey Oliver teeth. I was grateful enough for a new pupil without flattery.

But it would be unladylike to say so. "Thank you, my lady, you are very kind."

"You grew up in Portsmouth, didn't you? Are you fond of the sea?"

"Yes, my lady," I said, wondering at the question. "We came here when I was thirteen, after my mother died."

I rarely thought of the sea these days, but as a girl I had loved to walk along the harbor in good and ill weather, watching the men at work in the boats. My mother and I had shared a passion for combing the beach for shards of glass and pottery, worn smooth by the terrible endless friction of the waves. There was nothing so vast in Lively St. Lemeston. Low green hills bounded the horizon close on every side, and the River Arun barely deserved the title.

Yet I knew Lively St. Lemeston would wear me smooth and small enough in its time.

"Tassell Hall is only six or seven miles from the coast, but it's too far to smell the sea," Lady Tassell remarked. "At our lodge in Rye Bay, you can see the cliffs from the front windows."

I made a polite noise and took another sip of chocolate.

"One of my Rye Bay neighbors wants a governess for his little girl. I could think of no one else qualified for the role, who might be brave enough to travel so far from home. You have always struck me as a self-reliant young woman."

This was flattery, too—more dangerous than the first. If Lady Tassell truly thought me pretty, she would never recommend me for a governess. Iphigenia, more scholarly and accomplished, had been refused half a dozen such posts over the years, precisely for her incandescent beauty.

But self-reliant? I could almost believe that of myself. I crunched my toast smugly between my big Oliver teeth.

I should have been wary. I should have known better than to think a little independence of spirit could arm me against all the danger of the wide world. But I was seduced by salt and sugar, chocolate and white flour.

"The pay is twenty-five guineas per annum, with room and board. I am told the child is obedient enough, though she's struck me as a little peculiar." The countess chuckled. "But what child isn't peculiar?"

I smiled back, mentally turning over that *room and board*. A governess wasn't family, but she was not a servant, either. Surely the food would be good, and the bed soft. A salary to be received on quarter-days, instead of rent to pay. "Is her mother dead?"

A shadow passed over Lady Tassell's face. "No, but very ill. She does not much leave her room."

My heart went out to that obedient, peculiar little girl. An image formed in my mind: a solemn, dark-eyed child, perhaps a little resentful of her lot, inclined to throw stones at birds and make up secret languages. "How old is she?"

"Five."

"Young for a governess, surely."

Her eyes searched my face. She tapped her pen against the desk, then set it down decisively. "Allow me to be blunt. Lady Palethorp is foreign. Sir Kit wishes his daughter to have a good genteel English education." She screwed up her mouth. "If you will forgive me for offering you a very awkward piece of advice, it might be better not to speak of your mother to him."

My cheeks heated. No one in Lively St. Lemeston had ever met my mother. Few of them troubled to remember anything about her. But of course Lady Tassell was the exception.

"These John Bull country squires can be small-minded," she said ruefully. "The Olivers' unimpeachable respectability and your good schooling should satisfy him."

In all honesty, I was unlikely to have discussed my mother in any case. I wasn't ashamed of her. On the contrary, I hated to expose her to slights. She had borne enough of those, alive—from the unimpeachable Olivers, no less. I knew better than Lady Tassell ever could, about the small-mindedness of John Bull squires.

I could almost smell the sea. I *could* smell a generous breakfast.

And that little half-English girl needed someone to take care of her. "I'll go."

"I'm glad to hear it." But to my surprise, Lady Tassell did not look entirely glad. She fussed with her pen again, then leaned in. "I hope you will write me and tell me of your progress. Please believe I mean to stand a friend to you, Miss Oliver."

I drew back—not physically, but in my mind. I felt my grandmother's fingers dig into my shoulder, felt her hot breath in my ear: *They'll say they're your friends. Don't believe them! They lie, they lie...*

I could never hear the word *friend* without remembering. Perhaps that was why I had so few. "Thank you, my lady. I am sensible of the honor you do me."

"Then you'll write?"

I nodded reluctantly, already itching to leave—to tell Iphigenia about the position, and be reassured by her admiring exclamations.

I felt a pang. Iffy and I weren't as close as we had been at school, but I would miss her.

The countess produced a little tin box, and held it out with a smile. I made myself take it, reading the neat motto on its lid: "*A Gift* FROM A *Friend*." It had been painted, no doubt, by some other not-yet-desperate lady trying to wring a living from her accomplishments.

I twisted open the lid to find a hot cross bun inside. The sweet Easter rolls were lucky, people said; keeping one by the hearth protected a house from fire. Every Good Friday I considered saving one—and every year some faint scruple prevented me.

I turned the tin until the cross was only an enigmatic letter X. "What a kind thought, my lady. Happy Easter."

"Happy Easter, dear. Please don't forget to write."

2

I arrived in Rye late on a Saturday evening, after having spent the better part of twenty hours in a coach with a guitar case clutched between my thighs. The lesser part, I had spent in a London hostelry full of rodents. My arse, stomach, and eyes all ached, I was in desperate need of a piss, and I would have given half my first year's salary to unlace my stays and crawl into bed on the spot.

I wished with every fiber of my being that I were spending the night in Rye, and journeying on in the morning. But—ignorant of my new employers' sentiments towards travel on the Sabbath—I had waited for them to suggest it, and they had not.

Lacking the wit or patience to look about me at the town, I relieved myself, bought a sandwich, and returned to the rapidly darkening innyard to tip the porter and await the cart that was to take me to my new home.

I smelled the sea, though. Fish, too—but even that was familiar, if not quite comforting.

It was the *only* familiar thing. I had not been in a new place in years. One or two men made lewd remarks, and that was enough to set my heart racing and my mind busily picturing to me my fate if the cart did not come—several dozen fates, in fact, all dreadful. I was pitifully grateful to hear a simple Sussex voice asking, "Miss Oliver, been't it?" and to give over my trunk to a hale-looking man of middle years.

Mãe's guitar I kept by me, which offended him—and to no purpose, really. The instrument had been cheap when it was made, and was now worth next to nothing. I ought to have brought my handsomer one, but great houses usually had a guitar or two lying about, and I had no more been able to leave this one behind, than I could hand it over to a stranger now.

I ought to have made myself agreeable on the drive, too, to pacify the coachman after my stubbornness, for I was sure the people among whom I was going to live would hear his report before church was over tomorrow. But I barely managed a few perfunctory sentences before we lapsed into silence. The landscape trotted by—not *flat*, but somehow stunted, in the way of countryside at the edge of the sea.

I drew my cloak tight, feeling very small, and liable to be extinguished by a sudden gust of wind. Longing seized me for my narrow bed at Mrs. Humphrey's, and for Iphigenia to exchange wry glances with over the breakfast table.

"Her's Camber Castle on your left." The driver pointed proudly at a few squat lumps, casting long spindly shadows in the twilight.

I had been studying my gazette on the journey, and knew the castle had been built by Henry VIII near the second town of Winchelsea—for the sea had swallowed the first, half a millennium ago. I strained my eyes until great menacing stones loomed out of the dusk. "Is that New Winchelsea?"

He grunted. "What's left of her."

We passed a ruined gate, half a church, and a few abandoned streets lined with empty houses—*mostly* empty. Lights flickered in a window or two, where dire necessity had driven human beings to shelter with ghosts. I shuddered; desperate people did not watch their fires, and empty towns burned easily.

At last it grew quite dark, the waning moon cowering behind the clouds' skirts like a frightened child. When the cart stopped at the end of a long drive, I could make out only a vague jumble of chimneys, towers, and gables. I saw no lights. The shutters and curtains must be closed against the damp, chilly air.

Surely it was only my own mood that made the house look ugly.

The driver gave my guitar a glance as I lifted it out myself—in the darkness, I imagined it a disapproving one. Shouldering my trunk, he carried it into a deep arched doorway, and having once wielded the knocker—not on the wide main doors, but in the recessed porch's left wall—he climbed back into his cart.

The sweating horses could not be left standing in the night air, so with a last touch of his cap, the man drove off, and left *me*.

I saw again the dead buildings of Winchelsea. *The house is abandoned*, I thought. *No one will come.*

But in another moment lamplight was trickling through the opened side door, barely limning the flagstones. A bowing footman wrestled my trunk through the narrow aperture, then returned for my guitar.

My fingers spasmed on the handle. "I'll carry it, thanks," I said as pleasantly as I could. He held the door for me with another shallow bow, and I crossed the threshold—*a* threshold, anyway—of my new home.

As I did, I knocked the instrument case against the stone jamb. Not hard, but I knew the footman must be laughing up his sleeve, and felt it as a small agony.

The porter's room was a low, plain chamber. As the footman barred the door, the dim light turned his livery, which had been black and silver in the moonlight, to brown and bronze. I would know the true colors in the morning.

"If you'd be so kind as to wait half a moment, madam. Of course you are welcome to the chair." He disappeared with the lamp up a crooked flight of spiral stairs.

The only chair was directly before the fire-screen, but I was weary enough to take it gratefully. The seat was still warm, crumbs and a game of patience strewn on the table. I tried to commit my brief glimpse of the footman's face to memory, but it was gone already. Dark skin and a friendly expression. Had his face been square? He was very tall, but so were all footmen, and some great houses even hired their liveried servants in matched pairs, as though they were not men, but horses. I hoped very much my new employer would not be that sort of fellow, who valued appearances over everything.

My new employer could be any sort of fellow.

I looked about the room for some clue as to its owner's character, and saw only faint dancing shadows on dark walls. Did the curtain on the room's rear wall cover a painting, or a window to an inner courtyard? I lifted my hand—and dropped it hastily in my lap at the sound of footsteps on the stairs. *Tomorrow*, I repeated to myself. Tomorrow I would look about with curious eyes, ready to be pleased.

A middle-aged woman bustled in, keys jangling at her waist. "Miss Oliver?"

I leapt up like a jack-in-the-box.

She thrust the lamp in my face, to look me over. I forced myself to be still, the lamp searing my cold nose and cheekbones as she took in my mussed appearance.

She nodded in satisfaction, and I had the poisoned-dart thought that she had been afraid the new governess would be pretty. "Welcome to Goldengrove, Miss Oliver. I am Mrs. Cross, the housekeeper here."

I set down my guitar to shake her hand, and did my best to smile and memorize her face. In her youth she must have been, if not beautiful, then pleasant-featured in English fashion, with apple cheeks and a button nose. "Thank you, madam. I hope I shall…"

I foundered. I could hardly say *do well here* when she did not employ or direct me, or *be very happy here* before she had expressed such a wish for me. "I am glad to be here."

My elbow protested as I lifted my guitar once more, and I wondered glumly how far off my room would be.

"You've no need to carry that yourself, ma'am. Peter will come back for it when he's settled your trunk." She glanced behind me at the crumbs and cards, mouth pursing. "I'll speak to him about the mess, as well. I'm very sorry. I assure you, I keep a very clean house."

"Oh, that's all right," I said, trying to sound gay. "We've been through a lot together, this instrument and I. I like to keep her close. And—" She would not like me to tell her how to manage the servants, I was sure. But what could I do? "Please don't scold the footman. I am very grateful to him for waiting up."

She sniffed. "That is very good of you, ma'am." She turned a heavy key in the barred outer door before she led me up to the first floor, where she locked the stairwell behind us. I followed her down a short passageway, and across a large chamber into a small one.

"This is just for tonight, ma'am. We can't reach your usual room without waking the family." She dipped a spill into her lamp, lighting the candle on the bedside table before blowing out the spill and replacing it in its vase.

I watched to be sure the smoke dissipated.

"The household will assemble in the chapel at eight tomorrow, with breakfast to follow. What time shall the maid wake you?"

The door opened behind her to admit a bed-warmer, followed by a pair of hands on its long handle, and finally a young housemaid.

At Mrs. Humphrey's I had insisted on a hot water bottle, for newspapers regularly reported bed-warmers as the cause of house-fires. Not long ago, I had read of a servant who tripped on the stairs while carrying one and "expired within twenty-four hours" of her burns—an unadorned little phrase, passing over a day and night of screaming agony. I pressed my back to the wall as the maid passed, trying unobtrusively to see whether the pan had air-holes to feed the coals inside—and permit sparks to get out.

I silently recited Iphigenia's oft-repeated reassurances: *The holes are too small for sparks. If there are sparks, they'll go out. You'll catch your death of cold if you indulge all your fears.* But laughing, sanguine Iffy was not here. My throat felt tight.

"Miss Oliver?" Mrs. Cross sounded impatient.

"I beg your pardon?" I sucked in a breath as the maid turned, the warmer passing...well, not very close to me, really.

"What time would you like to be woken?"

The maid stifled a yawn, her unwieldy burden wobbling.

I gave Mrs. Cross an answer, then regretted it and gave another. "I'm sorry, I've been up since dawn." I realized belatedly that the poor housekeeper had likely woken just as early.

She clucked sympathetically anyway. "Shall I help you with your stays, ma'am?"

I did not want her help. But there was no alternative, so I retrieved my night things from my trunk and stripped, my skin pebbling. I felt her hands on my laces.

I held the stays awkwardly over my breasts as she bid me good night. When the door had closed behind her, I dropped them with relief, slumping onto the bed in my shift.

"I'll lock you in now," she called.

I went rigid. "Mrs. Cross!"

"Yes, ma'am?"

"I beg your pardon, wh-what did you say?"

"I'm locking the door," her muffled voice came again—but not so muffled I could be in any doubt as to her words. "You'll find the chamberpot under the bed."

I rushed to the door, and yanked it open. "But what if there's a fire?"

I had ripped the knob from her fingers. She cradled her hand in her other elbow, her impatient expression shading into active dislike. "Master's orders, ma'am. All doors are locked at night to keep out thieves."

"May I keep the key?" I pressed, heedless of her lamp stoking my hectic flush, and pitilessly illumining my muddy shift and shapeless chest.

"I'm afraid not, ma'am, I'm sorry. Master's orders. But you're quite safe. We've never had a fire in all my years here. Goldengrove has good stone walls, not like the flimsy wooden buildings you're used to in town."

I could not argue any more. "Very well," I said with feigned cheerfulness. "Good night." I shut the door very slowly.

The lock turned loudly. Mrs. Cross's footsteps retreated.

I flew to the room's other door to try the handle. Locked. My shaking fingers could not make sense of the curtains' tasseled pulls. God, I hated my weakness. Seizing the curtain itself, I dragged it back to examine the window.

There was no window. The smooth paneled walls extended behind the curtain—white, blank, and impenetrable.

3

My heart leapt into my throat, choking me.

I lifted the candle. The flame trembled and nearly went out—but I saw my mistake, and managed a shallow breath. I was gazing at interior shutters, carved to match the wall.

Blood surging in my ears, I opened the hook-latch, but could not budge the shutters. Locked, but the key was not in the little keyhole, or on the mantel, or in the night-table's little drawer. The opposite window—the house did have an inner courtyard, then—was the twin of the first, and also locked.

If the house burned, I would burn with it.

Why had I not considered this? I knew some households locked the servants in at night. How far above a servant *was* I, really? Evidently not as far as I had fancied myself.

I snuffed my candle, first. Then I checked that the fire was banked, and searched the bed for sparks before climbing in. I shut the bed-curtains and my eyes. The ticking of the clock goaded on my rapid pulse.

Other people could be peaceful behind a locked door, if they knew it would open in the morning. But not I. If this was to be my fate every night, I could not stay here. I would have to go back to Lively St. Lemeston, and beg my pupils' parents to hire me again. I would have to explain to Iphigenia what had happened. Lady Tassell would certainly never do me another favor.

I tried to conceal this nervous tremor in my constitution from the world. I *did* conceal it. I had fooled Lady Tassell into believing me a self-reliant young woman. I had half fooled myself.

I shut my eyes tighter. I *would* sleep. I would.

I was awakened by the sound of the bed-curtains opening. My anxious glance flew past the housemaid to the door.

It was shut.

But it must be unlocked, or the maid could not have entered. I took a deep breath, willing the tickling tension at the back of my throat to subside. "Is the door unlocked again?" I tried to sound amused.

The girl laughed obligingly. "Oh yes, Mrs. Cross unlocks them all first thing in the morning. Here, I've brought up some warm water." She laced my stays for me, and I washed and dressed. How should I arrange my hair?

I raised my eyebrows at the vain creature in the mirror. A governess need not—*should* not be pretty.

No pinned waves at my temples could improve my appearance, anyway. Wondering for the millionth time if a fringe would soften my high forehead, or draw attention to it, I coiled my hair primly at the crown of my head and tied on a clean cap. Iphigenia would have made its frayed ribbons charming; I merely looked shabby.

"Chapel's about to start, ma'am."

I jumped, ashamed to be caught fussing in the mirror. The maid—a rosy-cheeked, golden-haired child—must pity me in her heart. "Ought I to wear my bonnet?" I inquired, my embarrassment deepening at my ignorance of the etiquette surrounding a private chapel.

"Mrs. Cross wears hers, but most of us girls just wear our caps."

"What about Lady Palethorp?"

The girl hesitated. "Her ladyship don't leave her room much. Her health been't strong. Last time I saw her in chapel…I think she wore some sort of veil."

I decided to imitate Mrs. Cross. It did seem silly to settle my bonnet on my head and draw on my gloves when we were not to go out-of-doors, but I had rather be over- than underdressed for a solemn occasion.

"Follow me, ma'am."

The opposite door opened on a handsomely furnished music room. My heart lifted a little to glimpse a pianoforte, a shrouded harp, and a couple of music stands as we rushed past. Traversing a neat library, we emerged in a stone passage.

"The family gallery," the maid whispered, indicating a door in the opposite wall. "But today you'll sit with Mrs. Cross." We descended a spiral staircase, crossed another passage, and at last I was curiously inspecting the chapel.

Windows upon windows ringed the large, lofty room, their glazing clear to admit the daylight. Behind the altar rose a vast expanse of mullions and diamond panes, each arch crowned with a gaily painted coat-of-arms. The Tudor and Hanover crests I recognized; the rest I supposed familial.

Despite this generous subscription to the window-tax, it seemed a sensible, low-church room. The walls were whitewashed, with the merest hint of gilt about the moldings, and the servants sat in sturdy wooden pews. Goldengrove livery, in the light of day, was a sober dark blue, with pale gold facings.

My escort pointed out Mrs. Cross's bonnet rising from the first pew—an imposing pleated tartan calash, calculated to block the view of as many inferiors as possible.

It was also at least twenty years out of date. I hoped my amusement was not visible as I wished her good morning and took my seat beside her, facing a simple lectern by the altar rail. At least I had not needed to worry about recognizing her again—or about the modishness of my own bonnet, for that matter, which was a warm but water-stained velvet with a third of its beaded trim gone, scattered across Lively St. Lemeston like Tom Thumb's breadcrumbs.

The family gallery perched on stilts behind us. I longed to crane my neck for a glimpse of my charge, and perhaps of my employer. But that would look impertinent—or worse, irreverent—so I folded my hands and mentally drafted my first letter to Iphigenia.

The room came abruptly to attention, conversation ceasing and faces turning resolutely forward. The renewed temptation to turn my head had nearly overpowered me, when a gentleman passed us and took up his place at the lectern.

"That's Sir Kit," Mrs. Cross murmured proudly.

The baronet was unprepossessing at first glance. Perhaps in his middle thirties, his dress was careless and his hair—the color of dirty straw—far too long for fashion. Like me, neglect made him look unkempt and not poetic.

His deep-set eyes and strong nose were placed too high in his head, creating a low, prominent forehead and long chin.

Worst of all, he was short—about my height, and I was not tall. The lectern, alas, emphasized the deficiency: his head and shoulders protruded, and not much else.

Then he grinned across his book at me, wide and boyish. His brows rose in eager anticipation, and his eyes twinkled infectiously, the lines around them deepening further. A smile spread across my face in involuntary imitation.

Recollecting myself, I pressed my lips hastily together and glanced at Mrs. Cross, expecting to be condemned for my forwardness. But to my surprise, she gave me a smile and a satisfied nod: *That's Sir Kit.*

"Good morning, everyone." His voice was loud and clear, his accent good but not drawling. "Today we welcome Miss Palethorp's new governess. Miss Oliver, would you be so good as to stand?"

I obeyed, face hot.

"Well, turn around and let everyone see you."

His eyes laughed at my hesitation. Somehow, I could not take offense. I made the room an awkward little curtsy, and Sir Kit started a ripple of applause.

Grateful for their apparent goodwill, I tried to look round in a friendly way and meet a few eyes, despite my shyness—but I could not help darting my eyes upward for my pupil. I gained nothing by it, but a glimpse of a little white dress and a few blond curls through the bars of the railing. The gallery's only other visible occupant was a young woman I took for a nursemaid, although someone sitting at the back by the fire, as an invalid might, would be hidden from my view.

I sat, disappointed, and Sir Kit began the Lord's Prayer.

I had rather dreaded church services in my new home. A pompous, long-winded, mumbling, or bigoted preacher could make Sunday mornings a torment. Even the simple lay preachers in Lively St. Lemeston's Methodist chapel had sometimes bored or infuriated me nearly to tears.

But Sir Kit read a short, plainspoken sermon with little in it to object to. His voice was clear and sincere, and the household's silence attentive. Despite my skepticism, the pale light streaming through the high windows, and the sure, good-humored voice, lifted me up.

Surely Sir Kit would not begrudge me a key to my room.

After the sermon, he came directly to me. "Miss Oliver!" He bowed over my hand. "Was that *too* much ceremony? I've never employed a governess before."

"I've never *been* a governess before, sir."

"Then we'll muddle through together." His eyes twinkled, as though he found the whole artificial edifice of propriety as meaningless as I did. "Come and meet Tabby, she's been eagerly awaiting your arrival."

I followed him up to the gallery, where my charge blinked wide, cornflower-blue eyes at me and said, "Welcome to Goldengrove, Miss Oliver."

Her curtsy was not graceful—she was five years old, after all—but it was done with slow, anxious solemnity. She held out her hand with a bright, abrupt smile.

She was unquestionably a beautiful little girl—more beautiful than I had expected, after seeing her father. And unquestionably, she knew it—I read it in the tilt of her head. Very fair, very soft ringlets fell about her heart-shaped face. *Her mother must be French.*

I was ashamed as soon as I thought it, but there was something affected about her, something coy and practiced, that I could not quite like. I also, in a corner of my heart, envied her that soft, pale hair.

I smiled at her. "Thank you, Miss Palethorp. What a beautiful curtsy!"

Her smile widened at the compliment, looking more natural.

Sir Kit crouched down, beaming at his daughter. "Miss Oliver is going to teach you to be a proper English lady. You must be very good and always listen to everything she says."

Tabby nodded emphatically. "Yes, Papa."

I was not quite pleased by this description of my employment, though I knew it was all most parents wanted from a governess. "I shall teach you a great many things," I said cheerfully, trying hard not to sound as if I was correcting Sir Kit. "History, mathematics, geography, music. I play the guitar, too. Would you like to learn to play?"

Her eyes flew to her father. She said nothing.

Sir Kit laughed. "You'll have plenty of time to get used to the idea. Well, run along with Clarice. Miss Oliver and I must discuss your education for a few minutes, and then she will come and breakfast with you in the nursery."

Tabby's eyes flashed indignantly. "I want to have breakfast with *you*!"

Sir Kit glanced sheepishly at me. "I know, moppet. I've been spoiling you since Rhoda left. But a little girl doesn't usually eat with grown-ups."

"You want me to eat with Miss Oliver, and *she's* a grown-up," Tabby said with undeniable justice. "I keep you company. You like having breakfast with me." The dark look she threw me said plainly whom she blamed for her loss of privilege.

With an inward sigh, I let the peculiar, clinging child of my fancy melt away like morning mist. Peculiar? Tabby was spoiled, that was all. A very ordinary failing in the pretty only daughter of a rich man.

"Tabby," he said warningly. "Miss Oliver will think I haven't taught you any manners."

She subsided resentfully.

"Go upstairs, and after breakfast Miss Oliver will hear your prayers and help you with your catechism."

"Sunday is a day of rest," she pointed out.

I smothered a laugh, liking her a little better already. It was not *her* fault if she had been too much cosseted.

Sir Kit did laugh. "So it is—a day of rest *and prayer*. After your lesson we can all walk down to the beach, how's that?"

The beach! I held my breath.

Tabby considered. "Yes, Papa, I should like that very much," she conceded finally.

Sir Kit held out his arms, and she rushed into them. He spun them both round, and set her down with her bow askew. "Who's my good little girl?"

"I am."

"Correct! I'll see you this afternoon. Take your leave of Miss Oliver for now."

"Good morning, Miss Oliver." With another careful curtsy, she ran off, nursemaid at her heels.

Sir Kit watched her go with obvious affection. "You see what a wonderful girl she is. I thought there was no harm in letting her run wild when she is so young—but I suppose a girl can't be too young for bad influences. Poor kid, she grew terrified of anything that looked like a circle in the grass, and what should I find but that good Mistress Rhoda was frightening her out of her wits with tales of faerie rings and changelings. Amazing how this pagan nonsense lingers more than a millennium after St. Wilfrid came to Sussex."

He led me across the stone passage and through the library. "I'd have had to let Rhoda go sooner or later—the Sussex in her voice was thick enough to keep you warm in winter—but she and Tabby liked one another, and she seemed commonsensical at least. My friends' nursemaids all seem to be coarse women who ply infants with gin."

We entered a spacious study, in which a comfortable clutter prevailed. The paneled walls were earthy blue-green, like the sea on a cloudy day, and the upholstery was the rich orange-yellow of a fresh egg yolk. I couldn't decide if the combination was bilious or inspired.

"I hope you weren't too bored by my sermon. The parish church is far worse, I promise you. The vicar is a young prig who preaches entirely too much hellfire—a debatable improvement over his predecessor, who was an old prig in the same style."

The inkstand, already half an inch from the edge of the desk, quivered as Sir Kit dropped his volume of sermons carelessly among his books and papers. Smiling at his absent-mindedness, I lifted my hand to push the inkstand back.

The thought came with sudden, peculiar strength: *That is for a wife to do, not a governess.*

A wife, or a servant.

I stepped away hastily, turning my eyes to the lit fireplace. Above the mantel, a portrait of Newton hung; on it, an alabaster bust of a middle-aged woman held sway alone.

By the low brow and long chin, I guessed she was a relation of Sir Kit's, but on her the features looked heavy; her lids hung over her eyes and the corners of her mouth were tucked sourly in. Perhaps her smile had been charming, or the sculptor unkind. But I heard my mother's voice as I studied the bust: *a doughy English face.*

"Who is that, sir?"

"My mother. The late Mrs. Palethorp."

Did I imagine that he laid a faint stress on *Mrs.*? The significance was lost on me, beyond the obvious implication that the previous baronet had outlived Sir Kit's father.

He flicked an affectionate finger at the bow threaded through her old-fashioned profusion of curls. "I suppose she wasn't a beauty, but I miss her."

He sat, trying to arrange his papers in some semblance of order and giving up with a wry shrug. "Well, well—sit. I tried to make the chairs for visitors as comfortable as mine."

It was a comfortable chair, but I could not *be* comfortable in it. "Sir, before we begin…I don't want to waste your time if…"

For the first time, he grew absolutely serious, folding his hands and regarding me with concerned sympathy. "Yes?"

I felt a little calmer. "I understand it is your practice to lock all the doors at night."

"Yes." Sir Kit scratched sheepishly at his jaw. "I have a horror of thieves and kidnappers. Smugglers roam the nearby beaches and fields after dark, and my house…Tabby…"

"I quite understand," I said sincerely, my hope growing. If I understood him, then he might understand me, might he not? "I have rather a horror of fire, myself. I cannot live in a house where I am locked in my room, unless I might have the key in my possession."

4

"Have the key?" His eyes searched my face. "Only myself, Mr. Christie, and Mrs. Cross have ever kept room keys. That has been the practice since I came to Goldengrove."

Lady Palethorp's illness must be worse than I had imagined, if she did not require a set of keys. But perhaps he considered that her inclusion in the list went without saying.

If I told him that my grandmother's family burned to death, probably he would understand—even be sorry for me. It would have sounded like an everyday tragedy, if I could have said it in an everyday tone.

"I have a horror of fires," I repeated. "I'm so sorry, I have tried all my life to get over it and I can't." The egg-yellow chair really was comfortable. Everything here was comfortable. "Please, sir—I had rather stay." I gripped the padded arms until I felt the wood beneath. "I will take any precautions you like, if I might have the keys to my room and Tabby's. If an accident befell her at night, and I could not reach her..."

"A key to your room would open Tabby's, too. All the family apartments in the old castle keep share a lock, for the sake of convenience. Just be glad I replaced most of the door fittings when I took possession. Some of those rusty iron latches took five minutes to wrestle open. My pocket linings lost a few fights to the heavy keys, as well."

My heart sank. Of course he wouldn't give me a key to his own chambers, or his wife's. "You might take the cost of new locks out of my salary, if you wished to change them."

Pushing his chair back, he came round his desk to look me in the face. I tried to meet his frowning gaze unflinchingly.

Leaning closer still, he set his finger under the knot of my bonnet-ties and tilted up my face as though to read my character. The knotted ribbon dug into my chin when I swallowed, but his touch steadied me, somehow. So did that insightful gaze.

I set my shoulders. If he *could* read my intentions, then I had nothing to fear.

He let fall his hand, turning to clear a space at the edge of his desk. Dizzy, I watched him lift the inkwell I had not dared touch, and set it down out of danger. He sat in the empty space, smiling at me. "You know, I think I shall make up my mind to trust you." He held out his hand. "Friends?"

My grandmother's fingers dug into my shoulder. *They'll say they're your friends. Don't believe them.*

I couldn't let an old woman's delirium rule me.

It had not *only* been delirium.

I released my grip on the chair, stripped off my glove as manners demanded, and shook his hand firmly. But I didn't say *friends*.

He kept hold of my hand. "If I find you snooping, I'll roast you alive myself," he teased.

I hid the hot electric shock I felt. He was only jesting. "The eventuality will never arise."

He dropped my hand, grinning, and wandered to the window-seat. Lacing his fingers around one bent leg, he let the other dangle, unselfconsciously boyish. "I'll send to the Rye locksmith tomorrow."

I relaxed into my soft chair at last. Beneath my ungloved fingertips, the bright upholstery was smooth as a baby's skin, a sharp contrast to Sir Kit's rough palm. I knew an impulse to kick off my slippers and tuck my feet under me. It wouldn't be ladylike, but I thought he wouldn't mind that.

"Well, take your hat off, madam, since this is your home now."

I smiled and obeyed, propping the bonnet on my knee with my gloves tucked inside. "Do you have a curriculum in mind for Miss Palethorp, sir?"

"You must know better than I do what's usual for a young lady. Nothing too heavy, please. I don't want her shut up all day, growing pale and listless. Girls need exercise and fun just as boys do."

"I couldn't agree more. Two hours in the schoolroom each morning and afternoon will be more than sufficient. Young children learn best out of doors. Geography, botany, natural history…"

"English history, too, so near Hastings," he said. "I am glad you do not mean only to teach her *accomplishments*. I ask nothing but that you follow your own bent in giving her a thorough education, and a thoroughly English one. Naturally she'll have to learn French, so her friends can't gossip about her to her face; but you must see her raised on right principles. Do you know the song *I leaned my back against an oak, thinking that it was a mighty tree…*"

"*But first it bent and then it broke.*" The rhyme dangled, incomplete: *just as my love proved false to me.* I shifted in my chair, but the ease of a moment ago eluded me.

It was half shame at my own pedantry, that hated to leave a quote unfinished. But that *thoroughly English* stung me, too.

Sir Kit nodded. "It's not an easy world, especially for a young woman. I want Tabby to have a solid English oak at her back when she enters it, and English bedrock at her feet."

There was much to admire in the sentiment. But I thought sourly, *Women do manage, now and then, to be virtuous even on the Continent.*

"Sir, does…?" I had been waiting for *him* to broach this next subject first, but I could not plan Tabby's lessons without an answer. "Does your wife also wish to speak with me about her daughter's education?"

He turned his head to the window. The pale sunlight of a cold English spring played over his face, along with a private sadness. "I speak for both of us."

I took a deep breath. "And does her ladyship listen to Miss Palethorp's prayers on Sunday?" We had never done that in my house, but many of my schoolfellows had.

Sir Kit sighed. I wondered what view he saw—only bright gray sky was visible from my chair, the clouds smeared together by thick antique glass. "Lady Palethorp's health is very fragile," he said stiffly. "Her ears are sensitive to high-pitched sounds. Tabby is too young to remember to speak softly." He kept his face averted.

I tried to look blank, but I felt a rush of pity for Tabby, whose mother could not bear the sound of her voice. I felt sorry for Sir Kit, too, obliged to divulge such a thing to a stranger. No wonder he spoiled his daughter. I couldn't help wondering if his wife was truly ill, or only indolent.

He did look back at me, finally. "You must believe she loves Tabby very much. The doctors…" He gave up on the sentence.

"Very well," I said with more false cheer. "I'm sure the doctors know best." That left one more painful question to be got over. "Might I borrow a Book of Common Prayer?"

"A governess without a Book of Common Prayer?" His eyebrows winged delightedly upward, chasing the sorrow from his face. "Are you an anarchist, Miss Oliver?"

"My father preferred the Methodist Church, sir." It was no more than the truth, though it was also *less*.

He *tsk*ed with mock gravity. "A Methodist! Almost as bad. Take as many prayer books as you like from the chapel. Oh, but I shouldn't say that—you'll make a bonfire of the lot, topped with the king's effigy."

I grimaced; the custom of burning effigies had always revolted me. "I have a horror of fires," I reminded him. "I used to hide under my bed on Guy Fawkes Day."

"Ah yes, of course. And thus you were obliged to become a governess, and not an anarchist. I hope your parents were not too disappointed."

I laughed. "I'll go up to the nursery, if you've no more instructions. What time shall we come down for that walk to the beach?"

Sir Kit glanced at the clock: not yet ten. "Why don't you order sandwiches for half eleven, and find me when you've finished your luncheon?"

At the door, I was faced with yet another awkward question. "Where is the nursery, sir?"

He was already spreading his papers across the desk once more. "Oh, I beg your pardon, of course you're still learning the house. Let Tabby give you a tour, she'll feel very important—but take Mrs. Cross with you if you're actually interested in our history. Can you find your way back down to the chapel by the spiral stair? Very good. When you have gathered your kindling, take the same stairs all the way up, to the very top of the keep."

I dreaded losing my way, for it would look like snooping, and I had not forgotten Sir Kit's humorous warning. Clutching my borrowed prayer book, I followed the stone stair swiftly up, barely allowing myself a glance at the now-familiar first-floor corridor, or the heavy oak door on the second-story landing.

The windowless stairwell seemed to swallow me. Between floors, I could see neither its beginning nor its ending; under my palm, the wall's stones were dry and smooth as scales in a dragon's throat.

But at last the tower spat me out, dazed, onto a little L-shaped landing with a slanted roof. Stooping, I rounded the final steps under the eaves.

There was another ancient oak door immediately on my left hand, and a paneled modern one ahead and to the right. I loitered by the railing until I heard Tabby's voice clearly at my left.

I set my hand on the knob, and paused. I could not knock, for neither Tabby nor her nursemaid had the authority to keep me out. But what if I had misheard? Who lived behind the other door? Myself, perhaps, but I could not count on it. Putting my ear to the door, I heard the nursemaid's voice and footfalls, near and growing nearer. I started back before she could catch me skulking.

I smoothed my dress, and pushed the door open.

5

Crudely arched hammer beams supported the nursery's plaster ceiling. To the left, a wall and a bricked-up chimney blocked off a portion of the eaves. Properly speaking, there was no right wall; only a few feet of dark oak paneling cut off the ceiling's sharp slope to the floor. Before me, a carved door—ornate without style or elegance, after the fashion of previous centuries—jostled a two-arched window with a single small casement. The house's immense age was borne in on me anew.

But someone had done their best to gloss over the harsh angles and rough asymmetry. A faded pink and black carpet, which must have been inordinately expensive a few decades ago, concealed all but a few inches of the uneven wooden floor. Sky-blue Chinese paper covered the walls, patterned with cherry blossoms and bamboo.

Those painted yellow songbirds were a type of oriole, I thought. Would it interest Tabby to search out the exact species in the Goldengrove library? It would have interested me, at her age.

Softest and most extravagant of all was the little crown-canopy bed, its gossamer clouds of netting drifting down from a half-coronet of gilded flowers affixed to the eave. With no need of bedposts, the padded silk head- and footboards curved to meet the sides' graceful upward sweep, the bedding nestled inside like a robin's egg in cupped hands. It would not have been out of place in the nursery at Versailles; I wondered what Sir Kit had said when his wife ordered it.

The floor creaked when I stepped forward, the hard edge of a warped floorboard pressing into my heel through the soft carpet and the worn sole of my shoe. I introduced myself to the nursemaid, since Sir Kit had not done it earlier. I thought he had called her by name, but to my relief she gave it anew without prompting. Clarice, yes, of course. She was a sturdy girl with an impossibly small nose and dark hair.

I turned to my charge. "What a lucky little girl you are, Tabby, to live in such a beautiful room."

She looked about like a little queen surveying her domain. "You live here now too," she said magnanimously.

"So I do. Do you know where I am to sleep?" I was sure it would be somewhere much plainer than this.

That made her scowl. She pointed behind me, where two doors, one old and one modern, flanked a neat little fireplace. I had entered through the old one; she was indicating the other. "I used to keep toys in there I'm too big to play with, but Papa put them in the attic."

I hid a smile. "Thank you for making room for me." I nearly asked, *May I go in and see?*—but I remembered in time that she was meant to obey *me*.

Despite sharing the nursery's rude hammer beams and warped glazing, the narrow space behind the door was newly whitewashed, and its north-facing window was twice the size of Tabby's. I knelt eagerly on the bed to survey the slate roofs and red-brick parapets, gables and twisted chimneys, rippling in all directions like a crowd below a queen's balcony. From up here, the central courtyard was a tiny patch of green and gray.

I had only been tired last night, after all, when I thought the house was ugly.

My room and its dividing wall were plainly an afterthought to the house. The slanted ceiling would not permit proper bed-curtains; a folded square of muslin lay on the bed, which I soon identified as a canopy I was meant to stretch between my abbreviated bedposts.

To my left, a closet protruded into the room. At least, I assumed it was a closet, but the door was locked. "What's behind this?" I asked Tabby, who had followed me to explain where she used to keep each surplus toy.

"The stairs to the roof. I have to hold Papa's hand if we go up there so I don't break my neck. And I can't drop anything over the side because it might hit someone. Not even a pebble."

I met Clarice's eyes in amusement. "Yes, it's not very nice to drop things on people. Do you like the roof?"

There was a pause. "You can see all the land that Papa owns. It goes right down to the sea." Tabby fixed her gaze on mine, expressionless. "I'm a girl, so I can't ever own Goldengrove."

I felt that she was waiting for my opinion of this. "It doesn't seem very fair, does it?"

She considered, then shook her head slightly.

"But after all, when you marry, you'll go live with your husband."

"Why can't he live with me?"

I had no answer I would want repeated to Sir Kit. "Do you think you would like to stay at Goldengrove forever? Sometimes it's nice to be among new people and places. I was glad to leave my old home and come live here."

"But your home probably wasn't as good."

"That is rather impolite," I said, feeling it was required of me as a governess.

"I beg your pardon," she said with equal halfheartedness, and sighed. "I think I have to stay here. That's all right. I don't like boys very much anyway."

At that, my laughter escaped. But I could hardly say, *My sentiments exactly*. "You might feel differently when you're older."

"Can I watch you unpack your things?"

I drew back sharply. Why did she stare at me like that? Perhaps she was peculiar after all—or perhaps, I scolded myself, I was only secretive. I remembered how often I had begged mãe to open her father's old peddler's box so we might pore over its enthralling miscellany of buttons, paste hairpins, pomanders, shells and sea-glass, her wedding slipper, and the corset busks Papa had carved for her while he was at sea. Even now, the box's scent of cedar, orange, and clove had not lost its power over me.

Tabby's mother did not even like her voice.

"'May I,' not 'can I.'"

"May I watch you unpack your things?"

"Of course—this evening," I added, hearing the arrival of the breakfast tray. "When we come back from the beach."

Breakfast was only tea and toast. But what tea! Richly aromatic, tinged with red. And what toast—white and soft and thickly buttered! Cream floated on the fresh milk, the sugar overflowed its bowl, and the wafer-thin slices of lemon shone like tiny rose windows.

My knife hovered shyly in my hand, but Mrs. Humphrey was not here to accuse me of greed. I smeared marmalade over my bread, enough to cover the surface completely and leave thick ridges at the edge. Candied bits of peel glittered like jewels amid the gold.

I took a bite—a *small* bite, since I was charged with teaching table manners. My teeth slid smoothly through the hefty layer of preserves and hit the crisp bread. I whimpered.

I was going to love it here.

Question: What is thy duty towards thy Neighbor?

Answer: My duty towards my Neighbor, is to love him as myself, and to do to all men as I would they should do unto me: To love, honor, and succor my father and mother: To honor and obey the King, and all that are put in authority under him: To submit myself to all my governors, teachers, spiritual pastors and masters...

The catechism of the Established Church seemed ill-designed to give children an affection for religion. But perhaps that had never been its purpose. Perhaps it was only meant to teach them to do as they were told—in this case, to memorize a long, dull series of answers full of words they didn't know.

I shut the book. "How much of your catechism do you know already?"

Tabby hesitated. "I know the Lord's Prayer," she asserted with a touch of belligerence.

"It's all right not to know things," I told her. "I don't know the catechism either."

She looked astonished, then suspicious—then afraid. "Why not?"

"My father was a Methodist," I said, taken aback by the strength of her reaction. "Do you know what that is?"

She didn't answer.

"A Dissenter or Nonconformist is a Christian who goes to a different church than the ordinary parish church, but is not a Roman Catholic. A Methodist is one kind of Dissenter. They follow the teachings of John Wesley."

She regarded me warily. "But you're a Christian?"

I felt a chill. *She's just a child*, I reminded myself. "Yes," I said calmly. "Do you know why it's important to learn your catechism?"

"So I can take communion," she said, still watching my face.

"Very good. And what is communion?"

"It's when you pretend to eat the body and blood of Christ. But it's only pretend. We aren't Catholics."

I decided there was nothing precisely heretical in that. "That's right. And when we eat the bread and wine, we feel the spirit of God within ourselves. It's a very special and very holy thing, and it's important to understand what it means before you do it. The catechism teaches you about that."

After she had stumbled through an "Our Father," I read her the Apostles' Creed. She was quite distressed by *I believe in the holy Catholic Church*. It required my most earnest representations to convince her that the English Church was meant, and that she was only obliged to repudiate the *Roman* Catholic Church. Even then, I suspected she would appeal to her father for confirmation at the first opportunity.

Soldiering on, I gave her a turn at sounding out the Creed herself, glancing at the clock over her bowed head. Five to eleven. At half-past I was to order sandwiches, and then we might go down to the beach.

I was used to tedium—had learned to find contentment, even, in sitting straight and still and hearing the same note plucked out badly a thousand times. But today the clock's steady ticking barely kept my restive heartbeat in check.

At quarter past eleven, I praised Tabby's progress. "Now it is time to look inward, and then I will hear your own prayers. Do you know the proper position for praying?"

She pulled over a cushion and knelt on it, clasping her hands with all the studied grace a five-year-old could muster. She looked like a cherub, and plainly knew it.

Iphigenia had laughed at me once, for saying she looked like an angel. *No, I look like an artist's model—that's all angels in paintings are.*

Still, that seed of dislike shook within me, trying to sprout. *Well then*, I told myself wryly, *practice what you preach*. I steeled myself, and looked inward.

My own younger self gazed unrepentantly back: a drab little girl, who had never looked like an angel and never would.

She is a child, I told her. *Iffy might have looked like her at five years old. You disliked Iffy sometimes, too.*

I wished I could give my child-self a few good thwacks with a hairbrush until she took the words back. No, it hadn't been easy to be friends with the most beautiful girl in school, but neither had it been easy to *be* the most beautiful girl in school. My skin crawled, remembering how hard some of our teachers had been on poor Iphigenia—and my own hot words, oft repeated: *She's only jealous, the ugly old shrew.*

My age and features were in the hands of Time and Fate, but whether I would be a shrew or no was up to me.

I smiled at Tabby. "Self-reflection is always the first step on the path of self-improvement. Close your eyes, and think: What are you sorry for in the week that is passed? What are your hopes for the week to come? Has something lovely happened, that you would like to give thanks for?" I waited. "Now, what would you like to tell God this week?"

Her eyes opened. "If I say I'm sorry for something and you didn't know I did it, will I get in trouble?"

A very pertinent question. I considered my answer. "For small sins, no. Most of all I want you to be honest. But it is my duty to care for your character, and teach you to tell right from wrong. If you have done something truly bad, like stealing, I shall have to inform your father so we can decide on a fitting punishment and amends. But you need not be afraid of that. You will find it's best, and *feels* best, to confess frankly at once when you know you have done wrong. There's a saying: a liar fears other people when she ought to fear God, Who knows the truth already."

I was as much a hypocrite as the Church and their catechism, wasn't I? Tabby's cool blue eyes seemed to see through me.

"Dear God," she began at last, "I'm sorry I kicked Clarice, it was mostly an accident."

Across the room, Clarice snorted over her mending.

"I'm sorry I ate an extra biscuit from the tea tray." Her eyes slid to me. "That's not *stealing*, though."

"I don't need to tell your father, no." I felt suddenly and uncomfortably like an interrogator. "This time isn't about punishment, Tabby, I promise.

It's for you to talk to God. You and I can talk later, if you're not sure what is and isn't stealing."

"I'm sorry I disobeyed Papa when we went for a walk. Thank you for Cook making pigeon pie for dinner. Thank you for good weather for the ships and playing cricket. Please make me a good little girl and let my father and my governess love me."

For a moment I was simply flattered, as no doubt she meant me to be. Then I realized what she hadn't said. "What about your mother?"

She stared up at me for a very long moment. Then she said dutifully, "Please, Lord, don't send my mother's soul to Hell."

6

The words sliced my chest open. "That isn't—" I pressed a fist to my heart. "Why do you say that, Tabby?"

Her gaze didn't waver. It was so impossible to guess the thoughts of children. "She's sick and could die."

I let my breath out. Oh, poor child! "We'll pray for her health together," I said shakily. "But even if she were to die, I am sure she would watch over you from Heaven."

That was more hypocrisy. Perhaps quoting the adage had been honest after all, then: I did lie because I feared other people, and not God. Men were crueler than God—for if I had little faith in Heaven, I had less in Hell. I could not believe that God set Himself up as a Grand Inquisitor, to torture His enemies and condemn them to the flames without compunction—but I *knew* that men had done so. And then they painted God in their own colors, as a convenient bugbear to frighten children into obedience.

Sir Kit had been right to banish superstitious Rhoda from the nursery, and employ me in her stead.

The sandwiches arrived at last, warm slices of tender beef slathered with mustard and tucked inside hot buttered rolls. But I ate only one, unwilling to spoil my walk by the sea with a stomachache, nor did I cajole when Tabby pushed half of hers away.

We found Sir Kit still in his study, washing down his own sandwiches. "Local beer," he said with a rather self-deprecatory grin, imagining that I looked at his pewter mug from curiosity and not because it caught the light.

"I suppose a proper baronet would drink claret." He shrugged. "If it's good enough for the men who work my fields, it's good enough for me."

I hid a smile. Maybe the baronet really was an unpretentious fellow, more at ease in the wheat-field than the drawing room, but I strongly suspected he had also found that ladies in drawing rooms were charmed by the performance. I wished I were less so, myself. "An Englishman's home is his castle," I said, as if Goldengrove were not a castle regardless. "Drinking whatever takes your fancy is simple patriotism."

He laughed, and I felt a sudden burst of happiness at being liked.

Downing the last of his beer, Sir Kit crouched in front of his daughter. "So, Mistress Christabel, what did you learn this morning?"

"The Apostles' Creed."

"Oh, very nice!"

I felt another glad burst. I would be a good governess, and please Sir Kit, and maybe in time Tabby and I would even love one another.

"I don't know it *all* yet," she added hastily.

"Of course not," he agreed. "It's only been a few hours since I saw you last. How pretty you look in your bonnet!"

Swinging his daughter's hand in his, he led us out of the house and across the wet lawn. Following, I tried to keep my petticoats out of the mud without showing my ankles, and failed in both aims.

Our path took us through a small wood, across a field and over a stile, past a marshy flat, over a canal-bridge, through a line of trees—and onto a shingled beach.

The glittering blue-gray bay curved on and on, dancing a minuet with the shore. The lace hem of her swaying silks trailed across the pebbles, catching them up and tumbling them down with a rhythmic grating sound. I drank in her scent, transfixed, transported, seduced.

I'd been half afraid it would only be pretty scenery now I was grown. But the sea was the sea. Age could not wither her, nor custom stale her infinite variety.

"Have you seen it before?" Sir Kit asked me. "The sea, I mean."

I blinked, trying to draw my attention back to my companions—or companion, for Tabby had run on ahead and was flinging pebbles into the water. "Yes. I've missed it," I said, walking faster to catch her up. "I grew up in Portsmouth. The Arun in Lively St. Lemeston is lovely, and thirty feet wide at a generous estimation."

He laughed. "I grew up in Rye—well, spent my infancy there. I suppose I grew up at school, like most boys." The laughter fled for a moment, his mouth twisting, before he shook it off. "I'm glad Tabby will be spared that, anyhow."

"Girls do sometimes go to school. I did, myself." Of course, that was because school cost less than a governess, which could be no object with Sir Kit.

"Yes, Lady Tassell told me all about your excellent education. But do you know, I don't think I could trust Tabby to such an establishment. I have it on good authority that through washing together, girls sometimes acquire indecent, immodest habits, and learn indelicate tricks." He gave an infectious shout of laughter.

It was an extremely improper remark. Yet there was something innocent, something unalloyed and pure, in his delight at his own joke. *I hardly think Mrs. Godwin an authority on propriety*, I almost replied. He would be elated that I had recognized the allusion, and I yearned—no weaker word would do—to look clever.

Instead I rolled my eyes, and maintained a dignified silence. A gentleman might read *A Vindication of the Rights of Women* himself, without wishing the lady in charge of his daughter's education to do so. Besides, it would invite teasing about my own girlhood, and I was afraid my face might betray my intimate knowledge of the truth of Mrs. Godwin's assertions. How Iphigenia and I had giggled over that passage, that first winter we were lovers!

"I beg your pardon, Miss Oliver. I hope I didn't shock you." His eyes glinted mischievously at me, his tone saying that he knew he hadn't, and liked me the better for it—perhaps, even, that he found the whole edifice of propriety a little absurd, that required ladies to pretend to such endlessly recurring, inexhaustible shock.

I wanted to ask him if he had read more of *Vindication* than the saucy bits. "We had better change the subject."

He complied, asking about Portsmouth and my father's naval career with every appearance of interest. Tabby ran up every half a minute with a seashell or a question. Sir Kit spoke to her with the same cheerful attention he gave me, with no trace of the irritation or impatience one often saw in parents pestered by their children.

"Can we go sea bathing this summer?" she asked.

He pretended to consider. "Hmmmm. Maybe, if you're *very* good and the weather is *very* fine."

"Can we bring the telescope to the beach? You said the smoke from the chimneys hides the stars at the house."

"Soon it will be warm, and we won't have to light fires at night. We don't come to the beach after dark, Tabby-kitten, you know that. Smugglers might be here then. It's not safe for little girls—or for big girls, or big boys, or anybody who isn't a smuggler, now I think of it. Even during the day, you shouldn't come here without one of the footmen, at least."

I suspected he was really worried about the soldiers in the squat Martello towers that dotted the beach at quarter-mile intervals, to protect against a French invasion. I sighed. The beach looked so peaceful. It would have been nice to imagine for a little longer that it truly *was*.

The drawers of my clothespress shut too far if I was not careful (probably why it had been relegated to my chamber), but a fresh sachet was tucked into each one. Lifting one of the little bags, I smelled—not even lavender, though that would have been luxury enough, but *strawberries*. Unable to believe my nose, I loosened the red satin ribbon and peered inside for proof. Yes, those were strawberry leaves!

"Are you a lady?" Tabby asked very seriously.

Cheeks heating, I took up the last of my four dresses and folded it very neatly indeed. "That isn't a polite question, but yes, I am."

Further protests could only lower my consequence. I laid the dress in the drawer to absorb the sachet's reflected glory, and shut the clothespress as deliberately as I shut my lips on *I went to a very select school. I speak without a Sussex burr.*

The Olivers are one of the oldest, most respectable county families, even if my father married a costermonger.

"'Lady' means a woman whose family ranks among the landed gentry," I explained. "She can be identified by the refinement of her mind and manners, not the number of her dresses."

"So you're a poor relation."

I snorted a laugh. "That isn't a polite question either. You must never ask it of anyone else. Have you heard the expression *noblesse oblige*?" I took her sullen silence as a negative. "It means 'nobility confers obligations.' You know that your father looks after his tenants and laborers?"

She nodded, curls bouncing.

"You are very lucky to live in a fine house and have many pretty dresses and a papa who is a baronet. So you must remember to show kindness and consideration to those less fortunate. Poor people don't like to talk about their poverty."

"Why not?"

"Because being poor isn't as nice as being rich." I was dying to see if my sheets smelled like strawberries too. But I could hardly sniff the bed in front of Tabby, if I wanted her to think me a lady.

"My mother is rich, but I don't think she's a lady."

This was why people avoided frank conversations with children—because something as dreadful as this might be said. "Your mother is Lady Palethorp. She has 'lady' right in her name."

It would be unworthy of me to trade on Tabby's artless confidences, so I turned back to my trunk, ruthlessly quashing my curiosity about what her mother was, if not a lady.

Out my things came in a sad little procession. An apron. Wooden pattens, down at the heels. A single extra pair of stockings. *Poor relation*, they seemed to shout. *Nobody wants you.*

A lumpy pair of mitts Miss Starling had made for herself, only they came out too small. Papa's tin lantern, wound in a shawl.

Tabby wrapped herself in the shawl as I explained that mica was a mineral from Russia, and that ships used it for lighting the powder magazines.

"Why?"

"Because it doesn't shatter even under cannon fire."

She looked as impressed as I had been as a girl, though the panes had been clearer and flatter then, and less scratched.

"This is for me to read with you." I held out *The Wise and Witty Governess*, a farewell gift from Phoebe Dymond. "It's for little girls. My friend wrote it."

She snatched it eagerly from my hand. I forbore to correct her manners, pleased to see her willing to be interested in a book—it boded well for lessons.

While she was poring over the frontispiece, I slid my commonplace book onto the top shelf of the clothespress's upper compartment. Of all my things, those notes and scraps of verse in different hands were the most irreplaceable. I didn't want them torn or wrinkled or covered in jammy fingerprints.

Swiftly, too, I stood my father's peg leg upright in the compartment and hid it beneath my bonnet. Only the one, for I had abandoned my summer hat, its lopsided straw liable to become more so in transit, unless I had piled a hatbox on top of my guitar case.

Another day I would answer Tabby's questions about the cannonball that took off Papa's leg when I was about her age, and how he had got about with a wooden one after that. Tonight I felt protective of my history, like a hedgehog curling around its soft belly.

Papa had curled up when he sat, in those early days, his shoulders rounding as he massaged his sore knee. *I've got to get used to it, that's all*, he'd tell mãe.

And he had, eventually. We'd saved for a better-fitted leg, as well—but I had buried him in that one, for on his deathbed he had admitted to a lingering doubt that his own limb, amputated and cast into the deeps, would be recoverable by the Almighty.

Blinking back my tears, I briskly lifted my avô's box.

Papa had long since removed the shoulder straps to let it sit flush against the wall, sanding and waxing the bare spots. *Isn't it beautiful, mamã?* my delighted mother had coaxed my more skeptical grandmother. *Pai's old box, so fine!* Even if someone did recognize its original function as a peddler's movable warehouse—which Tabby certainly would not—they had no way of guessing whom it had belonged to.

I still felt exposed.

"What's in there?"

Not much. "My favorite things," I told her. "Look, this is the slipper my mother wore when she married my father. The toe is stuffed with lavender to keep away moths." In the years since Papa's death, I'd pawned the paste hairpins and the carved busks, but thank God nobody wanted half a pair of shoes.

"It's a funny slipper."

The child was determined to be unpleasant tonight! But in truth, I preferred it to the winsomeness of earlier, for it seemed more genuine. "Fashions change. In thirty-odd years, somebody's going to say that about your shoes, too." I tweaked her toes.

Setting my hot water bottle on the floor, I took out Lady Tassell's hot cross bun in its tin. *A Gift* FROM A *Friend*. I grimaced, but I put it on the mantelpiece.

It was a bad night, but better than the one before it. Yes, I lay awake at least an hour under my luxurious eiderdown coverlet after the key turned in the lock, listening for the faint crackle and pop of flames. Yes, I bolted upright the moment I heard the housekeeper's footsteps in the morning, calling out, "Could you open the shutters, please, Mrs. Cross?" with a very weak semblance of composure.

But in between I drowsed and dozed, and the sheets did smell of strawberries. Though my body was tired and slow as I dressed in the morning, my thoughts felt sharp enough.

All day I swallowed a reminder to Sir Kit of his promise to make a fresh key. I would only look pushing, and more mad than I already did. My patience was rewarded, for a little after dinner the baronet poked his head into the nursery, hugged his daughter, and handed me two brass keys: one for the tower doors, and a smaller one for the shutters.

Relief flooded me, commingled with gratitude—for the keys, and for not forcing me to remind him. "Thank you, sir." My fingers closed tightly around my salvation.

"You are quite welcome." He gave me a conspiratorial smile. "Now if you will promise never to surprise me in the bath, I will thank *you*."

For a moment I was nonplussed. But it never did to let people see that their teasing bothered you. I looked him up and down, amused. "That I can promise with all my heart," I said dryly, wishing the idea were as distasteful as I implied.

He grinned. "How fortunate that I have no vanity to wound. How will you wear your badges of liberty?"

That embarrassed me far more than his remark about the bath. I had no jewelry. "On a ribbon, I suppose."

"My wife…" His mouth twisted. "Lady Palethorp sends her apologies, that her health prevents her from offering you a proper welcome." He drew a fine golden chain from his pocket. "She sends this instead, with her hopes that you will care for Tabby with all the energy and attention of which she is at present incapable."

Could I accept the gift? It was likely worth more than all my belongings together, though too delicate to be called ostentatious. Dangling from Sir Kit's hand, it seemed fragile as a sick mother's hopes for her child. The links were broken up every half-inch by a miniature pearl nestled between tiny, trembling leaves of beaten gold.

My mother is rich, but I don't think she's a lady. I had no wish to wound Lady Palethorp by calling her well-meant gift an impropriety. More prosaically, it was in my own best interests to wound my employers as little as possible in *any* manner.

I glanced at Tabby. She was watching very closely. I did not wish to wound *her*, either.

"Please convey my thanks to Lady Palethorp, sir," I said gently. The chain was so light in my hands—one quick jerk, and it would snap. "Tell her I am sensible of the honor she does me, and will do all in my power to deserve it."

I threaded it through the bows of the keys. The gold leaves shivered, but the chain held, stronger than it looked.

Unlike me.

No matter. I had a key now, and could sleep easier. I looped the chain over my head, comforted by its pressure at the back of my neck.

7

The next few weeks passed with all the expected awkwardness. I lost my way in the house, answered prying questions, and got used to a stranger lacing my corset, until by degrees the maid who lit my morning fire was a stranger no longer.

When I did not mock Clarice for carrying a tiny curled ammonite in her apron pocket—a "snakestone," as the countryfolk called them, to ward off evil—she unbent so far as to offer me a little round stone with a hole in it, which she instructed me to string with my keys to keep witches from using them. The extra weight around my neck was an irritant, but I thanked her politely for the gift and wore it, to keep the peace.

I almost wished for the chance to lose my way out-of-doors. But a footman accompanied Tabby whenever she ventured outside without her father—usually Peter, who had seen me knock my guitar into the doorframe my first night.

With Sir Kit's approval, I had settled on a varied plan of lessons, more intended to awaken my pupil's curiosity than anything else. I succeeded in doing so more rarely than I had expected. I thought Tabby was clever enough, and she generally looked with alacrity at what I showed her, but her eyes were always straying to my face, more interested in praise and admiration than learning.

Yet despite her efforts to please me, I could not tell whether she *liked* me or no. The child seemed more changeable than the moon, no sooner showing the beginnings of affection or trust than she did something to torment or spite me—putting raspberry jam in my slippers, or burying my gloves in the bucket of sand by the fireplace.

I could not even punish her, for there was never any evidence against her, nor did her protestations of innocence falter under questioning. I would almost have rather believed that one of the servants had taken me in violent dislike than that Tabby was such a liar, and I found myself unwilling to risk imposing an unjust sentence. I had not anticipated how far a governess resembled judge, jury, and executioner.

I thought of speaking to Sir Kit, and asking his advice—but that seemed like whining or, worse, seeking to impose the unjust sentence at second-hand, and wash my hands of it like Pontius Pilate.

If only… The useless words *would* intrude. If only I could ask Tabby's mother, and have her help in raising her daughter. I waited every day for Lady Palethorp to emerge from her room, or to summon us to it; but she never did. And if I mentioned her to Tabby, I seldom got more than a blank stare or a shrug.

Self-reliant, I reminded myself. *Self-reflection is the first step towards self-improvement.* Governesses were often the victims of these sorts of childish tricks. Why, I asked myself, had I expected to win over my charge as swiftly and completely as Miss Baillie, the Wise and Witty Governess, when I was neither wise, nor witty, nor a work of fiction?

Vanity, I answered truthfully, and persevered.

I could not quite relinquish my first impression of Tabby: that she was a cossetted, spoilt child who had never wanted for anything. Her expensive playthings were so plentiful that my and Clarice's best efforts could not keep the nursery from perpetual clutter. Yet Tabby treated her lovely toys with rough carelessness when she was not smugly showing them off.

Her doll, for example—a coquettish thing with a painted blush and several silk dresses copied faithfully from *La Belle Assemblée*. Tabby disliked her hard wooden body in the bed, and left her on the floor at night, where both I and Clarice repeatedly (and painfully) stepped on her. But when I offered to make a soft cloth replacement, Tabby said very seriously, *It wouldn't be as beautiful as Adeline.*

I nearly snapped, *Pretty is as pretty does*, but thankfully the absurdity of arguing over a doll's moral character asserted itself in time. Why should I resent Tabby's blessings, when I would not have traded my own for them? For one toy stayed at the bottom of the toy-chest, untouched: a box of unfinished wood, with *My MOTHER* neatly inked on its brown paper label.

Peeking inside, I found a dissected puzzle whose flat, irregular wooden pieces were decorated with illustrated verses, beginning:

Who fed me from her gentle breast,
And hush'd me in her arms to rest,
And on my cheek sweet kisses prest?
  My Mother.

The popular children's poem was too new to have been part of my own girlhood, but old enough that I had read it countless times in print-shops and magazines. I had even wept once or twice over its sentimental lines, remembering my own mother's tender care.

So when I found myself growing shrewish, I would lift the lid of the toy-chest and look at the box, reminding myself that Tabby did not have everything, after all. At her age I had roamed Portsmouth freely, with a pack of playmates, and come home to my family's affectionate welcome. Apart from the occasional afternoon with the head groom's daughter or the vicar's son, and the hour or two Sir Kit tried to spare her every day, more often than not Tabby's only companions were myself, the servants, and these extravagant, lifeless toys.

One morning I arranged with the cook, Mrs. Bishop, to show Tabby the larder and explain the planning of a menu. My pupil was entranced, so I tried to ignore the kitchen-maid's skirts trailing perilously close to the flames and congratulated myself on my sound pedagogy.

"If you're hungry, madam, I could fry a sausage for you, too."

I flushed at having been caught looking. Now I was obliged to approach the hearth to answer, for Tabby would never speak quietly indoors if I did not. I tried not to wrinkle my nose at the smell. "Thank you very much, but I don't really care for sausage. We never ate it when I was a girl." I hastened to turn the subject. "Are those for Sir Kit?"

"It's for her ladyship's breakfast." The girl jerked her head towards a tray holding a roll, a pot of mustard, and a dish of apple compote.

I blinked. "Isn't that hearty food for an invalid?"

She shrugged.

"Does she eat it?"

Another shrug.

Suspicion flared again, that Lady Palethorp was malingering out of a dislike for the responsibilities of a wife and mother. *She hopes that you will care for Tabby with all the energy and attention of which she is at present incapable,* Sir Kit had said. How nice, to be able to purchase someone else's energy and attention when yours flagged. Self-reliant, was I? What choice did I have? It was that or the workhouse.

"Miss Oliver," Tabby shouted, "come look at my menu!"

Mrs. Bishop looked harried. "I tried to tell her pigeon pie can't substitute for a roast, ma'am."

I huffed a laugh. At least Tabby was consistent in *something*. I went to her, glad to escape the pungent sausage, the hissing fire, and my own uncharitable thoughts.

But when we returned to the nursery, I could not get it out of my mind. What did *Tabby* think of her mother's defection? I still had to prompt her, every Sunday, to include Lady Palethorp in her prayers, which she would do only with a rote phrase I had myself suggested: *Please send my mother good health.*

Every Sunday, I remembered her saying, *Please, Lord, don't send my mother's soul to Hell.*

For weeks I had conspired with Tabby to pretend not to see the puzzle at the bottom of the toy-chest. But today I thought, *This is absurd. I must cut the Gordian knot with the sword.* Surely it would be better to learn what strange thoughts she was harboring, than to continue passing the matter over in such weighted silence?

I took the box from the toy-chest, and sat on the floor with it in my lap. "Have you ever put this puzzle together, Tabby?"

She didn't answer. Her intent gaze unsettled me; as I opened the box, I felt a thrill of trepidation, as though I reached for forbidden fruit.

Tabby watched me assemble the puzzle in silence. Silently, she followed my pointing finger with her eyes as I read aloud one of the poem's verses.

> "Who drest my doll in clothes so gay,
> And taught me pretty how to play,
> And minded all I had to say?
> > My Mother.

"Has your mama always been sick?" I asked her. Another vacant stare.

I glanced at Clarice, who, though she had been at Goldengrove barely longer than I had, must hear more gossip. But she kept her head bowed over her sewing—a pose that, for a moment, seemed as false and affected as the way Tabby bent over her slate.

"Did your mama sew Adeline's clothes?" I tried again.

Tabby shrugged. Then, remembering I had told her that shrugs were unladylike, she added, "I don't know, ma'am."

Hopelessly, I turned my gaze back to the puzzle. My eyes dwelt on the illustration of a child with her hands folded in prayer.

> *Who taught my infant lips to pray,*
> *And love God's holy book and day,*
> *And walk in wisdom's pleasant way?*
> > *My Mother.*

What a chasm between that and *Don't send my mother's soul to Hell!* My curiosity had fled, and like drunkenness or fever, it left behind a slight headache and a bitter taste. I wished I had left the box where it was. But it was too late for that.

In the countess's makeshift office at the Lost Bell, I had thought, *That little half-English girl needs someone to take care of her.* I had come here—I had left everything behind—to do it.

Lady Palethorp could not or would not hold her child, play with her, listen to her prattle, teach her right principles. Very well; I had undertaken to do it for her, and I would keep my word. *I* would not shirk my duties, only because they were onerous.

Honesty was not really part of a genteel English education. But that, too, was why I had come: so Tabby would have someone with whom she could share thoughts that might not be genteel or English.

I looked seriously into her expressionless face. "Do you have any questions for me, about your mother? I know she is sick, and cannot see you as much as she would like. That must be hard for you to understand, at times."

She said nothing.

I wasn't sure I was within my rights to suggest this, but I said, "I'm sure Mrs. Cross knows of a deserving child in the neighborhood who would love to have this puzzle, if you have outgrown it."

Tabby's mouth set. "It's *mine*."

"Yes, and that means you may give it away, if you like. Indeed, it would be kind of you to—"

Her eyes narrowed. "Everything in this room is *mine*. Not yours. You have no right to give away my things."

"That's true," I agreed with determined mildness. "I only asked your opinion." But surely she would not have so pointedly ignored the puzzle all these weeks if its presence did not distress her. "You have not played with it since I came here. Would you like to put it in the attic with the rest of your older toys?"

She didn't answer for long moments. Then she said, "It was better when my old toys were in your room."

Tears stung my eyes. To hide them from Tabby, I occupied myself in putting the puzzle back in its box. What weakness, to be overset by a child's clumsy insult!

When thou art feeble, old, and gray, said the piece in my hand, *my healthy arm shall be thy stay.*

The verse blurred. My own mother had not lived long enough for me to take such care of her. Could I have supported us, if she had? And at Goldengrove, I could perform a mother's duties as steadfastly as I liked, but when Tabby had outgrown *me*, I might be parted with more readily even than this puzzle—passed on to another deserving girl and forgotten. I could not count on even a quiet corner in the attic to pass the rest of my days.

I set the box back in the toy-chest. It stared up at me. "It's time to tidy the nursery," I said a little wildly. "Go on, put your things away."

To my relief, Tabby didn't argue. We piled dolls and hobby-horses and cricket bats and pennywhistles on top of the puzzle until we couldn't see it, and shut the lid.

For the rest of the afternoon, Tabby, aware that she had been rude—perhaps even that she had hurt my feelings—was rather more clinging than I had ever seen her, and gave me extravagantly affected compliments on my singing.

But in the morning, when I came through the door between our rooms, she had strewn marbles in my path. I caught myself on the door-handle and didn't fall, but my ankle throbbed all day.

My half-holidays were on Fridays. I avoided the nursery on those afternoons, locking my trunk and my doors to keep Tabby out of my things—with mixed success, for Friday was a wash-day, and the maids were always in and out changing linens, beating carpets, and freshening the strawberry-leaf sachets.

By the end of each week, I craved silence and peace as an addict craved gin. I found them in a little turret room, up a flight of stairs off the library. Its musty smell and lack of furniture convinced me I would be in no one's way there—and no one would be in mine. The weather had warmed enough that a pelisse and shawl did in place of a fire, and if I shut the library door behind me, my guitar would disturb no one but the squirrels skittering across the roof.

On dry days, I did fear that a northern breeze might carry my notes past the roof-peak to Lady Palethorp's windows, on a level with my hidey-hole. But Sir Kit never appeared, shamefaced, to tell me my music grated on his wife's tender nerves, so I tried not to think of it.

Alone, I could forgo the Robin Hood ballads and English carols I sang for Tabby, and give my fingers some real exercise. I even dared, now and then, to play soft Portuguese lullabies and tragic love songs. I sorely missed the circulating library in Lively St. Lemeston, for Goldengrove's music room turned up disappointingly little sheet music. But I promised myself that on the first mild day after Midsummer, I would take my quarter's wages to Rye and buy myself some new pieces.

I was glad I had brought mãe's guitar. I had needed the finer instrument to impress my pupils' parents, for this one had never been handsome, and outwardly the years had been unkind: scratched wood, chipped inlay, and pegs worn smooth and round as pebbles on the Rye Bay shore. But its tones were fuller and louder, the notes clearer and longer than a new instrument could match.

If the thought intruded, now and then, that what I really craved was not *solitude*, but mellow adult companionship—if I imagined slipping into Iffy's room at the boarding house and flopping onto her bed with an exaggerated sigh—if I called to mind the tone and pitch of her sympathetic murmur—*poor Livvy! what a week you've had*—I set it aside.

I carried my lap-desk up to my turret, though, and wrote to her. Three letters a week I wrote, religiously: the first to Iphigenia, the second to the Countess of Tassell—since I had promised, and accepted franked covers from her secretary for the purpose—and the last to one of my other acquaintances in rotation.

At first, I described to Iphigenia my conversations with Sir Kit (though I left out any mention of the key, embarrassed by my weakness) and complained of Tabby's pranks. But her replies came rarely, if at all, and at last when I lifted my pen to tell her that I had still not seen Lady Palethorp, or that Tabby had spilled chocolate on my dress *again*, the humiliating sensation would creep over me of continuing to speak to someone who has stopped listening.

So I would set the pen down uninked, or describe Tabby's lessons or another luxurious meal, despite a lingering dissatisfaction with how closely my letters to my friend resembled those to my patroness.

I had so relished Iffy's admiring exclamations and predictions of my great success at Goldengrove, and the pretty way she clung to me at our parting, enough to say she would miss me and not enough to be a reproach. I wanted her to smile over my picaresque adventures in a faraway castle by the sea, not fret over my trials—or worse, think me peevish and tiresome.

And what if she read my letters to the other boarders? My secretive nature writhed in agony at the idea, however unlikely, that Sir Kit might hear of me gossiping.

One Friday afternoon, I happened to be crossing the courtyard with a hunk of bread and cheese in my hand and my letters in my pocket, when I saw the Rye postman handing over our mail.

I generally gave my letters to Sir Kit to post—I felt grand, even, at handing him a franked envelope. But slow mail was another part of country living I had not yet grown quite used to. The mail coach only came to Rye three times a week, arriving from London early on Wednesday, Friday, and Sunday, and departing around four in the afternoon on the same day. This, coupled with the baronet's relaxed attitude towards the clutter on his desk, meant that letters I wrote on Friday afternoon rarely left Rye before the following Wednesday.

I dashed up the path. "Sir!" I called. "Would you do me a very great favor, and take these letters to be posted?"

"No trouble, ma'am," the postman said, reaching out his hand.

I realized that I had no money for a vail. "I'm very sorry to put you to the trouble," I said to the porter, "but might I borrow a penny? I'll run up to my room and pay you back directly."

He gave me a disapproving frown. "It's not the done thing, ma'am. All our letters go through Sir Kit."

"Yes, and I'm sure he'll be glad to be spared the bother. Lady Tassell is expecting my letter." I turned them in my hand so the earl's frank showed.

The porter's frown deepened at this transparent stratagem, but the postman smiled at me. "Don't fret, ma'am. You can leave something for me with old Phil here, if you like to, but I'd be a right ingrate to count pennies after all the Christmas boxes I've had from the Tassells."

I thanked him very sincerely, and could not resist a triumphant glance at the porter. As I did, my eye was caught by my own name on the bundle in his hands. "Look, that one's for me!" I said, pleased. "It's from my friend Miss Lemmon. I'll take it with me."

The porter was now nearly scowling. "The post goes through Sir Kit."

I looked at him, amazed.

"Master's orders."

Really, for a gentleman who prided himself on his independence of thought, Sir Kit did not seem to encourage the quality in his staff! "The post goes through Sir Kit because it is almost all for him," I said. "You see my name on that envelope."

The rider by this time had stuffed my letters into his mailbag and mounted his sweating horse, but at the sharpness in my tone, he pulled at the reins and glanced back. His horse, snorting, did the same.

I flushed, self-conscious. But I had not had a letter from Iffy in three weeks. Why should I slink away to wait upon Sir Kit's leisure? Instead I gentled my voice, searching for a charitable interpretation of the porter's attitude. "Can you not read it? I shall be glad to wait if you wish to fetch your wife, or your spectacles."

It was his turn to flush. "Of course I can *read* it," he said with a sullen glance at the postman, and let me slide the letter through the twine.

As I climbed once more to my hidey-hole, I felt that my behavior had been less than genteel, and further alienated the servants besides. But triumph overran my misgivings, and I tore the letter open with a smile.

Livia Drusilla, it began. I sat up straighter, eyes flying over the words, for Iffy only used that nickname when she meant to scold me.

*Yes, you see I'm very angry, for your last letter came late, and this week you haven't written at all. I *still* can't recall the rest of the tune for that song you used to play, which means the few bits I do know chase each other round my skull like courting squirrels, until I stooped to privately suspecting the new maid—that's eight since Sukey, now—of stealing my mail, which is a baseness I despise…*

I frowned. I had transcribed the song and sent it to Iphigenia two weeks ago. I knew she was only teasing, but I didn't wish her to think I had ignored her request. And now the letter I had just posted would come, and still no music in it!

Let her wait, a voice inside did whisper. *She is hardly a regular correspondent herself.*

But perhaps some of her own letters had been lost, like mine. I knew the post came less frequently here, but until now it had never occurred to me that it might sometimes not come at all!

I knew I was making too much of it. There was no hurry, and never had been. I lacked self-command—had lowered myself to argue with the porter out of sheer obstinacy, and was now working myself up over a matter of no consequence whatsoever. I ought to take a nap, and forget the whole thing.

But alas, I was better at giving myself wise counsel than taking it. The flush would not seem to leave my face. Hastily, I copied the song over again. If I set out now and walked quickly, I could reach Rye before the mail coach left at four.

I dug a penny out of my lap-desk to place under the seal, to pay the postage—and paused. I had no wish to suspect the new maid either, but if she *had* stolen a letter, it would certainly have been for the coin. Should I omit it? I had few left myself, to last me until quarter-day. I wished I could reconcile it with my conscience to use one of Lord Tassell's franked covers.

Livia Drusilla, I told myself, *stop dithering.*

I sealed the penny to the letter and tied my boots and my bonnet, checking at least a dozen times that the wax jack and the spill I had used to light it were extinguished. *A baseness I despise...* That summed up my fear of fire pretty neatly. The mania had been with me a long time, but its severity came and went; was it increasing?

The walk will calm you, I promised myself. *You have not walked above a child's pace in weeks. The lack of exercise is depressing your spirits.*

So, with serenity and improved spirits a sort of Fata Morgana on my horizon, I set out with my letter, past maids laying wet bed-sheets on the grass. Alas for the laundress, the sky had darkened and begun to drizzle before I was a mile from the house. I put up my umbrella, and was dithering over whether I ought to turn back when I heard hoofbeats behind me.

Sir Kit drew up beside me with a frown. "Where are you going, Miss Oliver?"

"I meant to walk into Rye to post a letter. Do you think the sky will clear?"

"I think it unlikely. You shouldn't be wandering the countryside alone."

I blinked. "In the country, even a lady may—"

"I'm concerned for your safety, not your reputation," he snapped. "Next time, take a footman with you. And tell him to bring one of the *good* umbrellas, not that leaky old tub. You're one of the family, for God's sake. Here, I'm going into Rye. I'll post your letter for you."

When I did not at once hand it over, he laughed, his expression lightening. "The porter was just informing me of how daringly you rescued your correspondence from his villainous clutches. Do you think I read your mail, Miss Oliver?"

After that, I could not refuse without looking as if I did think so. I surrendered the letter, and my walk. "My friend never received the letter I gave you two weeks ago," I said awkwardly. "She has been waiting for some music from me." The moment did not seem auspicious to ask whether he was sure he had sent it.

"The mail in this part of the country is not nearly as reliable as either death or taxes," he commiserated. "Well, I cannot answer for what will happen to this letter when I have posted it, but until then I will be like Sylvia's lover in the ballad, and consent to be shot by a highwayman rather than give it up."

I laughed, my nerves settling. It was not so bad, after all, to be smiled at, and saved from at least four hours' hard walking. I hummed the ballad to myself as I made my way back to the house.

In the event, the weather did worsen. Sir Kit put up in Rye overnight, and came home with a head cold. I gave up on long walks until summer set in.

―――※――※――

I began keeping a notebook of the weather with my pupil. Thrice daily, Tabby and I read the elegant inlaid thermometer and barometer in the music room. Climbing to the roof, we read the weather vane and examined the sky. We made our own predictions and copied out the almanac's, then compared the preceding day's guess with the actual weather.

Tabby was fascinated beyond my wildest hopes. She stopped merely attending to how charmingly she could *pose* with her slate, and began copying out her numbers in earnest, determined to win the privilege of writing in the precious notebook with her own hand.

I congratulated myself heartily on this success, made plans for crafting a rain gauge in the autumn, and was even privately gratified when Sir Kit said, "What a literal mind you have, Miss Oliver. I ask you to give my daughter an English education, so you teach her to talk incessantly of the weather!"

But as temperatures rose, I grew to dread the little ritual. The instruments became my private judge and jury—not helpfully warning of approaching storms or rain, but sentencing me to nightmares.

The warm eiderdown coverlet on my bed became my enemy, too,

as I had known it would. The solution was simple: ask Mrs. Cross for a lighter blanket. But I felt she would see at once the excess of sensibility that prompted the request. So I put it off, until I dreamed of being burned once, then twice.

The garrote was around my neck, but they had lit the fire too early. I choked, but did not die. I could feel the flesh melting from my bones, dripping grease into the fire with a hiss and crackle…

I woke in pitch darkness, my nightgown plastered to my skin and the chain of my keys wrapped around my throat.

"It wasn't real," I whispered, throwing off the blankets and tumbling gratefully through the flaps of my muslin canopy. The key fell between my breasts, dragging the chain with it, and I could breathe again. "You're safe. It was a dream."

It was dangerous to expose my damp skin to the chill night air, but I didn't care. Shivering, I crept to the nursery door and pressed my ear to it, listening for the even sound of Tabby's breathing.

There it was. But I also heard… What *was* that?

The murmur was so faint my mind patched the holes with tattered scraps of memory: my mother singing me to sleep. One of the tunes I had whispered to myself in the turret Friday. Tears filled my bleary eyes.

Perhaps Tabby had woken, and Clarice was singing her back to sleep. Yes, footsteps shuffled across the nursery, and hinges creaked. That must be Clarice going back to bed—

A floorboard creaked in the hall. But the landing stayed dark.

I worked my key over my head, afraid to snap a fragile link and gasping when the chain caught under my chin. It seemed an eternity before the door swung open. I rushed to Tabby—and stepped painfully on Adeline's pointed wooden toes.

I rubbed at my foot, cursing under my breath. In the darkness, I could see only a faint lightening of the air where netting swathed Tabby's bed. I could hear her breathing, though; she was sleeping peacefully.

Hobbling silently across the room, I cracked the door to Clarice's closet. My heart skipped a beat, for she was snoring softly.

I tiptoed to the door to the landing. The handle turned, but the door did not open. Locked.

Who had been here?

I summoned reason to my aid. My own pounding heart was not sufficient cause to suspect anything untoward. Sir Kit had said only Mrs. Cross, Mr. Christie, and himself had the key; the servants had no reason to visit; ergo, if someone had come through that locked door, it must have been Sir Kit. Perhaps he had wanted to hear his daughter breathing, just as I had.

Strictly speaking, it was even possible I had surmised correctly at the first, and his wife's keys went without saying. Still, it seemed far-fetched that she would have gone to all the trouble of creeping into her daughter's room in darkness, when the far easier task of sending for Tabby in daylight had thus far been beyond her.

Look at your syllogism again, the voice of Reason suggested—sounding rather like Iphigenia. I rubbed at my eyes, wishing Iffy were here to prop her chin on my shoulder and set her fingertip under the error in my copybook. *Think, Livvy. Do you see it now?*

It had been years since she did that; it was all these damn lessons that brought our school days so vividly to mind.

She was right, of course, that there was a gap in my logic. There was no proof anyone *had* come through the door, except my own brief impression of a creaking floorboard on the landing. Half-asleep and frightened, had I imagined the whole thing? After all, a moment ago I had thought I heard my mother, dead for over twenty years. The house was ancient, and its joints creaked in changing weather like an old woman's.

Glancing up, I saw the alternation of old plaster and warped hammer beams in the low ceiling, closer than seemed right. It was all so close—closing in—the ceiling, the air, my nightmare, my memories. I could not breathe. At any moment, the past might reach out of the darkness to brush me with its fingers.

I sank to the carpet by Tabby's bed. The room seemed a little bigger from the floor. Listening to Tabby sleep, I brushed the end of my left braid from the base of my palm to each fingertip in turn, back and forth, back and forth, until my feet were ice and my pulse had slowed enough to let me go back to bed.

But I did not put the key back around my neck, lest I dream again of strangling. After much deliberation, I put the chain in my reticule, and tied the strings round my wrist.

In the morning, I was even less sure of what I had heard. "Clarice, did you hear anyone come into the nursery?" I asked as we broke our fast. "Around two o'clock?"

"I don't remember waking, madam, but maybe it was me? I don't remember it, but I do get nervesome now and again that Tabby might have taken ill, and look in on her. I hope I didn't disturb you."

"No, not at all. I was already awake. Tabby, do you remember waking up in the night? I thought I heard someone singing you back to sleep."

Tabby did seem tired, even listless, but she shook her head.

As soon as our rolls and tea were finished, I went down and asked Mrs. Cross for lighter blankets.

"I know it's a great favor to ask," Sir Kit said, "but a few neighbors are coming for dinner Saturday. Would you pour the tea and all that, Miss Oliver?"

"You—you want *me* to serve as hostess? For Goldengrove? …Sir."

He smiled. "No, for my other house, just down the lane. Naturally for Goldengrove. Mrs. Palmer from Fairlight usually obliges me, but she's come down with a fever and begged off. I can't see anything improper in you doing the honors."

Truthfully, neither could I. But I might as well have been a mouse invited to take tea with cats, for all the enthusiasm I felt.

You were just wishing for adult conversation, I scolded myself. Yet this would be no musical evening at the boarding house, but a party of well-dressed strangers, to whom I could have nothing to say and who were unlikely to wish to hear it in any case.

"Have you asked your wife to do it?" I said weakly.

A muscle twitched in his jaw. "My wife won't even see her own child. No, I haven't asked my *wife* to do it."

There was a little silence.

Sir Kit went abruptly to the window, but I did not think he was really seeing the view. "That was unjust. She's really very ill. I beg your pardon, and hers."

Was she very ill? I thought of those sausages.

He let the window embrasure take his weight, shoulders slumping. "I can't stand the thought of them looking at that empty chair where *she* should be and…. When I was a little boy, I used to watch my mother get ready for her dinner parties. It was more of a to-do then, what with powder and false hair. I'd hide at the top of the stairs and watch the guests file in, proud of how beautiful she was. I thought one day it would be my beautiful wife holding out her hands to our guests."

He turned back to me. His eyes were very blue, and very troubled. "Do you think I'm a monster?"

"No," I said, surprised. "Of course not."

He sighed. "You needn't do it if you don't wish to. God knows I don't wish to do it myself, but I can't always be going to other people's homes without a return for their hospitality, as though I were a bachelor."

"I'm sure your neighbors don't mind."

He pushed off the wall and strode back to his desk. "They still send their footmen to leave cards for her," he said viciously, pulling a stack of them from the clutter. "And I send ours to leave hers."

He took the top card from the pile and held its corner to his oil lamp. I took a hasty step back.

He blew it out at once. "Christ, I'm sorry!" He crossed the room to drop it in the grate. "Forgive me. I'm sorry, I'm making an absolute ass of myself. Forget I opened my fool mouth."

He braced himself against the fireplace for a moment, before straightening. "My neighbors pity me, you know. *Poor Sir Kit, raising his little girl all alone!* I suppose I wanted them to see that Tabby is in quite capable hands."

Sir Kit wanted to…show me off? The compliment quite overwhelmed me, especially when I had just shown myself so craven. "I haven't anything to wear," I blurted out, and then blushed for how vain I sounded.

The laughter crept back into his face. "And here I thought you fully dressed. What a cunning glamour you have cast! Is there a counter-charm, that will allow me to pierce the veil?"

This was what came of vanity and blushes! I regarded him severely. "If this is how you mean to behave in company, sir, I had better stay in the nursery."

"Madam, I shall behave however you like in company. But if you wish to stay in the nursery anyway, we'll say no more about it."

I almost took him at his word. And yet—what did I suspect Lady Palethorp of, if not shirking any task that did not *please* her?

I had better mind the beam in my own eye, and not the mote in my neighbor's! *I* had my health; *I* was capable of self-exertion. What justification could I give for scurrying back to my mouse-hole, when my pupil's father asked for my help? Sir Kit's neighbors would not eat me.

He met my gaze, open and unguarded. "I don't want your pity too," he said softly. "I couldn't bear that."

And I found it easy, after all, to take up one more burden his wife had cast off. As I straightened my spine, the chain she had given me pulled at my neck—but a little tug at my collar sufficed to settle it, the keys nestling comfortably between my breasts once more. "I'll be glad to do it."

Sir Kit's face flooded with such simple gratitude that I started forward and put out a hand, for a moment remembering only that he was a suffering fellow soul.

Then I remembered the rest, and dropped my hand. "And I'll pray for your wife's health," I added hastily.

I wore my only evening dress. The dark blue lustring was too warm for the weather, and with every lady I greeted, I saw anew how out of style it was, with no puff to its long sleeves and hardly any train. Poor Sir Kit, who had dreamed of a captivating, gracious wife to perform this office! Even the footmen in their Sunday livery outshone me.

I was painfully conscious of the abrupt, narrow shelf of my bosom, seldom on display. My corset straps, shoved out of view and pinned there, bit into my shoulders each time I stretched out my hand to a new guest. Lady Palethorp's chain—my sole adornment—crept over my bony clavicle, falling into the gap between my breasts as often as I pulled it out.

My room key was wrapped in a strip of paper and pinned into my bodice for safekeeping. I welcomed the occasional pinprick and poke, a reminder of the words I'd jotted on the paper for courage: *Ah, Friend! to dazzle let the vain design / To raise the thought and touch the heart, be thine!*

I also reminded myself that I had seen the dinner menu.

The table was meant for a larger party than our eleven. The servants had spaced the chairs evenly, but Sir Kit's neighbors, not wishing to shout, moved their chairs closer to him, and left me alone at the foot of the table.

He gave me a wry, apologetic look, but though some minor girlish part of me was stung—and though I was conscious of failing in my promise to assist Sir Kit in entertaining his guests—I was really grateful to be left to myself, except at the laying of a new course, when my nearest neighbor was obliged to make up my plate.

Avoiding the duck wrapped in bacon, I gorged myself on white soup, tender lamb, and slender French beans, and watched Sir Kit wrap the company around his little finger. Pity him? Nobody in that room pitied him—or if they did, it was the warm, admiring sort of pity that comes from knowing a friend's blessings are less than his deserts.

Soon the toasts began, full of extravagant compliments and great good humor. I was touched to hear Sir Kit make a kind toast to his wife, and send one of the footmen to tell her we were drinking her health, and would she like anything brought up from the table?

I made a strange sort of game to myself of guessing what delicacies her ladyship might request—the duck, I thought, looking over the dishes, and the pickled walnuts—but the answer came back, "Lady Palethorp's compliments, and she has everything she wants."

Had the kitchen already sent her a share of the feast? Or was she lying in bed eating a sausage with her fingers, grease dripping down her wrist?

What did her sheets smell like? Pork fat and fever-sweat? Or the same starched strawberry scent as mine?

Maybe she wore perfume. She would apply it with a heavy hand—something French… Here my imagination failed. I had no idea how French perfume differed from English, never having bought anything dearer than orange-flower water.

No one toasted me. I saw Sir Kit remark it, and reach for his glass. I gave a slight, pleading shake of my head, and his hand fell—but I felt warm that he should think of it.

Dessert began, the footmen bearing in two great epergnes, nuts and sweetmeats overflowing their little silver baskets. I polished off an airy syllabub, lemony and sweet with a little spiced wine in the bottom of the glass. And then, scarce believing my luck, I plucked a whole orange from a tray!

I lightly scored the peel from stem to stern—but the skin was thinner than I expected, and my silver knife sharper. Blood welled from the cut and dripped onto my plate.

8

Was it a trick of the light? Casting table manners aside, I dug my thumb into the fruit, gouging out a chunk of peel and flesh. The wound gaped glistening and scarlet.

"What—?" My voice failed, though perhaps as much from shyness as horror. There must be a rational explanation. But I looked at the prize I had snatched up so gladly, and I wanted to spit and say *Ojo!* to ward off bad luck and evil omens.

I was not the only one surprised. Exclamations rose around the table, some dismayed and some delighted.

"Wonderful, aren't they?" one of Sir Kit's neighbors said. "My nurseryman brings them in from Malta for hothouse gardeners. Blood oranges, the natives call them."

I drew a relieved breath.

"They might call it something nicer," a lady said. Everybody laughed at her, but silently I agreed.

The orange was sweet, though. The sweetest I ever tasted.

At last Sir Kit signaled me to lead the ladies to the drawing room—which fortunately adjoined the dining-room, so I could not lose my way.

I had been in it only once, on my first tour of the house. It was part of the "modern" wing, added to the east side of the house by Sir Kit's grandfather and given over mostly to the servants, with the exception of a few receiving rooms. Filing past the dining-room's carved paneling and enormous medieval hearth, we emerged in a square, light room, with sash-windows paned in smooth new glass.

The wallpaper and curtains were silk damask the color of pease porridge, the matching carpet relieved by a sort of large pink cartwheel. China ornaments littered the room, right down to the Meissen candlesticks.

I could not help feeling that if *I* were mistress of Goldengrove, I should decorate rather differently.

The furnishings that interested me most were a pair of pink upholstered chairs flanking the fireplace, each with a single deep-cushioned semicircle in place of the usual back and arms. Mrs. Cross had informed me they were French (very fine), and mangled a name which I eventually deciphered as *bergère en cabriolet,* shepherdess in a cabriolet. The chairs indeed resembled these low-slung, cozy open carriages, and I tucked myself into one with great satisfaction, careful to keep my skirts away from the hearth.

My chair was separated from the other guests' by the fire on my right, and on my left by a lacquered stand for a shellwork flower arrangement, which looked so intensely artificial in its glass case that for a moment I forgot seashells were products of nature. I felt sure the work was the late Mrs. Palethorp's. It matched her marble bust's heavy-lidded, flat gaze.

Thus secluded, I occupied myself in ranking the portraits first by the degree to which the painter flattered the Palethorps' low foreheads and long chins, and then by the degree to which he or she had captured their mischievous smiles. The lists ran nearly opposite, a neat parable on the emptiness of vanity.

But all too soon the tea was brought in, and I was obliged to leave my perch for a hard sofa. *I want them to see Tabby is in capable hands,* Sir Kit had said. *Capable* my hands certainly looked in this company—I never saw such a collection of well-kept fingernails in my life—and yet how easily they might falter, and defile this English sacrament: overturn a cup, or chip a near-translucent cup on the spigot.

Why is it called bone china? Tabby had asked me, not too long ago. She had been horrified by my explanation that crushed bone ash gave it its warm, creamy translucence. Perhaps I should have lied...

"No lemon, please!"

I jumped. A few drops of scalding tea sloshed onto my hand.

"Oh, are you all right? I'm sorry, I didn't mean to startle you."

I forced myself to smile as I wiped my hand on my napkin. "Yes, yes. The fault was mine, of course you said no lemon."

At last the ceremony was concluded, and as I dropped a generous lump of sugar into my own cup, poured last, the ladies began what they probably imagined was a subtle interrogation.

"So you are Miss Palethorp's new governess!"

"What family were you with before?"

"Are you from Sussex, dear?"

"And how do you find Rye Bay?"

The answers could interest nobody—they barely interested *me*—but I did my best to smile and keep my brief replies both humble and ladylike.

"Which branch of the Olivers are your people from, dear?"

My heart beat a little faster. Could one of them have heard of my father's marriage? "My grandfather is George Oliver of Sele Priory."

There was a long pause as they all racked their brains.

"I met him once at Worthing," one of them said, triumphant at having remembered something to the purpose. "A kindly gentleman. Is he in good health?"

He had not been kindly to my mother, or to me. "As far as I know, madam. He and my father were not close, but he paid my school fees, for which I am very grateful." Like Sir Kit, he had wanted me to have a good English education.

The ladies eyed each other. Then one said with suppressed eagerness, "What do you think of Lady Palethorp?"

I didn't know how to admit the truth—that I had yet to see the lady. "I have been made very welcome in her home."

There was a murmur of disappointment.

"You must all know her far better than I could after so short an acquaintance," I added. Was there any potential slight to the lady in that?

"Oh, nobody really *knew* her, even before she became ill," said a gray, faded woman with a sharp chin, propped up by stiff peach satin.

The ladies glanced at each other again, as if deciding how far they might safely go. I disliked them all in that moment, and yet I was too fired with curiosity about Lady Palethorp myself to turn the subject as I knew I should. I stirred my tea, the half-dissolved sugar clicking against the spoon.

"I thought she was a little proud," ventured a pretty, dark-haired lady of forty. Mrs. Abbott, I thought? With any luck, *madam* would see me through the evening.

The girl beside her leaned in confidingly. "Mama is too diplomatic. She was *very* proud, and I'm sure I don't know what she had to be so proud of. My father might not be as rich as hers was, but he didn't braid straw hats for a living either."

They all tittered.

"I was ready to overlook the straw hats—I'm very fond of straw hats—but she didn't seem to want to be welcomed!" said a plump older lady I had rather liked during dinner. "She obviously thought Rye Bay terribly provincial. At our first meeting, I told her—well, I suppose it is a little funny, but—you know, I told her our house was near Cock Marling, and she laughed for five minutes."

We all laughed at that—but how dare Lady Palethorp do the same?

"She despised our food, too," chimed in the square-jawed blond wife of a justice of the peace. "She would be syrupy sweet when she dined with you and compliment your cook, but then you'd see her dousing everything in pepper sauce and cayenne at home. I heard she once shouted at her cook for stinting on garlic."

"I suppose everybody finds foreign ways peculiar," said Mrs. Abbott drolly. "Only to her, *we're* the foreigners."

Everyone laughed again, at the startling notion that Englishness was not the natural state of humanity.

"Nothing is more ruinous to a weak constitution than an excess of cayenne and spices," the magistrate's wife said sagely. "It heats the blood and irritates the whole system."

Your inglês self-righteousness heats the blood and irritates the whole system, I thought. But here was my first clue to Lady Palethorp's origins! Not France after all, then. Where were spicy foods eaten? Perhaps Italy. India.

Probably I only thought of Spain and Portugal because of mãe.

"Was she in good health when she first came to Rye Bay?" I ventured, hoping for some clue as to how long Tabby had been motherless.

"I thought she was strong as an ox," the magistrate's wife said flatly.

Mrs. Abbott turned to her daughter. "Do you remember when we all picnicked on top of the bluff?"

"She got all red in the face and had to sit down," Miss Abbott answered.

"Of course I was eleven and couldn't understand why everyone didn't wish to run about in the hot sun all day."

"At the time I thought how soft people got in town," her mother said, "but maybe she was already ill."

The magistrate's wife snorted. "I thought she was lazy. Used to being driven everywhere. She didn't want to scratch her shoe leather."

"I'm sure that made things worse." The sympathetic older lady shook her head. "Indolence complicates a disease so terribly. Convalescence requires resolution. I've asked Sir Kit again and again whether she follows the doctor's advice, and of course he tells me to mind my own business and he's quite right, but still I think a little fresh air and sun would do wonders for her. They do for Mr. Wakefield's gout. Well, that and eating one of our oranges instead of tipsy cake for dessert."

I thought again of that hearty plate of fried sausages. Of Sir Kit saying, *She won't even see her own child.*

But I didn't trust these women to have observed anything accurately about Lady Palethorp, except her foreignness. No doubt they would inform me with equal confidence that Nathan Rothschild had horns and Angelica Catalani was a poisoner, should they ever find themselves dining with those luminaries.

Indeed, their judgment would be as swift against me, if I gave them any reason to think me a gossip. Already, I judged myself. "Your husband is an avid gardener, is he not, Mrs. Wakefield?" I asked, pleased with myself at thus neatly changing the subject *and* passing myself off as someone who remembered names. "I never saw such oranges!"

All the ladies at once exclaimed at the strange foreign oranges, and soon after, the gentlemen rejoined us.

Sir Kit came at once to my side. I felt the company remark it, and kept my replies to him civil in tone but very nearly uncivil in their brevity. I prayed he would hear his cue, and follow it as he had promised me; for though his speech was none the worse for drink, his cheeks were flushed and his eyes bright—brighter than usual.

To my relief, he turned away to face the company. "Would you mind if Miss Palethorp joined us for a few minutes?"

"Of course not," Mrs. Abbott said warmly. "I should love to see the dear child." All the ladies added their voices to the chorus.

"She will be in bed this half-hour," I said quietly.

Sir Kit laughed. "Not on your life. She knows I always send for her, and so does Clarice."

Sure enough, Tabby ran in a few moments later in her most beflounced dress, every string of beads she owned clacking against each other, and began making her curtsy to all the guests in turn.

"Are you being good and listening to your governess?" Mrs. Wakefield asked her. I wished she had not; I had never seen a child who enjoyed leading questions of that sort.

Tabby nodded quickly, then glanced at me as if fearing contradiction.

I smiled at her. "Christabel is a very good little girl."

"And have you been learning a great many things?" Miss Abbott asked. "Sing something for us!"

Tabby preened.

"Yes, do."

"What a little beauty you are becoming, Tabby, to be sure!"

Sir Kit rolled his eyes. "Little girls are not performing monkeys or artists' models. Come, Tabby-kitten." Tabby's face fell, but she didn't protest as he hoisted her onto his knee. "It does a child good to hear rational adult conversation now and then—if you people can manage that." Everyone laughed, but despite his teasing smile, I thought he meant it.

Tabby listened eagerly to a conversation about parish business; the progress of the war; the health of the magistrate's mother; Fanny Musgrave, whose husband was sending her to the country for making a fool of him; and the Tassells' family affairs, especially their middle son's recent marriage to the author of *The Wise and Witty Governess*.

"Nicholas Dymond must love to be looked up to," a man opined. "I too might have married the daughter of a freeman, if all I wanted from a wife were gratitude and complaisance."

"If you *don't* want those things, you chose excellently well," said Mr. Abbott.

Sir Kit saw the look on my face. "Miss Oliver is from Lively St. Lemeston. Tell us, madam, do you think the new Mrs. Nicholas Dymond will spend her days licking her husband's shoes?"

"Hardly." I wished I knew how to keep the edge from my voice, as Iphigenia did. "Mrs. Dymond is a woman of strong character and firm principles."

"Oh, a shrew!" said the magistrate.

I had known someone would say it. Truthfully, Mrs. Dymond *could* be a shrew now and then, but she was broad-minded, and fair-minded too, as none of these people had shown themselves to be. No, I was forced to admit, not even Sir Kit. He meant well, that was certain, but—

"And how do you know her, Miss Oliver?" someone asked, rather meanly.

I knew they were all hoping for an answer just like the truth: *She rented attic rooms near my boarding house. Sometimes she stopped by of an evening, when she couldn't afford her own coal.* "She served with some of my friends on the Society for Bettering the Condition of the Poor's Committee for the Encouragement of Charitable Subscriptions and Bequests."

"Mrs. Dymond gave me a book," Tabby said loudly. "She wrote it herself. It's my *favorite* book."

I smiled gratefully at my charge, who looked furious that the guests were laughing at her. She was a good-hearted girl after all, and I ought to be more patient with her.

Sir Kit squeezed his daughter. "Gratitude is not such a bad thing, eh?" he said. "But Lady Tassell told me Mrs. Dymond is a very shabby dresser, kitten, so I know you won't take her *too* much as a model." He kissed her on the forehead and set her on the floor. "Now I think it's your bedtime."

Tabby looked as if she would have argued, but Sir Kit raised his eyebrows in admonishment and she came at once to me, reaching for my hand to go upstairs. I felt the peculiar pleasure, and the peculiar pain, of being momentarily singled out by a child not one's own. It was so impossible to know how much it meant, and yet it felt like such a blessing.

I looked to Sir Kit for leave to go, though I tried to keep the eagerness off my face.

"Miss Oliver is our hostess tonight, kitten, so she must stay with the grown-ups for now. Give her a kiss and go with Clarice."

Tabby's hand fell. She gave me an odd, calculating look, and then a pretty kiss on the cheek that was for her father's benefit, not mine.

My heart sank. Did she know it was her mother's place to do what I was doing? Had she noticed the warmth with which her father sometimes spoke to me?

I had done nothing wrong, wanted nothing more than to take Tabby's hand and let her lead me back to our attic. Yet I felt myself a usurper, suddenly.

Had I really thought to myself, *If I were mistress of Goldengrove…?* How had I dared?

"We will search the nursery top to bottom," I told Tabby again, getting on my hands and knees to peer beneath her clothespress for the missing embroidered hair ribbon, one of a pair.

Her inconsolable wails did not diminish in pitch or intensity, and my nerves were in shambles from the shrill, unceasing sounds of distress. "If we don't find it, we will ask the maids to look for it in the rest of the house."

I had given up on reasoning with her as to the insignificance of the loss or the ease of obtaining a replacement. At first, she had shrieked in reply, *Papa gave them to me!* and *Papa will think I'm careless!* By now, she had lost the power to speak or understand. In truth, I was beginning to feel frightened, though Clarice assured me that children sometimes carried on so, and likely she was just tired.

I thought the opposite was the case—the better rested Tabby looked in the morning, the worse her petulance and fidgets. I had thought perhaps she needed more exercise and made a point of taking her outside in the mornings, to no avail.

The excitement and agitation of the dinner party had not yet worn off, though nearly half a week had gone by; she could not sit still to study her numbers, and would interrupt my lessons to repeat her account of how each lady had dressed, and the compliments they had paid her. I would have lost my patience long since, if she had not dwelt particularly on Mrs. Abbott and her daughter, and how they had sat next to one another, and how they wore matching pink gloves, in a way that would have wrung a heart of stone.

Where else could I look for the ribbon? I had searched once already in the dusty, narrow space that ran behind the low wooden panels along one side of the room, and had hit my head on the eaves for my pains. In desperation I opened them again, dragging out a few crates of the old toys that had once been stored in my room.

Nothing.

I eyed the door to the emptied cupboard, afraid to put even my ship's lantern in such a close space, where a flailing hand could set the roof ablaze—or my hair, when I stuck my head in.

Tabby paused to draw breath. I yearned for that brief silence to last.

I stuck my arms into the low compartment and felt about. Dust and cobwebs clung to my hands, just as they always did to Tabby when she had crawled into the cupboard over my protests. The maids did their best, but they could hardly expunge spiders or dust from an attic.

Had Tabby been wearing the red ribbons the last time I stripped off her grimy dress to send it to the laundress? Had she been wearing *both* of them?

I crammed my head and shoulders into the tight space, running my hands over everything I could reach and getting splinters for my pains. Resentful tears pricked at my eyes. *Why me?*

At any moment, Sir Kit might come to find out why his daughter was crying, and I would not be able to answer him calmly. I might even weep myself. He would think me weak and excitable, not fit to raise a sensible Englishwoman.

I fetched my lantern and candle-stub, but when I had twice dropped my flint trying to strike it, Clarice took pity on me and lit the candle.

I shut the lantern and slid it slowly into the cupboard. I poked my head in after it, a hand pressed to my ear so I could feel the heat of the lantern and judge its distance from my skin.

The roofbeams glowed yellow, a miniature hellscape. I didn't see the damn hair ribbon.

But what was that rectangular shape wedged between a beam and the floor? A misplaced toy? Perhaps the ribbon was behind or beneath it.

Pulling out the lantern and lying flat on the floor, I thrust as much of my torso as I could through the little sliding door, stretching my hand out, feeling—there! I brushed a corner with my fingertips.

My shoulder cramped as I pulled the object free. I had to massage my arm for a moment before reaching back in to drag it out and carry it to the window for inspection.

Tabby's crying cut off abruptly.

I turned back in shock, wondering if Clarice had found the ribbon, or if Sir Kit had walked in without my hearing him. But Tabby was staring at me.

To my surprise, when I looked down, the object in my hands was familiar. It was the wooden box, with its label reading *My MOTHER*.

"It's your puzzle," I said slowly. It had been in its usual spot in the bottom of the toy-chest a few days ago. "You told me you wanted to leave it in the toy-chest. Did you change your mind and put it in the closet?"

Tabby shook her head.

I struggled for self-command; snapping at her for lying would serve no purpose. "Well, perhaps your ribbon is inside. We will check, and then put it back."

"I don't think the ribbon is in there."

"All right, but it can't hurt to…" I lifted the lid—and stared in horror. Beside me, Clarice started back, her hand flying to the amulet in her pocket.

The puzzle had been destroyed.

9

I'd seen my share of crumpled, torn, stained, painted-upon playthings. This was not that. Red and black crayon slashed across the pieces, the lines ending sharply as though the crayon had snapped in the holder's hand. Water must have been poured over it, too, for the paper rippled away from the swollen wood.

The word *Mother* was gouged out at the end of every verse.

Just yesterday I had asked Tabby how she had bent her sewing scissors. She had looked at me, blank and watchful, and said *I don't know, ma'am, perhaps it was someone else.* Assuming she was afraid of being punished for carelessness, I had sent the scissors to be repaired and thought no more of it.

"Christabel, did you—did you do this?"

She shook her head.

"It's best to be honest, sweetheart." My lips shaped the endearment numbly, my stomach aching as though I had drunk hemlock.

"A rat must have done it."

"Rats don't use crayons!"

"It wasn't me."

I looked at the vicious gouges in the wood, and felt almost afraid, as if she might plunge her little scissors into my flesh next. *I have charge of a monster.* "I must show this to your father," I said faintly.

She ran at me. I flinched, but she only dropped to the floor and began kissing the hem of my dress, as if just a few minutes ago she hadn't fought like a wild thing to get free of me, when I had tried to comfort her.

"Don't show it to him," she pleaded. "Please don't tell him. It wasn't me. I'll be a good girl and always do what you say."

"A good girl doesn't destroy her things."

Tabby gave me a look like a cornered animal and clambered up onto the window ledge, trying to scramble out the open casement.

Thank God I was already at the window. I dropped the puzzle, mutilated pieces scattering across the floor, and yanked her back so hard I felt her shoulder wrench in the socket.

Then Clarice had leapt forward and wrapped both arms around her waist. "The devil's in you!" she scolded, voice high. "You'd ought to be whipped, you little bitch!"

I shut the casement and locked it, heart racing. Tabby was small enough to fit through the narrow panel of glass, but it would take me some contortions to follow her, if I could manage it at all. If I had not been by the window…what act of desperation might she not have committed?

"Language, Clarice," I said weakly.

Tabby stared me down from within the prison of Clarice's grasp. "Don't tell Papa," she said fiercely. "I didn't do it."

Mindlessly, I bent and picked up a ruined puzzle piece: a little blond child, falling, arms reaching helplessly out for succor. My memory filled in the gaps in the depicted verse: *Who ran to help me when I fell, and would some pretty story tell, or kiss the place to make it well? My mother.*

I imagined showing this to Sir Kit, and the bleak look on his face. There was no delicate way to do it.

I imagined, too, telling him that his daughter had almost escaped from me onto a patch of roof bordered only by a low parapet and a long drop.

Tabby's rage had faded. Her red eyes pleaded with me, and her lip trembled. She just looked like a child, exhausted from crying. I felt exhausted, too.

I had hated being spanked. I had hated when my father looked me gently in the face and told me I had disappointed him.

My sense of proportion belatedly reasserted itself. Was this really so very dreadful? Children had tantrums. Stabbing a bit of wood was not the same as stabbing flesh.

I knelt to look Tabby in the eye. "Will you be still if Clarice lets you go?"

She nodded.

"Promise me."

"Yes, ma'am, I promise."

I nodded to Clarice to release her. The nursemaid raised her eyebrows, but she let Tabby go and began putting the puzzle pieces back in the box, holding them by one corner as though they would contaminate her.

"You have done a wicked thing," I said gently. "Are you very sorry?"

"It wasn't me," she said again.

"Do you remember what I told you on our first Sunday together?"

"That you would tell Papa if I was bad. But I didn't do it."

"Yes, and I also told you that you will find it feels best to tell the truth when you know you have done wrong. We must be honest with ourselves, and admit it when we have done wrong, if we ever wish to do better. I'll ask you again. Are you very sorry for destroying your nice puzzle, that might have made some poor little girl very happy?"

There was a long silence. Would I have to tell Sir Kit after all?

But when I shifted my weight to stand up, Tabby burst out in a small voice, "Yes, ma'am. I'm ever so sorry."

"Thank you for your honesty, Tabby. Can you tell me the Fifth Commandment?"

"Honor thy father and thy mother."

"Very good." I had taught her that. Surely I was not such a bad governess. Surely I was not ruining this child's disposition by too much leniency. Was it so strange, that she might wish to rid herself of a reminder of what others had, and she lacked? That she should resent her mother for being—as far as I knew—entirely absent from her life?

As far as I knew. A fresh chill assailed me. Might she have reasons to hate her mother I could not yet guess at?

But I said, "Will you strive to keep the commandment from now on?"

She nodded, curls bouncing vigorously.

"Then you may ask God to forgive you in your prayers, and if it doesn't happen again, we'll say no more about it."

Tabby hurled herself into my lap. "I love you, Miss Oliver. You're an angel. A beautiful angel, and God will reward you for your kindness."

My gorge rose at this shameless flattery. "I'm just a governess," I said, to show I wasn't taken in—but I *was* taken in. I had let a child get the upper hand of me. I didn't dare look at Clarice, afraid to see my own disgust at my weakness and hypocrisy mirrored in her face.

I rocked Tabby in my lap like an infant, humming a sad, slow ballad.

When her little body had relaxed, I washed her face, and brushed her hair until it crackled. Such fine blond hair! I wondered again where Lady Palethorp was from.

Tabby looked sad when we tied off her fresh braids with plain blue ribbons, but she didn't say a word, and let me kiss her temple without protest.

The knowledge that I was keeping something from Sir Kit prevented me from behaving entirely naturally in his presence. He felt it, and to my shame, he seemed to make an effort to charm me out of my stiffness. One afternoon, as I passed through the library, I heard him call me back.

I turned. "Yes, sir?"

He stood in the door to his study. "You're teaching Tabby to play the guitar, aren't you?"

"That would be an exaggeration. Her hands are still too small for the instrument." I did now and then let her hold it in her lap and strum at random while singing loudly. I smiled fondly to myself.

"I'd like to learn," he said, to my surprise. "It seems easier than the pianoforte, and more portable. A good thing for a father to know on winter evenings."

My smile widened. "My father played the recorder. He learned in the navy." I flushed without quite knowing why, only it seemed an oddly intimate thing. A soft, young piece of myself I hadn't meant to share.

"Will you teach me?"

I hesitated. That was an intimate thing too—at least, I felt that it would be with him.

"There's a spare instrument around somewhere. A fine one, I think, as such things are reckoned. Step into the music room with me."

A fine guitar! My eagerness overcame my usual dread of the music room and its thrice-damned thermometer. As we entered, I was able to meet the thermometer's eye boldly, for the weather remained cool and it read only 56.

I told myself it was not only my own little madness that made me dislike the room, which *ought* to have been my favorite in the house. No, I had plenty of better reasons. The designer's idiosyncratic eye for color had been happy for once—gray walls and carpet, a checkered floor, and crimson upholstery—but the bust of Handel and sketches of the Muses were straight out of a furniture dealer's catalogue. Moreover, the room adjoined the garderobe and smelled overpoweringly of lavender (and sometimes, faintly, of earthier things).

Worst of all, the piano was near to both the fire and the window, where heat and light would wreak the most damage—quite a feat in a room with only two narrow windows and a slim hearth crammed into the corner.

In short, whoever had designed the room, she could not have been a musician. If I had been mistress of Goldengrove, I would have put the instruments in the airy parlor adjoining the chapel.

Unlocking a cluttered closet and rummaging through, Sir Kit emerged with a dusty case, which he laid on the floor and opened.

I gasped, my fingers flexing covetously.

Sir Kit laughed at me, brushing cobwebs from his hair. "You can touch it."

The strings were old and snapped, but when I had wiped away the dust with my handkerchief, the instrument was satiny to the touch, voluptuous and gleaming. Mother-of-pearl and ebony inlay danced around the sound-hole, and swooped in delicate ribbons below the bridge.

"You can use this one, if you like, and I'll practice with yours."

I did not quite want to relinquish my own. But my fingers wrapped possessively around the ebony neck. "Are you certain, sir?" Oh, how sweet its sound must be!

His eyes twinkled. "I hope you don't doubt my word."

"It needs new strings," I blurted out. "I'll walk into town on my half-holiday." Oh, but that was days away! I laid the guitar flat on the shrouded pianoforte and bent to examine it from the side. The table had not bowed, and the neck looked straight. I pressed lightly on the body, then the fret-board; all seemed securely attached. "Have you any spare strings about? How long since it was played, do you know?"

He hesitated. "A few years? At a guess."

I took the instrument to the window. In the sun, the frets and pegs were well-used, but nothing worse. The whole instrument looked in far better condition than I had expected from those frayed, ancient strings. Perhaps they had been worn out through playing, not age. I took one half-string in my fingers and looked closely at the end.

I blinked, unsettled. "The strings look cut." I showed Sir Kit the sharp, clean end. "Do you know what happened?"

His brow furrowed, as if in pain. He didn't answer.

I thought sickly of Tabby's scissors. Could *she...*?

But no, he had said *a few years.* If his two-year-old daughter had cut the strings, he would laugh and call her a little hellion. He would tell me.

His blue eyes met mine, and darted away, as if afraid.

I thought of his gossipy neighbors. Did he have anyone in whom to confide?

"Could..." I bit my lip, gathering my courage for the leap. "Could your wife have done it?" I waited for him to tell me I was unforgivably impertinent and fanciful.

But he nearly sagged in relief, pressing his fingertips into his eyes. "Yes. My wife—how did you guess? The guitar was my mother's. My wife...didn't get along with her." He laughed shortly. "But why should I sweeten the bitter truth for you, Miss Oliver? My wife hated my mother. I suppose women often do hate their mothers-in-law, but I—I hadn't expected it."

I pressed the tip of my finger against the sharp string-end, feeling cold. Somehow, the precise little snips disturbed me more than if she had smashed the guitar to smithereens on the courtyard stones. Such a small, nasty thing to do.

Once, when I was very young, I had started awake to the sound of my grandmother's sobs. *Why couldn't they leave me my music?* she was saying in a clogged whine. *Such a little thing but they had to take it too...*

Hush, mamã, my mother told her, her own voice husky with tears. *Hush, I know, I'm sorry...*

I had been frightened to hear my capable avó wail into my mother's dress like a baby. Now, with the vantage point of years, I realized vó had probably been drunk. It struck me like a sudden vertigo, how strange it was to be an adult, and to have been a child.

What would Tabby be like when she was grown? Could she have inherited her mother's vicious streak?

No, I vowed. She might grow up headstrong, or quick to anger. But I had the raising of her, and she would grow up with a sense of justice, too.

The suspicion came back: had Lady Palethorp treated her unkindly? Was that the true source of Tabby's fury at the puzzle? I felt ashamed that I had thought her merely spoiled by overindulgence. I must be more patient, and more charitable.

"I've shocked you," Sir Kit said. "You're incapable of this sort of petty-minded feminine treachery, aren't you?"

I think that shocked me more than anything else—that he could see such pointed cruelty as a little thing, an ordinary fault of women. I felt offended on behalf of my sex.

I reminded myself that I was privy only to his words, not his thoughts. If he knew his wife to be a virago, he would hardly say so to his governess. "I'm not shocked. Only distressed on your poor mother's behalf."

In spite of everything, my eyes were drawn irresistibly back to the guitar. I wanted very much to test its sound. Conscious of my own selfishness, I knelt to rummage through the case for a spare packet of strings, and sat back on my heels with a smothered sigh.

A small, strained smile crept over his face. "Write down your order, and I shall visit the music warehouse for you this very afternoon."

My breath caught. "Oh, you really needn't." But my fingers were already curled around the pencil in my pocket. "I can go on Friday."

He laughed. "There, you have very civilly begged me not to trouble myself. I shall very civilly assure you I was going into Rye anyway, and now you may write your order acquitted of the terrible crime of allowing a friend to do you a favor."

They'll say they are your friends. Don't believe them!

My shoulder felt stiff as I wrote, and the words marched crookedly across the scrap of paper: *1 set of strings for a ten-string guitar*. Really, I ought to order two, but I thought with misgiving of the handful of shillings that must last me until the Midsummer quarter-day. "I do not know precisely what they will cost. I will give you two shillings, and if it is more than that—"

He plucked the note from my hand, eyes gleaming in amusement. "Shall I ask him to write up a receipt, too, so you know I have brought you correct change?"

But he did not bring a receipt. Instead, he brought three sets of strings and a stack of sheet music, which he presented to me when I had come down to take the final barometer reading after Tabby was in bed, for she could not abide an incomplete square in our notebook.

"Thank you, sir. What do I owe you?" I asked, embarrassed. Of course I wanted the sheet music, but my little purse would be quite empty if I repaid him now. "You may take it out of my wages at Midsummer…"

He waved a hand. "Consider it wages for my lessons. I arranged to have the pianoforte tuned next week, as well. Do you play well enough for Tabby to begin with?"

"Yes, sir." I felt that it was wrong to accept the present, but I could not hide my pleasure at it. New music, for my new guitar. I gave him a demure look. "And I am sure the ladies will be glad to have the instrument in playing condition at your next party."

He laughed. "It would make the evening less appallingly dull, you mean?"

I lowered my eyes.

"Well, you are right, it was very dull indeed, but to atone for your incivility in *saying* what we were both thinking privately, you must play a duet with me at my first musical evening."

My heart leapt. It felt like an eternity since I had last played a duet. "Do you play the piano, sir?"

"Obviously not, or it would already be tuned."

"Then you—sing?"

He let out a bark of laughter. "Your doubt wounds me, Miss Oliver. You don't believe I have the voice of a nightingale?"

I felt warm. *Too* warm. This was unwise. "We had better not," I made myself say.

There was a little silence. I dared not meet his eyes.

"Is this because I bought your music?" he asked gently.

"I don't wish to be guilty of impropriety, sir, that's all. I don't want to cause talk."

"What could anyone possibly say?"

"People will say anything," I replied a little bitterly. What had Sir Kit already told them at the music warehouse? Would the shopkeeper spread it about, that the baronet was giving presents to his governess?

I could feel his gaze on my face. "I didn't think you cared so much for the opinions of strangers. You and I are friends, aren't we?"

That word again! I drew back, rubbing at my shoulder.

He couldn't hide his hurt at my recoil.

"A governess and her employer cannot be friends," I explained, hating that this was my recompense for his kindness. "Friendly, yes, I hope—I hope very much we are that, sir."

"You don't really believe that."

Part of me yearned to say *no—no, I don't. I have a soul and a mind and a heart, and deserve friendship as much as a rich woman.*

"I thought you were a Methodist. A leveler of ranks."

The words were a knife in my heart. I remembered Papa saying, *Distinctions of rank melt away like dew in the light of Heaven.*

"My father was." I had meant to say it lightly, but I couldn't carry it off.

Sir Kit didn't laugh. He didn't speak.

If Iphigenia had answered Sir Kit as I had, he would have laughed. But Iphigenia was seventy miles away. I had no friends at all. I cast about for an olive branch, something to say, anything. "How was your visit to Rye?"

His eyebrows went up, just a little.

"The barometer is falling. I'm glad you made it back before the rain."

"What would we English do without the weather to cover up these little unpleasantnesses? Here, I will go to the window and make a show of examining the sky for storm clouds." But he only settled himself in the window-seat, and examined my face. "Were you fond of your Methodist father, Miss Oliver?"

"Very much so."

"I passed the house I was born in, today." He laughed mirthlessly, shoving his hands into his pockets. "I was birched in that house more times than I can count. Perhaps I *should* be fond of my father. He did more to prepare me for Eton than my Latin tutor." He fingered the fine brocade curtains. "Do you know I quarreled with my mother over what she spent on Goldengrove? How galling it must have been for her, to have her jackass of a son calling it *my* house, when it ought to have been hers—would have been, if my father had lived just a few more years, or my grandfather a few less. They even arranged their deaths to disoblige her."

"I'm sure she knew how much you loved her."

He glanced at me, his frown softening. "Thank you. I'm sorry. I didn't mean to monologue like the melancholy Dane. Such outpourings of the soul should be reserved for a *friend*, and you are only my music tutor." But he said it teasingly. "Can you spare time for a lesson for me tomorrow evening, when Tabby is in bed?"

10

Sure enough, the next day brought a summer storm. I brooded over the rising temperatures in our little notebook.

I brooded, too, over Sir Kit's hurt look, and presented myself promptly for his lesson.

He raised his head from his papers and stood, smiling at me. Did I imagine the hint of reserve?

"Sir," I said in a rush. "What I said yesterday. About our not being friends."

The smile faded. "If it will ease your mind, Miss Oliver, I will lie and tell you I have quite forgotten it."

I knotted my fingers nervously together. "If I left my employment, you would find another governess. But I don't know if I could find another post, if you showed me the door."

"I have no intention of showing you the door," he said impatiently. "Who cares if small-minded people talk nonsense?"

"You would, since I am raising your daughter."

He opened his mouth to expostulate.

"I only meant that true friendship requires equality," I said, defeated, "and there is not equality between us. That is *all* I meant."

He closed his blotter on a mass of paper and stood. "Come, let us go into the music room. That will be more comfortable for a lesson."

The lesson would be an agony, now. Did he really mean to insist on it?

Why had I reopened the subject? I was no Eliza Bennet, with a "mixture of sweetness and archness in her manner which made it difficult for her to affront anybody." Shy, stiff people like me and Mr. Darcy would never receive a like tolerance. Sir Kit had been willing to pass it off, and now he would be further offended, and dislike me for telling him the truth.

Was my most stimulating conversation henceforth to be with Clarice—practically a child herself—about whether Tabby ought to wear her warm coat today?

But as he watched me tune the guitar, my nerves making me fumble over the simple task, he spoke at last. "Aristotle agrees with you that the law of equality is the soul of friendship," he said gravely. "But he also says that a virtuous man may live in friendship with the great, if they will honor his superiority of virtue as much as he honors their superiority of fortune." His smile at last broke free. "Perhaps if I esteem your virtue very highly, and you heap scorn upon my riches, we may yet manage the thing between us."

I laughed with relief, eyes stinging. "You're not angry with me?"

"I believe I read out a sermon a few months ago, on a text to the effect that wise men love reproof. One day, God willing, I may be wise in truth, and in the meantime, I shall claim the gentlemanly prerogative of counterfeiting virtues I do not possess."

I didn't really think he understood what I had said to him. But he had heard me out, and bore no grudge. That was more than I had hoped for. If I avoided every man who was a trifle overfamiliar on occasion, I would soon find myself living in a hermitage. It was only natural for gentlemen to seek the pleasure of uninhibited social intercourse, when for them it was not followed by the pain of the world's censure. How *could* Sir Kit understand my fear? With what could he compare it?

And yet he maintained a respectful distance through our lesson, because he knew I wished it. I was grateful for that.

The next week, the sun blazed out all at once. I finally permitted Tabby to write the temperature in our notebook with her own hand, and for a moment her beaming pride swept away my distress at the bold, thick *78°*.

"Look how well you formed your numbers, Tabby! What a clever girl you are."

"That's the hottest it's been all year," she said, thrilled. "Do you think it's *ever* been so hot in May before?"

I blotted my damp brow, and smiled at her. "We shall look it up."

But our little rooms at the top of the old keep, where the sun beat down on the stone roof, became nearly unlivable. Only Mrs. Palethorp's guitar bore me up.

Once strung, it had a rich, sweet tone I loved to distraction, and the instrument fit my knee as if made for me. I played until my fingers threatened to bleed, and only stopped there from a reluctance to dirty my new strings. I can't put into words its effect on me: the notes filled up the air until I floated in a warm, welcoming sea.

After a few days, I even dreamed of it—a welcome respite from nightmares.

"Why don't you play 'Foi por mim' anymore?" mãe asked me.

"I don't remember the words, mamã."

"You don't? Well, give me the guitar, minha filha, and I'll sing it for you."

But she had only strummed a few chords when I woke. The floor creaked—

But I would not let my imagination run away with me again. I pulled the pillow over my head, trying to slip back into the dream. If only one could carry a pencil and memorandum book into the land of Nod…

Alas, the words still escaped me in the morning. Still, Tabby was in a good mood, and chattered happily to me over breakfast. I asked her if she could remember her grandmother playing the guitar.

"I was just a *baby*," she said, as if I were very stupid, and though she usually scowled when I laughed at anything she said, for once she merely looked pleased with her own wit.

"Let's have lessons in the library this morning," I said. "It will be cooler there, and the piano tuner is coming today. I think you will find that very interesting."

I brought down the guitar, hoping to sing its praises in counterpoint. But the man only shook his head when I showed off the instrument, in a lull between Tabby's eager questions. "That must have been before my time, ma'am. I'm only Mr. Shriver's apprentice."

"I am sure he is glad to have your help on his rounds," I said, to mask my disappointment.

"He would have rather come himself, ma'am. But Sir Kit said he wouldn't hear of it."

I blinked. "Why not?"

At this moment, the baronet himself entered. "Because I thought he would have more patience with Miss Christabel's pestering. Good morning, Jeremy. Poor lad, you've spared your master a sunburn as well. Have they sent up enough lemonade?"

"I wouldn't say no to another pitcher, thank you, sir. And I quite like children."

"I'm sure I'll pay you enough for the service to make you like anything."

"A man must make a living," the young man answered impudently, and was rewarded by Sir Kit's infectious bark of laughter. I thought again of Eliza Bennet's precious gift of archness, and sighed.

Somewhat to my surprise, Sir Kit exerted himself to practice on my guitar most mornings in the music room, slow and fumbling.

"Remember to keep your wrists straight, sir," I would chide when Tabby and I came in to take our readings, for it delighted Tabby to see her father corrected like any other pupil, and he would exaggerate his groans to please her.

"Who taught you to play, Miss Oliver?" he asked one morning, pausing in his playing to massage his cramping fingers. I suspected him of exaggerating that also, for he was as proud of his sore muscles as any athlete.

"My mother." I thought of Tabby's ravaged puzzle. Perhaps she did, too, for she ran to retrieve the album of last year's *Gentleman's Magazine*s from the piano bench, slipping beneath the piano with it. "That is her guitar in your hands."

Sir Kit's grip gentled, as if the idea gave him a deeper respect for the instrument; I was grateful to him for it. "And who taught her?"

"My grandmother."

"Did you know your grandmother, growing up?"

"I did, sir. She lived with us until her death when I was seven or eight."

"Did she play for you?" He glanced wistfully towards the piano, where Tabby was poring over temperature tables.

I was just a baby, she had said; poor child, to lose her grandmother so very young.

"No, sir." I lowered my voice so Tabby would not hear. "Her fingers were broken as a girl."

"Good God. What happened?"

I hesitated. Even a brief *There was an accident* would be false. "She didn't like to speak of it. I…I believe her first love broke off their engagement in connection with it." How innocent that sounded—an ordinary cruelty such as happens every day under the sun.

But then, what cruelties did *not* happen every day?

Sir Kit looked revolted. "Best to discover his character *before* the wedding, I suppose. But what a…" He cast about for a word he could say in my presence.

"Some things are unspeakable."

"How ruthless you look, Miss Oliver!" His smile was startlingly fond. "I believe if you could, you'd call the…*fellow* out yourself and shoot him."

I drew in a deep breath. I *would* shoot him if I could. But surely he had been dead for years by now. I could not bear to think of the alternative. If he had outlived her so long—if even now he was fishing and taking his siesta and doting on a pack of great-grandchildren, the Iberian sun bathing his ancient joints…

Vó had always been so cold in the winter.

That night I tossed and turned in my bed, sleepless. *Exert yourself,* I scolded. *Govern your feelings. Cease to voluntarily renew and increase a natural grief.*

But I could not stop picturing vó as a trusting girl, glowing with first love—or missing her as I remembered her, a cynical, stubborn old woman who bluntly corrected my playing and loved me. I missed my parents. At last I climbed to the roof so I might play her old songs to myself, the sweet notes of Mrs. Palethorp's guitar wrapping around me until I wept my heart out for all the things that were crooked, and could not be made straight.

At last, exhausted and cried out, I crept back downstairs. Softly, I shut the door behind me and locked it.

Some quality in the silence changed: a deeper hush, some rustling ceasing. It could not have been a mouse, could it? I stood very still, listening and watching my floor—faintly moonlit, for I had not yet closed the shutters.

A door shut softly. I gasped.

Be rational! That was no cause for alarm. The house had other inhabitants. The door had not been one of mine; that left Clarice's closet or the nursery's door onto the landing.

A floorboard creaked on the landing. Sir Kit, then, come to visit his sleeping daughter. The riddle was solved.

So why did my mind keep turning it over? I was no better than a mouse myself—

No candle! I realized suddenly: no flickering glow through the crack under my door. Sir Kit wouldn't climb the stairs without a light, would he?

My key was still in my hand; I rushed to the other door and opened it. "Who's there?"

Footsteps raced down the stairs. I ran to the mouth of the stairwell in time to glimpse a shadowy figure disappear around the first bend, trailed by—long hair? A cloak?

I pounded after it, but inky darkness swallowed me whole at the first turn. My heel slipped from the narrow end of a spiraling step. I nearly tumbled into the abyss, the wall scraping my palms and a hard stone edge slamming into my shin.

My quarry's footsteps and gasps for air echoed in the stairwell. I scrabbled for my dropped key, wrapping the chain between my fingers as I got to my feet, light-headed with fear, and limped on.

At last I stood on the second-story landing. I had never been in the interior of the house at night. No susurration of the sea, no croak of a night heron, no ray of moonshine, no snore of a fellow inhabitant penetrated Goldengrove's thick walls and doors and shutters. There was no sound, no light—only a presence. For a moment, I fancied it was the house itself I sensed, that I pressed my hand not against stone, but against the belly of the whale that had swallowed me.

What waited in the darkness with me? How close did it stand? Would I have time to scream before its hands were round my throat?

Afraid to disturb the thick hush, I pressed my fingers over my own nose and mouth until Lady Palethorp's gold chain scraped against my teeth. Pressure built in my throat. My heart threatened to burst. The implacable stones seemed to bunch and coil beneath my feet. One shove, and they would crack my skull with relish.

My nerve broke.

11

I fled downstairs, calling out for Sir Kit. I half slipped a dozen times, but I could not force my feet to slow. Before I knew it, I had tripped over the first-floor landing, barely managing to seize the door-handle before I plunged headlong down the remaining stairs. It took me several tries to get my key into the lock, and then I was in the corridor between Sir Kit's apartment and the chapel gallery.

I felt along the wall until my fingers passed over a doorjamb and onto paneled wood. I fell against the door, drumming on it with the sides of my fists. "Sir Kit! Sir Kit! Wake up, please, light, we need light…"

Why didn't he open the door? Had it been him I chased down the stairs after all?

If he wasn't here, and the shadow followed me—

The door opened. I stumbled blindly into a warm, breathing human form, and clung to it. I knew dimly that I should not—that he wore very little—but I could not care for that. I was safe, at last I was safe.

"Is Tabby ill?" His voice was terrible.

Oh God. I made a sobbing sound. Had she been smothered in her bed? Why hadn't I gone into the nursery? "I don't know. Someone was in her room. They ran and I went after them. I don't know—I was frightened. I couldn't see. I've got to go back…"

I turned away from his warmth, towards the impenetrable darkness—and froze, trembling.

"Let me light the lamp," he said.

Each strike and bright spark of the tinder made me jump, but at last he had lit a spill, and then an oil lamp. I was so grateful for the light that I did not even object to the smoking wick when he held the lamp out for me to take: a shining brass thing of Dutch manufacture with a round reservoir atop a tall stem, its spout split to catch stray drops of oil. And a good thing, too, for the flame jumped in my shaking hand, and I must have blistered my toes if the lower fork of the lamp's tongue hadn't lapped up the spatter.

"Go see to Tabby," he said. "If she's all right, lock the doors and go back to bed."

"They have a key," I protested.

"Do as I say, Miss Oliver."

The lamp's naked flame showed me nothing outside its narrow circle—and made *me* horribly visible. I inched my way up the steps, ears straining. I heard only my own breaths, the rustle of my nightdress, the faint slosh of oil in my lamp.

The thing had fled; why did I imagine it had crept back up the stairs, and was waiting for me? Slowly, I slid the key into the nursery door—slowly, because if I had tried to do it quickly with my shaking hands, I should never have managed it.

The trembling, smoking lamp made the nursery a miniature Hell as I crept across the floor. Afraid to bring it near the bed-curtains, I set it on Tabby's little writing table and inched towards her queenly little bed, ready to push Adeline aside with my foot, but she wasn't in her usual place. Slowly, I drew the muslin curtains open—and barely swallowed a scream when my fingers brushed flesh.

Tabby was sitting up in bed, motionless. I stepped aside to see her in the light. She held Adeline in her lap, and child and doll stared up at me, unblinking.

Unharmed, I told myself, trying to still my heaving chest. *She looks unharmed.* "Are you well?"

She nodded silently.

My heart finally slowing, I took up the lamp to swiftly look about the room. I found nothing except for Tabby's marbles scattered across the floor, ready to break someone's neck.

I was painfully aware that if Tabby had not already been frightened, my present behavior must alarm her, and I bit my tongue on a sharp reprimand for her carelessness. It would keep until morning. Now I merely gathered the marbles up in my nightdress before peering into my own room and Clarice's closet. The nursemaid was sleeping peacefully.

I knelt beside Tabby's bed. "Who was here before, sweetheart? Did you see?"

Her face was a smooth mask. "No one was here."

"Are you sure? You can talk to me."

"No one was here," she repeated impatiently.

"What woke you?"

She shrugged.

I was sure she was lying. But why? The only explanation I could see was that the visitor had been Lady Palethorp. But why on earth should the mistress of the house steal into the nursery like a thief, and flee like one? Why should Tabby try to conceal a visit from her mother?

And Sir Kit had told me to simply lock the doors and go back to bed. How could I? Didn't I deserve to know who had been in my charge's room—who had frightened me out of my wits?

I jumped again, marbles rattling in my lap, as voices swelled below us, a muffled but rising rumble. Sir Kit, and someone shriller. I could almost make out the words…

"Are you frightened, Tabby?"

She shook her head.

I ought not to leave her alone—ought at least to wake Clarice—but I didn't want the maid to know I was eavesdropping.

"Call for me if you need me." I slipped back into my own room, locking the door behind me and dumping the marbles temporarily on my bed. Without the nursery carpet, the voices were less muffled, but not enough to be intelligible.

I hesitated. Could I leave Tabby alone? But surely the intruder was the person currently arguing with Sir Kit, anyway. To get back to the nursery, they would have to pass me on the stairs—which I now descended, leaving my lamp behind me.

The stone stairwell swallowed most of the sound, and made the rest echo so that I could make no sense of the sounds, or their direction. Vertiginous, I wished with every step to turn back. But having chosen my path—having exhausted the last of my mental energy in the choice—I was powerless to deviate from it.

The voices came abruptly into focus as I passed through a few degrees of curve, still muffled, but no longer echoing. I stepped onto the second-floor landing where panic had overwhelmed me—and barely caught the smooth, well-oiled sound of Lady Palethorp's door-handle in time to dart back into the stairwell and press myself against the wall.

The hinges, however, groaned under their heavy load as the door cracked open. Sir Kit's low voice came to me distant and distorted, but I thought he said, "…knew what to do with bitches like you in Spain."

Shock pushed me forward to peer around the corner. But my eyes could see only the black door, rimmed in flickering light like the mouth of Hell. Had Sir Kit said what I imagined? Or had my mind arranged disjointed sounds into a false tune, of significance only to myself?

He was answered by a hysterical shriek. There was a heavy thud, a few scuffling noises, guttural shouts unintelligible through wild sobs.

"Hellcat!" Sir Kit said between his teeth. *That* I heard clearly.

He would be furious if he saw me. But I could not move.

The door slammed shut. I gasped audibly—but the light had winked out, too. Sir Kit had stayed inside his wife's chambers.

Reading myself a sermon on the text *Curiosity killed the cat*, I crept back upstairs, trimmed the smoking lamp-wick, and carried the light into Tabby's room. She was still sitting up in bed, singing quietly to Adeline, but she stopped when I came into the room.

Guilt smote me, that I had left her twice this evening. "Shall I sing to you?" I asked her.

"Maybe you could read Mrs. Dymond's book."

I crawled into Tabby's bed with the book, expecting soft down. Instead I sat on a hard wooden edge. "What on earth is that? Did a toy get stuck in your bed? Why didn't you say something?"

"I don't think there's anything there," Tabby said.

"Of course there is." I lifted up the mattress. "There, you see?" I pulled out a flat straw-marquetry box.

"It wasn't bothering me," Tabby said stridently. "Put it back."

My heart sank, all at once. Would I discover more vicious destruction? Perhaps it *would* be better to just put the box back and forget it.

But my curiosity, already so thwarted tonight, would not be silenced. I raised the hinged lid, and breathed a sigh of relief. It was only a mess of odds and ends: a thimble, a scrap of paper, a dented wax cherry, a crumbling biscuit, a dirty handkerchief, a string of coral beads such as small children wore for luck, and the like.

I lifted the paper scrap to see if it was a preserved note or just a bit of stray trash, grimacing at a knotted clump of Tabby's hair that clung to the corner. I removed it with thumb and forefinger.

Tabby's sharp intake of breath caught my attention. But when I glanced at her, she dropped her gaze and sat motionless.

"What's wrong, sweetheart?"

"Nothing," she mumbled.

"Did you…?" *Did you want this?* was an absurd question to ask about a clump of hair. I held it nearer Sir Kit's lamp.

A stray hair—far longer than I had expected—wafted into the flame and caught. Tabby squeaked, and I snatched my hand back and pinched out the spark. Damn this lamp! It barely gave enough light to read by, anyway. I lit Tabby's candle and fitted the glass chimney over it, then set the extinguished lamp on the mantel, where we wouldn't overturn it and spill the oil.

Upon closer inspection, the hair was much less fine than Tabby's, and possibly a few shades darker, though it was hard to be sure in this light. And it was long. I pulled, shuddering, at the end of a strand, and had drawn out nearly two feet before the knot stuck. It sprang into a wave when I let go—and left grease on my fingers.

Trying to hide my disgust, I now examined the scrap of paper. Judging by its shape, it had been the corner of a sheet, with a single curling stroke of ink cut off by the torn edge. There was no way to tell what might have been written on the larger sheet.

Gingerly I poked through the box, picking out new details: some crumbled dust that might have once been a dried flower. A small blond baby doll in a whitework gown, of a size for Adeline to hold. A bit of thread. A rabbit's foot caked in old powder.

"Are these…" My gorge rose. "Are these things from your mother, Tabby?"

Tabby's eyes were fixed sullenly on her lap. "I don't think so."

Another possibility occurred to me. "Are they from Rhoda, your old nursemaid?"

Tabby shrugged.

It might only be forgotten litter. But I could not shake off my suspicion that this sad assortment was for Tabby what vô's box full of mementos was for me.

I steeled myself. "The biscuit crumbs and the hair must be thrown away, for they are dirty and attract vermin. And the handkerchief must be laundered. The rest we will put back, and keep in your toy chest so you can sleep more comfortably."

Tabby's mouth trembled. "The handkerchief isn't dirty."

I felt worn out. "Are you afraid if it goes to the laundress, it won't come back?"

She nodded.

"Then in the morning we shall have a lesson on how to launder clothes, and clean it ourselves."

"Yes, ma'am."

I felt anger rising. The sounds from downstairs had died out, and Sir Kit had not come with explanations. *Lock the doors and go back to bed.* Fine advice! It seemed to me that the Palethorps were both very happy to neglect and overexcite their daughter by turns, and then lock me in with her out of their way, to let her vent her agitation upon me alone.

I had agreed to care for Tabby, and I was willing to give her all the attention and energy *they* chose not to expend. But it galled me to do it half at random, because *they* left me in the dark. Did they think the exertions *they* withheld cost *me* nothing? The pair of them were as childish as Tabby, blithely strewing marbles in my path.

Then it struck me. *Had* it been Tabby, who spilled her marbles? Could the babyish prank conceal a sly purpose: to give the furtive midnight visitor time to run, if I surprised her?

But why should the mistress of the house hide from *me*?

I looked at the little baby doll. It was simple work, but cunningly and charmingly done. If Lady Palethorp had made it…

I could not reconcile it with the woman who ordered sausages for breakfast, cut the strings of her mother-in-law's guitar, yet said her nerves were too weak for a visit from the nursery. Was it possible—

No, surely my imagination was running away with me. And yet the thought formed: was it possible she was forbidden to see Tabby, because of some bizarre cruelty that had not been confided to me?

Could her illness be of the mind, and not the body?

"I am here to care for you and protect you, Tabby," I said, without much hope of my words having an effect. "I can do that best if you are honest with me."

"Yes, ma'am. Thank you, ma'am." She folded her hands in her lap.

I took up *The Wise and Witty Governess*, hoping Tabby could not hear in my voice how much I hated smug Miss Baillie tonight. Let her come to Goldengrove, and see how far her wit and wisdom got her.

In the morning, I took Tabby to read the barometer early. As I had hoped, Sir Kit had not yet brought mãe's guitar into the music room. "Wait here a moment."

I slipped into his study. "Good morning, Sir Kit."

"Good morning, Miss Oliver." There was an unaccustomed coolness in his voice, or perhaps only an absence of welcome.

"Last night—is everything—" I quailed inwardly, suddenly remembering what I had imagined I heard him say: *they knew what to do with bitches like you in Spain.*

He drummed his fingers on the desk. "Yes, I'm sorry my wife frightened you. But really I don't know which of you was more terrified. Her ladyship was quite hysterical. I asked her not to go creeping around in the night without a candle, but sometimes pain keeps her awake. I can't confine her to her room like a servant."

So it *was* Lady Palethorp who had been in Tabby's room.

Sir Kit's explanation seemed straightforward, so why did I feel as if the world swayed around me? What other explanation could there be?

Yet Lady Palethorp hadn't sounded frightened to me. She had sounded murderous. I could not say so, however, without admitting to eavesdropping.

I took a deep breath, and forced myself to see reason. People did row with their wives. Was what I had heard any worse than, say, the time I had seen Mrs. Dymond and her first husband shouting at each other at the Whitsuntide fair?

Poor harried Sir Kit—straightening his papers and lining up his pens because he was too embarrassed to meet my eyes—didn't have it in him to tell his wife she ought to burn at the stake. Even if he *had* said "bitch" or "Spain," he might have meant anything. It was my own disordered fear that made me think at once of the Inquisition, my own fear I had read in Sir Kit's grim looks last night, when he had been only weary and annoyed—very natural, when woken from sleep by one's hysterical governess.

Perhaps, even, it was my own madness I suspected in Lady Palethorp.

Tabby was out of sight when I slipped back into the music room. I knew she was only hiding under the piano as usual, but my heart raced anyway until I leaned down and saw her safe.

I crawled under the instrument with her. "Tabby, about last night."

"No one was in my room," she said instantly.

When I pulled her close, she held herself stiff in my arms. "Are you frightened?"

"Of what?"

"Of the person who was in your room last night."

I couldn't quite bring myself to say, *Are you afraid of your mother?* If it was false, and I put it in her mind… If she repeated it to Mrs. Cross or Sir Kit…

"There wasn't anyone there," Tabby insisted, after far too long a pause.

I gave up. "What does the barometer say this morning?"

❋❋❋❋

I thought often of Lady Palethorp in the following days. I lay awake listening for her footsteps. I heard nothing.

I wanted to know where she was from. If it was Spain, did that mean Sir Kit had said what I thought I'd heard?

My real question, of course, was *Is she de nação?* That was how my mother used to refer to people of Portuguese Jewish extraction: *of our nation.*

I didn't want her to be. I didn't want to be like her in any way. I reminded myself of the sausages— But some Jews ate pork, after all. Perhaps she had become a Christian upon her marriage.

Please, Lord, don't send my mother's soul to Hell.

Every time I descended the stairs, her door drew my eyes. Bolted crudely into the keep's original wall, its squat arch and thick, warped planks stood in brutal contrast to my own new door and Sir Kit's, whose elegantly insubstantial panels were crisp and right-angled as fresh sheets of paper.

Strange to think that this door had been young once, too.

Sometimes I crept to it, and softly fitted my cheek to the deformed oak. But I never heard anything within.

I threw myself into Tabby's education with renewed energy and attention, determined that in this, at least, I should have nothing in common with Sir Kit's wife.

Once, during a lesson with the globes, I asked Tabby where her mother was from.

"London."

"Can you show me London on the terrestrial globe?"

I felt lower than a worm. *She is from London,* I reproached myself. *The rest might matter to Sir Kit's neighbors, but to* you *it ought to be nothing. And to put a child to the question, about her mother!*

But soon my banked curiosity flared up uncontrollably once more, this time during a drawing lesson. We had visited the vinery, and carried away a bunch of half-ripe grapes. I allowed Tabby to arrange them with some other objects—Adeline, Mrs. Dymond's book, a cut-glass bottle, and the shell of a Channel sea hedgehog—to create a little still-life on the library table.

"It's a *portrait*," she corrected me indignantly.

"I beg your pardon, Adeline," I told the doll. "As you sketch, Tabby, remember to look at things very clearly, without prejudice, and draw it as it *is*, not as you imagine it. Look at the grapes, for example. Are they circles?"

She eyed them. "They're ovals."

I smiled. "Very good."

She disliked being watched at her lessons, so while she was busy with her pencil, I roamed the library in search of books with pictures that might interest her. I hoped in particular for an image of a living sea hedgehog to compare to its shell.

To my delight, I soon opened the first outsize volume of a natural history set to discover brilliantly colored plates. Aha! There it was, just as I had hoped: the shell at the top of the page, and below, the spiny denizen of the sea. I turned to the title page to see if it was up-to-date.

The book was inscribed *To my pretty Jessica,* Sir Kit's large sloping letters swallowing up the author's Greek epigraph. That was a quote from *Merchant of Venice,* wasn't it? Jessica was Shylock's daughter, who had married a Christian.

But there must be a thousand pretty girls named Jessica in England. Probably it was only coincidence, and not a quote at all.

The publication date was given as MDCCCIV, nine years ago. I showed Tabby the sea hedgehog, and then, hating myself for it, the inscription. "Is your mother's name Jessica?"

Tabby shook her head.

"Do you know anyone named Jessica?"

Another shake.

"What is your mother's name?"

Tabby pushed her drawing towards me. "Don't you like it?"

The maids had aired out the nursery in the cool of evening, before night fell and unhealthy miasmas from the coastal marshes suffused the damp air. But despite their best efforts, the night was too dark, too still, too hot for sleep. I felt ensnared by my low muslin canopy, my own warm exhalations a weight that kept my lungs from expanding.

I would have welcomed even Lady Palethorp's step on the stair, to distract me from my thoughts.

I threw back the sheets, took off my cap, and pinned open the netting round my bed. At last my wakefulness outlasted my resolve to keep the shutters closed, in deference to Sir Kit's fear of thieves. Any burglar would have to scale four stories and climb across the roof to reach my window.

Since I had dreamed Lady Palethorp's chain was a garrote, I had not slept in it, but kept the little shutter key in its keyhole, with the other dangling in easy reach. I reached up and turned the key.

I folded the hinged shutters' twin panels flat against the sides of the deep embrasure, climbing onto the wide sill with my ancient fan. I dared not ply it very vigorously, for two of its ivory ribs were snapped, and the paper brittle. And the sight of the heavens' glittering expanse, though welcome, could not thin the close, heavy air. *Master's orders*, I scolded myself, even as I cracked open the casement.

My first cool breath carried the acrid smell of smoke.

I leaned out of the casement, fearing to see the house on fire—and recognized the smell and glowing red tip of a cigar, floating above me.

"Is that you, Miss Oliver?" Sir Kit's form detached itself from the shadows and leaned cheerfully over the edge of the little parapet.

Don't smoke on the roof, I wanted to say. But I knew the parapet was stone and brick. If he was even a little careful, a cigar was no danger.

I had to pull my head back in before I could fit my arm out the window to wave at him. Caught out and flustered, I cracked my skull in the performance of this operation. "I couldn't sleep," I called quietly. "I'm sorry, sir, I'll shut the window."

The red dot swooped as Sir Kit brushed this aside. "It's too hot to sleep. Come out and bear me company."

I hushed him urgently. "Tabby will hear you."

Sir Kit flapped his hand again. My heart skipped a beat as a bright speck of ash drifted down and extinguished itself—I hoped—on the sloping roof. "I'm being quiet."

I remembered suddenly that Sir Kit was a short flight of stairs from my room, and had the key to it. My heart skipped another beat. I could almost hear him saying lightly, *If the mountain will not come to Mahomet…*

"The night air is unhealthful." It was a weak excuse, when I had plainly meant to sit by an open window.

"We've had no marsh fever here since they dug the Military Canal."

He would laugh if I said it wasn't proper—and it wasn't so very improper, was it, if we were outdoors? A lady who couldn't afford a chaperone could not be too precious about requiring one. And I was so hot! "Very well, sir, I'll be up in a moment."

I locked the shutters and regretfully replaced my nightcap. How tight should I tie my dressing gown? It must neither hang open, nor reveal my figure too clearly. I was terribly aware of my breasts—entirely covered, but free of stays, and he would know it.

Sir Kit laughed when I climbed out of the trapdoor. "How insufferably modest you look!"

"Modesty is never insufferable, unless it's false," I said blandly. "Castor oil to keep away the flies?" I rubbed some behind my own ears, glad of my poor looks and unflattering attire. Surely nothing could be less seductive!

I caught the white flash of his teeth from where he sat between two merlons of the parapet. "My cigar seems to do the trick."

I could not have sat with my back to nothingness in the presence of another person. Of course I would not push Sir Kit over the side—but how could *he* be sure of that? I might trip over a loose stone and tumble us both over, quite by accident.

He had told me that Aristotle believed one sort of ascendancy could be balanced out by another: awe of wealth by awe of virtue, for example. Aristotle had been a private tutor in a king's home; he must have tested his axiom by his own experience.

Sir Kit trusted me, and I did not trust him. That was its own kind of upper hand, and it gave me a sense of spiritual security, a safety within myself.

"It's hot as Hades in that attic, I suppose?" he said ruefully, knocking the ash from his cigar. "And there, that was a shiver. You have gone too abruptly from heat to chill. Forgive me. This solitary house makes me value company too much, and the welfare of others too little."

I didn't want to go back inside. "I'm fine."

"If the nursery becomes really uninhabitable, we can move you all into a spare bedchamber until the heat breaks. But I should warn you, we tried it last summer, and Tabby wept until we carried everything back up the stairs. The footmen were disgusted with the both of us."

Keeping his cigar at the edge of my field of vision, I rested my forearms on the brick parapet, chest-high and reassuringly immovable. The sea danced in and out along the barren shingle, the spangled hem of her black domino glittering in the moonlight. I matched my lungs' rhythm to her grating music.

"There's something about the sea on a starry night which demands poetry," I said, ready to be laughed at.

Instead Sir Kit said, voice full of emotion,

"…Look how the floor of heaven
Is thick inlaid with patines of bright gold:
There's not the smallest orb which thou behold'st
But in his motion like an angel sings."

I thrilled to the words—then placed the quotation, and wondered if it had been a chill. *Merchant of Venice,* spoken by the Jewess's Gentile husband. That first line was short of syllables, because it was meant to begin with *Sit, Jessica.*

"Sir Kit," I blurted out. "Tabby is very taken with a set of books we found in the library today. *The Naturalist's Miscellany.* They are inscribed to someone named Jessica. We wondered who she might be."

I had not managed to sound casual. My folded arms trembled under my chin.

There was silence. The glowing tip of his cigar rose to his mouth, illuminating nothing but the faint outline of his nose. He exhaled smoke, obscuring even that.

Then he ground his cigar out against the parapet with a sharp twist of his wrist, and stood. "I called my wife that sometimes. It was a private joke between us."

"Forgive me," I said in a stifled voice. "I didn't mean to pry."

"There's nothing to forgive," he said with an approximation of gentleness. "But I'm growing drowsy. I had better take pity on my waiting valet, and go to bed."

He bowed, and left me.

I sat on the ground farthest from where he had dropped his cigar and tried to relish the cool. But my head ached—whether from smoke or self-recrimination, I could not say. What a pleasant evening I might have had, if I had minded my tongue and my manners—if I had been *kind.*

I did not want to attend chapel that Sunday, but there was no help for it. I examined Tabby for dirt acquired since the previous evening's bath, wove ribbons into her braids (Tabby's favorite part of the Lord's day—and mine too, if I was honest), and let her set our pace on the stairs. A crawl, naturally.

Despite my reluctance, I really anticipated nothing worse than my own itching boredom and self-reproach, and Sir Kit's eyes on me now and then. Perhaps a few slighting references to the Jewish religion in the borrowed sermon—a common fault, alas, in such publications. But the sight that met my eyes when at last Tabby led us into the family gallery brought me up short.

Sir Kit did not usually visit the gallery until after the service, but his unaccustomed presence was not why shame flared up and swallowed me—shame and a horrible curiosity. My employer's hand rested on the shoulder of a sitting woman.

Thick, exquisite folds of lace cascaded from the straw brim of her tall, rose-wreathed bonnet, hiding her face and most of her figure. Butter-soft pink gloves, spotless as a sample in a shop window, protruded from the veil's hem and lay lifelessly in her lap.

She might almost have been a waxwork, the quivering of her silk rose-petals the result of a drafty window. I had to look very hard to catch the weak, rhythmic flutter of her veil.

But I must not jump to conclusions. Ladies did not generally wear gloves in their own house in the heat of summer. Perhaps it was a stranger—a visiting relative—

"Miss Oliver," Sir Kit said in a flat voice, "Lady Palethorp."

12

I dropped a deep curtsy. "I am honored, my lady." My lips were numb, and my fingertips. "Give your mama a kiss, Tabby."

My charge clutched at my skirts. I nudged her towards her mother. Now—now the veil would be lifted—

"I don't want to," Tabby whispered audibly.

My heart plummeted. "Christabel Palethorp," I said reprovingly, glancing to Sir Kit for help.

He did not move. The bleak satisfaction in his face frightened me.

I knelt. "Tabby, your mother will think I don't teach you manners. Be a good girl."

The waxwork stirred, reaching out her hands with unnerving slowness. The veil rose as they did—but no more than a few inches. "Tabby," she said in a low, dreamy voice. "Come here, minha filha."

Tabby exploded into tears. "I won't!" She ran and hid under Clarice's apron, only her little arms peeking out, wrapped like iron bands around her nursemaid's legs. "Please don't make me, Miss Oliver."

I felt cast in iron myself, or stone—something heavy and brittle. My mother used to call me "minha filha": *my daughter*. Sir Kit's wife spoke Portuguese.

The spotless pink hands flopped back into Lady Palethorp's lap, and lay trembling. My gorge rose.

Clarice tried to pry Tabby's arms open, but she was afraid to jerk too hard with Sir Kit looking on. She looked to me for assistance, and got none.

At last Sir Kit said, still with that bleak satisfaction, "Miss Oliver, take Tabby and sit below with Mrs. Cross. Only dutiful little girls have a place in the family gallery."

Poor Clarice shuffled into the hallway, and we dragged Tabby off her and into the library, out of earshot. She was still sniffling, face red and set, and said nothing in answer to our questions or expostulations.

I hesitated, glancing at Clarice. "Were you afraid, Tabby?" I still didn't dare finish the sentence with *of your mother*.

There was a pause. "Maybe," Tabby hiccuped.

"What were you afraid of?"

She only stared at me.

I had never felt my position so keenly—only a governess, a blinkered pawn in an intricate game of kings and queens. Why had I pried? *You chose the wrong quotation from Pope*, I told myself. *It ought to have been "Fools rush in, where angels fear to tread."*

Now I saw no choice but to inch forward in the file assigned me. After much persuasion, bribery, and hypocritical moralizing, I extracted a promise from Tabby to apologize to her mother after chapel, on condition that I would accompany her.

The service was well advanced when we slipped into the front pew. I half expected Lady Palethorp to have vanished, but when I glanced up at the gallery, I glimpsed her rosy bonnet crowning her veil like a mantilla's comb.

I turned my eyes to the front, and realized Sir Kit had caught me gawking.

His sermon, by some evil chance, was on the subject of gossip, and he read it grimly, with none of his usual humor. "Some so-called Christians, impelled by curiosity, search out every petty transaction of the neighborhood, sift it again and again to the very bottom, and treasure up in their memories each particle of intelligence which they have collected. They pry into the interior of families; worm out every incident of the day…"

I felt bitterly ashamed—and, distantly, sorry for the baronet, remembering how his own neighbors had clustered around me like carrion crows: *What do you think of Lady Palethorp?* I was consumed even now with guessing at his wife's features beneath her veil.

Minha filha.

I kept my eyes firmly fixed on the lectern, but the back of my neck prickled. Was she watching me?

The sermon was half over before it occurred to me that she was far more likely to be watching Tabby, huddled against my side. I was nothing to her—I was nothing to anyone. The sermon wasn't aimed at me either. Sir Kit read them from the book, one after the other.

As the servants filed out, I led Tabby to her father. "Sir, Miss Palethorp is very sorry and would like to apologize to her mother."

Sir Kit knelt, face softening at last. "Come here, Tabby-kitten."

Tabby catapulted into his arms, sobbing afresh.

"I know you didn't mean to hurt Mama's feelings, and I know she will be very glad to hear your apology. But it will have to be tomorrow. She has taken a sleeping draught to calm her nerves."

I glanced up in surprise, searching for the pink roses. But she was gone.

His words made sudden sense of Lady Palethorp's languor, and the queer, acrid smell around her, spicy and corrupted, that I hadn't remarked at the time, except to think it closer to my imaginings of her than her neat dress. She had taken laudanum even before coming to the chapel.

Tabby must have sensed the difference in her mother at once. No wonder she had recoiled. I thought of my own fear at vő's drunken weeping. How could a child comprehend such a thing?

Poor little girl! She clung sweetly to me all day, and I squeezed her hand when we presented ourselves in the music room the next morning, to ask if we might tender her apology.

But Lady Palethorp was still indisposed, and when we asked again that evening, she had already retired. The next morning she felt unwell—the next had a headache—the next had been up all night and was resting.

Tabby was impossible all week, restless, inattentive, and spiteful. But this time, I laid the blame squarely where it belonged: at Lady Palethorp's door.

I grew to hate that door, day by day. Somehow I never caught the servants going in or out. It was an unchanging, malevolent blank. I stepped up to it, now and then, when I was alone—hesitated, then pressed my ear to it. I never heard anything.

Did she sit like a waxwork all day, squandering her precious hours in drugged indifference while I toiled thanklessly? How much she had been given, and instead of striving to merit it—instead, even, of enjoying it—she shunned her splendid home and sprawling estate to hide behind this door.

I could not help thinking that if I had been mistress of Goldengrove…

if I had met Sir Kit before *she* had disappointed his hopes…if I had been Tabby's mother from birth…how much happier everyone would be! But of course, *her* father had made a fortune in straw hats, and mine had only been a kindhearted half-pay naval officer.

I dreamed of burning twice that week. The rest of my dreams were merely crawlingly unpleasant. When the clock chimed midnight on Wednesday, I was still awake, sweaty and full of dread.

Someone scratched at my door. She had come again! I shot upright, and tangled myself in the low-slung canopy.

I clawed myself free, heart racing, and sprang to my feet. This time I would not let her frighten me. I would give her a piece of my mind, for neglecting her daughter all week—

There was a warm glow along the lower edge of my door. Lady Palethorp had not carried a light before.

My heart raced for another reason, now. "Who's there?" I whispered through the keyhole, but I knew.

"I put on my banyan to keep things proper," Sir Kit whispered back. "And I hope you are grateful, madam, because it is smothering me."

I felt almost light, despite the heat. I had expected Sir Kit to avoid our little turret, after my tactlessness. Or rather—I had expected he would avoid *me*. He had been, hadn't he? Perhaps he had only been busy. I raced to wrap my cumbersome robe around me and open the door.

The banyan he complained of was an airy thing; I must have sold all I had to scrape together the price of so much pale silk. But I swallowed the bitter taste of envy.

He locked my room behind me and led me to the library, lighting the bright glass globes with his little oil lamp, darting boyishly conspiratorial glances my way.

He was not handsome, and never would be. But I felt a frightening fondness for him, and an answering delight in sneaking about while everyone else was snug abed, the doors locked upon them. I hoped my face was less easy to read than his, and turned away to climb into a window-seat.

The paneled shutters were closed, and my vertigo from that first night at Goldengrove—when I pulled aside a curtain and saw an unbroken expanse of wall—flashed upon me once more.

"Read to me," he said. "Would you? I hear you reading to Tabby and you do it so well—you almost make me like that insufferable Miss Baillie."

I hoped he couldn't see my rush of pleasure at the compliment. I liked the idea of him listening to my voice from the next room, and wishing I was speaking to him. It transformed my dull hours into something charming. "What shall I read?"

He flung himself into a wheeled library chair, rolling himself across the floor with one foot. "We're in a library. Take your pick."

I wanted to choose something funny. But humor was rarely entirely proper, and I could not dare one inch beyond being alone with Sir Kit in my dressing gown. I took up a volume of Pope, but skipped past all my witty favorites to the *Essay on Man*.

He skittered about the room as I read, rearranging a shelf or clearing dust from a gilded title with his finger. But I knew he was listening. It was not only that he chuckled in the right places. I *sensed* his attention.

Indeed, I sensed little else, for reading aloud permits me little true comprehension; giving the words proper expression requires looking ahead. The verses flowed meaninglessly past, as I tuned myself to his reactions.

After perhaps a quarter of an hour, he sat beside me in the window-seat. I hardly dared to breathe, putting all the life I could into my voice while the rest of me was a statue. I thought of Lady Palethorp's motionless hands, and the faint flutter of her veil.

At the pause between epistles, he tugged the book from my hand and laid it on the cushion. "Miss Oliver, will you grant me a very great favor?"

The lamp did not show me his eyes' true color, but their expression of earnest supplication made the nape of my neck prickle. "You quoted *Merchant of Venice* recently," I said lightly. "I think that play illustrates nicely the dangers of blanket promises." Was that apt? I hardly knew what I said.

"I have not been allowed to share my wife's bed for two years." His low voice was terrible in its naked honesty.

I turned my flaming face away, embarrassed as much by his sincerity as by the confession.

"I haven't touched a woman in *two years*. Seven hundred and—God, it's too late for arithmetic. You can't know what it's like, to be in Eden and be driven out with the flaming sword." He swallowed. "At least—I know nothing of your past. *Do* you know?"

He meant, was I a virgin. I flushed hot and cold, thinking of Iphigenia. Would he consider that a yes or a no? I shifted away a few inches. "I shall not dignify that question with an answer." But I darted a glance at his face—and then I could not look away.

Tears stood in his eyes. "I'm desperate simply to feel close to another adult human being. Can you understand that?"

My breath caught, and my own eyes stung. I had never understood anything so well. I was a flower dying in cracked earth, for want of a little cool rain. I thought of my dream, not so long ago—my mother casually sharing my guitar—and the tears almost spilled over.

"Let me sit by you and hold your hand," Sir Kit whispered, and I did not pull away when he laced his fingers through mine.

How can I tell you what I experienced? I remembered the lines that followed his quotation about celestial music:

> *Such harmony is in immortal souls;*
> *But whilst this muddy vesture of decay*
> *Doth grossly close it in, we cannot hear it.*

In that moment, flesh and blood and bone melted away, and I heard the sweet counterpoint of our souls, as clear and true as golden stars suspended in crystal spheres. I felt God's love.

I don't know what he felt. At last he brought my hand to his lips, and let it fall. His eyes shut for a moment, and then he stood. "I should get some sleep, or I'll be good for nothing in the morning." He grinned at me. "More so than usual, anyway."

I stood, trying to seem unaffected—yet somehow, not wanting to overdo it. I could not quite wish to deny what I felt. "Good night, sir."

"I'll walk you to your door."

"Better not, sir." I braced for an argument.

But he only said, "I'll light you a candle."

I hesitated, not wanting to pass Lady Palethorp's landing in the dark, where I had panicked not so long past—where she might be hovering at the stairwell's mouth even now, listening to me with her husband, as I had listened to her.

But I wanted to curl quietly in my bed and examine my own heart, not check a dozen times that the candle was truly extinguished. "It's only two flights of stairs," I said, and went as steadily as I could into the darkness, trying not to think about what I could not see.

In the morning, I resolved that Tabby had made enough attempts to apologize. I helped her write a note instead, and I slipped it under Lady Palethorp's door. No reply ever came.

Either Tabby had learned to hide her disappointment, or she had never expected better. But on Friday evening, carrying my lantern up the tower stairs after my half-holiday, I could restrain myself no longer. I stopped on the second-floor landing and tried the door-handle, heart in my throat. Locked.

I had a key, of course, but that—*that* I could not do.

I listened at the door, its oak familiar by now against the whorls of my ear. Nothing. Was she in a stupor even now? I pictured her in her bed, stripped of her Sunday finery, the laudanum bottle in pride of place on her night table, Tabby's note crumpled and forgotten behind it.

I still had not seen her face, but I pictured her sallow head on the pillow: her eyes smoldering coals, flashing fire intermittently and winking out as she sank into oblivion. I saw her nose curving and jutting with malevolent energy, and her mass of hair curling thick and vibrant across the sheets like parasitic vines, sucking the life from her enervated frame.

Could she sense my presence at her threshold—the upstart who dared to be admired by her husband—like a spider when the fly brushes some distant filament of her web?

I went into my room, and saw something crumpled on my bed. Papa's old lantern was so scratched and darkened with age that it took my eyes long moments to understand what I saw: the precious sheet music Sir Kit had given me ripped to shreds, and tea-dregs poured over them.

My throat closed. *Such a little thing, but they had to take it, too…*

Probably it had not been *her*. Probably it was only poor Tabby, miserable at her neglect.

Had Tabby heard Sir Kit scratch at my door? She had looked at me so strangely the night I served as hostess. Did she think I tried to usurp her mother's place? As though one *could* usurp something that had already been abdicated so completely!

But I thought of Lady Palethorp cutting Mrs. Palethorp's guitar strings, the flash of the scissors reflected in her eyes. I bundled the ruined music into my coverlet and pushed it under the bed to deal with in the morning, and tucked my own scissors within easy reach beneath my mattress.

13

Tabby wielded the sugar nippers under Mrs. Bishop's narrowed eye. She looked darling in her pinafore, tongue between her teeth in concentration.

The pinafore was still too large for her, but barely. She was already taller by an inch or two than when I came to Goldengrove. I ought to begin keeping a record of her height. Had anyone done it before?

Had Lady Palethorp, before…?

I tried to put her ladyship from my mind. Tabby strained her little arms with all her might, and a bit of sugar crumbled to the plate. Mrs. Bishop and I cheered.

Once enough of the hard brown cone was broken into small lumps, she would be allowed to pound the sugar into powder for a cake. Martha, one of the kitchen-maids, was laying out the other ingredients at my elbow. The morning seemed to be going well, but my unease persisted.

My gaze fell on the sugar loaf's crumbled blue wrapper. That usually meant sugar from the Americas, the paper dyed with indigo. My family had given up sugar when I was eleven or twelve, not long before mãe died. She'd explained that slaves made sugar and coffee and chocolate, and that was why the cake tasted so strange. *And don't eat the cake at Beth's house, either. I know I brought you up to eat whatever your hostess gives you, but morals come before manners. Here is a circular for her mother.*

Mrs. Bishop was explaining to me how she calculated and ordered the food needed for the household each week, as I took notes for a future lesson. Disjointed ones, unfortunately, for not only did clarifying questions appear to offend Mrs. Bishop's sensibilities, but Martha was humming in my ear, just quietly enough I could not place the tune.

"…All the mutton I serve is our own, see. I've just to let Mr. Kirk, the overseer, know to pen up so many pounds, and the butcher slaughters them when he brings the beef."

"The lamb last night was very fine," I murmured ingratiatingly. Martha's tune wasn't "Hugh of Lincoln," was it? I edged away from her.

"Oh, I hadn't ought to take the credit, it's grazing on the salt marshes that gives it such flavor." She sighed. "You'd think with the sea so near, salt would be cheap, but I daren't tell you how much we'd save if Sir Kit would consent to buy it smuggled from Ireland. And the sugar! Sugar for tea and sugar for cakes and sugar for pickles. When I think of the harvest preserves, I fear for my purse."

Mãe hadn't lived to see the revolutions in France and Saint-Domingue break the sugar boycott. The Tories had shouted accusations of Jacobinism and sedition until respectable English grocers and housewives gave in, and once more put manners before morals. Papa had kept to honey for a year or two longer, in memory of mãe.

I'd been angry about that, I remembered suddenly. He'd kept so many of mãe's little household arrangements, but *me* he sent away. *The cake at school is better*, I'd told him vengefully, that first Christmas vacation.

Then I'd got used to school, and forgotten about all of it. It was too late to apologize to Papa now.

But I could still teach Tabby that morals came before manners, though my heart was already sinking at Mrs. Bishop's anticipated reaction. I opened my mouth to say, *Have you asked the grocer if this is slave sugar?*

The kitchen-maid screamed.

I spun towards the hearth, ears ringing, sure I'd see one of the girls on fire. But they were only staring at Martha, whose gaze was fixed on her creamware bowl. I leaned over to see what all the fuss was about.

Blood spilled from a gash in a snow-white egg.

"Her be an omen of death," Martha breathed.

I secretly agreed. Fortunately, my superstitious shock was interrupted by Tabby climbing half onto the table trying to see. Lifting her down, I explained that shoes and kitchen tables must be kept as far apart as possible.

"It's just a bloody egg," Mrs. Bishop said, exasperated. "Charity, come here!"

Tabby giggled. "You said a bad word."

We all laughed, my heartbeat finally slowing. Mrs. Bishop showed Tabby the little bowl. "This is why you'd never ought to crack an egg straight into your cake."

Charity rushed up, looking chastened. "Did you know, Miss Palethorp," the cook said with a pointed glance at the kitchen-maid, "that if you hold an egg up to a candle, you can see right through the shell?"

I felt sorry for Charity. Mãe had always checked our eggs with great care, for Jewish law forbade the eating of blood. But when her kitchen chores fell to me, I had shirked the task, for in my youthful grief, my fear of fire had entirely mastered me.

Tabby's eyes grew wide. "Can I try?"

"Charity will show you some morning," Mrs. Bishop said. "Since *she* is tasked with sorting our eggs in the morning, to take out the ones with spots and the ones that will be new chickens."

"I did, ma'am, I swear. I must've missed one."

"Just one, I hope and pray."

"I'm sorry, ma'am. I'm that sorry, Martha."

Martha had regained her composure, and soothed her friend's conscience with a whole heart. Only I was still unsettled by the smooth egg nestled in a crimson pool, stark against the pure white dish.

Mrs. Bishop sighed. "It's rare to find one so bloody. We eat the spotty ones for breakfast ourselves. It's too late to keep this one for that." She shook her head. "Put it in the slop bucket for the pigs, Martha, but save the shell."

"What do you do with the shells?" I asked.

"We dry them, crush them, and feed them back to the chickens, madam," she said comfortably. "It gives them strong bones."

I concealed my horror, for the servants already thought me a town mouse, naïve and citified. Of course I understood that foxes ate chickens, but must the chickens be obliged to eat each other, too?

In all likelihood the chickens didn't notice or object, but that reflection did nothing to decrease my horror—rather the reverse, in fact.

Sir Kit's nighttime visits were becoming—not a bad habit, exactly. They were not frequent enough for that. An occasional vice, then, or a dark ritual. He scratched at my door, and then he talked, or I read, or I played the guitar. He asked to hold my hand—I went upstairs alone—I catechized my heart and received no answers. But I thought about it unceasingly, and on days when Sir Kit was abstracted or cool, I was in agony. I waited up, listening for his footsteps, and woke scattered, fuzzy, to the echo of his voice: *I'll be good for nothing in the morning.*

Was that infatuation? Warm friendship? Or only loneliness and nerves? I never felt again that perfect harmony of souls. I listened too hard for it, and was too aware of his eyes on me.

What did he see? I had always counted on my plain face, spinsterish dress, and unsentimental air to shield me from designs on my virtue. If they failed…

One morning, worse for nothing than usual, I forgot to knock on Clarice's door before entering. "Have you mended Tabby's stockings?"

She fisted her hand—which she had been holding to the window—and hid it in her apron.

"What's that, Clarice?"

"Beg pardon, ma'am?" she returned, a little defiantly.

It had been an idle question, but now her manner lent it significance. I had no wish to meddle, but she was so young. If she got into trouble, I would answer to my conscience—and perhaps to Sir Kit as well. "Let me see it, Clarice."

She set her jaw and spread her fingers. A little sapphire ring winked at me.

My heart sank. "How lovely! Where did you get it?"

Her face was mulishly wooden. "It were a gift, ma'am."

"From whom?"

"I don't reckon I have to answer that, ma'am."

Who on earth could have given Clarice such a thing? I reached for her hand with both of mine. She closed it so I could not take her prize, and I cupped her clenched fist, looking her seriously in the face. "Have you been doing anything you shouldn't?"

"Have *you*, ma'am?" she returned rudely. "That's an awful nice chain round your neck."

My breath stopped. Did she think me Sir Kit's mistress? Had she heard him come to my door at night? How reckless I had been, and what a fool, not to have shut my window and gone back to bed that first night.

Then a new possibility struck me like a blow. Did she mean *she* was Sir Kit's mistress? Who else could she have met, and kept meeting, who could buy such a ring? She looked very pretty in her anger, bright eyes snapping and cheeks rosy.

Perhaps it had not always been Lady Palethorp's footsteps in the nursery at night.

I tried to breathe, and think. "What do you mean by that?" I got out.

"I mean I didn't steal it. And I mean you'd best not tell anyone I have it. I haven't told anyone about *you*. Yet."

For a moment, I felt only intense relief that no one else knew. How selfish I was! If I submitted to Clarice's blackmail, I as good as gave her carte blanche to do as she liked, in everything. It was a wrong to Clarice, a wrong to Tabby, and a wrong to Sir Kit, who trusted me.

"If you are in any trouble," I said uselessly, "if you need any help—come to me. You're so young." I could not go on. How could I help her, if she did come? What if she got herself with child? I found myself almost hoping she *had* stolen the ring.

Her face softened. "I'm tol-lol, ma'am. But *you'd* ought be careful, I think, if you'll forgive me for saying it."

I might have preferred a threat to the pity in her eyes.

Sir Kit's first musical evening was fast approaching. To my relief, he had never again suggested a duet, but he did insist that I prepare a few pieces on the guitar. "You must give me something to look forward to, Miss Oliver," he said with a twinkle, unmoved by my demurrals. "Unlike you, I have heard my neighbors play and sing."

It had been ages since I had performed for any audience less forgiving than children, or my own friends—or Sir Kit himself. I spent my evening polishing a Carulli sonata, a very English piece adapted from Handel (who wasn't English, but the English liked to forget it), and a sentimental Scots ballad that was *almost* in my vocal range.

I need not have bothered. The guests talked through everything, barely excepting the performances of their own family and particular friends. But Sir Kit watched me—listened, even—and looked proud of having me in his employ.

If it *was* more than that, I counted on the general inattention to conceal it, for he gave me no special applause. Indeed, unlike his partial neighbors, Sir Kit clapped for each piece equally, first and loudest, in warm salute to the musician's effort and courage. I liked him the more for it, having shepherded so many nervous children through their first public performance.

But when I had once more taken my seat in the corner, Mrs. Abbott sidled over. "Sir Kit seems very fond of you."

My cheeks flamed—no pretty blush like the one painted on her pale cheeks, I knew, but blotches of dull red. "I hope he is satisfied with his daughter's progress under my care, madam."

She bit her lip. "My dear, you're alone in the world, and I am a mother. I hope you'll forgive my impertinence."

The skin around my eyes and mouth tightened with the effort of not grimacing. Ever since I lost my mother, kindly older ladies had been assuming that the vacant position might be filled by all comers.

Taking the empty chair at my side, she leaned close. "You must not look at him like that," she whispered. "He will remark it."

My ears burned, and the back of my neck. My stays crushed my ribs. I realized, mortified, that I *had* been watching him—that in my fear of some indiscretion on his part, I had been indiscreet myself. "If I have looked at him more than the rest, madam, it's because I don't know anybody else."

She frowned. "Don't be offended. I only want to warn you of your danger. A girl in your position can't afford to be careless."

I knew she was only trying to be kind, but anger swamped me. As if I could forget my precarious position for a moment! And to call me a *girl*, when she could not be more than five or six years older than me… "No *woman* can afford that, madam." If my reputation was truly in danger, could she *afford* to hire me to teach her own daughter?

Ask her, I thought suddenly.

But I couldn't bring myself to trust a stranger—and who was not a stranger to me?

My gaze fell on the candelabra. Even that little flame, which would extinguish itself in falling, terrified me. Yet it let Mrs. Wakefield see her music.

Without fire, we would yet be beasts, huddled into caves in summer and winter, tearing at raw meat with our teeth and fingernails. Was human affection any different? It had the capacity to strike me down where I stood, but could I live without it?

I sat very still and let Mrs. Abbott take my hand—but as she patted it, Sir Kit appeared at my elbow.

I briefly raised my eyes to his, and thought I read censure in them. Had he heard her? The unfairness of it smote me, when I had not even wanted to talk to her. I merely couldn't afford to rebuff his neighbor, and my superior in rank.

"Mrs. Abbott!" he said, handing her a little dish. "I hope you will eat several dozen more lemon tarts before you go, beginning with these. Cook made them specially for you, and no one here can abide them."

She fluttered a little, smiling up at him. "I do love Goldengrove lemon tarts. My cook makes them too sweet. But Lady Palethorp used to be so fond of them! I know they're rich for an invalid, but one or two… We can't avoid *every* indulgence for the whole duration of a long illness, surely."

Sir Kit's expression set a little, but his voice didn't change. "That is a very kind thought, madam. I will send Luke up to inquire." He offered his arm. "I believe your daughter needs help with her train."

She popped up at once. "Poor girl, trains are so difficult at first! I could see her struggling earlier, but she is forever telling me not to interfere…"

And off they went, leaving me and the half-eaten pastries behind in our corner. Sir Kit had not even looked at me after that first glance. Was it chivalrous discretion, or indifference?

Lost in self-pity, I started violently when Luke announced, "Lady Palethorp's compliments to the company, and she has everything she wants."

No doubt she does: sausage and laudanum, I thought bitterly. Or perhaps she had already sent for a plate of cakes hours ago, and was cozily dropping crumbs into her book. *She* didn't have to practice sonatas or wear stays or be polite to Mrs. Abbott. *She* could afford whatever she liked, without lifting a finger.

That week the warm wind blew towards the sea, and my room was hot and close. Instead of sleeping, I listened for footsteps on the stairs.

Was Mrs. Abbott right? Should I leave Goldengrove?

It's only hot, I told myself. I would be no cooler in Lively St. Lemeston; running away from my post would not make me rich enough to summer in the Lake District.

And the idea of leaving only brought Goldengrove's comforts and beauties more sharply before my eyes. My slice of buttered toast with marmalade in the morning, my borrowed guitar, Tabby's blunt remarks and silly affectations.

Sir Kit's jokes, my conscience accused me.

Round and round I went, debating with myself as, for the dozenth time, I recounted to Tabby the story of Phoebe Dymond's whirlwind courtship by a lord's son.

She clasped her little hands soulfully over her heart. "It's better than King Cophetua and the beggar maid, because it's true."

I swallowed a laugh. "Her gowns weren't as shabby as all *that*."

Having heard the obscure authoress opined upon by every adult she knew, Tabby imagined Mrs. Dymond a person of considerable celebrity, and I wasn't above basking in the reflected glory of a slight acquaintance with her. But I really knew very few details, and was forced to draw out such minor points as Mr. Dymond's gift of a ham, which Phoebe had served to some of the boardinghouse women at a sewing circle (Mrs. Humphrey thought it oversalted, but Miss Starling disagreed).

Fortunately, Tabby was an undemanding audience, and always insisted that the ham must have been perfectly salted.

As I talked, she pored over the frontispiece of *The Wise and Witty Governess:* Miss Baillie expounding on the beauties of nature to two children in near-identical white gowns, their golden curls haloed by little round hats. It was prettily drawn, but I was unsettled by the poses, clearly copied from antique paintings of the Christ—Miss Baillie's uplifted arms spread wide, the girl's folded over her chest, and the boy's at his side, palms out and fingers pointing Heavenward.

"I want a little brother," Tabby announced suddenly.

I blanched, for I knew far more than I should about why that was impossible. The best answer would have been *You must ask your papa about that*, but I could not bear to think of Sir Kit's face, if she did.

Had he wanted a little boy? Well, of course he had; all gentlemen wanted heirs, and titled ones more than most.

Miss Baillie would have known what to say; *I* looked imploringly at Clarice. Her face said *This one's all yours.*

I sighed. "Do you know where little brothers and sisters come from?"

"From under cabbage leaves," she said dubiously. "I look there when we go to the kitchen garden, but I never find a single baby."

I realized with a kind of vertigo that if I stayed at Goldengrove, one day it would fall to *me* to tell Tabby the truth about men's and women's bodies. Yet I could not do it now unless I asked Sir Kit's permission—which would be, at the very best, awkward.

"Only mamas can find babies," I said without conviction.

Tabby's frown deepened. "Mama is too sick to go in the kitchen garden." She narrowed her eyes at me. "If Mama died, would you be my mama?"

Clarice snorted. I stood lightning-struck, split open to expose my rotting core. I could not pretend even to myself that the thought had never crossed my mind.

What was wrong with me? I could not have married Sir Kit even if he were a bachelor. I did not even dare to tell him about mãe. What would my mother say, if she knew how I had disavowed her?

That little flight of melodrama finally made me laugh at myself. Mãe would say I was a smart girl, and to be careful, because you never knew, and there was no one else de nação for miles—with the probable exception of Lady Palethorp. Then she'd tell me it wasn't too late to go back to Portsmouth and marry a nice prize agent, or perhaps a baker, so my children never went hungry.

That was what Tabby needed—less delicacy of mind, and more honest motherly advice. "Do you remember my first day here, when you asked the Lord to save your mother's soul from Hell?"

She watched me, unblinking.

"Is your mama Jewish, Tabby? Is that why you're afraid she'll go to Hell?"

Tabby shook her head.

Clarice made a scoffing noise.

Tabby glared at the nursemaid. "I'm not lying," she insisted to me. "Mama *isn't* Jewish. But my grandpapa was, and Rhoda said demons are pulling his long beard."

There went my shreds of calm. "Don't say that, Tabby. You mustn't think it. People don't go to Hell for being Jewish." I didn't look at Clarice, for if I saw skepticism in her face, I would never be able to forget it.

Tabby hunched her shoulders at my vehemence. "But Rhoda said…"

I took a deep breath. "Ignorant people say many things," I said gently. "Ignorant people even become ministers and publish sermons sometimes. But I am right. Come into my room with me. I'm going to show you something special."

Now I did glance at Clarice. Would it be wise to invite her along, so she wouldn't be suspicious, and invent worse?

I reminded myself not to be fanciful. This wasn't Portugal, and Clarice wasn't going to denounce me to the Inquisition. Still, I left the door wide open.

"I'm going to show you my commonplace book, Tabby." I drew it from the top shelf of the clothespress—and then remembered my sheet music, and resolved to start locking the album in my trunk from now on. "Do you know what that is?"

"…Maybe."

"It's a big blank book, for copying out poems or quotations that I want to remember. Friends write in it, too. That way, I always have a collection of beautiful thoughts to look at, and memories of my friends in Lively St. Lemeston."

Tabby reached for it.

I already half regretted letting her see it. "This is only for me to touch. But we can sit together and look at it. Would you like to start your own?"

She nodded emphatically. "And you have to write in it."

"I would be honored." I lifted her onto the edge of my bed, gratified anew when she curled against my side. "Would you like to see what Phoebe

Dymond wrote in my book?"

Her eyes lit up. "Phoebe Dymond wrote in your book?"

I found the page I wanted easily. "To Mercy, Pity, Peace, and Love all pray in their distress," I began, trailing my finger below the line so Tabby could try to decipher the words.

"…For Mercy has a human heart
Pity, a human face:
And Love, the human form divine,
And Peace, the human dress."

The poem was from a favorite book of Mrs. Dymond's, which necessity had obliged her to sell to the local bookshop; she'd tried to talk me into buying it once, when we happened to run into one another by its shelf. I couldn't afford it either, but I'd admired the hand-colored plates to please her.

I'd lingered on this page.

The next time we passed round our commonplace books in Mrs. Humphrey's parlor, Mrs. Dymond copied it out from memory. I hadn't told her what it meant to me. I wasn't going to tell Tabby, either.

"Then every man of every clime,
That prays in his distress,
Prays to the human form divine
Love Mercy Pity Peace.

"And all must love the human form,
In heathen, Turk or Jew.
Where Mercy, Love & Pity dwell
There God is dwelling too."

Tabby peppered me with questions, including what sort of dress I thought Peace wore. Then she said, "Let's tell Papa."

"Tell him what?" I tried to speak cheerfully, and failed.

"That Mama isn't going to Hell. So he doesn't worry."

"He already knows," I said quickly.

"Are you sure?" Tabby asked.

"I'm sure."

Perhaps I was doing Sir Kit an injustice, and depriving Tabby of a better understanding with her father. Perhaps he would even say, *Hell is a great deal of nonsense, kitten. Just don't tell Clarice.*

But as much as I liked him—and I liked him far too well—I didn't deceive myself that he was a devoted friend to the children of Israel. And I had heard him be very bitter against his wife.

Not, to do him justice, in front of Tabby. But if he were asked point-blank…

What would Tabby feel—what would she believe—if her father told her that her mother was bound for torment?

What would *I* feel, if I heard Sir Kit say the Jews were damned? How could I live under his roof? How could I live under the same *sky* as him, and believe it would not fall and crush me?

And I had been reminded, now, that it was my duty to stay at Goldengrove. For who would raise Tabby, if I did not?

※ ※ ※ ※

So I wrote *Christabel Palethorp's Commonplace Book* in a new notebook. Tabby requested several verses and songs for me to copy in, among them Mrs. Dymond's poem.

After that, nothing would do but to show it off to her father, and beg him to write in it. He exclaimed over it as much as she could desire, solemnly examining every page.

"Very Unitarian sentiments," he said of the Blake poem, glancing at me.

"It's Mrs. Dymond's favorite," Tabby said loudly.

My chuckle sounded nearly natural. "Mrs. Nicholas Dymond copied that into my own commonplace book—it *is* by a favorite poet of hers. I think Tabby would have rather ripped out the hallowed page and kept it, but we compromised."

He laughed. "I want to write something in your commonplace book."

"Write in Tabby's first," I teased.

By the time he'd composed a silly limerick for his daughter, he had forgotten all about mine. I breathed a sigh of relief.

That night, I dreamed the Inquisitors were tearing off my fingernails. I screamed as the pincer drew near, my own blood smoking on its red-hot jaws.

I woke gasping, to find that my arm had fallen asleep. I cradled it as I inched my way to a half-reclined position against the headboard. My sweaty nightdress clung unpleasantly to my skin. At last my fingers regained enough feeling to manage the canopy.

It was barely cooler without it, but at least I had left the shutters open. The moon was nearly full, and the light calmed my racing pulse. I looked longingly at the casement latch.

Then I heard voices in the nursery. I held my breath. Tabby's childish tones, and a soft voice…

Not Clarice, and not Sir Kit. I was sure of it.

A fresh flood of nervous excitement. Yet there was already so much in my veins, had been for so long. It was all one hot, buzzing blank inside my skull.

I considered for a moment. Then I unlocked the door to Tabby's room and, flinging it open, raced in. Of course Tabby had strewn a shuttlecock and jackstones on the floor, but I managed to skid to a stop at a point between the doors, ready to lunge at her if she ran. A narrow column of moonlight galloped in after me and surrounded her: a round little woman crouching barefoot by Tabby's bedside.

She blinked owlishly as she stood, stumbling a little. "Miss Oliver? Is that you? Perhaps you don't remember me—I'm Jael Palethorp."

14

Free of intoxication, her husky alto voice was pleasant and surprisingly solid. I had not remembered her accent being so impeccable—except for that Portuguese *Zha-el*.

I curtsied. "My lady." I recalled abruptly that she was no thief, but my own employer. However strange her behavior, what could I say to her? My ears rang faintly, as though from some loud percussive sound.

Tabby sat up in bed, Adeline in her lap. Child, doll, matron, and governess regarded one another, silent and lifeless.

"I'm sorry I woke you," her ladyship said. "Sometimes I feel stronger at night, and I couldn't sleep."

Her words rang hollow. But was the fault in her voice, or my ear? If she had been the most engaging, sympathetic woman in Europe, could I have been sensible of it in that moment?

My fancy had been right to give her a serpents' nest of curls that seemed to breathe with her. But it was lighter than I had expected, dipped in molten silver by the moon. And where I had expected sunken features and wasted flesh, her broad cheekbones and wide jaw were soft and rounded, and her nightgown pulled tight over breast and hip.

She could afford to be careless and let the world clearly see the points of her nipples; *she* did not feel obliged to smother herself in a dressing gown on a hot night. Why sweat under that thick blanket of hair, then, instead of braiding and twisting it away from her neck and shoulders?

Her hands fluttered, trying to straighten her crooked nightdress across her hips. But the tug made her collar gape, and she let her hands fall.

That little self-conscious human gesture startled me, brought my gaze up to the dark pools of her eyes.

"Don't tell Kit," she said. "He would be angry and say I'm endangering my health."

Jealousy rushed up my throat at that careless *Kit*. Perhaps they were no longer happy, but she was his wife, and he had loved her. *You can't know what it's like, to be in Eden and be driven out with the flaming sword.* She was lush and beautiful, and he longed for her bed.

I would never be anybody's Eden. Nothing green grew in me; no well sprung. I was a desert, and if I left this house, in a few weeks no one would miss me.

Tabby got up and stood between us—facing me, her watchful eyes on *me*, the outsider. "It's a sin to be a talebearer, Miss Oliver."

That was from Sir Kit's Sunday sermon against prying into other people's family affairs. I might live here, but I wasn't family. Goldengrove wasn't my home—it was *hers*. *She* had carried Tabby in her own body.

"Of course, my lady." The words were ash in my mouth. I fussed with looping my key-chain over my head. "You're Tabby's mother; it's not my place to tell you when to visit her."

If it had been, I might have suggested a time other than the middle of the night. Tomorrow, *I* would bear the brunt of Tabby's lost sleep, her fretfulness and ill temper.

Then I remembered that Tabby's temper was worse when she had slept than when she was tired. I had thought her excess energy made her restless and wicked, but no: it was disappointment at her mother's neglect. Clarice and I did everything for Tabby, and still the child's affections were hoarded for this selfish, fickle creature, who gave me a queenly nod and resumed her seat by Tabby's bed as though she had never left it.

"Shall I light the lamp?" I asked blandly, to shame her for creeping about in the dark.

I wished I had no other motive than that. But I did. I wished to see her features clearly—to guess her age, and the color of her eyes.

She shifted, uncertain.

"You can write in my commonplace book," Tabby said eagerly.

Her face softened, her smile that of any mother indulging her child. I thought suddenly of the destroyed puzzle. I had not wanted to show it to Sir Kit, and see his face change; but I knew a hot, vengeful impulse to show it to *her*, to say, *This is what Tabby really thinks of you.* She had no right to that smile.

It quickly faltered, anyway. "My handwriting is very bad, minha filha. I don't want to mess up your book."

Tabby drooped. "*Mama.*"

I remembered that people used to say my mother's writing looked foreign—*Continental*, if they were inclined to be polite—though she was born in Portsmouth. I had carefully mimicked my English friends' handwriting, the letters very short and wide and their tails very long, so that the space between lines stretched snowy and prim.

"Why don't you write something on another paper, and when you are satisfied, we can paste it in?" I suggested.

Tabby nodded eagerly, and her ladyship gave in.

I labored over my tinderbox to light the candle; I did not trust her to do it. Each strike of the flint was a gunshot.

But at last I melted the base of the candle to fix it in Tabby's tin candlestick, and fitted the glass chimney over it. I would have felt safer with my old ship's lantern, but it was a matter of opinion whether the mica let through enough light to write by, these days—and I wanted to see her clearly.

I snapped the tinderbox shut and tucked it out of sight behind the candle, where I would be less tempted to check too soon whether the char had suffocated and gone out. The room filled with the sweet smell of beeswax. If I left Goldengrove, I would have to go back to greasy tallow and lard.

I looked at Lady Palethorp, digging cheerfully through Tabby's writing desk for ink and a pen. Her eyes were lowered; I still could not see their color. Tabby hovered at her elbow as she began to write.

My own feet crept nearer, bit by bit, until I could read her words upside-down.

Her letters were angular and her lines meandered up as they neared the right margin, instead of marching straight. But for all that, it was a fair English gentlewoman's hand.

I felt an unexpected stab of grief for my mother's swooping slanted *f*s like the holes in a violin, that I'd left behind and could never now recover. What had Lady Palethorp forgotten, to make room in her memory for the neat poem flowing from her pen? *I wandered lonely as a cloud...*

It was not one I would have chosen to memorize—was not even fashionable, for everyone had very much enjoyed lamenting that Mr. Wordsworth's long-awaited second collection was such an unworthy successor to his first. When was that? Some five years ago, perhaps.

Around the time of Tabby's birth, I realized with a strange vertigo. I had been living with Papa in Lively St. Lemeston and teaching guitar, and she had been at Goldengrove putting cayenne in her food and laughing at bawdy English place-names. Memorizing poems—maybe even dreaming of one day reading them with her daughter. For it *was* a motherly choice, a poem that Tabby could understand, enjoy, and reflect on.

Lady Palethorp recited it in her musical voice. "You see, minha filha, he keeps the daffodils as a happy memory to think of when he's alone." Her voice thickened with emotion. "You're my daffodils, baby."

Tabby squirmed. "Don't *cry*, Mama."

She laughed shakily and screwed her eyes shut, pressing a kiss to her daughter's temple. "I won't. Just remember, I love you and I think about you."

Tabby wriggled free. "Yes, Mama. I love you, too." She sounded more polite than sincere, to my ears. I wondered if Lady Palethorp would even know the difference.

But she did: her mouth spasmed and her eyes darted to mine, to see if I had noticed.

I understood in that moment that whatever had blighted Lady Palethorp's life—illness, or madness, or selfish dissipation—it was a tragedy. Too many talents and virtues went to waste in this world, too many precious things left behind and lost.

"Shall I paste it into the book?" I asked.

She cut her eyes at me. "Perhaps you could copy it in for me."

Only then did I understand that she wasn't really ashamed of her handwriting. *Don't tell Kit.*

"Yes, Miss Oliver, you copy it in," Tabby directed me.

"How do you ask politely?" I asked woodenly.

"You copy it in please."

I shouldn't have found that as adorable as I did. "Very well. In the morning."

"Please do it now." She pulled me towards the table by my skirt. Lady Palethorp stood to offer me the chair.

If I carried tales, it would only make matters more awkward between Sir Kit and me, or cause another dreadful scene in chapel. It would only hurt Tabby. I sat, the wooden seat obscenely warm through my thin nightdress.

I went slowly, for if I made an error, Tabby would want me to do it again from the beginning. Indeed, when I was finished, she pointed out several imperfections in the formation of my letters and deliberated for long moments before giving my effort her nod of approval.

I pushed the open book away from me to dry. There was a little silence. Lady Palethorp forced a smile. "It's late. I ought to let you sleep."

That, Tabby didn't argue with. How many times had she watched her mother go, to have learned that protest was useless? My heart broke, and I wanted to ask on her behalf: *Will we see you again soon?* But it would sound like criticism, and if the reply was a negative…

I went politely to the door and set my hand on the knob, ready to open it for her.

Her ladyship put her fingers over mine, to stop me. It reminded me, with a warm rush of conscious guilt, that I had let her husband hold my hand.

Her eyes were wary. She had been creeping in the shadows and seen Sir Kit come to my door, or heard us in the library—she knew all about it, and now she would charge me with it—

Instead she reached out with a pretty confiding gesture, to take my other hand in hers too. "Thank you," she said in a low voice. "I won't forget your kindness."

My breath caught at how like Tabby that was, the same quick burst of cloying feminine falseness. I was growing fond of it in the child in spite of myself, the stratagem too transparent to seem dangerous. The lady, on the other hand—if I had not seen her wariness, I would have believed her smile and the appealing pressure of her warm fingers.

She's your daughter every day, not just when you're bored and can't sleep, I wanted to say.

But I thought of the cut guitar strings—and Tabby's twisted scissors. Vicious, ungovernable rage ran in their blood, too. Safer to offer no provocation. I inclined my head, still as a mouse, until she released my hands.

When I turned the knob, I found that she had locked the door behind her. We both put our hands to the bosom of our nightdresses at the same time, but hers fell first. She was the lady, after all, and I the servant. As I put the key in the lock, the chain was dark and gleaming against my hand, the tiny pearls dotted with golden pinpricks.

Her lips parted, and her eyes widened in recognition.

It hadn't truly been her gift, then. My face flamed. "Sir Kit told me about how you wanted me to have this." I tried to say it with false warmth of my own, an innocent recitation of events, but it came out as a taut, eager excuse. "It was a lovely gesture, to welcome me. Thank you."

Her lips pressed tight together, and when she gripped my hand again, it hurt. "Look after Tabby for me," she said in a hard voice.

She shut the door very softly, leaving me to lock it behind her.

15

"You look tired," were Sir Kit's first words when I presented myself in the study for his guitar lesson.

I had tried concealing the dark circles under my eyes, but in this heat, the powder caked and ran with my sweat. At last I had washed it off in despair.

I would have liked to say *I am tired*, short and flat. But if I did, I would have to be twice as warm and smiling after, to appease him, and I was… so…tired.

"Is the heat in the attic bothering you? Would you like me to move you and Tabby downstairs?"

I would. But I remembered that Tabby had wept when it was tried before, and I wondered—had she missed her mother's visits? Did Lady Palethorp have all the house keys, or only the same one I did?

And I wasn't sure it was wise, to put my room any closer to his. "No, thank you. I only had a bad dream."

He came around the desk, eyes soft with concern. He *looked* at me, the only person who ever did. "Tell me about it."

I was disarmed and flattered even as I lied with a self-deprecating little laugh. "Oh, fire. What else?"

His eyes crinkled. "I always dream I have an exam at Eton, and I've been playing truant all term and know the headmaster will birch me." I was already forgetting to keep my distance.

Just the other day, I had read Tabby an account in the *Naturalist's Miscellany* of American rattlesnakes rendering squirrels immobile with the fascination of their gaze. Perhaps it was not only a frozen fear; perhaps there was something pleasant in it, too. "If you had had a son, would you have sent him?"

"I don't know." Taking up mãe's guitar, he picked out from memory one of the more complicated scales in his primer—not well, but he was applying himself. "Jewish fathers circumcise their sons, don't they? But then, they no longer remember what it felt like."

I did not find the comparison apt. Circumcision was a sacrament; the same could hardly be said of public school. A single moment of pain, soon over, and your parents comforted you.

"I've heard it's worse now even than it was in my day. Not long after I went to university, a new headmaster flogged so many boys in a day that he was too sore to move for a week after. And the fellow there now spatters the front row with blood, when he gets going."

It sounded like one of Papa's stories about bad ships' captains. But floggings at sea were mostly reserved for the common sailors, not the officers. I could understand the logic in that kind of unjust cruelty: its victims had no power to stop it.

This, I could lay out no syllogism for. *A priori*, I would have reasoned:

The more money parents pay a school, the more tenderly their children will be treated.

If a man loves his son, he will do all in his power to keep him safe.

Gentlemen rule the world, therefore they will make it as comfortable for themselves as they can.

A posteriori, I would have been wrong on all counts.

Sir Kit saw my face, and grinned. "A rather different education than you're giving Tabby, isn't it?"

"Good God, I hope so!"

"Men are fond of calling it a fearful burden, to protect a daughter from the world, but at least you can keep her safely at home. I was so happy when Tabby was born. My mother told me to try for an heir again right away, and my wife was game, but—well, I thought it would be hard on her health, and I didn't care so much about an heir. I have cousins."

I didn't point out that cousins would not allow Sir Kit's mother, wife, or daughter to live with them. "Did Lady Palethorp want a boy?"

"Oh, dreadfully. She wanted to rub her success in my mother's face, I think." He chuckled. "'A big, bouncing, healthy boy, and I'll spoil him rotten,' she used to say. Once, when we were on the roof, she whispered to her round belly, 'You'll be taller than your father, and one day all this will be yours.'"

Now I knew what she looked like, knew her voice. I could imagine it very clearly.

It was more than I had ever heard him say about his wife. Had her remark wounded him, or had they been close enough that it was funny? I remembered Iphigenia running her quill over my brow, teasing, *Stop frowning, you'll frighten away all the young men.* It would have annoyed me from anyone else.

Despite my jealousy, I wanted to think Sir Kit had cared for his wife. Of course people married for money all the time, but…I did not want to believe it of him.

He sighed. "I never talked to her about school. You have a face that invites confidences, I think. Does Tabby confide in you?"

In point of fact, my face frightened away young men, and led fellow stagecoach travelers to pass me by when they shared out snacks from their hamper. Tabby met my questions with a blank stare. But Sir Kit trusted me. I felt a curious pain in my chest.

Maybe I should tell him about Lady Palethorp's visit.

But he had never quite said he didn't want Tabby to see her mother. He had told me, in fact, exactly what the lady herself had: sometimes she felt stronger at night. If I told him, he would probably only ask what I thought of her.

I could not speak to him about that.

I realized I had forgotten his question. "I'm sorry. Do you mind if we omit today's lesson? Tabby wants to play at Rapunzel, and she says Clarice can't look mean enough to be the witch." I knew she mostly meant *Clarice is too pretty, and her nose is too small,* but I mostly didn't mind.

He laughed as if he guessed my wounded vanity. "No one ever accused a Palethorp of tact."

I tried to remember the precise shape of Lady Palethorp's nose, so I could combine it with his and guess how Tabby's might look one day. If it didn't look English enough, would that trouble her? Would it matter to Sir Kit?

He frowned, sharp-eyed, when I failed again to answer him. "Well, go on. Don't let Tabby burn you at the stake."

I felt the blood drain from my face. "Wha—" My voice gave out.

"Why do you look like that?" He set mãe's guitar down and reached for me. "Miss Oliver? Are you well?"

I retreated, stumbling over an egg-yellow chair. As I righted myself, it dawned on me that he had meant, because I would be playing the part of a witch. He had not meant anything at all by it. As usual, my fear was all smoke and no fire.

"*Oh.*" He pressed his knuckles to his mouth. "Your terror of fire. What an ass I am. Let me pour you a swallow of brandy, you look faint."

"It's nothing." I tried to give a light little laugh. "I'm sorry. So silly of me. Good morning."

And I fled.

Lady Palethorp came again a few days later.

"Miss Oliver, you should play your guitar for Mama."

Lady Palethorp's eyes dwelt on me.

"We'll wake Clarice," I mumbled. I was secretly pleased that Tabby wanted to show me off, but if Lady Palethorp decided she had reason to be jealous of me, would I find my strings cut next?

"Play Robin Hood and the bishop."

Reluctantly, I brought in the guitar. In the candlelight, the honeyed wood shone and the inlay gleamed. How I wished for mãe's modest instrument, locked in Sir Kit's study! Beauty only made people envious.

Lady Palethorp's expression was neutral—too neutral. I laid my palm protectively across the new strings.

Suddenly, I remembered that her husband had bought them for me. Her delicate chain was a brand on my skin.

Tabby bounced impatiently, and I played the opening chords softly. The A was a little sharp, but tuning it would only draw this out, as would moving to a stool or chair so I might settle the instrument properly against a raised thigh. I played the ballad doggedly through, eyes on my fingers.

Tabby clapped when I was finished, with pointed glances at her mama. I laughed, thinking of Sir Kit doing the same at his musical evening. Lady

Palethorp smiled at her, too, pantomiming enthusiastic applause. Fear of discovery? But perhaps it was only consideration for Clarice, in case she was miraculously still sleeping.

"Do you play the guitar, Mama?"

"N…" She glanced between us, and then said in a rush, like any coy lady hoping to be coaxed into a performance, "I used to."

Tabby bounced again, thrilled. "Play something!"

Lady Palethorp and I regarded each other in silence.

I rubbed my thumb soothingly over the smooth wood, against my body where she couldn't see—an apology to the instrument for giving it to someone who had hurt it, a promise that it was only for a little while. I handed it to her.

She tuned the A with a little sigh of relief. She dragged over a footstool, too, and contrived a creditable posture, her left thigh raised—displaying, in the process, a great deal of leg, the more so since Tabby and I still sat on the floor.

And softly—very softly—she stiffly played "Foi por mim."

I did remember the words, now she sang them. They rose from my mind's deeps like a drowned sailor on Judgment Day, and knit themselves together into a perfect whole.

How long before they sank again? Would they last until I got back to my own room?

What a pretty song! I imagined saying. *What language is that? Would you write down the words for me?*

Lady Palethorp's hands lingered on the instrument as a man's hands might linger on his wife when he kissed her farewell at their door.

"Sir Kit loaned me the guitar so I could play for Tabby," I said. "My own is not nearly so fine. Whose is it?"

"Mine. I brought it with me from London."

I felt as if I had washed down a rock with hard liquor.

He *had* said the guitar was his mother's, hadn't he? Had I misunderstood, or misremembered? Perhaps he had confused two different instruments. Or—was Lady Palethorp lying to my face?

If it *was* her guitar, then who had snipped the strings?

She passed it back to me, too abruptly—the base thunked on the carpet, and we both started. "Do you like your music lessons, Tabby?"

"Play the cherry tree song, Mama."

"I don't think I know it. Can you sing it for me?"

Tabby heaved a disgusted sigh. "Miss Oliver will teach you."

Lady Palethorp's smile flickered. I felt a chill, deep in my belly.

"I'd better go," she said. "I feel as though I could sleep. You're better than a tonic, minha filha."

Better than laudanum, she meant—or lied. Her face was smooth and perfectly sculpted in the golden candlelight, her eyes shining like glass, and the thought came to me that she was empty inside, like a doll.

The heat seemed only to grow, and no matter how tired I was, I could not sleep for listening for footsteps. When I reflected that Lady Palethorp had come before, who knew how often, without my knowledge, I shivered as though someone had walked over my grave. Was Tabby entirely safe with her?

And so a few nights later, I again dragged myself into Tabby's room to light the candle and sit sweating on the floor as Lady Palethorp read aloud from *The Wise and Witty Governess*.

She seemed so ordinary.

Someone knocked. Not on Tabby's door—it came muffled from the other room. Lady Palethorp's voice died mid-word.

Sir Kit, knocking on my door. It could be no one else.

His wife's eyes fixed warningly on me. Then she rose, very deliberately, and pressed herself against the wall between the fireplace and the door to my room, out of sight from the other side.

She meant to listen to our conversation, then, and judge for herself what this nighttime visit meant. The shadows jittered dizzyingly as I took the lamp in my shaking hand. Tabby sat, still and watching.

I left the connecting door ajar—I dared do nothing else. I could see the faint halo of his candle beneath the door that led to the roof.

I could not get the chain over my head one-handed, so I bent over to awkwardly fit the key into the lock without taking it off. "Just a moment," I called softly.

I ought to set the candle down, but I was afraid of knocking it over with my foot. If I went back to put it on the nightstand and he unlocked the door himself—Lady Palethorp was listening—she would think—

At last I cracked the door. "Sir Kit? What brings you here so late? Is anything amiss?"

16

His eyes fell on my bosom, and I remembered that it was covered only by thin linen and a slight ruffle. I could not cross my arms because I held the candle, its light shining full on my chest.

He looked—and looked—and then he smiled at me, sweetly and with a hint of mischief, as though we had contrived together to bend the rules of propriety. As though it wasn't just that he saw, but that I showed him.

Fear flared in my belly. But something else flared lower, a sharp ache between my legs.

"I was reading to Tabby, sir." My voice was garbled, and thready. "She couldn't sleep."

"Poor kid." He brushed past me, and was in my room for the first time since I had lived in it.

That you know of, my mind corrected, spotting the logical fallacy. But Lady Palethorp had no way of knowing it was the first time. What if she assumed it was *not*?

Had *she* ever come into my room in my absence?

Pushing the nursery door the rest of the way open, he smiled at Tabby. "Why don't I come and sit with you for a minute, and Miss Oliver can read to both of us? Would you like that, kitten?"

I hovered at his elbow. "I think she's nearly ready to sleep again. You'll only excite her further if you come in." I prayed Tabby would not choose now for a tantrum.

Sir Kit rolled his eyes. "Well, I suppose Miss Oliver knows best," he said teasingly. "I'll just kiss her goodnight and go straight away again. Will that suit, madam?"

I would have resented how neatly he allied himself with Tabby against me, if I could have felt anything but shame and dread at the scene that would ensue if he caught sight of his wife. I stood frozen, a squirrel caught between two rattlesnakes. How could I possibly put him off?

Tabby popped up and ran to her father, wrapping her arms around his knees. "Good night, Papa! I love you!"

Five years old, and she was quicker at deceit than I was. How many scenes had she been called upon to prevent in her young life? And I must smile, and take the protection she offered me, when I ought to have protected *her*.

When he had kissed her, and wished her a good night, she ran back to her bed and pulled the covers to her chin. I shared another smile with Sir Kit—*how darling!*—and moved to escort him back out the door he had first knocked at.

He caught my wrist as I passed him. "Come to the library when she's asleep," he murmured.

All my relief turned to acid in my chest. "I can't. What if she wakes again?"

"Clarice is here."

"I *can't*," I whispered in anguish. I felt a deep, biting shame, that I would have gone, if his wife had not been listening.

With a glance towards Tabby, he released my wrist, crossed my room again, and went out. I locked the door swiftly, turning—but I was afraid to enter the nursery and meet Lady Palethorp's eye.

I didn't have to. She moved slowly into the doorway.

Since I held the candle, she could see me clearly. But she herself was a golden shadow, a silent, accusatory ghost. Her jaw clenched, her lip curled faintly, and one hand—she pressed her fingertips together, then curled the fingers in, thumb working convulsively over her knuckles. Not preparing to strike me, but as though putting forth all her effort *not* to. The tendons on her forearm stood out as she dug her fingernails into her palm.

I cringed back, but she only turned and knelt beside Tabby. "My good little girl. I'm so sorry." She opened her hand and smoothed the hair back from her daughter's forehead. "I'll stay with Tabby until she's sleeping, Miss Oliver. You can go back to bed."

I curtsied. "Yes, my lady. Good night."

I left the light with them, but still it seeped beneath my door; still I heard her speaking to Tabby, low and tender.

An abyss of loneliness cracked open at my feet: so catastrophic, so bottomless that if Sir Kit had come *now*, I would have gone with him anywhere, let him do anything, only to step back from its brink for a moment.

Instead I was locked in my dark, empty room, my dark empty life, brightened in flashes by someone else's child and someone else's husband. The hot, stagnant air constricted my ribs like stays, weighed down my legs like a thick quilted petticoat I could not take off.

I itched to move, to race up to the roof and lean out over the long drop as I had never dared, gulping in the dangerous breeze. But if Lady Palethorp heard me leave, she would think I had gone to meet her husband.

Now the tightness in my ribs became hempen ropes. With each breath, I imagined smoke filling my lungs, my soul winking out and leaving my body dark and abandoned, defenseless against a gawking crowd.

I rushed to open the shutters, then the casement. I tore off my nightdress and splashed my naked body with tepid water from the ewer. Clothes always burned first. But the Inquisitors liked to strip their victims anyway, for torture or auto-da-fé.

Don't think of it, why do you always think of it, it didn't happen to you—

I curled naked in my bed, trying to cool down. The moonlight fell on my skin like a gaze. I looked at my small breasts, just beginning to sag. Flatter and smaller than ever.

Sir Kit hadn't looked disappointed. I couldn't understand it, when his wife's were so...perfect. Round and fruitful as Eve in a painting.

Maybe he considered generous breasts inelegant, blowsy—too Jewish. The English gentry wanted everything restrained and modulated, even the unalterable, God-given shape of one's flesh.

"All must love the human form divine," I whispered to myself.

At length, the light went out next door, and I heard the door to the landing shut softly. I had to sleep, or I would be good for nothing in the morning. But my pulse would not slow.

At last I closed the casement and draped the canopy over my bed. Shutting my eyes, I put my hand between my legs, trying to imagine myself invisible and desired. I pretended it was possible to be both at once.

Sir Kit and his wife both stayed away in the days that followed, and my loneliness deepened until I worried it was a kind of madness. Maybe I'd caught marsh fever from my open window, and that was why I lay in my hot bed shivering from the chill inside me.

Sometimes I climbed to the roof—half hoping to meet Sir Kit—and curled up in a corner of the parapet, battered by the callous hunger of the sea and the vast indifference of the stars.

I had never felt so sorry for myself, not even after Papa died and left me alone in the world. At least in Lively St. Lemeston, everything and everyone was familiar and knew me, offering their condolences in the street until I wished they would leave me in peace.

Round and round my thoughts went: vô and vó were dead, mãe was dead, Papa was dead. Iphigenia wrote me perhaps once a month to tell me how cheerful they all were without me, how fine the weather, how sweet the summer fruit, how much they missed my guitar on musical evenings—not me, my guitar—but the new boarder had a Jew's harp, which produced far fewer notes but was very funny to see played, and they made do.

That was the tally of all the people who had ever loved me.

This was why people believed in God: so they wouldn't feel so forgotten. I tried to pray that Sunday in chapel, but I felt nothing. Would a synagogue be different?

Mãe and vó had taken me to the Portsmouth synagogue once or twice when I was a girl. The front rows of the women's gallery were reserved for wealthier women, and from the back, the lattice screens were as good as opaque; I could see nothing but bonnets, fichus, and the ceiling. I'd spent most of the long, chanting service planning our escape if the building caught fire.

I thought of asking Sir Kit for my mother's guitar back. I didn't know whom the fine one in my hands rightfully belonged to, but I knew with each mellow pluck of my fingertip on a string that it wasn't mine. It was a loan I couldn't repay, and one day I'd owe a pound of flesh for it—yet I could not bring myself to give it up. I hid in the attic and played Portuguese lullabies, weeping, ashamed of my lack of self-command.

Sir Kit gave another dinner party for his neighbors. I was glad when he didn't ask me to pour the tea—or told myself I was. It was pleasant hiding with Tabby in the minstrels' gallery to watch the guests process through the Great Hall below, but when we had returned to the nursery, I felt flat. I missed the conversation of adults, even ones I didn't much care for.

Tabby, in contrast, was in high spirits as she put on her prettiest gown in confident expectation of being sent for. I took Clarice aside to ask her to take Tabby down in my stead, for my stomach hurt—which was not at all a lie.

"What's wrong with your eyes?" Tabby asked abruptly. "They're all purple underneath. You should use powder."

I sighed, but I let her powder and rouge my face until she pronounced me "a vision of loveliness." In fact, I would not have been out of place in a harlequinade, but by dint of not looking at Clarice—who was howling into her apron, much to Tabby's indignation—I kept a straight face through my speech of thanks.

I heard footsteps on the stairs, and Mrs. Cross came in as I was concluding. The spasm of amusement on her face did not look as kind as Clarice's. "The baronet's compliments, madam, and would you bring Miss Palethorp down to the drawing room."

"Clarice will bring Tabby, Mrs. Cross. Pray make my excuses. I'm not feeling well."

"He asked for you most particularly, madam." A pause. "But if you are ill, of course there is no help for it. I shall send for the doctor at once."

If I persisted, it would only be a greater fuss. I went quietly to the basin to wash my face.

"But—" Tabby began to object.

"This would be perfect for a ball. But at an informal dinner, I should be suspected of putting on airs."

Tabby considered this. "When you go to a ball, I'll do your hair, too." Since the occasion would never arise, I saw no harm in agreeing.

My face was still drying as the housekeeper led us down the stairs past Lady Palethorp's landing and Sir Kit's corridor, coming out at last at the chapel door. Swiftly, we crossed the dark space with its empty pews, into the empty dining-room, cake crumbs and walnut shells and half-drunk wineglasses scattered across the snowy tablecloth.

For a moment, I idly fancied Goldengrove a plague-touched castle in a Gothic novel, hastily evacuated in the midst of a banquet—but then I registered Luke, lounging in Sir Kit's chair and watching the clock.

In the same instant, the footman caught Mrs. Cross's glower and clattered to his feet, rushing to stand by the sideboard. I thought it would have been more to the point to finish clearing the dessert, but the poor boy must be dull-witted and aching, after toiling all evening in heeled shoes.

In the drawing room, Tabby was taken up at once to be fussed over. My beloved *bergère en cabriolet* was occupied by the magistrate's wife, so I took a chair along the wall, pondering how best to answer Tabby later, when she inevitably commented on that lady's unflattering hairstyle.

Luke entered the room just as I had finished arranging my skirts to hide my ankles—less than half a minute after we came through the door. "Lady Palethorp's compliments to the company, but she has everything she wants."

A wave of nausea crashed over me, so strong I could not at once understand its cause.

Luke had been loitering in the dining-room watching the clock—to see when a reasonable amount of time had passed. He had not been to see Lady Palethorp at all. I'd heard no footsteps in the stairwell but Mrs. Cross's, and surely those buckled shoes would have echoed. The whole thing was a charade.

Don't tell Kit, Lady Palethorp had said. She had hidden when he knocked.

She was not allowed to see her daughter. She was not allowed to speak even to the servants. She was not allowed a key to her own room—didn't want Sir Kit to know she had one.

I had suspected it so long I almost didn't believe it now the evidence was before me. There were other explanations. Luke might have *already* visited her ladyship, and only drawn out the errand to rest his feet.

My mind went round and round it—whether he would have met with Mrs. Cross on the stairs and known to expect her—whether he had been sorry to be caught by her, or by *me*—but I could not keep it straight in my head. There were too many suppositions and contingencies for a neat syllogism.

If it was true, then *why*? Why would a grown woman be locked up in her room?

One of them must be a monster: Lady Palethorp, or Sir Kit.

It was impossible to believe Sir Kit a monster. Self-centered, perhaps, a bit high-handed, but even his mischief had a boyish, innocent quality. The servants adored him.

Lady Palethorp, on the other hand…

I pictured her fist clenched with rage, her working fingers, her laudanum-soaked voice in the chapel. Was she dangerous after all? If she harmed Tabby, through my negligence… Or perhaps her illness was highly infectious, and I had exposed the nursery to contagion.

I would almost have preferred to think so, than what I *did* think. But I heard again Sir Kit's hard, flat voice, when he hadn't known I was listening.

Maybe he *had* said *They knew what to do with bitches like you in Spain.*

He passed by my chair without looking at me. "Sir," I choked out.

He turned, surprised—but his expression was kind. Sincere. No one could act so convincingly.

"I don't believe Luke really inquired after Lady Palethorp." I thought I might faint. "We should have met him on the stairs, if he had. I saw him tarrying in the dining-room."

Sir Kit frowned. "That is unpardonable shirking. I shall make Mr. Christie aware of it. Thank you for informing me."

It was what I had hoped he would say. It was more plausible, even, than my suspicions. But in my heart, I didn't believe him.

He stepped closer. "You are beginning to look really ill. Do you think it serious? Shall I send to Rye for the doctor?"

The idea panicked me out of all proportion—as though it were the first step to declaring *me* an invalid, and locking me in my room. "My mother died around this time of year," I remembered suddenly. "I suppose my spirits have been a little depressed. I shall be well presently."

He reached for my hand. I drew it back, conscious of Mrs. Abbott's gaze. There was a pause.

"I will tell Mrs. Bishop to make you up some arrowroot jelly," he said at last. "You must keep your weight up; you have no flesh to spare."

The kindness was poisoned for me, and the teasing. He did not even pretend to have foods fit for an invalid already on hand. I thought of those sausages, and for the first time, it occurred to me that Lady Palethorp might not have asked for them. That they might be sent up to goad her.

"Thank you, sir, you're very kind." My voice sounded strange to me, but he moved away. I let out my breath.

Mrs. Abbott, walking by a few minutes later, murmured, "Good girl." I felt that I heard her from the bottom of a well.

For a night and a day I could think of nothing else.

I wanted to ask someone, but there was no one at Goldengrove I trusted. For all I knew, Clarice's sapphire was her reward for spying on me. But on Friday, I sat down to write my letter to Lady Tassell—and paused, long enough I had to blot a shining drop of ink.

The countess would think I had lost my wits, if I confided such outlandish suspicions.

So I began the letter as I always did, assuring her of my continued good health and satisfaction with the position she had placed me in, then sharing any neighborhood news I thought might interest her, yet not brand me a gossip if repeated.

I told her that Mrs. Musgrave had arrived at Jury's Gap at last and wanted a lady's companion (leaving out that Mrs. Cross said she should thank her husband on her knees for only sending her away and not bringing a crim. con. suit, which I suspected Lady Tassell already knew).

Please believe I mean to stand a friend to you, Miss Oliver, she had said. She was a shrewd woman with a wide experience of the world. She would know what I ought to do.

At last I wrote, haltingly, *I hope I do not overstep—I beg your pardon very humbly if I do—but can you tell me the nature of Lady Palethorp's illness? I have not been informed of it, and can find no tactful way to inquire. Ought I to watch for symptoms in the daughter?*

There was time enough to confide more, when I saw how she answered that. I sealed the letter in a franked cover and addressed it to Tassell Hall, near Chichester, where the earl's household had removed for the summer. I tried to calculate how many days it would take the letter to reach her there, even if I gave it to Sir Kit straightaway.

I shrank from placing it in his hands. What if he delayed mailing it, or forgot? What if he opened it? He might even do it by accident, if it fell in among his papers. If I left the house now, I could walk to Rye in time to put it in today's mail.

So I went downstairs and asked Mr. Christie for a footman to accompany me to Rye.

"I'm afraid none can be spared, ma'am."

"In an hour, then."

"No, ma'am, I'm afraid they will be occupied all afternoon."

I was strongly tempted to inquire after particulars, for I knew he would have no answer. There were always far more footmen than the house had any need of, excepting on formal occasions. But what was the use? Mr. Christie plainly did not wish to oblige me, and I could not command his obedience.

Steeling myself, I went to Sir Kit's study. But he was out on some errand at the home farm.

Very well. I had tried to follow the *master's orders*, and been thwarted. Why should I wait upon everyone else's convenience, when they never thought of mine? I did not need *permission* to go. It was my half-holiday, and England was a free country.

I tied my bonnet tightly on my head—too warm for the weather, how had I been so foolish as to sell my summer bonnet, only because I left my home in spring?—and stuffed my letter into my reticule.

Sir Kit and Mrs. Cross would both have preferred to keep all the outer doors locked and barred except the one to the kitchen-yard. But forcing the maids to lug their mops and pails through the house would have soon ruined the carpets, so two more doors were open during daylight hours. The first was the small door within the great front double doors, where the porter kept watch.

The other, of necessity, was the door at the base of the tower, for the only other entrance on Goldengrove's west face was in the dining-room, with its opulent Persian carpet.

So I marched down the spiral stairs onto the square lower landing. Only a gray, empty corridor, perhaps twenty feet long, separated me from the lawn. At the end of it, warm yellow light spilled around the edge of the door, propped open with a brick.

I hesitated. It was cool here at the base of the tower, and hot out there, and to walk seven miles, even with a parasol...

Self-reliant, I reminded myself, and scurried out the door. I was perhaps a hundred feet down the path, my eyes still adjusting to the sun, when someone called my name.

I turned, heart sinking. At first, I only saw a tall, dark shape and a blinding glitter. But in a moment it resolved into Mark pulling on his gloves, his livery's pale-gold buttons and buckles catching the light.

"You hadn't ought to go out alone, ma'am." He didn't meet my eyes—but then, footmen weren't supposed to. He removed his hat respectfully as well.

"It is my half-holiday, and I wished to mail a letter. I would have been glad to take an escort, but Mr. Christie said all the footmen were occupied." A touch of irony crept into my tone on this last phrase.

He took his hat nervously in his hands. "Yes, ma'am. I'm supposed to watch this door."

"To keep out thieves, surely! Not to keep me in." The irony lasted until the last few words—but those came out uncertain. Nearly a plea. I pleaded with my eyes as well, but he would not meet them. Was the sweat on my face only summer heat, or incipient panic?

He was sweating too, dripping down his forehead from under his wig. "Sir Kit wouldn't like you to go out alone."

"Let me be sure I understand you. I ought not to go out alone, but I cannot take a footman with me, because he is stationed at the door to be sure I do not go out alone?"

"I couldn't rightly say, ma'am. You'd better ask Sir Kit."

"And so I shall, when I return from Rye." I spun on my heel.

Mark came after me and blocked my way. Plainly he did not like it—he kept his head deferentially lowered, and his hands tight on his tricorne so he could not be accused of molesting me—but he repeated stubbornly, "Sir Kit won't like it, ma'am."

I could go round him. Surely he would not truly dare to stop me. Would he be disciplined for my willfulness, though?

If he did raise an ill-judged hand to me, I would have no choice but to demand his dismissal—and probably Sir Kit would be quite ready to pronounce that harsh sentence for the crime of daring to touch a gentlewoman, never mind that it was on his own too-broad orders. The staff would hate me, more than they already seemed to.

And what if—what if Sir Kit refused?

Even if it only meant he was a lenient master, I would have no standing in the house left. I would be laid open to every impertinence.

If it meant I was a prisoner, and they all knew it…

I nearly threw myself on Mark's mercy, and asked him what orders Sir Kit had given him. He was only a gangly boy. He had always been polite.

But if he *was* my jailer, he would probably lie, and if my imagination was running away with me, he would know it, and tell the household. He would tell Sir Kit.

I did not dare give Sir Kit the letter now.

Drawing myself up, I turned back to the house. I could hear Mark's noisy sigh of relief behind me.

I went upstairs. I copied the letter, omitting my question about Lady Palethorp's health, and set it on Sir Kit's desk. I burned the original to ash in the grate, terrified that a glowing flake would flutter across the floor and set my skirts or my sheets on fire.

When I was sure the ashes were completely out, I took a book to my dusty turret room. It was not so cool as it had been, but I wanted solitude—did not want even the sound of my guitar to alert the house's other inhabitants to my presence.

But just as the light was growing too dim to read by, I heard footsteps on the stairs. My heart began to pound.

Sir Kit's head appeared through the hole in the floor, and then the rest of him. He sat on the edge, legs dangling. "Good afternoon, Miss Oliver."

"How did you know I was here?" I asked, then felt foolish. "Sir."

He smiled crookedly. "You always come here on Fridays. Sometimes I stand at the bottom of the stairs, and listen to you play."

In another mood, I might have been flattered. But my heart pounded harder. Had he heard me singing in Portuguese? Had he recognized it? Why could I never be alone, when Goldengrove was so spacious?

He leaned towards me. "Is everything well at home?"

I froze. *Iphigenia—a fire at the boarding house—* "Why, has there been news? Did Lady Tassell write?"

He shook his head. "I thought perhaps something was amiss, that your letter could not wait for the next post."

I exhaled. So, Mark had reported me. "I appreciate your concern, sir. I only had the letter written, and wished for a walk." I gave the last words a waspish emphasis.

"Yes, I'm sorry about that. I spoke with Mr. Christie, and told him that next time he must give you a footman, if one can at all be spared."

There, I told myself. *Iphigenia has not burned to death, and Goldengrove is not a prison.* But my nerves, once roused, were not so easily soothed. "And if he tells me none can be spared?"

He laughed. "I confess, I cannot understand it either. Surely we could do with half as many; it is not as though—" He cut himself off.

"Not as though?" I prompted.

"It is not as though my wife requires them to welcome her guests and carry her bandboxes," he said in a low voice. "I remember they were a good deal busier, when she was well." He shook himself. "I'll send a rider to Hastings with your letter in the morning, if you like. They have a more frequent post."

I shook my head, eyes stinging. What was wrong with me? Sir Kit had always been kind to me, and my suspicions were absurd—cruel. How hurt he would be, if he knew of them.

He tipped my chin up. I looked away, but that could not hide that my eyes were swimming. "If nothing is wrong at home," he said slowly, "then perhaps something is wrong here. A depression of the spirits, you said. I—if you will not let me be your friend, let me—" He tried to laugh. "Let me do *something*, to make you smile again."

I could feel Iphigenia's quill tickling the bridge of my nose. *Stop frowning, you'll frighten away all the young men.* My throat relaxed a little, and the tears retreated. "On my half-holiday, I'm afraid I arrange my face to please only myself," I said, in almost a normal tone of voice. "You can order me to smile tomorrow morning."

His finger tightened beneath my chin for a moment—but he dropped his hand, and hoisted himself onto the stairs. "The arrangement of your face pleases me quite enough this afternoon. I shall take you and Tabby to the beach tomorrow morning instead, before the heat sets in. The fresh air will do you good."

I tried to get fresh air today! But we had been over that already. More sharp remarks would be mere shrewishness. "Thank you, sir."

I woke from unpleasant, confused dreams to light under Tabby's door. Lady Palethorp did not usually light a candle. Was it Sir Kit? I listened until I heard her ladyship's voice before I went in.

My charge was making an even greater mess of her mother's hair, lumpy braids of varying thickness protruding haphazardly from her head like snakes digesting a large meal. Lady Palethorp winced painfully, but without protest, as Tabby struggled with a tangle.

"You should cut your hair," the little girl instructed. "Then it will be easier to wash and brush and keep neat. Hair grows better when you care for it."

A shadow passed over the lady's face. I felt guilty, for Tabby was repeating my own words, when she had wept inconsolably over trimming two inches of her hair. Some sympathetic impulse made me say, "She advised me to wear powder to hide the circles under my eyes."

I didn't know why I bothered; her ladyship merely glanced at my eyes and said nothing. Probably she agreed.

Tabby gave up and wove the knot into the braid. "Miss Oliver won't wear powder or let me arrange her hair unless there's a ball. You should give a ball, Mama."

"I can't, sweetheart."

"You should."

"I can't. I wish I—"

Tabby dropped the half-finished plait. "You can too! Mothers give balls. Mrs. Abbott gives balls. Grandmama gave balls. Why can't you?"

I had never seen Tabby throw a tantrum with her mother as she did with me, but it was hot, and late, and Clarice had told me she had barely eaten any supper. I stood. "Now, Tabby. You are out of sorts, and will regret your words in the morning. Why don't you wish your mother good night—"

"I hope she has a *terrible* night," Tabby said under her breath.

"She doesn't mean it, my lady."

Tabby's chin set, for she *hated* to be contradicted. I should have known better, but I was also hot and tired and had barely eaten any supper.

"I'm sorry, my lady. Perhaps you had better come back another time."

"It's all right," Lady Palethorp said, but I could see very well that it was not. She was rigid herself, and her voice shook. "You're like me, minha filha. We get angry, and then our tongues run away with us. I understand. I'll see you soon."

She had barely shut the door behind her when Tabby burst into tears and ran to bury her face in my skirt. "I'm *not* like her. I'm not! When *I* grow up, I won't be sick or fat. I'll go to parties and Papa will buy me pretty dresses, not some old nightgown with a hole in it! I wish *you* were my mother instead of her!"

The door swung open again with a terrible creak. Tabby fell silent; we both turned, trembling, to look at Lady Palethorp.

"You shallow, nasty little brat." She had flushed deeply enough to show by candlelight. "Do you think about anything but dresses? I don't sit in my room in old-fashioned clothes for *fun*. You don't like my nightgown?" She yanked viciously at the shoulder of her nightdress. Stitches tore loudly, and one heavy breast tumbled out.

I tried not to look at her wide brown nipple, soft from the heat. I could not swallow.

"I fed you from this bosom while your *Grandmama* called me a milch sow with my piglet, and your darling Papa didn't say a word. I should have spared myself the trouble and kept my breasts from sagging."

They stared at each other, the mother's eyes slitted and the daughter's wide. I was afraid even to give Tabby a squeeze of comfort. *I wish* you *were my mother instead of her!*

Lady Palethorp looked away first—turning on *me* as she shoved her breast back into her bodice. "In there." She jabbed a finger at my room.

Heart pounding, I rushed to wake Clarice. "Tabby is upset. Come watch her." The nursemaid blinked, bewildered—but I watched her face when she came into the nursery. She was not shocked by Lady Palethorp's presence, only sighed and gave her mistress a sleepy curtsy.

What conclusions could I draw from that? It might mean her ladyship's visits were permitted after all. Or it might mean she had bought Clarice's silence with a sapphire ring.

I followed Lady Palethorp into my narrow room. She wrung her hands, her mouth working, vibrating like a plucked string. I shut the connecting door without locking it. *If she comes at me I'll scream, loud enough to wake Sir Kit. Clarice and I can hold her off long enough for him to get up the stairs.*

But Clarice might not help me. How much loyalty did a sapphire buy?

"Are these the manners you're teaching my little girl?" The words hissed from her lips like splashes from a boiling pot. With Tabby's clumsy braids sticking out from her head, she should have been pitiable, even ridiculous. But I retreated until my legs hit my bed, genuinely frightened. Her eyes burned a hole in me. "She never spoke to me like this before *you* came."

Abruptly, my own anger flared. She behaved like *this*, and wanted to blame her daughter's tantrums on *me*? "She is a child, and has not yet learned to *govern her temper*."

Her jaw dropped. "What does Kit see in you, you preachy, dried-up old maid? How dare you? How *dare* you? You think I don't see you trying to step into my shoes? You're not Tabby's mother, and you never will be. You think I'm nothing? I will burn this house to the ground before I let you steal my child from me." She thrust the candle at me.

A column of intense heat poured from the glass chimney, making the ruffle at my neck shimmer—a trick of the light, and my eyes were watering. Or was a loose thread already smoking? I could not breathe.

"Do you hear me?" she spat at me. "I will *kill* you."

17

The bedframe dug into my thighs. If I leaned any further back, I would fall, and perhaps knock the flame from her hands. At least it was not oil…

She pushed the candle closer, a burst of heat on the underside of my chin.

I suppose I might have darted sideways. But mouse that I was, I froze under her gaze. "Please go. I'll—" My voice gave out. "I'll scream," I whispered hopelessly. "Tabby is listening."

She bared her teeth at me like a caged animal—but she whirled away, setting the candle on my nightstand, and stalked back into the nursery.

I braced for a bang. But even in her rage she remembered to close my door softly. Next, Tabby's door gave a drawn-out, faint creak, and shut quietly. I barely heard her turn the key in the lock.

She had never raised her voice.

I had been right. She was confined to her room—or was supposed to be.

I could do nothing, could not even think, until I had put out the candle. Twice I cupped my hand around the opening of the glass chimney—and twice I snatched it away from the heat. Finally I steeled myself and blew, but my breath came too weakly, and the candle only flickered and sputtered, safe in its prison.

At last I blew the damn thing out, and went to the mirror to look for sparks in my clothes and hair. Nothing glowed in the dark.

She blamed *me* for her daughter's ungovernable temper?

I lifted the nightgown off, keeping the ruffle from my hair, and pushed the whole thing into the basin. Water splashed onto the wood as I shoved each air-bubble of linen down. At last it was drowned and still.

I raised it, dripping, to my burning neck. But the water was too warm to give relief. I wrung it out as best I could and hung it from a chair.

My cap was baptized next. I felt for sparks in my hair.

And I had sought to spare her feelings, like the sap I was. What feelings? Hot blood and a cold heart, that was the sum of her.

I had squeezed myself dry of energy and attention, trying to teach her neglected child right ways. If I made little progress, who was to blame?

She was the one who kept Tabby from her rest, not I. By her own admission, Tabby's spiteful temper was inherited from her—and was plainly being further corrupted by her own influence and example. After that laudanum-soaked scene in the chapel, *I* had persuaded Tabby to apologize, and she would not even hear it—

Or…had Sir Kit not permitted it? My racing thoughts tripped over the old riddle.

But surely tonight had answered it. One of them must be a monster: Lady Palethorp, or Sir Kit. Had she not shown herself a monster tonight?

I got on my hands and knees, naked, to check the floorboards for any stray spark. I knew it was a kind of madness, but at least if I did it—twice—three times—I would be done.

The worst accusation lodged in my bosom like a jagged splinter. *Before you steal my child.*

She raved at me and her husband pursued me and her child played cruel pranks until my nerves were in shreds, and *I* was at fault? Was I a dried-up old prune, or a scheming Jezebel? She could not have it both ways!

Oh, but she can, my conscience whispered. *You are a frustrated, unnatural spinster who hates mothers and pretty women. You have dreamed of being mistress of this house, and having Tabby call you "Mama."*

The splinter pierced deeper, the wound suppurating.

I knew I should go to Tabby, to see if she needed comfort or explanations. In the morning, in sunlight, it would be too late. We would both pretend it hadn't happened.

I will burn this house to the ground before I let you steal my child. I will kill you.

I took my shift from its overnight peg and pulled it on. The hem scraped against my raw chin, smelling of yesterday's sweat. I held my breath, as though that could starve the sparks of anger and fear in my chest. They spread, heedless. My nightgown dripped onto the floor, a repetitive, distracting sound, out of time with my watch.

I wasn't fit to go to Tabby.

Whatever my idle daydreams might have been, they could not justify violence or threats of murder—threats whose sincerity was impossible to doubt.

I was ashamed to remember that I had been half ready to take Lady Palethorp's part against Sir Kit—that I had suspected him of horrors. And she had reduced me to this trembling wreck for nothing!

Things could not go on like this. None of us could sleep peacefully in our beds while she walked the house.

In the morning light, I found a few singed threads on my nightgown's ruffle. I would have to keep wearing it; I had no other.

Tabby was breaking her fast when I entered the nursery. I hugged her anyway. "What happened last night was not your fault."

She squirmed out of my grasp and returned to her toast without answering.

When I had forced down my bread and marmalade, I hurried to the study, not daring to look at Lady Palethorp's door as I passed the second-floor landing.

Sir Kit was making short work of a stack of buttered muffins, his correspondence spread over the desk. The bitter smell of his coffee turned my stomach.

He held up a finger ruefully as he chewed and swallowed. "Good morning, Miss Oliver." He gave me a welcoming smile. "How may I help you?"

My nerves settled a little. I had wronged him first to last. He had not even seduced Clarice. "Sir Kit, is your wife's illness contagious?" I ventured. "Is she…is she dangerous?"

It was a jumbled speech, but Sir Kit did not look confused as he wiped the butter from his fingers and raised a sober gaze to mine. "Why do you ask?"

"I thought perhaps…after last time…that you did not like her visiting Tabby."

His frown deepened. "*Has* she been visiting Tabby?"

I found myself reluctant to confess the extent of it. "She came last night."

"I see." He rubbed at his forehead. "And how did she behave?"

"She became angry. She upbraided us both."

His eyes closed briefly—and opened, fixed on me and full of concern. "Is Tabby well? Are *you*?"

My eyes stung, and the red patch on my chin burned. It hurt when I nodded.

His shoulders sagged in relief. "Thank God for that." Pushing back his chair, he was at my side in a few swift strides. "I ought to have been honest with you from the start, but I was afraid it would frighten you from the post. Can you forgive me? I can hardly forgive myself. If she had hurt you…" He took my hands.

His solicitude was a balm. I stepped back to a more proper distance, but I didn't pull my hands away.

"No one outside this household knows the truth," he said. "And very few inside it. Discovery would dash Tabby's prospects. A devoted suitor might overlook an invalid mother, but not madness in the blood."

My imagination was swift to show me Tabby as an overeager, overdressed debutante. How keenly she would feel the affront of being shut out, whispered about, judged unworthy to bear a man's children.

His fingers tightened. "I thought her safely confined to her room." He let me go at last, and then seemed not to know what to do with his empty hands, drumming on the edge of the desk as he resumed his seat. "Her cunning is beyond anything."

"Has she ever injured anyone?"

There was a pause. "Not seriously." He rubbed at his cheek, as if remembering scratches. "She is given nothing sharp. No glass. No candles. In winter…" He glanced at me. "Never mind."

But I caught his meaning: in winter, when fires were necessary, precautions had to be taken.

"Why don't you send her away?" I blurted out.

"Send her where?" he asked wearily. "I'm not the Earl of Tassell, with the funds to keep as many households as I please. An asylum…well." The ghost of a smile flitted across his face. "I've heard they're worse than Eton."

But I can't say I haven't thought of it. She's threatened— God. A better man would have steeled himself to it by now." He turned his coffee cup round in his hands. "She's threatened to abduct Tabby."

My blood ran cold. He was not only afraid of burglars and smugglers, then.

"I don't think she'd attack our daughter. But if I'm wrong—if anything happened to Tabby, or to—" Sir Kit's gaze locked with mine for an instant, and fell.

He swallowed his coffee in a gulp. "You had better take Tabby for a long walk. I'm sure Peter can be spared; ask Cook to make you up a basket for your dinner. When you come back this afternoon, the matter will be dealt with."

I wanted to offer a word of support, or comfort. But I could think of nothing, only be sorry for his ruined morning. How many hours—how many days—how many *years* had been poisoned by the one unalterable mistake of having given his heart unwisely?

When had the madness come upon her, and how? Swiftly, or in fits and starts? Had she felt it herself—dreaded it—hated her pulse that would not slow, and her thoughts that would not resolve? How long had it taken Sir Kit to extinguish the last ray of hope in his breast, and face the truth: that the one person who had the right to offer him comfort would never be any comfort again, but a torment?

I remembered how he had chafed under his neighbors' pity: *Poor Sir Kit, raising his little girl all alone!* Yet they did not know the half of it—could not guess at the burden he shouldered alone.

Even I was relieved to slip away, and leave him to it.

I kept us out of doors until the worst heat of the day was past. Despite my insistence that Tabby retain her bonnet, and my efforts to keep us in shade, I could see sunburn rising on her cheeks, and feel it on my own.

The house was quiet when we returned, the staff no more than usually cross with the heat. Supper arrived in the nursery as usual. No sound rose from the apartment below.

When Tabby was in bed and I had put on my nightgown, dry now and stiff, I pressed my ear to the floorboards. Silence.

I fell into bed and slept like a stone.

I was awakened by the door opening. Through the gap in my canopy I saw light leap over the threshold, yellow and alive. I tumbled to the floor, drawing breath to scream.

"It's me. I didn't want to knock any louder."

My heart did not slow. "Sir Kit?" I scrabbled for the sheet, wrapping myself in it like a shawl. My feet could not locate my slippers.

He was still fully dressed, his hand cupped around his lamp to shield the open flame; the light shone pitilessly on his haggard face. "Come keep me company a while. You can't imagine the day I've had."

At last I went barefoot to the door, gripping the knob too tight. "I shouldn't. Don't you want your daughter raised by a woman of principle?"

"As if you could ever be anything but," he said. "How will it violate your principles, to sit with me in the library for half an hour? 'The narrow path of truth and virtue inclines neither to the right nor left—it is a straight-forward business, and they who are earnestly pursuing their road, may bound over many decorous prejudices, without leaving modesty behind.'"

Each facet of the glass door-knob cut lines into my palm.

"I need you," he said, very softly.

I went. I read him Thomas Gray, singsong and meaningless as a lullaby. And when he sat beside me and reached for my hand, I let him take it.

At length he brought my hand to his lips, as he always did. But after the chaste kiss I expected, he softly dragged his lips to the tip of my index finger, and sucked it into his mouth.

I snatched my hand away, scrambling to my feet. "Sir Kit!" My averted face felt as hot and pink as the inside of his mouth.

He sat quite still. Out of the corner of my eye, I saw his hands pressed flat to the window-seat. "I'm sorry. I forgot you were a Methodist."

He spoke lightly, but I could hear his hurt, and I knew far too well how he felt. I too longed to be forgiven for a fault I could not remember committing. I, too, longed to be welcomed into Eden—not because it was Paradise, but because it was *home*. I wanted to be naked without shame.

"Your *wife*—" I protested in anguish.

He was on his feet like a shot. "What wife? You think about my wife more than I do, and much more than she deserves."

I fled up the stairs in the dark. I made sure all three of my doors were locked, as though it mattered. As though that could make me modest. I stood very still in the center of my room, listening.

I had expected to feel safe, knowing Lady Palethorp was locked in her room. Now I thought, *If I scream, there is not a single person in earshot who could get to me.* Had I made a terrible mistake?

I heard Sir Kit's footsteps on the stairs. My heart climbed into my throat.

No, I told myself. I had not been wrong to tell him about his wife. He had not meant to frighten me just now. I had encouraged him. He had thought I would welcome his touch. He had done nothing truly wrong. There was nothing to be afraid of.

Yet I unlocked the door between my room and the nursery, against the master's orders. I cracked it for good measure.

He tapped lightly with a finger. I held my breath, listening for his key in the lock.

He tapped again.

Would Clarice come if I called her? What would Tabby do, if her father said *Shut the door and go back to bed, kitten, everything's fine*?

What would Lady Palethorp hear, in her apartment below?

At last his footsteps turned, and walked away.

I dared do nothing the next day, or the next. But when three long nights had passed, I asked Mr. Christie to have the footmen carry up a sofa to the nursery.

Sir Kit appeared as they were settling it against the wall. His eyes went to the daybed, and then lingered on me. "Has Tabby unexpectedly grown a few feet?"

I chuckled nervously. "No, but she has been having nightmares. I'll sleep in here for a while, to be on hand."

I hadn't coached Tabby beforehand. That seemed too low. Now this scruple appeared not only unwise, but nearly Jesuitical in its disingenuity. I was relying on a little girl to make herself an accomplice to my lies, whether I said so outright or not.

I thought of Sir Kit's quotation from Mrs. Godwin: *The narrow path of truth and virtue inclines neither to the right nor left—it is a straight-forward business.* I could see no straightforward path, unless I quit my post at once.

I watched Sir Kit go swiftly to his daughter and kneel beside her. "Have you been having bad dreams, Tabby-kitten? What are they about?"

I deepened my hypocrisy by praying.

Tabby looked at her father. She looked at me.

Clarice stepped forward, opening her mouth. Tabby said loudly, "Burglars coming in my window."

I thanked her with my eyes, and Sir Kit quite melted. "Oh, Mistress Christabel. You poor kid." He picked her up, big as she was, and set her on his hip. "It's really very safe up here at the top of the house, if you keep the doors locked and the shutters closed."

Tabby, gratified by the interest she had generated, expanded on her theme. "They take Adeline and say they're going to *sell* her, and then they take my dresses, and my books, and my shoes, and my chair, and my toys, and they say *Be quiet!* Burglars have knives sometimes, Papa…"

Sir Kit listened attentively, exclaiming in all the right places. There was no denying he loved his daughter. Perhaps…perhaps he even loved *me*.

Tabby was now asking for a strongbox for her best toys. "Like you have in your study, Papa." I could not leave her alone in this crooked house. I didn't *want* to leave her. She needed me.

"I'll see if I can find one the right size," Sir Kit said. "Remind me next week." This was his usual tactic, since Tabby forgot most things within five minutes. If she persisted two weeks running, he generally gave in.

I remembered suddenly how he had promised me Luke would be punished for his shirking.

Why had I been so certain that Tabby's talent for duplicity was inherited only from her mother?

In Tabby's room, I couldn't leave the shutters open or sleep naked. I woke from nightmares two or three times a night. All afternoon I dreaded the evening, and all night I dreaded the morning, when I would have to admit my attempts at rest had failed. I began to apply a dusting of powder below my eyes, after all, and hoped Tabby would not remark on it too loudly in her father's hearing.

Sir Kit had kept his distance, so far. I was glad of it—but wished I could be gladder. Without his conversation, there was nothing to distract me from my thoughts.

Lady Palethorp was in the family gallery on Sunday, hands fisted in her lap and veiled face turned towards me and Tabby. I could hear her stifled sobs all through the service, and see the flutters they made in her veil.

Tabby hung on me, eyes carefully averted from her weeping mother. My own gaze was dragged back, unwillingly, again and again.

"Thou shalt not wholly reap the corners of thy field…thou shalt leave them for the poor and stranger," Sir Kit preached below us—a sermon on the gleaners, women so poor they would inch across the fields behind the harvesters from eight in the morning to seven at night, bent double, collecting stray grains of wheat. Such a small prerogative, yet English justice had overturned it when I was a girl.

It would have been a fine sermon in the parish church, but here, too nervesome to be charitable, I could not but find it self-congratulatory; the only person present with the power to permit or prohibit gleaning was Sir Kit himself.

Lady Palethorp's weeping stopped for a few breaths—and resumed before my shoulders could relax. Why was she here? Had she begged to be near her daughter? Did Sir Kit think prayer would soothe her troubled spirits?

Or…the thought *would* come…did he want to spite her for her Jewishness?

All afternoon, as I listened to Tabby's prayers and taught her the catechism, I inflamed my weary brain with nervous imaginings, until my eyes could not judge the distance between myself and objects. I would reach out to touch something and it would not be where I expected. Perhaps I was feverish. My senses could not be trusted, or my thoughts.

Vó had rarely talked about Lisbon, though I had always known the Inquisition had broken her fingers, and burned her brother and uncle. But after she died, my mother had sometimes told me more, including that vó had given evidence against her own family.

But how could she? I had demanded. *It would be better to go to the stake!*

Mãe slapped me. I had been shocked—she almost never raised her hand to me once I was old enough to understand words.

God willing, neither of us will ever know what we'd do in her place! she said fiercely. *How dare you judge her, safe in England? If they thought you were really sorry and ready to be a good Catholic, they'd let you off with a few broken fingers. If you wouldn't confess, they didn't even strangle you before they burned you. All the children were coached—'admit to this but not that, don't mention your aunt who's been reconciled with the Church once already, because they always burn backsliders.' They gave her the name of a woman who'd been burned in Lima, for if she was asked who first brought her into Judaizing, because the harshest sentence was for that. That's what they called it,* judaizante. *You think her family wanted her to go to the stake to protect them? Anybody arrests you, you tell them, 'I'm a good Christian girl, it's all my mother's fault, she lives on Albion Street, if you go now you can get her before she leaves for market.'* And then mãe burst into tears and hugged me so hard I went rigid and embarrassed in her grip.

Something else I remembered from mãe's secondhand stories: the Inquisition jails drove some people mad. Even if your bones stayed whole, you could go in an ordinary person with a secret, and after a few years locked up alone, your spirit might break, or your mind, or your heart.

Vó's aunt had been in prison with a man who, after eight years, saw things that weren't there. He screamed and sang in his cell until even the other prisoners wished secretly that someone would come and take him away.

This man had confessed a dozen times, and retracted as often. Once, on the point of signing his confession, he'd torn it up and tried to eat it, saying, *Why would I sign such a thing? I'd have to be mad. These are my friends I'm sending to the stake!*

I felt a kinship with that man that I couldn't explain—didn't want to explain. I admired him, trying to reverse his deadly mistake with the last glimmer of clear sight left to him. A traveler lost in a thorn forest, doggedly forcing his gangrenous feet towards the distant, moonlit ribbon of the path of virtue.

I admired him, and I was afraid to see his face in the mirror. I, too, could never say, *I decided. Now it's over.*

Now I dithered about going to Sir Kit about Lady Palethorp, when I had done it and could not take it back. I tried to remember everything he had said about his wife, and compare it for consistency. I racked my brain for forgotten scraps of conversation, and doubted my own memories.

I was almost sure he had said the guitar was his mother's.

He had insisted the music shopkeeper send his apprentice to Goldengrove, instead of coming himself. Had he wanted to keep me from inquiring about the guitar and its owner?

But if it was a lie, what purpose did it serve? Surely it would be not merely wicked, but imprudent?

Round and round I went, unable to judge if the path was smooth beneath my feet, or glimmering in the distance.

I had seen Lady Palethorp's violent, uncontrolled behavior for myself. She had threatened my life, while Sir Kit had done nothing worse than to indicate that he would like to take me to bed. Men did, sometimes, want to bed women.

But if Sir Kit *had* locked her up, then she had been in her room for years, with only a nurse—a jailer—for company. Without candles, without a needle or pen-knife, without fresh air—for I was sure Sir Kit kept her shutters locked.

If that was true…then how strange was her behavior, *really*? Mãe would have burned down a thousand houses to keep me.

Tabby's tantrums grew worse and worse, now that her mother's visits had ceased. I felt an awful stab of guilt when I reflected that she might think her mother was angry at her. But if I confessed that *I* was to blame, what would my pupil do?

Had I signed my confession, and sent Lady Palethorp to the stake?

If it had truly been too late, maybe I could have found a way to forget it. But of course it wasn't. I had a key to her room.

18

"I'd like to take a holiday," I said.

Sir Kit blinked.

"Just for a week," I rushed on. "I'd like to go home for a few days and see my friends."

I could not think clearly at Goldengrove. I needed desperately to hear an outside perspective, if only to have something solid to measure my own against. Iphigenia could never really understand, especially since I already knew I couldn't bring myself to tell her most of it. But a moment to catch my breath—who knew how much good it would do me? After a week away, this might all seem a tempest in a teapot.

"Your friends," he said slowly. "Of course."

I felt at once that I ought to have used another word—that I had hurt him.

I could feel his tongue curling around my finger, and wished I wore gloves, though it would have been absurd.

He sighed. "Can you pay for the journey, or shall I give you an advance on your salary?"

I took in my first deep breath of the morning. He was going to let me go. That weighed in his favor. "I still have most of my wages from Midsummer, thank you, sir."

"I'll ask my cousin to come and watch Tabby." He uncapped the inkwell, pulling a sheet of paper towards him. "Now I see her improvement under a gentlewoman's care, I don't wish to leave her in Clarice's sole charge."

The days dragged on, dry and hot. The "Domestic Occurrences" section of the newspaper was full of house-fires. When a week had passed, I thought I might fairly ask, "Have you heard from your cousin?"

He looked at me for a moment, uncomprehending. "Oh! Of course, I meant to tell you. She will be glad to come at Christmas."

I felt no shock, for I had half expected it—only a kind of dull despair, and a conviction that at Christmas, Sir Kit would say *I'm sorry, but she has a worrisome cold*, or *The roads are impassable*. He had never written the letter.

"Mrs. Cross, I saw Lady Palethorp weeping in chapel, Sunday before last," I ventured to the housekeeper. "Has her illness taken a turn?"

Mrs. Cross looked impatient. "She's nervous, is all." She glanced around to see if the maids were in earshot. "You wouldn't believe what the master has had to put up with from her. And without a word of complaint!"

I had thought so myself, not long since. Yet I felt a flash of contempt, as though for a dupe—or an accomplice. He had complained to me a great deal, hadn't he?

That was all I saw, everywhere I looked—dupes and accomplices. The servants, the neighbors, my own face in the glass: I suspected them all. I even mistrusted the barometer. Why was its needle so steady, when I could feel the air growing thick and heavy?

I tried to escape the house for a solitary walk, and heard a footman hurrying after me before I'd gone fifty paces. I felt hunted, spied on. I remembered how Sir Kit had joked, *Do you think I'm reading your letters?* Why would such an idea occur to him, unless it was true?

Even the chapel assumed a sinister aspect. Sir Kit wanted to keep us at Goldengrove; he didn't want us listening to any voice but his.

Every turn of Mrs. Cross's keys in the shutters and doors tightened my vocal cords to the breaking point. I was afraid of screaming involuntarily. Not a shrill cry for help, but a guttural shriek of fury.

Then Sir Kit handed me a letter from Iphigenia.

It was dated over a week ago. Had the mail been slow, or had it been languishing on Sir Kit's desk?

But even if it had, that was hardly evidence of malice. He and I had been avoiding one another.

You won't believe this, but I've taken a post near you! Lively St. Lemeston just isn't as lively without you, Livvy. (Now I've written it out, I see there's a joke there, about Livvy and Lively sharing so many letters, but I'm too undisciplined to find it.) I'm going to be lady's companion to Mrs. Musgrave at Jury's Gap. I suppose it isn't so very near—eleven miles, Lady Tassell says.

I'll be in Rye for a few hours on the twenty-ninth before traveling on in the morning.

The twenty-ninth! That was tomorrow.

Do you think you might be able to get away? I'd love to share a glass of huckle-my-buff...

I was surprised into a laugh. Huckle-my-buff was an unremarkable hot drink of beer, brandy, and eggs, but at school Iffy and I had made *huckle-my-muff* our private cant for licking between a woman's legs. It was years since we'd done any such thing together, but we were still in danger of helpless giggles if we caught each other's eye while someone downed a glass in particularly enthusiastic or noisy fashion.

Longing welled up in me to see her beautiful face, with its crown of golden hair, breaking into a smile at the sight of me. And she would be in Rye tomorrow.

It wasn't my half-holiday, but I went to Clarice and told her I would have to go out on Thursday afternoon this week, and got her promise to watch Tabby. Then I went to Sir Kit's study.

I had considered not mentioning the matter to him at all, but in the end, I didn't dare. I explained—wondering all the while if he already knew—that Mrs. Musgrave's new companion was an old friend, that she would be stopping over in Rye, and that I meant to take supper with her.

"You can't possibly walk home so late," he said at once.

"Then I shall stay overnight, and walk back at first light," I said, unyielding. "I'll give up my half-holidays for a fortnight to make it up."

He leaned over his desk. "But Tabby has been having nightmares."

"Clarice will do for one night, sir. Miss Lemmon is my oldest friend. I can't let her pass so close by without some courtesy from me. It would be an insult." I saw no sign of softening, and added in dulcet tones, "Lady Tassell would think it so strange."

He tilted his chair back, grinning crookedly. "And that would *never* do. Very well, if you insist on going, I'll send you in the carriage."

His easy concession left me adrift, and full of self-doubt. "Thank you, sir. That would be wonderful."

He winked at me, and turned back to his work.

I curled up in my daybed, happier than I had been in—I did not care to think how long. Tomorrow I would spend a whole night away from Goldengrove. I would breathe fresh air. Well, perhaps not *fresh*, for Rye's fishy atmosphere must be worse than ever in the heat. But I was prepared to gulp it down like champagne. For once I managed to fall asleep before midnight.

A clamor of bells woke me. The parish church, ringing the bells for morning prayers... Had I overslept? But when I pushed aside my canopy, the nursery was dark, and I realized this was no melodic chime. It was a frantic clanging in one high note, each new peal battering my eardrums before the last had faded to a resonant whine.

Clarice stumbled in. "The French fleet. Help me with my stays, if they find us in our shifts—"

"*Clarice*," I interrupted, for Tabby was listening wide-eyed. "Don't borrow trouble. It's probably only—a fire. In—in the neighborhood. Wait here."

From the roof, I would be able to see the whole countryside at once. Was the floor beneath my bare feet warmer than usual as I dashed through my room? If she had set the apartments below us ablaze, the stairs might become impassable at any moment. We should all go down at once.

That bell is not tolling for you in any literal sense, and you know it, I scolded myself.

As I bolted up the stairs, Sir Kit came round the corner above me. I flattened myself against the wall, and he raced past without slowing. I hurled myself up the last half-flight.

I saw the light at once. Three blazes, separate, but close by one another. Perhaps half a mile off and low to the ground, I guessed, but it was hard to be sure in the dark. I could smell smoke; we were downwind of the fire.

I could dimly see the fire bell, too, thrashing and shrieking in its tower like a living thing. It struck me as strange, all at once, that I had never seen its bell-ringer's face, or set foot in its church.

Hooves rang on the gravel, suddenly near enough to break through the alarm. The iron knocker clanged, a deeper note. I went back to Tabby and Clarice. "Some buildings a ways off are burning. Cottages, perhaps."

"I'll go and help," Clarice said at once. "If you don't mind, ma'am."

"It's all right with me if it's all right with Sir Kit. I'm sure you'll find him below."

It was two in the morning, so I bundled Tabby back into her bed, but it was hopeless. Even after the bell stopped, even with the shutters bolted and curtains drawn, we heard an uneasy clatter of horses and wagon wheels from without, raised voices and booted feet within. At half past three, I suffered her to rise and dress, and go below where the excitement was.

Sir Kit had gone out to fight the fire, taking with him most of the young, able-bodied members of the household. Even my ineffectual aid was welcome in the kitchen. Mrs. Bishop gave Tabby toast and tea, and set me to shaping rolls while she sliced up joints of meat for a cold collation in the Great Hall.

"Has anyone…been injured?" I asked *sotto voce*.

The cook sighed. "It started in Joe Pilgrim's cottage, and poor Barty Vickers burned off half his face trying to get the old drunk out. That lad always had more Christian charity than sense. Old Joe must have gone up like a plum pudding." She pressed her lips together. "If you see the master afore I do, ask if he means to set up for a makeshift infirmary here, or only send out baskets."

I could not seem to avoid stretched, rough patches on the surface of my rolls, like burn scars.

"Flour your hands and go slow," Mrs. Bishop told me. "You'll get a smoother crust and softer crumb."

I obeyed. Tabby's attention was absorbed in prattling to the scullery maid about the practical uses of sea monsters in extinguishing fires, so I asked quietly, "Is the fire still spreading?"

The cook's knife paused, flush against a ham bone. "With this dry weather, Mr. Kirk says we might lose the corn."

The chances of our own sturdy hall being set ablaze by a floating bit of thatch were slim, but vicarious fear and horror oppressed me. A dry wheat-field would be an inferno. If Barty Vickers had sacrificed his face for an aging drunk—*Old Joe must have gone up like a plum pudding*—what would men do to save the harvest?

Tabby could no more think of anything else than I could. At last I took her up to the roof to gaze at the conflagration, and read the weather vane. Still an east wind blew the fire towards us. We descended to read the barometer. Still the glass foretold no rain.

Next, we catalogued the weapons being used to fight the fire. I sketched Lively St. Lemeston's fire engine and fire-ladders for her, and explained the workings of a volunteer fire company, and why they were better suited to towns than to the country. I tried to keep my voice steady, and my hands.

With the steady application of seawater and the fire's natural progress, the cottages were damply smoldering rubble by dinnertime. A smoky haze hung over the neighborhood; the sun's unnatural, radiant crimson became another lesson.

Sir Kit returned soon after, trailing weary firefighters. They descended on Mrs. Bishop's collation like locusts.

I knew my employer had slept little and done much. I watched the clock like a cat at a mousehole, hoping he would remember on his own, and I should not have to pester him. But at last it was quarter past five, the latest possible moment I could set out on foot and still reach Rye before dark.

I found him in his study, all over soot, talking to the vicar about what the parish might do for the unfortunates who had lost their homes. "Might I speak with you a moment, sir?"

Sir Kit rose at once, instructing the vicar to treat the brandy decanter as his own. He shut the study door behind him and leaned heavily against it. "Has the hullabaloo overset Tabby?"

"No, she does very well," I said honestly. "Do you have a prism, by the by? I touched on the principles of light to her, by way of explaining the sun's strange appearance, and she was much interested."

He blinked bleary eyes. "Good Lord, you're well educated," he said, and then stopped, as if struggling to recall my question, and blinked several times more. "I'm sorry. I don't know," he said at last. I could not seem to remember why I had suspected him of villainy. "Let me poke about the place, and if not, there's a Jew optician in Rye."

That *Jew* was like the prick of a cold steel pin; it jolted me awake. "Thank you, sir. I don't know if you recall, but my friend is stopping in Rye tonight.

You had meant to give me use of the carriage, but…"

His face fell. "Oh. Oh…yes. I'm afraid it's out of the question. The horses are jawled-out, and the air is foul; I wouldn't like to send even fresh beasts out in it."

"I quite understand. I shall be glad to walk."

"Walk!" he said in astonishment. "Of course you won't walk. The air is as unhealthy for you as for the horses—worse, for you're smaller."

"Sir, Miss Lemmon leaves Rye in the morning. She is my dearest friend, and she is expecting me. My veil is thick. I'll carry smelling salts, if you like. I'm quite healthy."

He stared at me. I felt the beginnings of panic.

"I can't countenance it," he said with finality. "I'm sorry, it's deuced bad luck. Worse for Old Joe, though, eh?"

I knew I ought to leave off, but I had rested too many hopes on this evening. "Please, sir. I want terribly to see my friend. I'll be quite all right, it's only a little haze. *Please.*"

"What has got into you?" he demanded. "I thought you were a woman of sense. Am I to have two hysterics on my hands?"

"Then may I go see her at Jury's Gap?" I persisted. "In a week or two—"

"At Jury's Gap?" He rubbed at his forehead, then wiped his grimy hand on his coat with a curse. "Miss Oliver, you must see that is impossible. Mrs. Musgrave is no longer respectable. Her own son is not permitted to visit her at Jury's Gap, let alone her dependents' childhood acquaintances. Now, I'm sorry your outing was ruined by *three homes burning to the ground*, but kindly leave me to speak to the vicar in peace."

I mumbled an apology and fled. But I did not stay chastened long. How much more dangerous *really* was the air outside than in our own kitchen, with its blackened walls and charcoal stench? At worst my eyes and throat might be sore for a day or two. *He* had been breathing in the smoke all day at close quarters, along with half the neighborhood.

His apprehension was not for my health. He didn't want me to leave the house, or to speak to a friend away from his watchful eye.

My anger fizzed and curdled all evening, like yeast in hot water. I lowered my eyes and curtsied quietly when Sir Kit came to bid Tabby good night, still in his top-boots and planning to ride out again. Then I waited at the window to see him ride off, mumbled an excuse to Clarice, and made my own way down the stairs—only one flight.

I turned my key in Lady Palethorp's door, and slipped inside.

19

The smell must have begun as the faint natural odor unique to any room's occupant—embarrassingly intimate, perhaps, but otherwise inoffensive. How long had Lady Palethorp's windows gone unopened, to allow the atmosphere to concentrate and ripen into something so thick, sour, and suffocating? I wished myself less a lady, so I might have forgotten my manners and tied my handkerchief over my nose and mouth.

Sir Kit had forbidden me to walk abroad because of some smoke, and he kept his wife in *this*? Even if she *were* mad, he might contrive to air out her room—indeed, I felt that if she were merely out of her senses, he *would*.

The room had once been the height of elegance, its crown-canopy bed fit for a French queen. Now there was a deep depression in the thick down mattress, where the mistress of the house lay in a slovenly heap, plump legs splayed and nearly entirely on display. Her mass of hair wriggled like a sea anemone over the embroidered coverlet.

She sat up on her elbows to peer at me through the dim orange light that always leaks through closed shutters, made dimmer and redder by the haze outside. An eager light came into her eyes—she began to smile, her gaze dropping down to my side—

She slumped back on the bed, realizing Tabby was not with me. "Oh. It's you," she said flatly.

I tried to swallow the lump in my throat.

"If you want to stick me with pins, you'll have to bring your own," she said. "I'm not allowed them any longer." A sort of satisfaction came into her face at this, and I remembered Sir Kit qualifying that she had not injured anyone *seriously*.

The sooner I got this over with, the sooner I could go. I hurried to the bed. In my eagerness, I even sat on it, heedless of stains and crumbs and odors and my shocking proximity to Lady Palethorp's bare legs. My lips were already open to speak—and then our eyes met, and a hot wave of physical awareness stopped my mouth.

Even this bad light was better than a lone taper. I could make out the ordinary ash-brown shade of her hair and the true shape of her face, not smoothed and softened by candlelight. Her complexion was unhealthy, her flesh puffy, her expression sullen. Her fingernails were bitten to the quick. One of the little braids Tabby had made lingered in her hair, half unraveled.

In that moment she ceased to be a phantom or a succubus, and became flesh-and-blood to me.

She swung her legs over the side of the bed, not bothering to pull her shift down. Her matted hair fell around her like a cloak as she looked cynically back. "Does Kit know you're here?"

I shook my head.

There was a guttural sound in the corner of the room. I started violently, whirling towards it. Lady Palethorp laughed unkindly.

I don't know what I expected, other than something dreadful—and it *was*.

I had thought us alone. But a woman sat in the corner, cheek propped on her knees and limp hands trailing on the floor. When our eyes met, she nodded vaguely, her dreamy smile never wavering. For a moment I could not understand, and then I did: she was soaked to the gills with laudanum.

Lady Palethorp rolled her eyes at my horror. "Oh, you can speak freely in front of Nurse Churchill. I trust her implicitly."

"Y-you do?"

"I trust her not to remember you were here." She flopped back on the bed, already bored of me. "Why *are* you here?"

My shock had somehow extinguished my urgency. I could find no words. I thought longingly of the warm taproom in Rye, where I might have spent the evening in talk and laughter, and where now Iphigenia was enjoying a hot drink without me. She might still be hoping I would come—perhaps had asked the barmaid to watch for me. Outside the sun was setting, the room growing dimmer and redder.

"How is Tabby?" she asked at last, stiffly.

"She's well, my lady. She was very taken this morning with my explanations of optics; I must find a prism for her."

Lady Palethorp smiled at the ceiling. "Wouldn't it be funny if that coquettish child grew into a bluestocking?" The silence stretched until I thought she had forgot me, but her next words were, "You ought to borrow the stopper on Kit's brandy decanter. It won't do for experiments, but it will make a rainbow."

For a moment I was pleased at the aptness of the suggestion. Then came nausea. My fingers rose to the nape of my neck, tracing her delicate gold chain.

Sir Kit had said when he gave it to me that she was incapable of aiding with Tabby's education. He had told me it was a gift from her, when she had not known I had it.

Her expression sharpened. "Not happy with my lord and master?"

He admits that he lied, I reminded myself. *He admits she is lucid sometimes.* But I pictured him coming into this reeking room and rifling through her jewel-box, and I could not conquer my horror.

"Why…" I looked to see if the nurse was listening. She had not moved, except to tip her head back against the wall. "Why does he keep you here?"

She popped up like a jack-in-the-box, leaning in close. I almost reared back at the smell. "He wants my money," she said rapidly. "But he won't get it. You'd do better to throw in your lot with me. You can't trust him. You can't. Surely you're clever enough to see that. I'll pay you. He hasn't taken *all* my jewels yet. What's he promised you? Even if he wanted to, he can't marry you unless he kills me. You really want to be Bluebeard's second wife? You think that's a good gamble? I'm…"

But already the acquisitive glitter faded in her eyes. "But I suppose you think that because you're English, he'd *never*. Not to a good girl like you."

Her gaze met mine as though she saw me for the first time—as though she read my future in my face, and was distantly sorry for it. Her mouth twisted, too exhausted to be bitter. "You'll find out when it's too late. At least I tried to warn you."

Wandering to the window, she put her eye to the crack between the thick shutters. I had done it often enough myself to know she couldn't see anything. "Why did they ring the alarm bell?" She paused. "But I suppose it tolled for me."

I laughed, startled.

She glanced over her shoulder, looking startled, too. There was something so strange in the moment—or rather, something so ordinary—our eyes meeting in pleased surprise, two strangers thrown together by chance, wondering: *Will we be friends?*

We wouldn't, of course; but I could not catch my breath. How long since she had seen the sky? Years? "There was a fire in the neighborhood." I drew her chain out of my bodice and went to the window, shuddering when my skirts brushed the nurse's ankles. The opium-eater herself did not appear to notice.

Desperate hope flared in Lady Palethorp's face—and then she slapped her hand over the keyhole. "Someone might see. It's not worth it."

"Only an inch," I bargained.

Desire warred with calculation in her eyes, and desire won. She took her hand away.

I fitted the little key into the lock with a crushing sense of undeserving, that I had it when she, with so much better a right, did not.

I drew the shutter open a crack, and Sir Kit's wife—his wedded wife, whom he had sworn to cherish for richer for poorer, in sickness and in health—pressed her face to the gap with a heaving breath, as though someone had been holding her head underwater and taken away their hand. A band of red light curved over her hair and forehead.

The shutter rattled. She drew a second breath, and then she flung herself away. "Lock it again."

I wanted to get out of this room. I was choking on its thick red air. Outside, the sun must be staining the world crimson with its blood.

It was worse to guess at the horror happening out of sight. If I could bring myself to look full upon it, it might hurt my eyes, but I would be less afraid.

I could not be *more* so.

I turned the key crisply in the lock and faced her. "You said he wants your money."

"Yes, I…" She tilted her head. "What do you want to know?"

"I want to understand. I want to understand what's happening in this house."

She laughed bitterly. "Only the usual fate of Israel. What's to understand?

I have something he wants, and he's decided it's rightfully his. Or haven't you noticed he feels the same way about your twat?"

My ears rang. I felt as I had when my mother sat me down and told me she was dying. I hadn't wanted it to be true, I had protested, but—it had felt *real*. When I had imagined her being cured, I'd known *that* was the dream.

I believed her. But my belief was proof of nothing; I had believed Sir Kit. There was no way to *know*, ever, whom you could trust. If Lady Palethorp had read my own parentage in my face, she knew this was a story that would always sound true to me.

She shut her eyes and clasped her hands before her, taking a deep breath. Then she pasted on a shy smile. "I beg your pardon for my coarseness, Miss Oliver. It's been a long time since I've needed my manners. I'll explain as much as you like. Please forgive me."

I tried to think of a question that might tip the scale with its weight, but instead my mind filled with trivialities insubstantial as feathers: *Do you like pork?* and *What was he like when he was courting you?* and *Who taught you to play the guitar?*

"And you mustn't think I'm angry." The conciliatory words were expelled from her mouth one by one, stones falling into the silence. Beneath her furrowed brow, her eyes were intent on my face. Too intent. "I don't blame you for taking my husband to bed. You have seen me behave very badly, and I..."

Her brow contracted further—her lips trembled—and Lady Palethorp burst into tears.

She put up her hands—not even to cover her face, for that would have implied a decisiveness, a control, entirely lacking in her movements. Her shoulders hunched, one hand curled at her temple and the other curled helplessly outward beside it as she turned her face away.

"Tabby hates me," she gulped between awful, wheezing sounds. "I meant to be such a good mother, I meant for my little girl to be happy..."

I have transcribed the words all together, but they were much separated by sobs, and scarcely intelligible. It was several seconds before I could decipher each one, and longer before I could piece them together. I didn't know what to do. I wanted her to stop. Someone would hear. They would come in, and then—

I didn't know her. I didn't want to touch her. I didn't want to give up all my comfort to help her.

I built one last castle in Spain: her red face would go suddenly purple and she would drop to the floor, stone dead. The doctor, when called, would inform us that she had suffered an apoplexy. Any strange statements made shortly before her death ought to be disregarded, the morbid result of pressure on the brain.

Sir Kit would give me his coat and a swallow of brandy to stop my shivering; he would mourn discreetly; and after a decent interval, he would confess that he worshipped me. The banns would be read, and I would be Lady Palethorp. I would air out this room until it smelled of nothing but strawberries, change the mattress for a new one, and—

And Sir Kit still wouldn't let me leave the shutters open at night.

Would he even consent to be married in the parish church, or would he marry me by license in the drawing room, and shoo the vicar out the door with his fee before the ink was dry in the register?

I had rather live in a hovel in England than a castle in Spain, anyway. I took a deep breath, and released it. I went to the water pitcher, past the unmoving nurse with her misty half-smile.

It was empty.

My own eyes filled with frustrated tears. Nothing would go right today, and it was such a petty, petty cruelty.

Why couldn't they leave me my music? Such a little thing, but they had to take it too—

"Don't look at me like that," Lady Palethorp raved. "The nurse is supposed to fill it, but what's the point in washing when you won't see anyone, when you won't go out, when you… What's the use in being pretty? I don't *want* him to think me pretty. God, you're so clean. I hate you for being so clean…"

The narrow path of truth and virtue inclines neither to the right nor left— it is a straight-forward business. I straightened my spine and handed her my own clean handkerchief. She sank to the floor.

But that was too much like the nurse, and too near her. "Come over to the bed," I urged. "Sit where it's comfortable."

It wasn't comfortable. The mattress was lumpy, and dipped inexorably into the hollow where her ladyship must sleep. The once-fine coverlet was torn and stinking, though it would have made a year's work for an entire French convent.

Had *she* spent her girlhood stitching it, for her trousseau?

I thought of the twice-weekly wash days, the bedsheets drying on the lawn, the maids refreshing the strawberry-leaf sachets in my clothespress. Why did they pass this room over?

I cast about desperately. The remains of a meal sat by the bed—the sausages, I saw with a sinking heart, untouched.

The tea was lukewarm and oversteeped, but I mixed it half and half with milk, and gave her the cup.

She took a sip politely—and set it down with a clatter. "I can't drink that. *You* drink it and see how you like it."

"Very well, I will," I said, at my wit's end.

Taking up the cup, I choked it down, one cool, bitter mouthful at a time. I thought I would be sick before I finished, but she stopped crying to stare at me, and my relief at the silence was so intense, I cared for nothing else.

Her damp mouth curved. "You're an odd duckling."

I looked away. "You need nourishment." I spread jam thickly on some cold, half-eaten toast and pushed it towards her. I poured her another cup—nearly all milk this time. I even dropped in some sugar, though I had little hope of its dissolving.

The amused lines around her eyes deepened at the futility of the gesture, but she downed the milk obediently, and then sucked on the sodden sugar.

"Well, Miss Bountiful?" she asked around the lump. "What would you like to know?"

But my nerves had risen as hers calmed. The sound of hoofbeats on gravel propelled me to my feet, though I could not know if they were his. "I have to go. If he found me here—"

"Kit doesn't visit me unless he has to."

There was an embarrassed pause, as I tried to think how to say that he might come looking for *me*. "I'll come back."

Her face closed even as she nodded.

Consumed with urgency to be gone, I peered through the keyhole. The landing seemed clear. I was reaching for my key when Lady Palethorp threw herself after me, bursting out in a low voice, "When can I see Tabby?"

Shame swept me. She had waited until the last possible moment, as I had waited to ask Sir Kit to let me go to Iphigenia. She had hoped I would think of it myself, and I hadn't. I still couldn't think. I couldn't pry my hand from the door-knob. "How did you judge when it was safe to visit?"

"An earthquake wouldn't wake Kit once he's asleep. I wait an hour after I stop hearing sounds below."

"What about his valet?"

She shrugged. "I bribe him now and then. Mostly, though, he hates rows. He won't stir up trouble for nothing."

"But Sir Kit almost caught you," I protested. "You had to hide behind the door."

Her eyes fell. "I got impatient. He's been staying up late. Wandering the house." She glanced back at me a little ironically, as if to say *But you know all about that.*

"You must be patient now," I whispered harshly. "If he gives me the sack, then where will you be?"

Eyebrows shooting up, she gestured at the room. "Right here."

"Well, you must look after your own interest," I snapped. "It is for you to judge what that may be. When you think it safe, contrive some way to knock on the floor under Tabby's room."

"Tabby's room? Will you hear that?"

My face heated. Would she never let me go? "I've moved my couch there temporarily. Tabby..." The lie I had told so cavalierly to Tabby's father stuck in my throat. If I said her daughter was having nightmares, she would worry.

Of all people on earth, she would best understand the truth. Yet it stuck in my throat too. "If I judge it safe, I'll fetch you."

She glared at me. "If *you* judge safe? Nothing is safe. I'd still have a key if not for you, you—"

"You may call me Miss Oliver," I interrupted. "You'd have kept your key if you'd kept your temper."

Her glare gave way after a moment to a soft laugh, in a fashion that reminded me uneasily of Sir Kit. They had been well-matched, once. "Is that what my husband calls you?"

"*Yes.*"

She snorted. "I suppose you look like a Miss Oliver. Let me guess your Christian name."

My skin itched with wanting to be gone. But I lingered.

"Minerva," she suggested. "Priscilla—"

"Prissy for short," I finished, foolishly disappointed that her guesses were not in earnest. Did I imagine it possible to read a person's name in their face?

"Euphemia." She tapped a finger on her chin. My heart pounded. "Theodosia. Hortense." Her mouth curved. "Oh, I have it—Olivia! Olivia Oliver. Come now, admit I have guessed it."

I laughed in spite of myself. "I do have a friend who calls me Livvy." But I could not stay one more moment. The light in the room was fainter than ever, and barely red.

Once more I put my eye to the keyhole. Nothing.

"I have no Christian name," I said rapidly. "But my given name is Deborah. 'Bore,' for short." And I hurried out.

I had nearly waited too long. I had not yet reached the nursery when I heard Sir Kit's boots echoing up the stairwell. Hastily I turned, and pretended to be descending.

We met on the wide stair by Lady Palethorp's landing. "Oh, there you are, Miss Oliver."

I refrained with difficulty from glancing pointedly at his wife's door: *Told you so.*

I smiled at him. "I'm glad to see you, Sir Kit. I wanted to borrow the stopper of your decanter, until we can find a prism."

He grinned back, relieved I did not bear a grudge. "That's clever. And you know I never drink brandy if I can help it. I think my copy of Newton's *Optics* is in the library somewhere. I remember using lenses to start fires when I was a boy. Perhaps you'd better not teach Tabby that."

"I hadn't planned to."

"No, of course not. Well, come down, and I'll give you the stopper from my room." He laughed at the look on my face. "Ever vigilant! I commend your dedication to the path of truth and virtue. You have foiled my villainous plot to lure you into proximity with a bed and ravish you." He scrubbed a hand over his eyes. "I'm too tired to know what I just said. I beg pardon on my knees if it was truly improper. I ought to get some sleep before I scandalize any more virgins, but unfortunately they're making a hospital of the Great Hall and I've got to see everyone settled…" He trailed off, blinking. "What did you ask me for?"

"The stopper of your brandy decanter." I wished I could hate him more—that I could dislike him, even! It would have given me confidence. It would have been a *decision*, of sorts.

I had been so sure, a few minutes since. But I could not hold fast to it. If I had been gullible before, what cause could I have to think myself wise now? Was I unkind to doubt him? If so, the only remedy was to be unkind to his lady.

"I shall ask Mrs. Cross for the stopper tomorrow," I told him. "In fact, I will ask her for it now, after I inform her that you have gone to bed, and that you wish her to finish overseeing the infirmary."

He wavered. "I want to give them every attention."

"And I will tell Mrs. Cross so," I said firmly.

"You are a jewel, Miss Oliver." Turning to go back down the stairs threw him off balance. He was obliged to pause and grip the banister to clear his head. "The prop of my old age. I shall leave you everything in my will, and Tabby will squander the estate in a Chancery suit."

I could not help it; I laughed.

These are my friends I'm sending to the stake! the prisoner who ate his confession had said. But friendship could not guide *me*. I had no friends at Goldengrove. My choice was only whose pawn to become, in a game where I could never be a winner. I set nearly as little store in Lady Palethorp's eager promise of jewels as I did in Sir Kit's idle jest. My reward would be to find my way back to the path and out of the forest, alone and empty-handed.

I descended the stairs behind him, one foot in front of the other.

20

When I finally returned to the nursery, Clarice had put Tabby to bed for me, true to her promise when I had planned to spend the night in Rye.

I carried Newton's *Optics* into my room, but the diagrams would not resolve. The present hour blurred into the past, and my chamber dissolved into the one below me.

Lady Palethorp's sharp longing had glowed in that dull squalor like a coal in the dark.

Could a man keep his wife prisoner in such a way? Goldengrove was no anonymous slum, free from servants and prying eyes—

Yet I had believed Sir Kit, when he told me no one knew she was mad. Was it any less plausible that no one knew she was healthy—or as healthy as a woman could be, without exercise or fresh air or nourishing food?

Sir Kit was popular, and his wife was not. Her parents were dead, as far as I knew, and I had never heard mention of another family connection in this country who might intervene on her behalf.

The servants might perhaps suspect the truth, but what of that? There had been countless small abuses and scandals at our school, well known to all the girls, of which the teachers were wholly ignorant. Even now, I hardly believed it would have been of any use to inform them.

Or take Albion Street, where I grew up: Tom Parrish spent his mother's pension on drink, and Lily Mussina always had bruises on her arms. We had all clucked our tongues and gone about our business. What else could we do?

I wasn't certain this was even illegal. An Englishman's home was his castle, and if he beat his wife bloody in it, the constable couldn't cross the threshold to stop him unless she cried *Murder!* A man could force his wife to live with him, couldn't he? Though the newspapers spoke of legal separations on grounds of cruelty, sometimes…

In short, I was wholly uninformed, and it was unlikely many people in the neighborhood knew more.

Suppose, then, that some Goldengrove chambermaid did take her suspicions to Mr. Munk, the magistrate. Would he lift a finger?

But I would be charitable, and suppose Mr. Munk a man of conscience and deliberation. I would suppose he brought a panel of physicians, good Christian gentlemen all, to examine Lady Palethorp.

Sir Kit would say she was mad. She would say she was not. He would be calm and charming. She would rail and weep, and make cutting remarks. I could not stretch charity far enough to suppose a happy conclusion.

More likely Mr. Munk would go straight to Sir Kit and lay the whole before him, and the only result would be the poor servant turned off without a character—a vivid object lesson to all would-be Quixotes of her station.

I found it in me, even, to admire Clarice for letting Lady Palethorp buy her silence. Contrasted with my own servile allegiance to Sir Kit, it seemed a mark of discretion, and independence of spirit.

Did I dare do more? What *could* I do? I only knew one person who might be both willing and able to intervene: the Countess of Tassell. And "know" was a generous estimation of our relationship. Would she believe me? Had I even the means to inform her?

Perhaps Lady Tassell already knew of it, and had clucked her tongue and given it up as a lost cause. Perhaps she was in possession of facts that would discredit Lady Palethorp's account. Perhaps she would even show my letter to Sir Kit, and *I* would be the homeless Female Quixote.

For now, then, I saw no path but to hold my tongue, and try to offer the only help Lady Palethorp had actually asked for.

By Saturday, a sea breeze had cleared the air. Mr. Kirk, the overseer, was too occupied with the fast-approaching harvest to give us a promised lesson in crop rotation, so the nursery party had spent a pleasant morning watching beans climb their poles on the home farm, and was now at the shore. Tabby was absorbed in making rainbows with Sir Kit's crystal stopper and speaking to the wooden occupants of her toy ark in the voice of God—deep for Tabby, but a theologian would probably have judged it rather squeaky for the Lord.

I was alone with her save for Peter and Clarice, dozing on each other's shoulders a hundred feet off. I gathered up my courage in both hands. "Tabby, I would like to speak to you about something important."

She glanced at me.

"Your mama misses you very much. She wants you to know she is very sorry for losing her temper with you, and she would like to visit you again."

Her face went blank, her gaze stony.

"You don't have to see her. You can say no."

Tabby had told me over and over that she was not afraid of her mother, and I wanted to believe her. But could a five-year-old child truly understand and answer such a question? If I had asked, *Are you afraid of your papa?* I was sure she would deny that, too, yet I had seen her lie to mollify him.

I was sick of roundaboutation. How could I ask *her* to speak plainly, if I could not? Could the truth be a more painful burden than this suffocating silence?

She was only a child, but she knew *something* was wrong. Worse, she lacked anything to compare her home to, to know this wrongness was not the natural order of things.

"You may already know this, Tabby, but your papa and mama are quarreling with one another. Your papa doesn't think it's good for you to see your mama. I think your mama loves you, and that it's good for a little girl to see the people who love her, unless she doesn't want to, or doesn't feel safe in their company."

I took a deep breath. "You should know that if your papa finds out I'm letting your mama visit you, I'll have to go away. But I won't ask you to lie for me. What do you think, Tabby? Grown-ups have to make decisions for little girls sometimes, but not always. Only you know what is in your heart. Do you think seeing your mama would be good for you, or bad?"

The surf rattled in and out, grating on the shingle and my raw nerves.

At last she said, "Why doesn't Papa love Mama? Is it because she's sick?"

How could I say to a half-Jewish child, *Your papa hates your mama because she is Jewish*? What if I was mistaken after all?

"I don't know, sweetheart. I don't think it's because she's sick. Sometimes when people are married, they find they don't like each other as well as they expected, and they wish they didn't have to live together."

"Maybe it's because he thinks her soul is damned," Tabby said eagerly. "Maybe if you explained to him that people don't go to Hell for being Jewish, he would love her again."

My heart broke. Here was an illustration of the futility of shielding children, indeed. "Sweetheart, that wouldn't help. I'm sorry."

Tabby's eyes narrowed. My stomach sank, even before she said loudly, "You're a liar!"

"I know you're very upset." I sat still and serene despite my racing pulse. Once the storm broke, there was nothing to do but wait it out.

"You don't know anything!"

"You're right, it's not fair."

"If there's a flood, I won't let you on my boat. Only blood relations and animals are allowed."

"What about me?" Clarice called over in some amusement, woken by the noise. "Must I drown too?"

I sighed. "Please don't, Clarice." Laughing at Tabby only made her worse.

Sure enough, she exclaimed passionately, "Yes! Drown, drown, drown!" and began throwing her little wooden animals at me, using the worst language she knew.

Clarice and Peter wobbled resignedly to their feet and gathered up our belongings.

The toys were too small to hurt me, but by the same token, they were small enough to be easily lost on the pebble beach, and she might refuse to go home without them. Luckily, the servants had nearly reached us. I put out a hand for the little wooden houseboat. "Clarice, if you would come and hold Tabby while I put the animals away?"

"No!" Tabby shrieked, dodging Clarice's outstretched arms, and took off running for the surf.

I leapt up and chased after her, but I tripped over the hem of my gown on the uneven shingle. I scrambled up, bruised and terrified, to see Peter scooping Tabby into his arms. She thrashed violently.

Clarice gripped her chin to hold her still for a scolding, and got a kick for her pains. "Self-destruction is a sin! Do you want to—"

I gave Clarice a sharp kick in the ankle myself, before she could say *burn in Hell.*

It was a long tantrum, even for Tabby. Just when she'd at last nearly calmed down, we discovered that in the scuffle one of us had stepped on a leopard and broken its leg.

In the end, we dragged her by force to the house, where she refused to eat her supper or change her clothes for bed. Hours later than usual, she at last fell asleep in her dirty pinafore. I was tossing and turning on the sofa as quietly as I could when something thudded faintly against the floor.

I froze, heart pounding. Had I imagined it? But the muffled knock came again through the floorboards.

I could have wept. Lady Palethorp could not possibly come up now. I imagined the hopeful agitation in her breast as she waited for me, and felt her disappointment like a blow.

I rose, and put on my wrap. Should I light a candle, to avoid the appearance of sneaking? I decided against it; Sir Kit wouldn't find it strange that I avoided a flame.

I could hear noises far below. For a moment I was startled, and then I remembered the infirmary for Sir Kit's poor burned tenants. I crept down the stairs in my bare feet, and fit my key into Lady Palethorp's lock by touch.

She must have been waiting just inside, listening intently. As I braced my shoulder to the heavy door to push it open, it swung inward, and I nearly toppled into her arms.

"Wait! You can't visit Tabby tonight. She was in a rage all afternoon and is only just now sleeping. God knows how she'll behave if we wake her."

I heard a heavy exhale, then nothing. I wished for a candle after all, to see her face.

"Of course she must sleep." The attempt at lightness cut me to the quick. "We shall try another evening. Thank you for coming to inform me." The door pushed at my palm.

I held it open. "I... Would you care for a little company?"

21

There was a long pause. The door wavered.

"Oh no. I am afraid her ladyship is not at home to callers." But I could hear the smile in her voice, and I found myself smiling too as I darted in and locked the door upon us. For a moment it felt like school, tiptoeing about after hours with racy chapbooks and contraband blackberry wine.

"You do like Tabby, don't you?" she asked wistfully.

There was that curious vertigo again. Was I a free woman offering comfort to a prisoner, or a governess being called to account by her employer? "Of course," I said in surprise. "I thought—"

But I could hardly say, *I thought you knew I wished she was mine*. "I am very fond of her." I could not help smiling again. "A few weeks ago, I taught her the story of Archimedes…"

It had done what nothing else could—namely, interested her in long division. Tabby had taken great delight a dozen times since in weighing each of my meager ornaments, immersing it in water, helping me to calculate its density, and informing me with pitying relish that the piece was not pure gold and I had been cheated.

Lady Palethorp was giggling softly by the time I finished.

"I brought a candle," I blurted out. "And a book."

There was silence. I felt inexplicably crushed by shame. Why had I been so eager?

"What book?"

"It's a novel." The slim volume grew heavy in my pocket. "I hope you like novels?"

"Oh, light the damn candle," she said. "I don't know why I asked; I'll like anything that isn't one of the five books I've got. Nurse Churchill—she's fast asleep in the dressing room, by the by—sometimes condescends to pull something off the shelf for me, but she won't trouble herself about what it is. The only thing duller than the plodding translation of Dante is *View of the Greenland Trade and Whale-Fishery, with the National and Private Advantages Thereof.*"

I blinked.

"I've read it six times already."

Somehow, we both laughed. I hastened to light my candle stub and jam it into a porcelain candlestick. "I thought these must be the late Mrs. Palethorp's." I prodded one of the worried-looking cherubs that clung to the stem of the candlestick as though fearing a strong wind.

"They are." She stroked a little haloed head with her finger. "But I don't hold that against them. Don't you like them?"

Our eyes met across the flame. I snapped my tinderbox shut and dropped it hastily into my pocket, hoping she could not read in my face that I was remembering her threat to burn me alive.

As I passed her the book, I noticed that one handspan of her hair looked soft, fluffy, and loosely waving. The rest looked as knotted as ever—except, I saw suddenly, the bottom half of another hank.

Would I embarrass her by drawing attention to it? "Did you—wash your hair?"

She hunched in on herself. "I tried to comb it. But I got bored. It's so damn long. I wish I could chop it all off." She made a snipping motion with her fingers, just above her shoulders.

Who cut your guitar strings?

I contemplated fetching my own scissors. But it would be remarked if her hair lost eighteen inches from one day to the next—and I still felt uneasy giving her a weapon.

"I can bring you hair oil for your next bath," I suggested, for wet hair would be easiest to untangle. "Or…I can do a little now while you read."

"Would you really?" Her face fell. "Only…my comb…"

A dirty comb is a trial to its owner, and a horror to anyone else. "I'll use my fingers for now."

She opened the book. "'It is a truth universally acknowledged, that a single man in possession of a good fortune, must be in want of a wife.'" She laughed rather bitterly. "Whereas a rich single woman is assumed to be content with her lot?" She did not wait for my answer before reading on.

I was beginning to think the dreamy quality in her speech, which I had thought madness, was more like the careless, disjointed way I talked to my mirror, when I had no need to arrange my thoughts so as to be intelligible to a mind separate from my own. Lady Palethorp had got out of the habit of communication.

I had read the book thrice already. The familiar words in her mellow voice wrapped around me like a warm quilt as I—oh, I had not thought, why had I not thought? Why did I never, ever think?

As I buried my fingers in her new-washed hair.

From a purely sensual perspective, the experience was imperfect. The knotted strands were dry or greasy in proportion to how much soap had reached them, and while they smelled infinitely cleaner than they had at our last meeting, they were hardly the perfumed waves of poesy.

It was the intimacy that affected me, I think. This hair was hers—it grew from her head—she felt my fingers in it. Not *too* much, I hoped, doing my best to be gentle.

The imperfections of her hair had long since been known to me. Its perfections I discovered now, gradually. Thick, plentiful, not entirely straight—the sort of hair that made a show of conforming to a brush, but would lapse into curls in the rain, or fresh from the bath, or in the close, secret space beneath a cap.

As a little girl combing my own thin hair, I had wished for just such a vibrant mass, so thick you could not find the part or see between the tresses. It was not—and this, perhaps, was half its charm to me—a texture common to Englishwomen. It was de nação.

Her hair had seemed monstrous to me once: the outward mark of our concealed affinity. I had shuddered when it brushed against me, as though it had been a spider. Tonight I wanted to rub it against my cheek, and tell her, *My avô's hair was like yours—well, his wasn't so long.*

Why had I wanted so badly to have nothing in common with her? So Sir Kit and his neighbors might approve of me? Now my throat was so parched with longing that I could not speak. All these months at Goldengrove—

But it felt longer. It felt like years I had gone without kinship, and here the feast was before me, and I could not feel I deserved a crust.

Lady Palethorp paid me no mind, but read until her voice gave out—not very long, disused as it was. Then she read in silence, hungrily, turning the pages with an eager ripple.

In silence, I loosened the tangles in her hair. A few stubborn knots had to be pulled out. Once or twice she started at the sting, but more often a cluster of dead hairs had wound themselves round a living comrade, and slipped out painlessly in my fingers.

I had made my way round perhaps two-thirds of her hair when the candle began to gutter, and she shut the book with a sigh. "May I keep it?" she asked hoarsely.

"If you think it safe. I—er—where shall I—?" I gestured at my lap full of her shed hairs.

She made a little face, rubbing at her scalp. "Shake them onto the floor, and I'll put them in the chamber-pot." Then she smiled at me, soft, grateful eyes shining through her lashes. "Thank you, Miss Oliver."

I felt the smile was a bribe, a blandishment, and still I knew a foolish pang that she had not called me Deborah. "I'll bring you a wide comb with the hair oil, my lady," I said quietly. "You can finish it wet."

She laughed. "Oh yes, and make papillote curls at my temples, for my next ball." But she ran her fingers through it and ducked her head with shy, secret coquetry. "It seems so silly to dress at night, but perhaps… Tabby would be pleased, don't you think?"

I felt a sharper pang, for her words laid bare an unacknowledged fancy that *I* had inspired her desire to improve her appearance.

But what was I to her? At best, her daughter's governess; at worst, her husband's mistress. Of course she had been thinking of Tabby—whom I ought to be thinking of myself, and was being paid to think of.

She wandered over to her clothespress. "I'm sure she'll know at once that everything is years out of fashion, even if the servants and the moths have left me any dresses intact."

She began to pull out the drawers—too many, for the chest tipped and she was obliged to shove them all back in, with a crash that made us both freeze and listen for long seconds. The shadows jumped wildly in the light of the guttering candle.

There were more gowns in those drawers than I had ever seen in my life outside an old-clothesman's stall, but she slumped to the floor with a bitter sigh. "They don't even fit me now. It's a judgment on me, I suppose, for thinking the Rye Bay ladies terribly provincial when I came."

"Don't fret."

I meant to be such a good mother, she had wept. No words of mine could close the gulf between what ought to have been, and what was. But an English gentlewoman was drilled in platitudes for every occasion, so I said, "You know Tabby has no real taste yet. Besides, a mother isn't a paper doll, to be dressed and undressed and paraded about. She only imagines that's what she wants because…"

Here my training failed me—or I had failed it, by beginning to speak the truth.

"Because she knows no better," she finished for me. "Because she has no mother."

"She has *you*. And every time…" I laughed hopelessly. "Every time we look at your *Naturalist's Miscellany*, she asks to see the daffodil. She says, 'Mama thinks I'm as pretty as that,' and begs for a yellow dress."

Lady Palethorp's eyes filled. "I want to see her." She half turned away, making an abortive cradling motion with her arms. "I want to see my baby."

My own tears spilled over. What would I have given to see my mother again? "I know," I whispered. "Soon. I promise."

The candle went out. I could hear Lady Palethorp's labored breaths. "You should go. Please."

I would have liked to stay. But I felt a delicacy—perhaps a foolish English one—at overstaying my welcome, and intruding on a private grief.

"Yes, my lady," I said deferentially, and curtsied when I bid her good night.

But when she closed the door behind me, I had to lock her in.

Two of the burns being treated in the Great Hall had become infected, requiring continual nursing and doctors' visits. The other sufferers were too much recovered to be confined to their beds, yet not enough to be sent away. Strangers roamed the house.

The strain told on Sir Kit, who hid in his locked study when not obliged to play the role of Squire Allworthy. And though he strove valiantly to check them, I could see his suspicions growing, prodigal as the bean-fields. More than once I caught him counting the silver with his eyes, or carrying some treasure upstairs "to get it out of the way."

At first, he had made no objection to Tabby visiting the hall's patients, provided she did not pester them; now he took me aside and hinted with a faint, unspoken embarrassment that she was becoming unwholesomely agitated, and hearing rough language.

How well I understood that inward struggle against unreasoning fears, and the shame when you uprooted one, only to find another had shot up while your attention was diverted. Just this morning, I had spied the heroic Barty Vickers reading *The Newgate Calendar*, and snapped *Keep that wretched thing out of Miss Palethorp's sight!*

The poor boy had looked so startled and sorry, I'd felt obliged to explain that the engravings had terrified me as a child. He'd laughed. *They're horrid, aren't they?*

But I could not laugh, even now. Those pictures and their neat copperplate captions were branded into my mind: *Catherine Hayes burnt for the murder of her husband*, and *The punishment formerly inflicted on those who REFUSED PLEADING to an Indictment.*

That last had terrified me most: a half-naked man chained spread-eagled on a stone floor, while a jailer arranged iron weights in neat rows on a tray laid over his bare torso.

I could still see the anatomy-lesson precision of the prisoner's strained form—ribs and muscled arms and bare feet, one hand clenched and one open in supplication—contrasted with the loose posture of the turnkey, hip cocked and key ring dangling from one hand, profile contracted in mild pity. I knew an impulse to go to my desk and sketch a copy, to see how far my memory would serve.

Of course it was Sir Kit, not Tabby, who was unwholesomely agitated. But I assured him with a warm smile that I would conform to his wishes, and felt rewarded for my benevolence when his brow smoothed out, and his shoulders relaxed.

Only when I was out of the room did I remember what I suspected him of.

I had always thought myself a sound judge of character—had often seen through stratagems and insincerities opaque to acquaintances. Mistrustful by nature, I was not readily to be won by winning ways.

I had not even trusted Sir Kit! I had known he was not my friend, had known there were points on which he was heedless, narrow, even selfish. Yet I had believed him *sincere*. I had thought him kind, well-meaning, candid, humane. His movements, his expressions, his voice—all rang true to my instincts; they produced a pure golden sound when my senses struck them.

Even now I could find no false note. And I despised myself, that at thirty-four I could feel so shocked and hollow at a fresh proof of the worn adage *Appearances can be deceiving*.

Had I deluded myself that only lovely women could stoop to folly? A lack of attractions did not make me wise or virtuous. It only made me untried. It had been easy to see a mask's strings, when the face was turned towards my neighbor; let it be turned on me, and I was as blinded as anybody.

The worst of it was that vó had been deceived by a lover. Had I, in my heart, still thought myself above her—told myself *I* would not do as she had?

Out of Sir Kit's presence, however, I could remember to resent him. And as nights passed and I heard no signal from Lady Palethorp, I did so with energy. Night after night, his footsteps echoed on the stairs, on the landing, in the passageway, and the second volume of *Pride and Prejudice* gathered dust in my room beside the comb and the vial of hair oil. By now she must have read the first part ten times over, and be dying to learn whether Mr. Bingley would prove true, or Miss Lucas regret marrying for advantage.

Once, he unlocked the nursery door, and came in with his oil lamp to watch at Tabby's bedside. I kept my eyes tight shut, my heart beating an alarm. I had rashly dispensed with my canopy, which hung awkwardly over the daybed and tickled my face.

There was a faint clatter and a muffled curse. I prayed he did not see me start.

After a moment, I let one eyelid flutter open. He had stepped on Adeline, and was laying the doll gently back in her place, a weary peace in the set of his shoulders.

I buried my face in my pillow, ignoring how my skin stuck to the pillowcase. I tried to smooth out my brow, and keep my limbs loose. How much of my legs could he see? It was too late to pull my nightdress down. Why had I thrown back the sheet? My breathing sounded unnatural to my own ears.

His footsteps drew near my sofa. The space behind my eyelids lightened; I felt the lamp's heat on my cheek. A bead of sweat rolled down my nose. I wished I could see his unguarded expression as he looked at me. Was it covetous? Triumphant? Or only fond?

It was long moments before the lamp receded, and he left the room.

I gasped for breath. I did not dare get up to wash my face.

And then, one night, it happened.

I heard a thump from below the floor. I ran to put on my wrap and gather up my little trove; it was nearly a minute before my trembling fingers managed to wedge the book into my pocket.

I did not wake Tabby yet. I thought it best not to raise her hopes.

I crept down the stairs in my bare feet, hugging the wall. I was nearly to the landing when I heard footsteps. My eyes caught a faint brightening—then a dim halo of light—

If he came into the stairwell, he would see me. There was nothing for it but to hasten down the last few steps and meet him, praying he would not remark my bulging pockets. "Sir Kit! I'm so glad to find you up."

If I had been alone and wearing shoes, I would have given Lady Palethorp's door a good kick. The first shock past, it was plain to me that she had grown tired of waiting, and signaled indiscriminately. I did not trouble to lower my voice as I said, "Would you let me into the library a moment? I finished the second volume of my novel, and was hoping to change it for the third."

He grinned at me. "It would be my honor. Is your heroine in *very* dire straits?"

"Elizabeth is going to tour Pemberley, and I'm afraid Mr. Darcy will be at home after all," I said, still louder. "It would be so awkward after she turned down his proposal of marriage!"

I fancied I heard a muffled cry of rage pierce the oak door.

"An awkward conversation is the most dire strait of all," Sir Kit agreed gravely. "I see that it would be wanton cruelty to allow you and your alabaster toes to linger in suspense."

My face burned. In fact, my toes were long, with a dusting of hair at the joints. I wished miserably that I had worn slippers. I wished it were nothing to me whether Sir Kit thought me beautiful, and I breathed a sigh of relief when he let me return alone up the stairs, doing nothing more than lean against the wall and gaze after me.

I ignored Lady Palethorp's next signal.

The house was quiet, for we had seen off the sufferers in the Great Hall two days before, laden with ointment, clean bandaging, and jiggly cold beef-broth to tend their itching scars and shiny, pink new skin. But I thought it wise to punish her ladyship a little for her recklessness, so as to prevent a repetition.

I pictured her to myself, weeping as the minutes passed and still we did not come—tearing her hair, and writhing in her bed with rage at me. I almost wished I dared to take laudanum, so I might sleep.

Before she knocked on the floor again, Sir Kit announced he was going away on business, and would be gone a week.

At first, I could be sensible of nothing but agitation, for without his house key, in a fire we should all be dependent on Mrs. Cross to wake, and traverse the whole house to free us. Her room was at precisely the opposite corner of the huge square house, with at least seven or eight doors in between that my key did not open. To reach the porter would be almost equally difficult.

I had debated with myself whether we had any chance of breaking the doors down, and always decided that we did not: some opened in the wrong direction; some were stout, ancient oak like her ladyship's; and even the lighter modern ones were crisscrossed by thick oak beams. Even if we *could* smash out a decorative panel, only Tabby had any chance of wriggling through the gap.

In going over this eventuality (as of course I had a thousand times), I usually concluded that we might jump from Sir Kit's room on the first floor—not a *short* drop, but I had examined the windows from the lawn and found them of a size with the library's, whose stone mullions I had once successfully pushed my shoulders through, feeling deeply foolish but as deeply relieved by the result.

Lady Palethorp's stouter frame did give me pause, but I had resolved to help her through first, in case shoving was required. She and Clarice could hardly let Tabby fall between the two of them, and I could go last.

Of course, this presumed the fire had not started in Sir Kit's empty room. It would be no good descending to the keep's windowless ground floor, meant to stand against a siege. And even if the first-floor corridor were passable, its windows were small and my key did not open their shutters. With the fire so near, it would be false prudence to attempt it.

No, in that case—my heart quailed—I had determined on crawling through a little window in Lady Palethorp's room, that opened onto the chapel's roof.

This crenelated promenade was rarely used. Sir Kit had offered to open it for the nursery party, but I had been too afraid of Tabby falling—or jumping. But in a fire, a rope tied round one of the parapet's teeth…

Of course, I had no rope. Plucking up all my courage, I went to see Sir Kit before he left.

He laughed outright at my request. "If you mean to run away, better do it in daylight."

The comfortable egg-yolk armchair had long since ceased to calm my nerves. I wrung my knotted fingers, and fixed imploring eyes on him.

He still looked good-humoredly incredulous. "And what is to stop you or Clarice from lowering half the contents of my house through the windows?"

I shot to my feet. He rose too, politely. "What is to stop me murdering you in your bed? If you trust me so little, I—" Tears threatened. "I can go."

My voice broke on the final word, but in my heart of hearts, I wasn't afraid. He didn't want me to go.

Sure enough, his face softened. "Tut, Miss Oliver, don't cry. At the rate you go, you can't have enough handkerchiefs to last you wash-day to wash-day. When is your birthday? I shall give you another set. For God's sake, sit down so I can write a note for Peter. He'll obtain a rope for you from the gardener, if that is my only defense against a stack of new applications for your post. I don't believe I possess a single acquaintance without at least four poor relations of exceptional erudition. It is a sad commentary on my own sex, to find so many clever women unmarried."

He had scrawled the note as he spoke, and held it out to me. "You must stay, Miss Oliver, and educate my daughter very well indeed, to frighten away trifling, self-important fellows who don't deserve her."

"Thank you, sir." I sniffled, feeling bruised and tender and unable to shield myself from the sting in his words. "But perhaps she'll be an old maid like me, and you'll wish you had kept her ignorant."

I ought not to speak so waspishly to my employer. But in truth, I thought it safe. He would not mind a little display of feminine vanity from me; he would flatter himself I cared for his masculine opinion.

Safe, perhaps, was the wrong word. Glad triumph flared in his face—but he dropped his eyes, pushing some papers about.

"You *cannot* be unmarried for lack of opportunity," he said quietly. "At least—if no man has offered, it cannot be because none wished to. Perhaps there was someone who wished very much to ask, and was not free to do so." He left off fussing with his inkwell, and raised his eyes to mine.

22

Heat bloomed in my cheeks and beneath my breastbone. I could think of nothing to say.

"If you mean, because he was married," I stammered at last, "then could he be constant? One hopes…for a *lasting* attachment."

His jaw spasmed. He nudged the inkwell onto a clear patch of desk, like a chess piece. I remembered my first day in this office, my wifely impulse to keep it from tumbling off the edge. "A fair question. But sometimes…" I had to strain to hear him, so low did he speak. "Sometimes people change so much after marriage, that I cannot believe it inconstancy to have loved who they *were*, yet not to love who they *are*."

The tumult in my breast matched the emotion on his face. Was he in earnest? Was *I*? Or were we both playacting, weeping for Hecuba like Hamlet's player?

"Your wife is a clever woman, is she not? Those books you gave her—she took an interest in the natural sciences?"

His face was suffused with emotion. "'O, what a noble mind is here o'erthrown,'" he whispered, and I started, that we should both be thinking of *Hamlet*. "'Like sweet bells jangled, out of tune and harsh.'" He scrubbed at his eyes. "Tabby has inherited her intelligence, and will inherit her money. I pray to God she inherits nothing else."

My own heart echoed his grief. I saw Lady Palethorp baring her breast in a rage—weeping like a child—brandishing her candle at me. Like sweet bells jangled…

I meant to be a good mother. I meant for my little girl to be happy.

I heard her musical voice, reading to me in the dark until it gave out.

My own voice scraped in my throat as I asked, "Does she enjoy books, still?"

He blinked. "I don't—I don't know. Her nurse might fetch her anything she liked from the library, if she wished it."

I took a deep breath. My sight cleared, as though I had stepped from a hazy room into fresh air. I recalled the pitiful stack of dull books, the dry ewer, the rank, dirty room, the opium-eating nurse.

Even if he spoke the truth—even if he had loved her, and she had gone mad—even if, in her madness, she had hurt him—he might have been kind. If it pained him too deeply to see to her comfort himself, he might have paid someone to do it. He might have asked—*Does she want books?*

I had felt crawling revulsion at my grandmother's drunken weeping. I had seen my family sicken and die, each in turn. I understood the impulse to turn one's face away from a loved one's pain and weakness. I could pity, even, such terrible human frailty.

But the vows Sir Kit had sworn were for sickness as well as health, and he had broken them.

I relaxed my sweaty grip on his note for Peter, slipping it beneath my kerchief. "You spoke of Tabby's portion," I said slowly. "Is it large enough she truly need not marry? Can Goldengrove pass to her?"

He laughed mirthlessly. "Oh no, Goldengrove will go to the next baronet, and I wish him joy of it. The rents and the home farm don't come to half the income on my wife's dowry. He'll be in the hands of the Jews within five years. Or—" He glanced at me, and I guessed he had thought better of a sardonic remark, such as *Or he may marry one, as I did.*

He opened his blotter, sloughing off his self-pitying mood with a visible effort. "But you have not told me your birthday yet. I shall write it in my almanac."

There was no polite way to refuse, but the scritch of his pen as he copied down the date gave me an inward crawling feeling.

The full import of his words only struck me as I climbed the tower stairs, coil of rope in hand. His life interest in Lady Palethorp's money amounted to more than twice his own income.

Here, then, was his account of events: he had needed money to maintain his inheritance—he had married a very rich woman entirely for love, though she was a member of a race he openly despised—now he lived off her money and kept her locked away out of sight—and this convenient state of affairs was not of his choosing nor to his liking—in fact, it broke his heart.

If another woman had told me such a tale of her married lover, I would have been hard-pressed not to laugh.

Kit wants my money, Lady Palethorp had said. *But he won't get it.* A life interest, then, was not enough for him. He wanted to take the principal—to steal it from his own daughter.

It mortified me that his bright gaze could still so fascinate my will and immobilize my thoughts. Was I born, then, to be a squirrel, and make prey for stronger beings?

But I comforted myself with the reflection that he would never suspect me of subterfuge if he saw me still under his sway, and carried my rope upstairs with me in triumph. I began to store it beneath the nursery daybed—and then recalled that, with Sir Kit out of the house, I might sleep in my own bed! I might open my own window and enjoy a few blessed hours of invisibility. I might even find a moment to give myself pleasure.

But would Mrs. Cross inform him I had abandoned the daybed in his absence?

Well, and what if she did? I crafted a polite lie, polished it to a shine, and tucked it beneath my bed with the rope.

And so Sir Kit rode away. Tabby wept, and insisted on climbing to the roof to wave a lace handkerchief.

As our part of Rye Bay was made up chiefly of ploughed fields, marshy flats, and trees stunted by the wind, we could follow the dusty white road for the better part of two miles. I was wilting by the time his horse, and the coach bearing his luggage and valet, dipped out of sight, and could hardly conceal my dismay when Tabby declared she would wait for Papa to reappear on the hill to Winchelsea. But after a minute or two she began to fidget, and allowed Clarice to persuade her to go down and wade in the sea.

I had already remarked that the nursemaid wore her Sunday cap and kerchief, and quickly realized her proposal was more than an impulse. There was a holiday air about the house when we reached the bottom of our stairs, and at first sight of us, Peter left off polishing a stack of shoes and produced a broad-brimmed hat from beneath his worktable.

Even Mr. Christie only smiled indulgently. "Why don't you take Jenny too, she's been looking peaked. A spot of sun will do her good."

By the time we traipsed outside, we were quite the little party, and bearing food for a much larger one. Peter carried Tabby on his shoulders, and Clarice elbowed out one of the chambermaids for a place at his side, with a pious, "Miss Palethorp might have need of me." I supposed it was always so, when a master went away.

Of course, the mistress of our house was still in residence; but no one regarded *her*.

I looked up at her shuttered window—nearly the only one at this time of day, for casements all over the house were flung wide as maids shook out dusters and emptied basins, letting the breeze cool their upturned faces for a moment before ducking back inside. That window was a blank dead eye in the living house, and we all passed it by without remark.

Yet I could not stay gloomy long. The sun shone, and tonight we might visit with Lady Palethorp as long as we liked in perfect safety.

The servants soon waded barefoot into the water with Tabby, with quite a bit of shrieking and splashing. I sat on a log, watching Tabby and sweating under my parasol.

Clarice dripped over in seaweedy feet and rucked-up petticoat. "Come on in."

I tried to think how to explain without giving affront. I wished I could hug my knees; my decorous posture, with ankles neatly crossed, had been comfortable at first, but now my buttocks tingled unpleasantly and my knees ached.

She threw up her hands. "Why *won't* you?"

"If I let the footmen see my ankles, I will lose their deference."

Clarice laughed at me.

"You don't understand," I muttered like a sullen adolescent.

"Oh, I understand right enough. You'd never want people to think you was the same as me, now would you?"

I pressed my fingers into my eyes. "Clarice, if I am not a lady, I cannot educate young ladies, and if I cannot educate young ladies, I must starve."

"I'm not starving."

"You are sixteen!" I said in exasperation. "I'm sure you don't still wish to be a nursemaid when you are four-and-thirty."

She looked at Peter. "No, I mean to have my own babies to nurse by then." She winced, glancing back at me with pity—for my plain face no one would ever love, my meager bosom that would never feed a child.

If I said *I hope you will wait until you are married,* I would sound more incomprehensibly old and staid than ever. She was only young, I comforted myself. I remembered at school, how shocked we had always been to discover that a teacher had once had a beau.

Perhaps I would teach in a school when Tabby was grown. It had always made me shudder to think of returning as a grown woman to that atmosphere of starch and chalk-dust and squabbling over the dancing master, but perhaps it had been youthful ignorance to paint my teachers' lives in colorless tints. Perhaps they enjoyed one another's society, and shared cakes and ale in their rooms while the children were pretending to be in bed.

"I don't know why ladies' ankles must be such a holy mystery. It's just a knobbly bit of bone." Clarice's tactful change of subject was pity on top of pity. But my hurt had passed, and I could find it funny again, something to laugh over in my next letter to Iphigenia.

"I have often wondered the same thing," I said cheerfully. "I suppose it is Mr. Smith's principle of supply and demand again. As ladies' ankles are generally hidden, the supply is low, and the demand rises in proportion."

Clarice snickered. "Maybe it's because your stockings are white. If you wore hems like mine, everyone would see the dirt."

"Yes, and our stockings are white to advertise that we need not do our own washing."

She crowed. "Eureka, you've got it!"

I blinked.

"I was there when you explained about that Greek fellow," she said dryly. "In fact, I was the one giving Tabby her bath, *and* the one who's had to stop her leaping out stark naked and running about dripping on the carpet every Saturday night since, so thanks for that."

I laughed, and apologized very sincerely, feeling ashamed and surprised at myself. Once again, I had looked down on another woman for no reason at all—for worse than no reason. Snobbery in a costermonger's daughter was hypocrisy indeed. Sir Kit was away, and the sun was shining; I nearly bounded over a few decorous prejudices and went wading.

But my habitual mistrust rushed back, when I put my hands to my bootlaces. I had already spoken too freely to Clarice. I thought her too self-interested, maybe even too kind, to outright betray Lady Palethorp. But she might very well gossip about me with her friends.

I looked over the frolicking servants. Mark had barred my path to Rye. Luke had lingered in the dining-room and watched the clock.

I would come back alone, I promised myself. Surely no one would bother to bar my path this week. On Friday afternoon, if there were not too many soldiers on the beach, I would feel the sea between my toes.

Tonight, I would see Lady Palethorp. I smiled at my delicately crossed ankles.

I waited until the clock struck ten. Mrs. Cross had turned her key in our locks promptly at nine-thirty, but I was afraid she might dawdle in her rounds, or help herself to a glass of Sir Kit's brandy, relishing the cat's absence as much as the rest of us mice.

At ten-thirty, I rose from my bed. Lady Palethorp thumped on the floor as I was shoving my feet into my slippers.

I knew an impulse to kneel down and beat a reveille with my knuckles—but if *that* were overheard, how could I explain it away? She thumped again as I lit my lantern, and louder still as I unlocked my door.

I went past her landing to the first floor, and opened the door to the stairwell to be sure the three in the corridor beyond—the library, the chapel gallery, and Sir Kit's apartments—were all shut. I saw no glimmer of light but mine. I tried the door-handles, and found them locked.

Still I could not break the habit of secrecy; I raced lightly upstairs on my tiptoes and crept to her door, fitting my key into the lock and turning it so slowly that the tumblers eased open with barely a click. I felt my gorge rising, so full was my breast of nervous excitement.

I think she had already despaired of me, for when the door opened she bolted upright from the bed, a dark round shape held in her teeth.

When I held out the lantern, the thing gleamed blood-red, the cracks in its surface pale as bone. I blinked at it without recognition—and then she took it in her hand with a wet crunch, chewing, and my overheated mind understood that it was an apple, and that she had been throwing it against the ceiling for our signal.

I could not see the nurse, but I heard her unnaturally loud snores.

Lady Palethorp gulped the fruit down, and gasped, "Can I see Tabby?"

"Yes! Yes, come upstairs."

She began piling things into a shawl and knotting it.

"Quietly, mind. I brought you—"

But she darted past me to the stairs, outpacing the light, and I heard a thud, a clatter, and a curse as I locked her door again.

Gritting my teeth, I caught her up, and found her reknotting her shawl, mouth twisted with pain. She straightened and set her foot on the first stair, not meeting my eyes. I nearly obliged her by pretending not to notice her stumble. I would not be easy myself until we reached the safety of the nursery. But the risk was too great; I swung my lantern over the floor and handed her a stray ribbon, embroidered with pansies.

To my relief, she let me go ahead with the light. I climbed as swiftly as I dared, listening every moment for pursuit—glad to have her flaming cheeks and watery eyes out of my sight, yet wishing every moment to glance back like Orpheus, and be sure she still followed.

I let her into the nursery, and listened for stirring below before I went in after her.

Tabby was already squirming free of her mother's embrace. "Don't *cry*. You always cry."

"I'm sorry, minha filha, I'll try. I'm just so glad to see you." Lady Palethorp dashed her tears away. "I brought some things for you. Scarves and ribbons and my fans, you used to love to play with my fans."

Neither of them looked at me. I lit Tabby's candle at my lantern, and fitted the glass chimney over it. "If you need me, I shall be sewing in my room."

Lady Palethorp flashed me a distracted smile.

So I sat in my room, mending Tabby's pinafore—my sea lantern open for once, to give more light. My sailor Papa used to do the same for me, a row of pins in his mouth. One winter, when I was ashamed of my patched coat, mãe had embroidered a pomegranate on the patch and added six little seeds out of sight in the lining, recounting the fable of Proserpina and adding her own motherly moral: *…and that is why you should never trust strange men.*

I know, mamã, I had said impatiently, preening in my old coat.

When Tabby's coat needed patching, it would be given away. At Goldengrove, mending was not a *parent's* duty. Clarice's look of pity came back to me, the wound sharper in memory than it had been in life. I blinked to clear my vision, before my seam went crooked.

Lady Palethorp knocked on the door.

My heart leapt in spite of myself. "Come!"

She poked her glowing face in, brushing fringe out of her eyes from the scarf wound haphazardly round her head. She and Tabby were playing at fancy-dress with brocaded silk worth a quarter's salary. "Might I borrow the guitar?"

This time it was I who averted my face, hoping she would not remark my too-bright eyes as I handed her the case. Alone once more, I scolded myself for my envy and covetousness, when the poor lady was obliged to entreat me for the loan of her own guitar.

For I no longer questioned that it *was* hers. She played jaunty English tunes and popular ballads—out of practice, full of missed notes, but she knew them.

Then came a familiar rhythm: a Portuguese song with pauses, for translation into English. Not a melody I knew, yet I was transported with jarring swiftness to our rooms in Portsmouth—saw the punched-tin lantern draping the dark walls in golden lace, sensed the shadowy bulks of our furniture—

Lady Palethorp shifted into a cradle song, tuneless and spellbinding, unaccompanied save by the flat of her hand striking the soundboard. I set aside Tabby's pinafore before I stained it with tears.

Lost in self-pity, I did not even notice when the music stopped. When my door-knob turned, I started violently and blew out the candle.

The room did not lighten when the door opened; she must have already blown out Tabby's candle. Her voice was hard. "Why did you put out the candle? What are you doing?"

I sat still and silent as a mouse when the cat is at the bolt-hole.

She slipped into my room, and shut us in together. "I know you aren't sleeping. I can smell the candle smoke."

I felt for my handkerchief, and stabbed myself with the needle I had left in Tabby's pinafore. "I don't know what on earth you could suspect me of." My voice sounded clogged.

"Then my imagination is better than yours. Relight it."

Her hostility radiated from the darkness. If she struck at me, I would have no warning. I felt for my tinderbox. "Stay over there," I blurted out when her dress rustled.

The pressure of unshed tears and the late hour made me scatter sparks on my night table, and though they went out instantly, my nerves flared up just as my tinder stubbornly refused to. But at last a tiny orange flame caught, and I could light my candle and seal the box in my pocket.

In her eagerness to check for secrets beneath my pillow, Lady Palethorp snatched up the lantern still open, and the light went out.

I could not go through it again. "I'll open the window."

I heard her sharp intake of breath.

The first shutter jammed as I tried to fold it flat. A few frustrated tears scalded my cheeks, and I shoved violently with my shoulder, snapping the panels into place against the embrasure. Before I could turn towards the second one, Lady Palethorp had already wedged herself beside me and pressed her nose to the glass.

"It's fogging." She sounded as childishly thwarted as I felt. "I want to see the stars."

"Don't breathe on it," I told her. "Sit sideways."

She seized the casement's latch.

I laid my hand over hers to keep it shut. "The night air is insalubrious." She might not be an invalid, but she was hardly in the full bloom of health.

Her face turned towards me. I was suddenly conscious of how close we were—of the tiny movements of her fingers below mine. "I want fresh air," she said through her teeth.

"You are susceptible," I protested.

Her eyes were pools of darkness, her laugh a husky, insinuating sound. "Susceptible to what?"

I snatched my hand away, as if burnt. Did she suspect, then? "To infection," I said sullenly. "To miasma."

She settled onto the sill. "Why did you blow out the candle?" That husky laugh came into her voice again. "If I intruded on a private moment, my apologies."

I flushed hotter, for she obviously meant the sort of "indelicate trick" Mrs. Godwin had written of. Yet I almost played into her joke, to avoid the truth.

I had avoided a lot of truths, since coming to Goldengrove. "My mother used to—" My voice cracked. Not from fear, for once. From simple grief. "My—mãe—"

Would she throw it in Sir Kit's face the next time they quarreled? *That good English girl you're so fond of? She's not good and she's not—*

Lady Palethorp let her hand fall from the latch, turning to look at me with genuine curiosity. "Used to what?"

Despite my misgivings, I was resolved now to tell her—as resolved as I was capable of being. But when I tried to speak, my throat spasmed on a sob. I felt a flash of panic: *will she still be listening when I can say it?*

Sure enough, she turned away, curling into the embrasure with her temple on the glass and gazing, quietly transported, at the starry sky.

Unwatched, my panic faded. Melodrama for an empty theater was ridiculous indeed. I forced my larynx to relax, my wheezing inhalations loud in the silence. "Used to sing that song."

She glanced at me. "Which one?"

I didn't know its name—was not even sure I remembered the words, or mere phonetic approximations. I did my hoarse best to hum a bar, wishing for the honeyed tea Papa used to give me for a sore throat, with a half-stick of cinnamon and an orange slice.

Her stillness changed, sharpened. She brushed the fringe out of her eyes. "You said you didn't have a Christian name."

I shook my head.

She leaned towards me, elbows on her knees. "Was your mother of the nação?"

It had never even been a secret until I came to Goldengrove. I hated that I was so slow to nod. "She was beautiful," I blurted out defiantly, and then felt ridiculous.

Lady Palethorp smiled. "Of course she was. We're a much handsomer people than the English."

The sudden easing in my body nearly undammed fresh tears. Yes! Yes, we were a handsome people.

Say what you will, but it was not vanity; it was not shallow. It was deep and clear, springing from a place within me I had never plumbed. For more than half my life I had lived surrounded by the conviction, deep-rooted and unshakable as an oak, that there was one beautiful way to look, one beautiful way to live, and one beautiful way to understand Heaven and Earth—and with it, a certainty that I must agree. Of course I must know my mother was not pretty! What other opinion was there? Of course I must grieve that demons were pulling my grandfather's beard in Hell.

I pushed open the window. "Just for a minute."

It was only fair. She had opened one for me, and let me breathe fresh air.

23

With Sir Kit from home and the servants idling, I allowed myself to shirk my duties, too, just a little. When I felt my patience with Tabby's endless questions ebbing, I would find some pretext to slip away from the nursery, and wander the house with a purposeful air. At first the footmen asked after my errand or offered me escort, but they soon ceased, and besides, I saw less and less of them.

One morning, about halfway through our holiday week, I had gathered up my courage and approached the chatting maids sprawled across one of the great stone hearths, to ask if one of them would wash my window.

A girl barely in her teens had trooped cheerfully upstairs to scrub each tiny diamond pane, dragging with her a gangly friend, who thrust herself out of my casement to the waist to clean all the outer glass she could reach, giggling and shouting all the while, *Hold fast my legs—no, don't you dare let go—I'll get you for that, you slut—begging your pardon, ma'am!*

It would have comforted me, I think, to believe the Goldengrove servants uncommonly obdurate and hardhearted, for their indifference to their mistress's plight. But these girls had been undeniably kind to me; evidently callous cruelty required no special corruption. I had been no better than any of them, and ready to hate Lady Palethorp sight unseen.

Now, however, I had seen her—seen a great deal of her—and *indifference* was not the word.

You think of my wife a good deal more than you ought, Sir Kit had told me. What would he say now, if he knew I thought of nothing else?

She had been visiting with me a little at night, after Tabby at last yawned herself back to bed. It was for her sake I had the window washed, so she might see the sky clearly—as clearly as possible, anyway, through the ancient glass. And that night, as she combed her hair in my narrow bed, the stars' bright, clear gaze seemed to meet hers in mutual delight, while my homey lantern conspired with the moon to wreath her in gold and silver.

"Elizabeth is a fool," she said. "Mr. Darcy will be just like Lady Catherine when he's old, driving over the Pemberley grounds in a fussy little equipage and instructing his curate on the arrangement of his closets."

"Maybe," I conceded, though in my heart I did not believe it. "But if Elizabeth does not marry *somebody*, she'll have to live on one-fifth of her mother's portion—twenty or thirty pounds a year."

She waved this away. "People live on twenty or thirty pounds a year."

"*You* have never lived on twenty or thirty pounds a year." Once again, I failed at archness. The words sounded as dried-up and brackish as my heart.

She looked at me, the sudden, intense regard I craved and shrank from in equal measure. Eyes were lenses, after all; it seemed a mere principle of optics that her focused gaze would burn me if it rested on me too long. "But *you* have, haven't you? Would you really prefer marriage to a man you didn't love?"

Marry for love, like I did, mãe used to tell me. *Better a crust of bread in a house full of love.* As though it were that easy; as though you had only to take the crust, and the love would come.

I could have told Lady Palethorp of a hundred freezing, sleepless dawns in my rented room, imagining myself in the workhouse. I could have told her, *I never had an offer of marriage, and now I am too old, and never will.* But I was too afraid—afraid to let her burn away my flesh and expose my heart. My fingers found the scorched threads at my bosom, and worried them.

"My salary is twenty-five pounds a year now," I said, rather clipped. Her money must pay that too. "And it is far more than I earned before. That is why I came to Goldengrove."

There was a little silence. She shifted away from me, moving the lantern—which I had placed carefully near myself—closer to her, the better to see her hair.

I felt hollow. My fingers twitched with wanting to snatch the lantern back—or bury themselves in her curls, which seemed to glow from within.

"Well, Jane is sure to marry." The bright tones of her voice had lost some of their fullness; I heard a tinny quality, now. "Elizabeth can always live with her."

"I never met a woman who was happy to live in her brother-in-law's house."

"How many are happy to live in her husband's?" she countered. "At least a brother-in-law doesn't generally expect to share one's bed."

I could think of nothing to say. Or rather, I could only think of one thing, which I had no right to ask: *Does Sir Kit still visit your bed?*

He had told me he did not. Though he had importuned me, he had never tried force. And yet the cynicism in that word *generally*—her ready assumption that of course *some* brothers-in-law stopped at nothing—spoke volumes.

She frowned at me. "You welcome Kit's attentions, don't you? He hasn't… hasn't done you any—I don't know what I could do if he has, but I…"

"I am not his mistress." I thought bitterly of Aristotle's tenet that a wealthy man could befriend a virtuous one, if each looked up to the other. Could a rich woman and her dependent perform the same alchemy, if they only pitied one another sufficiently? "I wish you would believe me."

She set down the comb in dismay. "But that is worse! If you are not, he shouldn't speak to you as he does."

"Sir Kit is not here. Let him be absent from our thoughts and conversation, as he is from the house."

Her imperious eyebrows arched. They were thick, and did not quite keep to their bounds; once upon a time, her lady's maid must have plucked them. "Easier said than done." She twisted onto her stomach to examine the items on my windowsill, and reached for the knobs on vô's box.

I dug my nails into my palms. I did not want to watch my little store of riches suffer a sea-change in reverse, turning to low-tide detritus as her gaze passed over it. Nor could I bear to pull the box away, and see her eyes dim or hear that thin, tinny cheer in her voice again.

"You have been abusing this defenseless box," she said in some amusement. "It's all over dents."

As a smitten schoolgirl, I had told Iphigenia it was Papa's, battered from years at sea. Though I'd eventually admitted my low connections, I'd never wanted to admit the lie. I was tempted to lie now—but Lady Palethorp's eyes lit at my clove-studded orange, and fluttered shut as she raised it to her nose, smiling.

"My avô…" The word felt affected in my mouth, as though I were putting it on for her benefit. "He carried his wares in it. He was a peddler."

She nestled the orange back in its place. "And what did your grandmother do?"

I swallowed hard at her simple, unsneering assumption that my grandmother had worked. "She was a costermonger. Oranges and spices."

She pursed her lips in admiration. "The better sort of costermonger. My grandfather sold straw hats. Later, he and my father sold a great *many* straw hats, which made it *almost* respectable."

I watched her, heart in my throat, as she spread my sea glass on the counterpane, and held each shard to the lantern to see its color. But she lost interest soon enough, and only turned the glass absentmindedly in her fingers, opening and closing the drawers with little clicks and smiling to herself.

Very little seemed to absorb her for long. She had already forgotten the last uncombed strip of her hair. I suspected that either she would plait those ancient knots into her fresh braids, or never braid it at all, because it was not finished.

"Did you know," she said, "straw hats weren't even fashionable in England before vô talked the Gunning sisters into wearing them?"

"What did they wear before?"

"Felt, mostly." She dropped my glass back into the drawer, *clink… clink…clink*. "When Kit first brought me to Goldengrove, I went over all the portraits to see what their hats were made of. I thought it would amuse him. It would have when we were courting. But he didn't want his family to see my gaucherie. Not just his mother—I think he wanted to impress those flaking portraits, too."

"May I finish combing your hair?" I burst out.

She rolled over and sat up on her elbows, weighing me.

I flushed hot, ready to energetically deny any ulterior sapphic motives. But she sighed and turned so her uncombed hair was towards me.

Even in her fatalism I sensed a coiled energy—another kind of impatience, that had rather choose wrong than waste time in vacillation. "I hope you are kind to me out of cupidity, and not virtue. Self-interest is so much more predictable."

My cheeks burned hotter at the word *cupidity*, though of course it meant greed and not Eros.

"I haven't forgotten my promise," she said.

I stiffened, my eyes going to the lantern, out of my reach and within hers.

She looked confused—and then she laughed. "For Heaven's sake, Euphemia, not *that* promise! To give you some of my jewels. They're in the toe of my slipper."

Did she use the wrong name to tease me, or because she'd forgotten the right one? Caught up in wondering, I did not fully understand her words until she was dangling a pair of earrings before the lantern, filigree and pendant emeralds trembling with the slightest motion of her hand. I'd never seen such lovely things come from such a prosaic place—

—unless it was her feet.

The thought was both unseemly and fanciful: her toenails were overgrown, thick and opaque, and her wrinkled soles were yellow. *But the shape*, I protested, *the shape is perfect, and the ankle—* I swallowed a laugh, remembering my conversation with Clarice about ankles.

Her lower lip pouted, that I did not show a proper enthusiasm for the gift.

The stones were dark and flat in the dim light, the gold glinting dully, each unreflective pearl flecked with a single bright dot. They might have been a treasure unearthed from the deep. If I put them in vô's box, my plain sea glass would whisper spitefully, jealous of their beauty.

"I never pierced my ears," I said, too late.

The delighted pity in her laugh was rich and full; it lingered in my ear. "They aren't for you to *wear*, Olivia. They're to sell."

Oh. Of course. What a vain, foolish craving I nursed in my breast—not even for the earrings, but for them to be a gift and not a bribe.

She saw it in my face. "I *could* pierce your ears, if you liked."

My cheeks heated. I *would* like it, her fingers cool on my hot ears as she cooed at the result—and that gleeful schoolgirl mischief would still be a bribe.

She leaned in, mouth curving slyly. "I'm sure you've got your needle handy, in case another of Tabby's pinafores should need mending."

Did she mean to mock me for a servant, or only tease me for a Goody Two-shoes? And was there any difference? If I had been rich, I would not have needed to be industrious.

I reached for the rag she had been using to dampen her hair, and plunked it in the basin. The water had grown unpleasantly warm in the hot room. "I don't require payment."

"But then you are being kind out of virtue, and that is precisely what I did not want!" She said it playfully—flirtatiously, even—but not quite to *me*. Her attention had slid away again. She was toying with the ends of her hair, sliding a clean curl through her fingers, her eyes crinkling when it bounced back.

Since she was not listening, I said the first thing that entered my head as I wrapped a hank of her damp, fragrant hair around my fingers, so the comb would not pull. "'Yet I am very proud, revengeful, ambitious, with more offenses at my beck than I have thoughts to put them in, imagination to give them shape, or time to act them in.'" It was pleasurably mindless work, just varied enough to hold the attention, and soon my mood lightened. So did her drying hair, taking on the warm golds and bronzes of autumn leaves. And like a child falsely imagining a pile of dry leaves will give a soft landing, I wanted to lay my head in it.

"I don't think I'd fare well in a nunnery," she said.

It took me a moment to realize she was responding to my quotation from *Hamlet*. "A girl at school told us that 'nunnery' is cant for a brothel."

She laughed. "And you imagine I'd do better there?"

"That's not what I meant." This was the trouble with not sticking to platitudes.

"I suppose it makes sense." She hugged her knees. "Denmark isn't a Catholic country, to be full of convents. At least, it isn't now. When do you suppose *Hamlet* takes place?"

I turned the question over as I shifted to reach the last of her hair. "They must be Catholic, for the old king is in purgatory for dying unshriven. Protestants don't believe in purgatory. At least, English ones don't."

"What does 'unshriven' mean?"

"Not having confessed one's sins."

She snorted. "And purgatory...that's where they torture you just for a little while, before admitting you to Heaven?"

I thought of vó's hands.

"Why don't Protestants believe in that? Not as fond of torture as the Catholics?"

"Protestants don't believe one can work off one's sins like debt. One must be saved by faith and love for Christ."

She looked doubtful. "Is that better?"

I felt tired; I knew more about the subject than I really cared to, and less than I needed to prepare Tabby for her confirmation. "I don't know."

To me—as, apparently, to Lady Palethorp—the great difference between Catholic and Protestant was the Inquisition. Yet here she was, imprisoned so Sir Kit could take her money.

She made a small pained sound, and I realized my hand had tightened on the comb.

My fingers I could force open. My thoughts did not loose their grip so easily. "Have you heard the story of Little Hugh of Lincoln?"

Not long before I left Lively St. Lemeston, a pupil of mine—a friend of our old maid-of-all-work, Sukey—had sung me a particularly gruesome version of the ballad, in which the Jew's daughter cut off the boy's head with a penknife, drank his blood from a golden cup, *and* drowned him in a well. I'd been giving the girl lessons at a sharply reduced rate, as a favor to Sukey.

"Hasn't everybody?" I could feel Lady Palethorp's sigh. "I brought a beautiful new green muslin to school one term. Whenever they saw me in it, the other girls would sing, 'The old Jew's daughter she came out, all dressed in apple green.' I loved that gown, and after a month I stuffed it in the bottom of my trunk and never wore green again." She poked at the emerald earrings on the windowsill. "I didn't tell my father, or he wouldn't have given me these."

I knew the facts of what happened at Lincoln: the King had sold his right to tax the Jews and, being unable to profit from them alive, had executed eighteen men on trumped-up charges and confiscated their property. But if I had known nothing, I would have guessed the truth from the song. Mãe would not even eat a bloody egg. It was Christians who imagined their red wine turning to blood in their golden cups. Any story about Jews spilling Christian blood was a prelude to our slaughter, a call to arms as systematized and intelligible as the navy drum-calls Papa used to beat out on the table.

I could still hear the relish in my pupil's clear adolescent voice: *He tossed the ball in the Jew's garden, and the Jews were all below.*

"They accuse us of drinking their blood," I said, "but it's they who have been drinking ours for centuries."

"It seems to agree with their digestion," she said wryly. "Or do you think one day I'll give Kit gout? He'd hate it; he was always so smug about poor Mr. Wakefield and his French sauces."

"Do you think that's why he's so afraid of burglars?"

"Because he's a thief?" She laughed. "Perhaps. I'll tell him so, next time he brings his papers for my signature."

Don't mention me! But there was no use saying it. Such a slip, if she made it, would hardly be premeditated. I set down the comb. "It's done."

She fluffed her hair delightedly. "So it is. Thank you—you barely pulled! *My* governess was never so gentle." She shook it forward over her face, to part it for braiding. "Your father was English, wasn't he?"

"Yes, he was a disabled naval officer. My mother sold salep in front of the Prize Office."

She tied a ribbon round half her hair, revealing half her smile. "Was she pretty, or was her salep very good?"

"Both, I think."

"But I forgot, you already told me she was beautiful! Have you any picture?"

I shook my head. "She had a silhouette done once at the Free Mart Fair, but she didn't keep it. The artist thought to flatter her by entirely altering the shape of her nose."

"Perhaps your looking glass is her picture." She leaned out to look at the moon, fingers slowing in their plaiting. "My father used to say that to me, when I reproached him for never having her portrait taken."

"Don't be absurd." If anything could have made it clear she had stopped thinking of me at all, it was that. "I told you she was beautiful."

She blinked at me. "Oh." She shook her head, turning back to her braid. "I'd forgotten this part of feminine companionship, where we're forever obliged to lavishly compliment each other's looks to shore up our fragile vanity. I seem to have lost patience for it."

Perhaps I should have been glad of any ray of clarity, after grasping so long at truth's flickering shadow. But my eyes ached at her candid avowal that a compliment to me could be nothing but *politesse.*

I recalled my talisman: *Ah, Friend! to dazzle let the vain design. To raise the thought and touch the heart, be thine!*

Yet I had done none of the three. I had only combed her hair, and now she made a coronet of her braids and tucked them into a cap of Mechlin lace. "I forgot hairpins," she said happily. "But this will do for now." She looked like a lady again, someone who belonged to the world. Not to me—never to me. My shame choked me, to realize I had been thinking of her as my private property. I was no better than Sir Kit.

"But I wanted to ask you…your father was English. Do you wish…do you believe…" She tapped a finger nervously against her ribs. "You say 'us' when you speak of the Jewish people. But you might as easily…"

My own fingers beat a nervous tattoo on my mattress. "Not quite as easily. I rarely give the matter much thought." How candid did I dare to be? "I don't—that is, I don't really believe…"

Her eyes widened in delight. "Are you an atheist?"

In spite of myself, I smiled at the word. Many people imbued *atheist* with as much horror as *patricide* or *anarchist,* but to me, it held fonder connotations. "Not in any principled way. At home I sometimes went to the parish church with my friends, or to the Methodist meeting with my father, when he was alive. There may very well be a God. I simply…am not particularly troubled by the question. Either I shall learn the answer when I die, or I won't, and be past disappointment." I felt a pang. "I did think I was saved, once." I said it softly, and then hoped with all my heart she would ignore it.

"Saved from what?"

"I—you know. That I was assured of salvation."

"What…" She squinted at me, unsure what even to ask. "Pardon?"

"I was fifteen," I muttered. "Papa kept taking me to meetings during the summer holiday. It was exciting, crowding in to hear a visiting preacher who'd walked across England."

"The *bettermost* sort of peddler," she said.

I blinked, for I had never quite thought of my admiration in that light. But more than that, I was struck by how easily I could hear the same jest in Sir Kit's voice, the same tone of warm-hearted cynicism. How well-suited they must have seemed, when he still called her *my pretty Jessica*. With difficulty, I found my place again in my tale.

"One day, it grew too hot and crowded, so we went outside. I—well, I don't know. I thought I felt His presence, listening to this woman preach." I had been watching the leaves moving on a tree, listening to her voice speak of God's love, and all at once I had felt—something. A warm hand at the back of my head. The heat spread, until my soul lit like a candle and rose shining from my body. I could still picture the tops of everyone's hats, as though I had been looking down from the treetops.

"Ah." Lady Palethorp nodded gamely. "Was the preacher pretty?"

I stiffened. "No! She was old. It wasn't—I wasn't—"

Lady Palethorp shrugged. "I thought maybe it was like being uplifted at the theater."

"I was almost baptized that summer."

She cut her eyes at me. "You have to be baptized *again* to become a different kind of Christian?"

"I never had been." I swallowed. Even Lady Tassell probably didn't know *that*. "Mãe disliked the idea, and Papa didn't care then." I didn't tell him I was considering it that summer, for fear his face would light up and the decision wouldn't be all *mine* anymore.

"But you didn't do it?" There was a curious tension in her voice.

"I went back to school before making up my mind. The other girls laughed at me for—" For a moment, a peculiar shame stopped my tongue. But I had confided in no one since coming to Goldengrove; I was starved for it. "For wearing a cross. And for my taste for low company." All most young ladies knew of Methodism was that rich and poor shared the same pews, and the same pulpit.

"But the real end to my devotion was something else. My friend Iphigenia—" My smile broke out again. "*She* became an atheist, and announced it to the whole refectory between bites of my pudding."

I had always given her my pudding, out of a sense of justice—for though I was no less ravenous, I was shorter by a head and got the same rations. It had seemed an easy enough bribe, to keep her sitting by me.

Lady Palethorp laughed. "There's always one, isn't there? Was she a vegetarian, too?"

"She might have starved if she'd tried it at our school." My smile spread helplessly, for thinking of that year always made me sentimental. Of course I was still very fond of Iffy, but at fifteen I had worshipped her: a freethinking giantess, all legs and eyelashes and smiles, unalloyed gold. The memory of my idolatry ought to have embarrassed me, but like Mr. Bingley boasting of his bad handwriting, I secretly thought the fault very charming. "I didn't want her to think me in thrall to superstition like the scandalized multitude. I pawned my cross, and gave up the idea of baptism."

But I had lain awake longing for a return of my ecstatic immersion in forgiveness as devoutly as I longed for Iphigenia to kiss me. Iphigenia did, eventually, but salvation never came back.

I still missed it, now and then, sitting in church and feeling nothing. Once I had been cradled in warmth, like a babe in arms, and I never would be again in this life.

"And your father never..." She was fussing with my box again, making stair-steps of the drawers. "You never felt he treated you differently because you weren't..."

Oh. Of course—she had asked about my life because of Tabby. I flushed hot, that I had knabbled on so long. "No, Papa wasn't that sort of Christian. He was always quoting the parable of the Good Samaritan."

She didn't look reassured. We both knew my father was no pattern for Sir Kit.

Sir Kit did not, as yet, seem to think of Tabby as Jewish, or even half-Jewish—as having anything to do with her mother at all. But would that last when she grew older, and less determined to please him?

I felt a chill. How might he behave when she grew old enough to marry, and take her mother's money with her?

"I *was* baptized to marry Kit," she said quietly. "He said it was a formality, a few drops of water to keep the peace with Mrs. Palethorp. 'We'll do it on a warm day, so you don't catch a chill.' And then after we were married, if I didn't take a slice of ham, he'd say, 'You'll depress the price of pork, and what will I say to Mr. Kirk then?' He pretended it was a joke, but it wasn't."

I could hear the words in Sir Kit's voice so clearly. "Who cut the guitar strings?" I blurted.

She frowned.

"The strings on that guitar." I pointed at the case, propped in the corner. "I had to buy new ones." With a wash of renewed shame, I remembered that Sir Kit had paid for them.

"Who did Kit say did it?"

"You."

She looked baffled. "Why would I cut the strings on my own guitar? ... Oh, because I'm mad, I suppose."

"He said it was his mother's guitar." He had, hadn't he? I wasn't misremembering?

She burst out laughing, rich and scornful. "Mrs. Palethorp said my guitar gave her a headache."

"Did it?"

"I hope so," she said callously. "But if she cut the strings, she returned from her grave to do it. I can't think who but Kit would have bothered, though I didn't see him do it. He told *me* it must have been Tabby, and I should have a care where I left my work-box. But she was so small then, I can't believe she could have worked the scissors at all, let alone cut all the strings to just the same length."

She wandered over and opened the guitar case, staring vacantly into it. "He was always quarreling with Mrs. Palethorp about something when she was alive. Politics, money, Tabby, the upholstery. And then when she died, he blamed *me* for tearing them apart. For a year I could do nothing right, and then..."

At last she carried the guitar to the bed, where she morosely plucked out a trilling seguidilla, strident and plaintive at once. Sir Kit was away, and yet he might as well have been in the room with us, passing off his unkindnesses as jokes.

Yet, note by note, my lady filled up the silence. Each vibrating tone attuned my flesh to this room, here, now, with only the two of us in it. The lingering bitterness died away; I stretched myself out on my bed and became a sounding board, resonating to her strings.

I felt missed notes, too, delays she could not pass off as syncopation. Her fingers had regained their confidence, but not yet their flexibility or calluses. Yet it was not pity I felt. It was consonance.

She winced and sucked on the ends of her fingers.

Why couldn't they leave me my music? Such a little thing, but they had to take it too...

Somehow the impulse to turn thoughts into sound had begun to feel almost natural, no longer the sick craving of the opium-eater. "My grandmother's family was arrested by the Inquisition," I said quietly. "In Lisbon."

Lady Palethorp damped her strings with the edge of her palm, to let my voice carry clearly.

I rarely spoke of it. English people always said something strange. Iphigenia had said wryly, *Oh, Livvy. If this is the best of all possible worlds, what must the others be?* That hadn't been *bad*, but still I had felt myself a stranger in a strange land, that an auto-da-fé made her think of a novel, not fear passed down from parent to child like an heirloom.

"Vó was fifteen. She loved one of her brother's university friends—a little older, a Catholic. When he asked to court her, she and her brother confessed to him that they still kept the Law of Moses. She told him she wanted to marry within the naçao. He said he loved her enough to take her faith. Her family welcomed him like a son, and after a quarrel he denounced them all."

Lady Palethorp strummed one last chord, and laid her hand flat on the strings. "Ah," she said, unsurprised.

"They put vó to the question. They broke her fingers. It hurt her to play the guitar after that. She'd teach me a little, sometimes, but she would wince and rub her fingers afterwards."

Lady Palethorp looked at her raw fingertips. "She lived, though."

"Yes. She was the first to be released, after—" Without music, speaking no longer felt simple. The walls absorbed my voice, and sent no reverberation back. I didn't say *after she gave up her family*. It felt like disloyalty to vó, to tell a stranger that. "She ran away to England. Later she heard that her brother died, and an uncle. Her parents only had to wear the sanbenito, I think, but her mother hadn't recovered from prison fever when she last had news of them. It wasn't safe to write."

"And the boy?"

"Who cares?" I snapped.

She shrugged, setting her fingers to the strings once more. But in a minute or two she laid the guitar aside, and stood for me to escort her back to her room, her sore fingers curled into her palm.

When I came back upstairs, I saw blood on the strings, dark as wine in the candlelight.

I knew an impulse to put my tongue to it. Not even an impulse—a fleeting image, a recognition that it was possible.

Unsettled and ashamed, I buffed the strings clean, scrubbing my handkerchief in the basin until the few drops of blood dissolved invisibly into the water. I left the cloth by the basin to be laundered, and leaned over my bed to blow out the candle.

Her earrings winked at me from the windowsill.

I did not want them. Would the pawnbroker in Rye believe they were mine? If he did, would he put them in his window for Sir Kit or one of his neighbors to recognize? And where could I hide them, here? Sir Kit had a key to my room.

Yet it seemed churlish to return them. Lady Palethorp would think it a boast of my virtue, when it was only cowardice.

I crumpled them into my only spare handkerchief—I had better not weep until the other came back from the laundress—and stuffed them into the pocket of my winter pelisse, burying it at the bottom of my trunk and locking it.

That did not satisfy me—it was the sort of lock that could be picked with a hairpin—but it would do for tonight. I slipped the trunk key onto Lady Palethorp's chain.

My sheets smelled like her hair. I dreamed that she was dripping hot candle-wax onto my breasts, and that I liked it.

24

I woke to a headache, and the maid dumping my basin out the window. I felt sluggish and shameful and unprepared to meet anyone's eyes, and wished I didn't need her help with my stays, so I could remain in bed.

I could not keep my mind on Tabby's lesson, and at last I pleaded my very real headache and escaped the hot nursery on pretext of asking Mrs. Cross for a powder. Clarice gave a longsuffering sigh, but I did not feel guilty. She had been disappearing quite as often as I had.

I crept softly past a parlor where Mrs. Cross stood with her back to the door, examining sofa cushions for evidence of illicit sitting, and fluffing them just to be sure. Soon I was on the bright green grass of the inner courtyard, putting my nose to one of the trellises of *rosa mundi* just coming into flower. The windows of the footmen's room were flung open, and there the menservants congregated with the grooms, livery hung carefully on the backs of their chairs as they played cards in their shirtsleeves, drinking iced rum-shrub.

If I had not been a lady, I would have begged for one of those cold, sweating glasses, ruby-red from more of Mr. Wakefield's blood oranges. The courtyard felt suffocatingly small, the grass unnaturally lush. How long had it been since I'd left the house alone? When I thought of venturing onto the open lawn, my heart failed me.

One such weakness was enough; I had better root this one out before it spread. I was a grown woman, a salaried employee—not a child, not a prisoner, not even a servant! I could walk in the gardens if I wished to.

Reluctantly, I walked to the grand entranceway, and put my hand to the latch of the smaller, inset door. It lifted—and I stepped through, heart pounding.

A knot of servants fell silent to look at me, mouths and fingertips stained deep purple.

For a moment I felt a thrill of horror, as though I had come upon feasting vampires. But the porter was only collecting his toll from a basket of swollen, sun-warmed blackberries. I saw he had put a heap of cushions and rugs between his arse and the stone bench, and his wife had carried her rocking chair out-of-doors to knit beside him: an innocent, cheerful scene, if not permitted when the master was at home.

"You hadn't ought to go walking by yourself, ma'am," the porter's wife said. "Not with all these strangers in to pick the hops. Wait 'til after Harvest-home."

I hated that I felt a touch of fear—as though it were only strangers who could harm me. "I merely wished to circle the house. I must stay in the shade, in any case; you see I forgot my hat."

I squirmed under their suspicious eyes, and their silence gave me a fresh thrill of horror. *Was* I a prisoner? How could they square it with themselves, to treat me so?

Yet there were houses in Lively St. Lemeston where the servants were locked in. Sir Kit was not the only master who behaved so, though I would have guessed it more common in towns than in the country. Perhaps this state of affairs seemed less strange to the servants than to me.

I stepped across the threshold. They did not stop me. Perhaps I imagined that their glances at each other held some hidden significance. But I hurried swiftly round the southeast corner of the house, and out of their sight.

For once I could see no one, hear no one. Yet I felt the house's windows behind me; I could not be sure no one was watching. When I breathed deeply and tilted up my face to the sun, it gave me no sensation of freedom, any more than praying made me feel God's love. Squinting against the light worsened my headache, and the wind whistled in my ears and stopped my breath. I did not dare risk grass stains on my dress by sitting, and when I thought of walking to the beach, my fatigue overwhelmed me—fatigue and a bone-deep sense of failure, weakness, and shame.

Like a mouse, I turned and scurried back towards my hole, through the tower door propped open with its loose brick. My tired feet dragged on the stairs, and the curving walls made me dizzy. When I had at last emerged in our attic, Tabby was napping. I crawled into my bed for a nap myself.

Lady Palethorp thumping on the floor woke me. I started up in darkness, mouth full of cotton, and sought my memories of the evening: there were none. My stays were on crooked, digging painfully into my ribs. Clarice had let me sleep through dinner.

I could not decide whether to be annoyed, or abjectly grateful. My head no longer ached. It swam a little, but I thought that was hunger. After I had fetched my mistress to the nursery, I retreated to my own room to devour some crackers and cheese from the nursery cupboard, and wrestle out of my stays and into my nightdress unaided.

Lady Palethorp looked tired, too, when at last she slipped through my door. "I wish you had the key to the cellars."

Visions of rum-shrub rose before my eyes—and then I remembered. "A pupil's parents gave me a third of a bottle of cherry bounce as a parting gift. They forgot to finish it after Christmas."

"Hand-me-down liquor," she said. "Well, beggars can't be choosers. Let's have at it."

I'd almost left it behind, afraid it would leak or crack in my trunk. Now, as my penknife slipped on the sealing wax and nearly sliced into my fingers, I cursed myself again for not giving it to Iffy, who carried a corkscrew about with her.

Lady Palethorp snatched it out of my hands. "Let me do that."

I did not like handing her the knife, and I think it showed. She kept her narrowed eyes on me as she plunged the knife deep into the seal and twisted, with a sound of tearing oil-paper.

I winced as bits of cork fell into the liquid, but the bottle came unstoppered with a *pop*. "There," she said pointedly, before taking a long swig. "Mmmm."

She tipped the bottle up again for long seconds, eyes closed and throat working, then held it out to me.

I tried to avoid spilling liquor down my chin; I expected to fail, and I was right. But the taste recalled lazy, companionable winter evenings—spiced fire in my mouth and belly, warmth spreading at last even to my chilly fingers and toes. Each Advent, when Harry Pengilly strained out the fruit and bottled his brandy for market, he never forgot to give Iffy a little jar of boozy cherries.

It made me nervous to see her flirt with the old smuggler—his father had been the terror of the district when we were girls—but I wasn't above sharing in the spoils.

Lady Palethorp laughed at me as I wiped my chin, taking the bottle and raising it high. "To victory!"

That was the first in a series of Navy toasts Papa had taught me. "To absent friends," I replied, taking my turn for a deep swallow. "To our ships at sea."

There was a toast for each day in the week, but I could only remember one more.

"To wives and sweethearts," I said with finality. "May they always meet."

"Hear, hear."

I had already begun to feel the liquor. As I passed the bottle, I watched her hands carefully, to know when to release my grip. I was entirely unprepared when her face lunged into my field of view, and she pressed her mouth to mine.

I froze, forgetting how to swallow. Brandy pooled under my tongue.

"No?" She laughed with an attempt at lightness. "Look at me, pressing unwanted attentions on the governess. A pretty pair, Kit and I."

In my haste to swallow and reply, I coughed brandy into my nose. "Yes," I blurted out, miserably feeling for my handkerchief. "I do—I—I *do* want your attentions. I am only not passionate."

"So you... What does that mean? That you don't like to be touched?" I could hear the confusion in her voice.

One of my handkerchiefs was with the laundress, and the other was wrapped around her earrings at the bottom of my trunk. I wiped my running eyes and nose on my sleeve. I could not look at her. I was repulsive.

If she only knew how I longed to be touched.

"I was sure you and Philomela must have…"

"Iphigenia," I corrected her. "Yes. I—we did. I do like—that is. I only—I cannot simply—do you even want to? You needn't bribe me. I know I am not—it is I who would be no better than Sir Kit—if I accepted—if I pressed you—"

She rolled her eyes and pulled her nightgown over her head.

I pressed my knuckles to my mouth. I was starving, and she was a feast: breasts dangling like ripe fruit, a sweet roll of flesh at her hips, lush dark hair between her thighs. My fingers curled, envious of the pale pregnancy scars cupping her rounded belly.

Did she even remember my name? My throat formed hers silently: *Jael*. I had no right, no right to sate my hunger with her flesh.

"It's been three years since anyone put their mouth on my cunt. Of course I want it! I want it *now*. If I could gorge myself on sweets and racy French novels at the same time, I would." She swept her hair away from her neck, to twist it into a rope. "I'm so sick of waiting for everything. Aren't *you*? Why be sensible and careful? Does God reward good little girls, in your experience?"

I looked at my hands in my lap, tasting cherry brandy on my tongue. "I…"

"What?" Her voice came nearer. I could feel the heat from her bare skin. "What *is* it?"

She'd already said she couldn't be bothered to compliment my looks. I couldn't ask her, *Do you think I'm pretty?*

The question was laughable, anyway, with her sitting right there with her cloud of hair and great dark eyes and pouting mouth, her curves graceful and swooping as a calligrapher's flourish. Of course I wasn't pretty. I was only hungry, and she had sensed it in spite of all my efforts at concealment. So had Sir Kit; that was why he never believed me when I sent him away.

What could I say to her? *Sometimes we talk, but you aren't talking to me. If we go to bed, and you aren't going to bed with me, I shall fade away to nothing. If you imagine someone else while my face is hidden between your legs, I shall starve to death.*

"I'm not a sweet jar," I said at last, obscurely, "or a French novel."

"No," she agreed. "You're alive. So am I. Why shouldn't we act like it? Maybe neither of us has any right to do anything. Yet we must do *something*, or atrophy and perish." She knelt to retrieve her discarded nightgown from the floor, and caught herself on the bedpost with a sound of pain. "Like the muscles in my legs."

"Like my heart," I muttered, still looking at my hands.

She snorted. "My legs will be strong again when I have space to walk. As strong as they ever were, anyway. Maybe you should give your heart a little exercise, instead of keeping it locked up."

I blinked, caught by the acuity of her remark and the frustration in her voice. "Maybe I should," I said quietly, before I thought better of it. "But I seem to have lost the key."

"I suppose you put it somewhere very logical, for safekeeping."

I let out a startled laugh.

"It will turn up again. Do you remember when you last saw it?" Out of the corner of my eye, I could see her hang the nightgown on the bedpost. "It must be here somewhere; we'd better have a look round." She tipped up my chin to untie my cap.

I sat very still. My braids freed, she tugged at the strings of my wrapper. The robe fell open, revealing—well, revealing very little. The ruffle at my bodice and the fall of linen below would have hung much the same if I had had no bosom at all, save that the points of my nipples showed.

I think she smiled. She slipped her hands inside my robe, feeling along as though searching for something at the back of a drawer. I squirmed, ticklish and self-conscious.

At last she fitted her fingers snugly to my ribs, her thumbs between my breasts. Then she swept her hands open like slatted shutters, with fingertips for hinges.

She leaned in and whispered to my heart, "Come out and look at the stars. I hear you weeping in there."

I inhaled sharply, and this time I let her kiss me. I kissed her back. I devoured her immoderate mouth, her pugnacious jaw, the corners of her eyes.

But when I followed the salty curve of her shoulder down to her breasts and put her wide nipple in my mouth, she jerked away.

"Stop, stop." She pushed at me with panicked hands. "It's too much."

I fisted my hands to keep them off her. My hunger clawed at my insides, when a few minutes ago it had been quiescent, sleeping. I should have let well enough alone.

She curled shut like a flower at night at the far end of my bed. Her babbled apologies reached me muffled by her hair, her arms, her knees. "I'm sorry. I'm so sorry. I thought I was ready. It's too much. My digestion isn't used to it, I'll vomit…"

Grief for her welled up—shockingly sweet and fresh, from a source so deep within me I could not find it. I was astonished at how it filled me up.

"There's no hurry," I said, knowing the tender certainty in my voice would embarrass me later.

I fetched a book from the back of the top shelf of the clothespress, and set it by her on the bed. "We don't have to do anything but kiss," I said. "We don't even have to do that." I moved the lantern to the windowsill and opened its little door to illumine the space around her. "Read to me."

She uncurled a little, tentatively, to open the book. "A racy French novel?" Her laugh was watery.

"I have a bag of pastilles, too, but it might make it hard to read."

She brushed her hair out of her eyes and held the book to the light—too close to it, and her hands were shaking. I kept my eye on the paper's distance from the flame, but I didn't protest.

"You must have lived such a restful, rational existence before you met me," she said ruefully.

"I can assure you I did not."

She slid an incredulous smile at me. My heart skipped a beat.

"Lettre première," she began. "Cécile Volanges à Sophie Carnay, aux Ursulines de —. Tu vois, ma bonne amie, que je te tiens parole…" *You see, my good friend, that I keep my word to you.*

I knelt by the bed. "Tell me if you want me to stop." I kissed her ankle—paused; her calf—another pause; her knee. There was a still, waiting moment—and she unfolded her legs a little.

Slowly, I kissed her shoulder again. Her round arms. Her back. Each bump of her spine.

Her muscles grew looser, and her voice grew calm. *I write to you from a very pretty desk, to which I have been given the key, and where I can lock away anything I wish to…*

I laid my palm on her shoulder, and pressed gently to see if she would shift. I told myself I must not mind it, if she did not.

She unfurled completely, stretching out on the bed with the little volume held above her head.

When I bent at last to taste her breasts again, she stroked my hair, taking her hand away only to turn the page. Her voice grew breathless—and not from disuse. I drank in every hitch as I suckled, gently thumbing one wet nipple as I molded my tongue to the other.

She was the strings. I was the musician, and the sound box. I touched her so gently, so gradually, waiting for her to warm, coaxing the notes from her one by one.

My own greed was mounting, but I subdued it. There *were* rewards for patience and caution, whatever she said, and I meant to have them. I set my hand on her thigh.

She jumped, and all her French consonants stuck in her throat. But she gabbled out softly "*…the gentleman was a cobbler!*" and edged her knees a few inches farther apart.

I fitted my hands at last to the scars on her belly, and traced them with my tongue where they extended beyond my fingers' reach. I tuned every sense to her faint vibrations. I could smell her desire.

Most of all, I listened. The rustle of her legs falling open on starched sheets. Her staccato inhalations when I trailed the backs of my nails over the crease of her thighs. Her French vowels slurring higher when I ran my thumbs up her *labia pudendi*. A soft overture had an urgency and tension of its own, after all. It foretold—it warned—it let nothing be lost.

Her voice died away; she pressed a fist beneath her breastbone.

"Read." Where my nails had been, I laid a rising broken chord of kisses.

"*You must—come urgently—to accept my orders on your knees.*" She squeaked.

"Read."

"If you wish me to read, stop tickling!"

I ducked my head, hiding my smile, and at last I gorged myself on her tenderest flesh.

The page ripped. I gloated to hear it.

She mumbled indistinctly on for another half-minute or so. Then she said clearly, and too loud, "*The self-restraint of blo-o-ondes!*" The last word was a high tremolo—and the last word indeed. She slapped the open book over her face, thrashing.

I took my fingers out of her cunt to hold her hips down, afraid she would do me some injury.

Everything was unvoiced sound now. An eighth-note gasp, the *ssh* of her hand fisting the sheet, her inner thigh rubbing against my ear with a sound like the surf. Her body bowed for a moment—then another.

She snapped back with a shock.

I did my best to sustain the note, but soon her pleasure was only a faint reverberation, and died away. The room was silent except for our breathing, hers still muffled by the pages of the novel.

I sat up, wiping my mouth. I waited for her to speak. To reach for me. Anything that would give me a hint of what this meant to her.

She snored.

I stood and gently lifted the book from her face, wiping the page dry as best I could. I wanted to press my face into the softness of her belly.

Instead I shook her awake. "You must go downstairs."

"I don't want to go back down there."

"I know. But Mrs. Cross will let the maid in at six, and it's nearly three now."

Her face crumpled. "I know I have to." Pressing her fists into her eyes, she took a deep breath. "Very well, Theodosia, let's go." She took her nightgown from my bedpost and put it on, tucking my French novel under her arm without asking.

I escorted her downstairs and locked her in, like a prison turnkey.

The next day was Friday, my half-holiday.

While I could not suppose the servants ignorant of Sir Kit's interest in me, I doubted that in his absence they would take whatever orders he had given on the subject too much to heart. What did they really care if I went for a solitary ramble, so long as their master did not hear of it? And how would he, if they did not tell him?

Sir Kit could not stay away much longer. This was a chance at freedom that would not come again. And I had already planned how I intended to make use of it.

So after our luncheon, I said to Tabby, "I will see you in the morning. Be a good girl for Clarice and Cook will give you a blackberry ice with your dinner."

This attempt at bribery was met with disinterested scorn, though I was rather sorry to miss the ice myself. Tabby crossed her arms and glared.

"You shouldn't go. Papa is from home. It isn't right to leave me all by myself."

Clarice snorted. "Dunnamany thanks."

"Friday is my half-holiday," I reminded her. "May I have a kiss before I go?"

"No. You don't deserve a kiss."

"Well, you must suit yourself."

"When is Papa coming back? I want Papa."

My own feelings were so opposite that I didn't quite know how to answer. "Soon. You must enjoy this time with your Mama, for when your Papa is home you will see her less."

"Ye-es." Tabby looked doubtful. "Mama can't put me on her shoulders or take me riding with her."

It was not Tabby's fault, I reminded myself. Sir Kit had labored for years to bring about this very state of affairs. "I am sorry you are disappointed. Enjoy your ice." I blew her a kiss from afar, having learned that if I tried to embrace her now, I might get a kick for my pains. "Clarice, I was thinking of going down to the beach. Do you mind if I look from your window to see if I might have it to myself?"

She laughed. "To see if the soldiers are flopping their"—she coughed—"their handkerchiefs about, you mean."

"Precisely," I said dryly. "You know how an exposed handkerchief discomposes me."

I stuck my head out her window. The door itself was out of sight, but the path towards the shore looked clear, at least. Hurrying into my pelisse and bonnet, I pattered down the stairs, barely even slowing to glance at Lady Palethorp's door.

My luck—and the staff's Saturnalia—held. I met no one on the stairs or in the stone corridor at the foot of them, though the footmen's raucous conversation carried through the wall. The loose brick still propped open the door.

I slipped out.

25

I made myself stroll unhurriedly towards the trees that would hide me from the house's windows. The sun was a burning eye in a clear sky, and I was grateful for my veil and parasol to shield me from its accusing gaze. By the time I saw the surf breaking—the sea's green skirts were sewn with diamonds today, too brilliant to look at—my scalp was as hot as if I had worn a fur cap, and my garters chafed my damp thighs.

There was no one to see, if I abandoned my planned mission in favor of stripping to my shift and wading into the water. Some local children splashed about a hundred yards off, but all the soldiers were swimming together, nearly to Cliff's End. I wavered, sweat dripping between my breasts, lusting after the sea's cool embrace.

In the end, like the Laodiceans whom God spat out of His mouth, I was neither hot nor cold, but lukewarm. I did wade into the cool water up to my ankles, holding my skirts in one hand and my boots in the other, and walked a little ways. But it wasn't how I had imagined it.

I tried to listen to my body, as I had to Lady Palethorp's last night. I could not manage it. The tide sucking at my toes and caressing my ankles was drowned out by *The shingle hurts my feet* and *What if I turn my ankle?* and *Watch out for razor shells, you'll slice yourself bloody.* At last I gave up and laced my feet back into their leather prisons, climbing up the beach to rejoin the road to Hastings, where it ran between the half-harvested wheat-fields.

For weeks the men had cut the clover and the sainfoin and tall grass to make hay. In full flower they cut it, that being the most profitable time. They had turned sheep onto the stubble, eating the land to the bone. Now they attacked the golden corn, and when everywhere that had been ripe and beautiful and sweet-smelling was bare and downtrodden, they would celebrate with a raucous Harvest-home.

I thought of Lady Palethorp as she had looked last night, sprawled across my sheets: young and soft, her breasts lolling sleepily. She had looked like Eden, sweet and wild. Sir Kit had seen that too, and he had thought, *She is mine, and I will till her. I will sow my seed in her, and profit from her rents.*

The dry wheat whispered and rustled as I passed. I knew the men to be absorbed in their work, yet I was afraid of their eyes on me, shrinking even from the gleaners, who never glanced up from the earth, lest a stray kernel elude them. I thought of Sir Kit's self-satisfied sermon. This awful drudgery was *charity*, and these hungry women must be grateful to the landowners for their aching backs and sunburnt necks.

Even the laborers' music grated on my ears, sung in the nose to carry across the fields, slow and dirgelike to match the rhythm of the swinging scythes.

It was seven or eight miles to Hastings—farther than Rye, but not too dreadful a walk, except that the sun was at its zenith, my nerves were agitated, and I would have to walk *back* again afterward. I soon grew miserably thirsty, but I didn't dare stop and beg a dipper of water from the harvesters. They might ask who I was, or what house I had come from.

While I was in Hastings on my errand, I wanted to mail a letter to Iphigenia as well. At first, I planned to stop in the shade and write it; then I meant to write it in Hastings with a clear head and a glass of lemonade; then I grew so faint my eyes could not focus on the road past my veil, and I was obliged to crouch down under a scrubby little tree after all, heart pounding.

Was I really exhausted by two miles' walk? Had I been at Goldengrove so long that the muscles in my legs were atrophying, like Lady Palethorp's? I thought of veal, penned up to keep it tender…

But after a minute or two I realized my breaths were shallow, and had been for some time. My nerves made me faint, not the walk. Even now, my thoughts raced faster than my pulse.

Miss Abbott's story came back to me, of Lady Palethorp worn out by climbing the bluffs, and somehow the simple speculation—*Had she been nervous?*—struck me sharply.

The answer didn't matter—only that when I heard the story, I had wished to have nothing in common with her, and now my wishing was all the other way. The possibility stretched from me to her like a catgut string, and I could almost name its pitch.

I forced myself to breathe deeply against the damp pressure of my stays. My head felt heavy, and a blue afterimage of the white road hovered vertiginously between me and my tree. Should I write my letter? I went round and round with myself, until at last I awoke with a jolt, realizing I might have written it twice over by now.

I had waited for this moment of liberty to open my heart to Iphigenia. But when I pulled pencil and paper from my reticule and took off my gloves to write—to write without anyone looking over my shoulder or anyone to hand my letter to but the postmaster—my constraint did not lift. How could I begin to explain it all?

And she was living with one of Sir Kit's neighbors. Could I be sure Mrs. Musgrave didn't make herself free with her dependents' correspondence? Could I be sure Iphigenia herself, concerned for my safety, would not pour out the whole?

Dear Iphigenia, I began. She opened *her* letters with *Darling Livvy*, but though I drank in the endearment gratefully, I could not copy it. If I did, it would be all too plain it was just that: an affected copy of her instinctive effusiveness.

I am so sorry I did not meet you in Rye as I promised. I meant to. I miss you dreadfully. There was a fire in some of the tenants' cottages, and a horse could not be spared. I meant to walk, was actually on the point of setting out, but my employer positively forbade it. It's true that the air was bad, but I…

…but I suspect…

I despised the taste of lead too much to chew my pencil. I bit my nails instead, pausing every other word to consider what would be politic—then what would be impolitic yet not merit instant dismissal—then whether I might risk the dismissal after all.

…but I suspect he was not sorry to keep me at home. Sir Kit is a popular master, and a generous one, but as he pays the piper, he does not stint to call the tune. When I remember that I left Mrs. Humphrey's, where I was free—and

blessed with your company [I added this last self-consciously, feeling that to omit it would be ill-mannered]—*because I was tired of scorched porridge, sometimes I wish I had heeded the words of Scripture: "Eat thou not the bread of him that hath an evil eye, neither desire thou his dainty meats: the morsel which thou hast eaten shalt thou vomit up, and lose thy sweet words."*

I don't mean to suggest that Sir Kit has an evil eye! On the contrary, he is a forward-thinking gentleman, free from all superstition save a distaste for what is not wholly English. *And who can fault patriotism in wartime? It is perhaps his wife's misfortune she was born a Jewess, but as she is confined to her room almost entirely, his affection (or lack of it) can make little difference to her, poor lady.*

Is it intolerant in me to wonder if her race has affected her health— some congenital predisposition? Nobody disputes that some diseases run in families, after all. My grandmother's troubles with her hands ran in hers, and though my mother escaped, I have imagined lately that I see signs of the same complaint in myself. But it might be only one of my nervous fancies, brought on by marsh air and seclusion.

A strong dose of your common sense would do me good. I regret dreadfully that I could not see you. Too much that I long to tell you cannot be committed to paper. I need not tell you to burn this.

Yours ever and always,
Deborah Oliver

Iffy would remember about vó, wouldn't she? It had been years since we spoke of it, but the story was outlandish to English ears, a playhouse tragedy. I remembered the conversation so clearly myself—but how much had I forgotten of *her* family history over the years?

Did she even remember that I was half a Jewess?

What difference did it make? What help did I hope for? When I had planned to meet Iphigenia in Rye, I had not wanted her to *save* me. Nothing prevented me from buying a ticket home this very afternoon. I had wanted her to tell me whether I was sane, and who I should believe: Sir Kit or Lady Palethorp. Since then, for all my irresolution, I had chosen.

I thought of tearing up the letter. Indeed, if the sun hadn't moved until I was no longer in the shade, who knows how long I might have sat there fruitlessly debating with myself over it. Already I risked walking home in the dark, and finding the door barred when I got there.

The sun was halfway to the horizon when I entered Hastings, and found myself on a broad, bustling parade overlooking the shore. Far above me the Conqueror's ruined castle glowered, showing off the town by contrast, like proud Mr. Darcy refusing to dance at the Meryton assembly. Below, fashionable visitors crowded the beach, and bathing machines trundled cheerfully in and out of the water, leaving tracks in the damp sand below the high-water line.

I had grown entirely unused to crowds—I was shocked by how entirely. It had only been a few months! But the cacophony hurt my head: voices, cartwheels, footsteps, snuffling iron-shod horses, children shouting and spoons clinking against fluted glasses.

Shoulders and elbows and feet jostled me as though I were invisible, as though I were *nothing*, and the implacable sea grated in and out and in and out and in and—

I ducked into a coffee-room. It was clean and elegant as a public coffee-room on a public promenade could reasonably be, and quiet enough that my panting breaths echoed. The change ought to have been welcome, but after so much sun, the dim light and dark wood made my sight flash blue and yellow, and when an amiable waiter escorted me to a table, his very kindness battered me by demanding a return. Though acutely conscious that he must think me proud and disagreeable, I still shrank from offering a friendly smile, with the same self-preserving animal instinct I'd have felt at a request to open a vein and drip my life's blood onto the gleaming floorboards. But he soon left me to poke at the newspapers scattered over my table.

Memories have an odd trick of attaching themselves to places, and sensory impressions. For me, the smell of coffee and a profusion of newspapers always recalled a childhood visit to a coffeehouse with my father. I'd been bored, barely tall enough to see the coffee-woman Papa chatted with over her counter. My eye had landed on an article in the nearest newspaper, about a woman burned at the stake for coining a shilling. The smoke from her body had made some people in the neighborhood very ill.

I don't think I knew until then that people were burned in England, too.

I had not quite understood Papa's explanation of coining, and for a long time after, I had been terrified of unwittingly passing a bad penny and being taken up by the constables. I remembered a hundred agonizing walks to the grocer's, palm sweating around the coins in my pocket, vowing that I would take full responsibility. I wouldn't tell them my mother gave me the money. I wouldn't even tell them my name.

I was inured to the memory, usually: one more exaggerated terror I had learned to roll my eyes at in the light of common sense. But today common sense deserted me. How exaggerated *were* my terrors, when no one blinked at Sir Kit locking up his wife? When a scant two decades ago, England had set a woman on fire for a shilling, and forced her ashes down its citizens' throats?

But at last a glass of orgeat and soda water was set before me with a plate of sandwiches. The food settled me, bite by bite. I had worked myself into a fever, and the crisis passed, as crises do. Soon I remembered my delirium of a few minutes since with as much distant, rueful perplexity as I felt at my childish worries. I sipped slowly, relishing the bright orange-flower fizz and the lingering taste of almonds, warm and languorous as a convalescent after being bled.

At last I roused myself to locate a locksmith. I gave him the Goldengrove tower key, and explained I had come into town on the last coach, and had misplaced my trunk key so often that I wanted a duplicate for my husband to keep. He chuckled indulgently, and told me to come back in half an hour.

I next made my way to the stationer's shop that served as the receiving house for the post. "Pardon me, sir," I asked, "might I use your wax jack?"

In my current good humor, I knew the Receiver of Letters would have forgotten me in five minutes. Even so, I had nearly crept into an alleyway to fumble with my tinderbox and candle-end, knowing that tomorrow or the next day I would be on the rack, imagining ways for Sir Kit to hear of my excursion.

I hesitated over whether to melt a coin into the seal to pay the postage. Iphigenia would not yet have received her first quarter's wages, and she had just made a long journey. But mightn't the penny tempt some enterprising servant to remove the seal—and then, perhaps, to read the letter?

Hoping Iffy would forgive me, I sealed it without the coin and dropped it in the iron box with the peculiarly sweet relief of no longer being able to change my mind.

I had considered writing the Countess of Tassell, too, but it seemed too great a step to take without Lady Palethorp's prior agreement. I ought to have consulted her the night before, only…she had never asked me to help her leave Goldengrove. She had only ever asked to visit her daughter, and barely trusted me to allow that. I could not think her eager for pitched battle against Sir Kit with such uncertain allies as myself and a little-known patroness.

Duplicate key safely in my coin purse, I made my way homeward, stomach hurting from one too many sandwiches.

I was afraid dark would fall before I reached Goldengrove, yet I dawdled, only hurrying whenever I came within whistling distance of a Martello tower. The land was already filing the first shaving from the sun's rim when I reached our beach—and I stayed at the shore until the golden disc melted entirely into the earth's iron crucible.

But at last I had no choice but to march myself up and over the canal, past the marsh and into the little wood. I emerged from the trees, and my sore feet turned to stone in my boots when I saw Goldengrove's great hulking silhouette in the twilight.

I could still turn and walk back to Hastings in the dark, to buy that coach ticket home.

The house had not been shuttered yet; the nursery window was bright. I thought of Portia's glad homecoming after making Shylock choose between baptism and death: *That light we see is burning in my hall. How far that little candle throws his beams! So shines a good deed in a naughty world.*

The floor below ours, where the shutters never opened, was in shadow.

If I went, Tabby would probably tear my possessions apart in betrayed fury, and carve gouges in Papa's peg leg. Lady Palethorp would wait in her room, and no one would come.

Lively St. Lemeston would be familiar, and safe as any place *could* be for an impoverished old maid. But who would be really glad to see me? Whom would *I* be glad to see? Really, heartwarmingly glad? Iphigenia was at Jury's Gap, and there was nobody else living whose welcome could make me believe good might outweigh evil in this world. I might never believe that again.

Yet candles must be lit despite one's personal inclinations, and good deeds must be done. If I did not believe *that*, it was all the same whether I took the stagecoach home or threw myself into the sea.

This hostile jumble of stone *was* my home now, the only one I had left. I went up the path.

The porter threw his door open at my first knock. "Thank the Lord you're back safe, Miss Oliver! We was that worried you'd turned your ankle or summat. I'll tell the master you're home."

My veins turned to ice. "The—master?"

"Yes, ma'am. He came home this afternoon, while you were away."

26

The strap of my reticule seared my palm like hot wire. Sir Kit would never demand I turn out my purse, would he?

"I didn't mean to worry anybody," I said, trying for bemused surprise. "Give me a candle for the stairs, would you? And please ask Sir Kit to give me a few minutes to get out my dusty things, if he wishes to speak with me tonight."

I climbed to the attic as quickly as I could without letting the candle blow out. Once shut up in my room, I turned out the coin purse myself. A half-crown rolled away; I was too frightened even to look for it.

I dug up my winter pelisse from the bottom of my trunk, shoving the new key into the pocket with Lady Palethorp's earrings. The trunk safely shut and locked again, I collapsed atop it, hands shaking too hard to undo the knot in my bootlaces.

If I were found to have made the key, I would be dismissed. I would never see Lady Palethorp again, or Tabby. I would never know what became of them.

And what would become of me?

Sukey Toogood's husband had been a Tassell servant. When the countess had judged him disloyal, she'd sacked him and told all her acquaintance to put him on the black-list. He'd had to take a job in a much smaller home for less pay.

Mortified at having recommended a thief to Sir Kit—her neighbor, her social equal, her coreligionist—Lady Tassell would not hesitate to crush *me* to remain in the neighborhood's good graces. For me, a much smaller home with less pay might be the workhouse.

My stomach swooped as another possibility presented itself: what if Sir Kit found out, and *didn't* sack me?

I pictured him coming up the stairs with the condemnatory key in his hand, which he had discovered in his imprudent wife's possession. He would use it to open my door, and lean against the jamb with it dangling from his finger. What penance could he not exact from me then? What would I dare to withhold from him?

His sense of honor gave me some protection now, when he still seemed to wish for my good opinion. If he realized he had irrevocably lost it, what motive would he have for self-denial?

I heard his boots on the stairs, putting paid to my faint hope that he would stay away tonight, to punish me. My eyes darted about the room. Was there any sign of his wife's presence? No, surely not, the maids had been. "Who's there?"

"Your lord and master, back from the wars," he answered, low and merry.

I forced myself to the door, and opened it. "Welcome home, sir."

"You gave us all a scare! Clarice said you had gone down to the beach hours ago. I half convinced myself you had drowned, when I could not spy you from the roof."

"I can swim," I said, nonsensically affronted.

He grinned. "I also considered the possibility that you had been abducted by a ruthless Italian. But just as I was on the point of saddling my horse and riding to your rescue, there you were, coming up the drive with very little of the eagerness *I* felt. Has Tabby been a trial?"

I was too worn out in body and mind to think of a witty answer. "I did not go very far," I said. "But I am sadly out of condition, and my legs were tired."

"Checkmated in one move. You know I could never be angry at your legs."

My face heated. "I hope you had a pleasant journey."

"Very pleasant, for I spent it imagining my homecoming. But alas, instead of a friendly handshake and intelligent conversation, I was obliged to listen to Mrs. Cross's *very* lengthy explanations of why the house was at sixes and sevens. Have the maids been very bad? I was going to say that your bed looks as neatly made as ever—but you have been sleeping on Tabby's sofa, so that proves nothing."

Was his gaze sharper than usual? Had Mrs. Cross already told him I had been sleeping in my own bed?

I was terribly aware of it behind us, and how many steps would take us to it. My bones ached after my fifteen-mile walk, and now I would have to spend the night on that hard sofa.

Would Lady Palethorp signal tonight? Would it be safe for her to come up? She must have heard his return. If she signaled and I did not come, she would understand why—wouldn't she? She would not think I repented of last night…

Why couldn't he have stayed away another day?

"I'm glad to see you home safe, sir, and I'll gladly shake your hand. But intelligent conversation is beyond me just now, I'm afraid." I held out my hand, feigning a yawn as I did it.

He didn't linger over the handshake—much. "Very well. But tomorrow I shall not let you off so easy. You and Tabby must dine with me." He cast an affectionate glance at the door to the nursery. "I missed her dreadfully."

"Of course," I murmured. "Good night, sir." I hurried into my night-things. But at the nursery door I turned back, looking at my trunk.

How had Lady Palethorp described me? Patient, and sensible, and careful? Those were kind names for my cowardice. *She* had tried to scratch his eyes out; *she* had come at him with any weapon to hand, until even her pins were taken away. If I gave her the key, what might she find the courage to do?

Could they bring *me* up on charges, if she used the key to exact revenge? Not long ago, the murder of an employer and the murder of a husband had both been crimes women were sent to the stake for—though the handful of burnings that had finally changed the law had all been for counterfeiting, some twenty years ago, the newspapers full of each one until even Parliament was ashamed.

But the three crimes were the same in the eyes of the law: differing degrees of treason. The punishment for such a crime must be swift and terrible.

I remembered an argument at the long refectory table at school about whether it was fair to burn women and hang men for the same crime. *It doesn't matter one way or the other*, one girl had said, *because they strangle them first anyway.*

Not always, another had replied with relish. *Sometimes they light the fire too early by mistake.*

I had already spent courage far beyond my means, to obtain my counterfeit key. I had none left. I pried open the tin Lady Tassell had given me.

To my relief, the hot cross bun had dried into hardtack without molding, the iced cross hard and shiny as glue. Very slowly, and as cleanly as I could, I sliced off the foot of the bun with my penknife. Then I scraped a hollow and laid the earrings in it, wrapped in two scraps of silver tissue. I nestled the key between them, and pasted the bun back together, pressing until it dried.

In good light the seam would be visible, but why would anyone look? I returned the tin to the mantel and spread the crumbs on my windowsill before I crept into the nursery.

My sore legs reproached me as I arranged them on the hard sofa.

Thankfully, I was not obliged to talk much at dinner the next day, for Tabby was full of things to say, and Sir Kit seemed happy to listen. I managed, even, to enjoy the food, and admire the pudding when it came: an enormous trifle of ladyfingers swimming in clotted cream, shot through with fresh cherries in the syrup from last year's preserves.

"Could we send some to Mama?" Tabby ventured. "Maybe she would like it."

His eyes crinkled as he gazed into her uncertain face. "Of course we shall, if she wants some. Peter!"

The footman stepped forward from his place at one end of the sideboard.

"Please go up and ask Lady Palethorp if she would like some trifle."

My heart flew into my throat; for a moment I almost hoped that *this* time—perhaps Clarice's suitor was not part of the plot— I kept an eye on the clock as I tried to keep Tabby from spattering the tablecloth with scarlet.

Sir Kit laughed. "Don't fret, Miss Oliver, the laundry maids need something to do. Eat your cherries while they're ripe."

I could barely spare the attention to wonder if I imagined the double entendre in his voice.

But after four minutes nearly to the second, the door opened, and Peter said, "Lady Palethorp sends her affectionate regards to you and Miss Palethorp, but she has everything she needs."

Tabby's face barely changed, but I felt her disappointment as if it were my own. It *was* my own.

She was a child. Why could I, who should know better, still not quite extinguish my desire for the world to become easy, different, transformed by my wishes? I barely tasted my trifle, and yet I sat resentfully eyeing the streaks of cream and little red pool of syrup in the bottom of the dish. To scrape the glass would be unladylike.

Lady Palethorp would have done it anyway.

It wasn't fair. She had paid for this dessert: paid for the cows, and the orchards, and the glittering cones of sugar lined up in the pantry in their indigo paper.

The blood of slaves was likely in this trifle, too. I had been eating it all these years, wishing I could lick my plate. Mãe had warned me, and I had forgotten.

I was not a child, to sulk because life was not *fair*. I opened my mouth to say, *Sir Kit, have you ever thought of asking Mrs. Bishop not to purchase West Indian sugar?*

But I did not want him to look at me, and closed it again.

<hr />

It took me nearly an hour after Lady Palethorp's first signal, to gather up the courage to go downstairs. Or perhaps I was ashamed to face her, after squirreling away her key.

Her drawn bed-curtains were a swooping cobweb shape in the darkness. I heard no sounds from within as I tiptoed towards them. The dusty, ruined room might almost have been ravaged by time—might have lain under an enchantment for a century. At my touch, a cloud of dust motes flew up from the muslin. I drew the curtain back in inarticulate fear—

But there she was, curled against the headboard, fidgeting with her unbound hair and glaring at me. "What kept you? It's too late to wake Tabby now."

"I was afraid of meeting Sir Kit."

She plucked at the coverlet, frowning. "Let's go down to the beach. It's hot enough for a swim."

In fact I thought the beach would be chilly. It was only here, high in the thick-walled tower, that the day's heat lingered. But that was beside the point. "I don't have a k—" My voice died. "A key to the outer doors."

She sighed heavily. "The roof, then."

I had been right, it *was* chilly outside. And she did not even look at the stars, though they were bright; the moon had nearly wasted away to nothing, and I had left my lantern on the stairs. She stood at the very edge of the parapet, and looked down.

"'This brave o'er-hanging firmament,'" she quoted softly, not quite to me, "'this majestical roof fretted with golden fire—why, it appeareth no other thing to me than a foul and pestilent congregation of vapors.'"

"I thought you weren't worried about marsh fever," I jested weakly.

She stepped onto the ledge. God forgive me, my first jolt of fear was not for her. It was for what would happen to *me* if she jumped.

"Come down." My voice was a thread.

"I'm not going to jump. Probably not. Some days I'd like to. But then Tabby would be alone with him."

Everything today had gone so wrong, when I had meant so well. If there *was* a Hell, I would pave my path to it in short order. "'Little more than half a day's journey,'" I whispered to myself. "'Yes, I call it a *very* easy distance.'"

"Pardon?" She stepped off the ledge—she stepped towards me.

I blew on my numb fingers. I was so tired of being cold, and yet dreading fire.

"Are you well, Miss Oliver?"

"Oh, I'm well enough," I said savagely. "But I'm not *good*. I can't be. I don't know if anybody can, but then what in God's name are we *doing* here?"

She jostled my shoulder with hers. "I thought we were looking at the stars."

She only wished to cheer me. But why could *I* not be melancholic for once? "Not here, on the roof," I clarified—out of spite, for I knew she had understood me. "Living. The whole human race."

"I thought you *didn't* want me to jump," she said in amusement.

Now, she looked at the stars, one plump shoulder against the edge of the merlon. The breeze caught her unbound hair. Tendrils of it wrapped around my arm and clung to the back of my wrapper.

She saw me looking, and tried unsuccessfully to tuck it over her far shoulder. "Wearing it up gave me a headache. What purpose did your atheist friend, Antigone, assign to humanity?"

I didn't bother to correct her this time. Instead I said, as if I must relieve my spirit by confessing *something*, "I wrote to her. She's a lady's companion in Jury's Gap now. For Mrs. Musgrave. I told her…"

Her body went stiff. "Told her *what*?"

"Nothing," I said quickly. "Or—everything. I don't know. I was vague. If she remembers that I told her my grandmother was tortured, she might understand…"

"But you think she might have forgotten," she finished dryly. "You had no right to tell her. There's nothing she can do but make things worse."

My shoulder blades pressed against the brick, painful as if the bones had been scraped clean of their encasing flesh. "I have no right to do anything," I agreed. "I have no right to walk down to the beach and watch the sunset. I have no right to post a letter. I have no right to confide in my dearest friend, and I have no right to love your daughter, but I cannot—"

I broke off before I said *lock myself in a drawer when I am not wanted*. That was no metaphor, but precisely what Sir Kit had done to her.

"We can leave," I burst out. "Tomorrow, when the doors are open. I'll help you. We'll go to Lady Tassell."

She didn't answer. She didn't even look at me. I caught at her sleeve.

She flinched as though expecting a blow.

I wrapped my arms around myself, wishing I had known better. "She outranks him. Or we'll find a lawyer. We can go down the beach to Hastings. The mail coach leaves from there every day at three in the afternoon, except on Sundays. We can—"

"What a host of irrelevant detail," she said flatly, face still turned away. "You ought to have been a lawyer yourself. But then, even if you were a man, you would have to be baptized for that, and *you* are too virtuous to convert for advantage."

Above us spread the sky, full of fire so remote I could not feel its heat.

"He can't keep you here like this."

I was so relieved when she finally met my eyes. At least, I thought she did. It was too dark to be sure. "You're afraid of him." She sounded surprised, almost pitying.

"Aren't you?"

She tried to hoist herself up to perch on the merlon, but her arms weren't strong enough. She sat sideways in a crenel instead, one foot on the roof and one dangling over the drop. "I was," she said after a while. "But it's burned out of me now. There's nothing left he can take from me."

I was learning that I was not the sort of person fear could be burned out of. Like the bush in the desert, I burned and was not consumed.

"Maybe I *could* get away from him," she said. "Maybe I could get a lawyer and a separation. *Maybe.* One of my father's friends in London would take me in. But the best lawyer in the world wouldn't get me Tabby, and you know it—*especially* if I went to my father's friends. Bad enough to take a child from her father, but to take her out of the Church, too? And I won't leave her alone with Kit."

"We'll take her with us," I pleaded. "We'll go where no one knows us."

Even as I said it, I knew she was right, and it was impossible. Even if we managed to leave the house unnoticed, could *she* walk all the way to Rye? Could Tabby? Even if Sir Kit, riding, did not overtake us on the road, it would be easy enough to track our coach—and if that failed, did I imagine Sir Kit would give up in a day? In a year? He had brains and energy enough to track us the length and breadth of Britain, and Lady Palethorp's money to do it with. "We could leave the country."

Her jaw set. "And Tabby would go quietly, of course. She wouldn't run off, or scream to the first stranger we met that we had stolen her from her Papa."

My mind's eye showed me Tabby raving with fury on the packet to Rotterdam, and hurling herself into the sea. "We could…" But I could not say to Lady Palethorp, *dose her with laudanum.*

"I could stay with Tabby," I choked out. But what was the use of such a promise? She didn't want that any more than I did.

I imagined the house without her. How long before my nerves went? Before either I gave in and allowed Sir Kit into my bed, or he dropped me and began harassing one of the maids? By then, perhaps, I would have wandered so far from the path that it would not even occur to me to lift a hand to stop him. I would be relieved.

"You can't stay shut up in that room forever," I said anyway. "There must be *something* we could do. I'd rather jump myself than live in a world where there isn't."

She swung round to face me, planting both feet on the stone and leaning her forearms on her thighs. "There is one thing that would free me."

My heart leapt. "Yes?"

"If something were to happen to Kit," she said, very deliberately.

27

My breath stopped. "What…sort of thing?" I squeaked.

She lost her patience. "I mean I'd have to kill him. Obviously."

There were only wells of darkness where her eyes should have been. Her gaze held me paralyzed anyway. My heart beat a frantic warning in my chest.

Of all the decisions that could never be amended or taken back, this was the most final. *Murder is a crime*, cried the voice of conscience. *You cannot. You **must** not.*

But *was* it conscience? Had God's finger really carved *Thou shalt not kill* in stone, on a faraway mountaintop?

If so, then He had written it in Hebrew, and yet it had been entirely legal to murder my great-uncle for praying in the same language. The English Crown had burned women at the stake for coining a shilling, and cynically slaughtered the innocent Jews of Lincoln.

Yes, murder was against the law. But only because, like poaching deer, it impinged on the royal prerogative.

We would be risking execution, if we killed Sir Kit. I swayed, lightheaded, and had to steady myself with a hand on the parapet.

But what was the use in trying to be safe? I was terrified when I was safe, too. Perhaps I was terrified of safety itself, as I was of heat and light and love. Safety was like Sir Kit: it smiled, and when it had coaxed you into smiling back, the pit opened beneath your feet.

I spread my fingers across Goldengrove's bricks, and stared at them. This house could crush my hands with its might. It had already begun to break my mind, and my heart. I thought of the prisoner eating his confession.

I will not let you break my spirit, I told Goldengrove. I set aside my decorous prejudices, and took an unsteady step towards the path.

"I'll help you." It came out a whisper. I could not stand quite straight. But for the first time that evening, I wasn't cold: there was a bright coal in my chest.

The corner of her mouth curved, sure and a little exultant, as though she had known what I would say. How, when I was astonished myself?

"Will you really?" she asked me. But the question sounded rhetorical; in just such a tone, Judith must have asked Holofernes, *More wine, my lord?*

Judith had not gone alone into the enemy camp. Her maidservant skulked through every painting, squeamishly averting her face as she pressed the general's shoulders into his mattress so he wouldn't jerk under the knife, or looking nervously over her shoulder as she held out her sack for his bloody head.

"Yes," I told her.

"Why?"

Because I am dying here. I could not say that. I was not sane enough to explain it. "It's self-interest, pure and simple."

To my surprise, it came out steady. She stood, eyes searching my face. Then she smiled and held out her hand.

When I shook it, she shivered and pulled away. "Your fingers are ice. We'd better go in."

I was afraid of dropping the lantern, and reluctantly let her lead the way.

"Did we drink all the cherry bounce?" she asked. "It would warm you."

"It's not the cold."

"You're too thin."

I huddled self-consciously into my wrap. "Thanks."

"You said you had pastilles. Where are they?"

It felt a lifetime ago that I had told her that. I dug the sweets out of my trunk, keeping one for myself and giving her the bag.

"Mine's raspberry," she said. "What's yours?"

I put it on my tongue. "Violets."

Violets meant faithfulness, for their color, preserved, never faded. Yet the flower bloomed early and died early: *sweet, not lasting; the perfume and suppliance of a minute, no more.*

I felt old suddenly, and withered. *Too thin.* Would there be any sweetness left for me, when we had killed Sir Kit? I would be the living incarnation of her guilt. Would the sight of me be too bitter?

Or she might keep me close out of mistrust, the better to stop up my mouth with bribes and sugared words.

"You ought to get some sleep," she said kindly, as though she had not just vowed to kill a man.

I wished she would not leave me alone. I could not open my mouth to say so.

I could not bring myself to sleep in the nursery. I put my hand on the knob, and heard Tabby's happy voice at dinner, her eager *Papa, did you know...?*

But when I had stretched myself out in the dark hollow space between my bed and my netting, a few feet of floorboards and a door could not protect me from my thoughts. The crushing horror of what I had agreed to descended, flattening me against my mattress.

I thought of *The Newgate Calendar*, the man pressed until he surrendered his estate to the Crown or died. I could feel Goldengrove's bricks being piled on my chest, one by one.

In the next room, poor unsuspecting Tabby slept peacefully, breathing in a miasma of fear and secrets. Like Sir Kit, I knew a moment of glad relief that she was a girl, and could not inherit Goldengrove. Yet where would she find a more salubrious atmosphere? She must either live with her mother's torturer, or with her father's murderer. And if we were *caught*—

It was useless to hope for good. I was not good, Lady Palethorp was not good, even Tabby was not good. Perhaps no one was; some only managed a simulacrum of innocence, through ignorance or lack of exposure to temptation. I could not even comfort myself that Sir Kit was evil. He had been an infant once, ignorant and untempted, and Britannia had nursed him on blood.

Why did it ever and always pain me, to relearn for the thousandth time that Justice's scales could not be balanced? She could only hack about her with her sword, blindfolded.

It was time I made up my mind to hack, instead of fussing with pennyweights. *We must act, or atrophy and perish.*

With a mental effort, I moved the tip of my index finger, then wiggled all the fingers of my right hand. I lifted the hand an inch, shifting it towards the edge of the bed.

The sack of sweets clattered to the floor. A few escaped the drawstring—rolled on their rims—slowed, teetered, and fell flat with a final little *click*.

My heart pounded, but Tabby did not seem to have woken. I wondered if Lady Palethorp, below, recognized the sound.

At least the little shock had jolted me out of my paralysis. My body was leaden with weariness, and my mind racing. I would be good for nothing in the morning if I did not sleep. Grimly, I put my fingers between my legs. I did not think of Lady Palethorp.

I was awakened by Tabby's garbled voice saying accusingly, "You have sweets?"

I blinked open bleary eyes and parted my canopy. She stood at my bedside, mouth stained purple. The clock said seven.

The maid must have woken me at six as usual, but I had no memory of it. "Good morning, Tabby. How do you do today?" I said with pointed politeness. My mouth tasted disgusting, and when I sat up, pawing at the netting until it fell to the floor, my sore legs cramped at once.

Tabby bobbed a hasty curtsy. "Good morning, Miss Oliver." The bonbon clinked against her teeth. "How do you do today?"

"Well, thank you," I lied. A red lozenge winked at me from the floor, a telltale blood-drop. "Clarice, please come and help me with my stays!"

When I opened the shutters, birds scattered. What—? Oh, there must still be some crumbs from my hot cross bun.

I could not understand how ordinary everything was. The sun was shining, and the barometer in the music room predicted another fine day. I copied it into our diary just as I had yesterday. The previous night might have been a dream, or a nightmare. I half expected my memory of my pact with Lady Palethorp to fade before luncheon.

But it lingered as Tabby and I sketched the birds that came to feast on my windowsill, and matched them to Bewick's woodcuts. I would forget it in my flash of delight at a scarlet-cheeked goldfinch in among the sparrows and starlings—but when the dread returned, after a moment I remembered why.

⁂

That night I forced myself to go down at Lady Palethorp's first signal. She met me eagerly at her door, novel in hand. "Do you have volume two? That marchioness is a bitch and I love her."

I felt a little shocked, and shocked at my shock. A remark like that would have been nothing to me at the boarding house. I was atrophying with a vengeance. "I love her too. I'm sorry, I was in rather a stupor today and forgot to fetch the next volume from the library. I'll get it for you tomorrow."

Then I was shocked again, that we could talk about books when we had made a pact to commit murder.

I wondered if my stupor—which did not seem to be abating—was part of the reason Tabby was so fussy and clinging tonight. Certainly Lady Palethorp's visit to the nursery was not a success. Tabby was clearly unsatisfied with our responses to her conversation, and threw a minor tantrum when I would not give her the scissors to make over Adeline's dress for Harvest-home. Then she refused to go back to bed. At last we had to take the candle, blow her kisses from the doorway, and leave her sulking in the dark. The silence was punctuated at intervals by a wail from Tabby, or the thud of an object being thrown.

But the noises had the character of lodging a formal complaint, with no sign of destructive frenzy, so I was not too concerned. "We love you," I called. "Good night!"

Lady Palethorp, however, sagged against my side of the door, despairing. "She hates me. I love her so much and she hates me."

"She doesn't hate you. She's only tired and confused. The middle of the night is the worst possible time to see a child. When the two of you live together in an ordinary way, she'll be calmer."

"Yes. Yes. When we're living together in an ordinary way."

Did that *we* include me? She made no move to touch me again, and I didn't dare reach out first.

"I slept all day. I don't understand why I'm so tired." She scrubbed at her eyes and opened them owlishly wide, as if to blink herself awake. "We'd better make plans. Let's go on the roof."

I hesitated. "When Tabby is asleep." Most likely Clarice had been wakened by Tabby's shrieks and would hear anything untoward. But I had rather not go back through the nursery to be sure.

"Of course," Lady Palethorp said hastily. "I should have thought of that."

Why, when you pay me to think of it for you? I thought. I was tired and fussy myself.

"Perhaps we might pierce your ears," she suggested.

"It would seem awfully strange," I said as gently as I could manage. "Besides, I can't wear the earrings you gave me, and I haven't any others."

She deflated. "Yes. I should have thought— Another time, then. After."

I warned myself not to place too much reliance on that "after." Her sentiments now could not predict her sentiments *then*. "I would like that, my lady," I said quietly.

"Oh, for God's sake. I want my own name back. You can pronounce it, can't you?"

"I would like that, Jael." *Do you remember mine?*

She smiled to herself as she curled up in my bed to wait, and was snoring within two minutes.

Tabby was now complaining audibly to Adeline about our behavior, so I settled on the hard floor against the door. In the navy, men alternated watch and watch, so two sailors could sleep in one berth without ever sharing it. Of course *someone* must take first watch.

I didn't really believe that anyone would ever watch while *I* slept.

At length the rustlings died down from Tabby's room. I peeked in with my lantern to be sure she was not about some mischief, and then shook Lady Palethorp—Jael—awake.

She startled upright. "I fell asleep," she said, far too loud.

I held a finger to my lips, feeling tired and crosser than ever.

She yawned and dawdled her way up the stairs and onto the roof. I was too tired to enjoy the breeze.

"We ought to do it the night of Harvest-home," she said abruptly, hair whipping about her shoulders.

I had not expected such a definite plan. "But that can't be more than a few weeks away," I protested, remembering those half-shorn fields.

"Oh, sooner, with the weather so fine. It's the only day in the year that Kit really drinks. The laborers toast for hours, and he's obliged to pace them if he doesn't wish to be thought proud. Every Goldengrove man will be drunk as a wheelbarrow, and away at the home-farm barns. They'll be no use in putting out the fire."

"The—fire?"

28

She nodded, tucking her hair into the back of her nightdress. "It's quick, it's easy, and it will look like an accident. Drunk men burn alive in their beds all the time."

Old Joe must have gone up like a plum pudding.

"Can't we do it some other way? I don't like fire."

"What's your plan, then?"

I didn't have one. "…Poison?"

"What sort of poison?"

I suggested laudanum. She pointed out that even if we managed to mask the smell and taste enough to administer it, any doctor would recognize the odor in the morning and ask who in the household was known to take the drug.

Arsenic could pass as violent indigestion, but I would have to either purchase it from a shop, or locate and burgle Mrs. Bishop's store of rat poison. And while I could name a few other poisons, neither of us knew anything about them.

It could not seem a violent death. No one would want to believe Sir Kit capable of suicide, and once they began looking…

I might be able to lure him to the beach, but unless he was literally insensible with drink, I would need her ladyship—Jael's assistance to drown him. Smuggling her out of the house, and then back in dripping wet, seemed an uncertain prospect.

If we smothered him, could we make it appear accidental?

We could drop or push him off the roof.

By now I was sick with nerves and horror, but I grimly examined the parapet. Three sides overlooked turrets, roofs, and chimneys; the fourth was a sheer drop, but he might catch at half a dozen ledges, gutters, gables, and eaves as he fell. Clarice or Tabby might hear him shouting. He might pull one of us down with him.

I imagined grappling with him in the dark, his fingers twisting in my nightdress. Could we smother him downstairs and then drop his body over?

I glanced at Jael, and found her already looking at me. *What's to stop her pushing* you *over too, and being free of the whole mess?* I stepped back from the edge. "It does not seem very sure," I admitted.

"We'll wait for him together after Harvest-home, smother him, and set the bed on fire," she said impatiently. "There isn't anything surer."

"I'm afraid of fire," I whispered. "I couldn't set a fire."

"I can." She frowned, calculating. "If he's still on his feet, you'll have to talk him into another drink or two. Could you stomach holding him down while I smothered him?"

My nausea worsened. If Sir Kit was conscious, that might require lying full across his body while he struggled for his life. I would feel every vibration of his death throes in my own flesh—would feel it when he was only motionless clay.

But I thought of Judith's handmaiden. If his strength was sapped by drink, and she was there and commanded it, then— "Yes. I could do that. What about his valet?"

"You'll have to get him out of the way." She came towards me. I took an involuntary step back, and nearly tumbled over the edge. With a hop-step sideways, I landed flush against the brick.

"You'll be splendid. Machiavel in a whitework cap." She smiled at me, reaching for the ribbons of said cap.

"You needn't shore up my confidence," I said unsteadily.

"I just want to touch your hair, Euphemia."

I didn't really believe her, but I let her unplait my thin brown hair. It was not much to look at, but I knew it was silky to the touch, and after all, the roof was dark. She ran her fingers through it and oh, I mewled like a cat. My head felt light; the breeze tickled my scalp and sent my hair into my eyes.

She pushed my wrap from my shoulders. At the top of the house, there was nothing to break the wind. It whipped at my shoulders and neck and hair. In a minute, I would be numb. I kicked off my slippers and went up on my bare toes, dizzy, floating.

Jael took a fistful of my nightdress, halfway down my thighs, and pulled the linen taut over my mound. A sharp fold sank between my nether lips.

It was perverse, to do this now. But I shut my eyes and tilted up my hips.

"Good girl," she encouraged me. I decided to take the bribe.

I tormented myself, slowly, half an inch up and half an inch down, clamping my muscles to heighten the sensation. She undid the button at my collar, to let the wind paw at my bared breasts with cold, greedy hands.

"Don't touch them," I gasped. "Don't do anything. Just this."

"Can I touch them after you spend?"

I nodded tightly.

I don't know how long it took—long enough for her to switch hands, rubbing at her sore shoulder. I didn't care. So much agony in the world, but this one was in my power, this one I wanted.

Even that small power was finite, and ended before I wished. I struggled, and was shoved into the abyss of pleasure.

Next I knew, I was curled on the stone floor of the parapet, trying to stretch my burning legs.

"Are you falling asleep?" she demanded, laughing.

I shrugged, eyelids heavy. "Maybe. You can take your pleasure."

"I'm not a husband," she said, affronted. "I'm not taking my conjugal rights."

I frowned and slid my hands round her waist, pulling her into my lap. I was a little amazed at my daring—though why that should take daring, I didn't quite know. Everything was cold and she was warm, and for once I went towards the flame and not away. "I want you to. I'm just tired."

"I don't think my knees can take this floor. Let's go inside."

So we were snug in my bed, Jael in my arms, when I heard Sir Kit's step on the back staircase that led to the roof.

I shoved her away from me with a curse.

Even in the dim light, I could see the moment she heard him too. She blanched, her hair seeming darker by the stark contrast. I should never have trusted her signal.

"Not afraid of him?" I murmured unkindly. "Under the bed, quick!"

Weaving a little, I forced myself to my feet. If he found her—oh, and I had let her take off my cap…

By now he was in the passageway, and must have seen the light under my door. Probably he'd heard sounds within. I had no chance of feigning sleep.

My eyes frantically searched the room for signs of Jael's presence. Sir Kit had scratched thrice before I found the nerve to snatch up the book she had brought with her, and open the door with a show of tying my wrapper shut, as though that were the cause of my delay.

He was still fully dressed. I cursed Jael with all my heart, for he had plainly never been to bed at all. She must have grown impatient and signaled regardless.

"Sir Kit, really!" I hoped he thought my breathlessness was flirtation. If Lady Palethorp sneezed—if he discovered her— "Can't a bluestocking stay up late studying the modern languages without being pestered by men?"

"Perhaps they have need of her civilizing moral influence. *I've* been staying up late playing billiards, like one of the brute creation." He looked at the volume in my hand with every show of interest. "What are you reading?"

I was too terribly aware of Jael, a few feet away, to think of an excuse. I dropped my gaze as I handed him the book, and remembered despairingly that my feet were bare.

He laughed softly. "So much for a moral influence! Well, I'm not such a hypocrite as to condemn you for reading a book from my own library. He's a fine writer, is he not? He says much with little. The scene of the poor convent girl's ruin, for example."

I went entirely cold, for the villain had contrived to take the girl's virtue by possessing himself of a key to her room. "Indeed," I said with an unwise sharpness. "I felt for her most extremely. To have trusted in a gentleman, to have looked to his honor for protection, and found he had none—"

He gave me back the book, and held up his hands in surrender. "I'm not going to hurt you," he said a little sadly. "I was on my way to the roof. Would you like to join me? Stargazing might overexcite the sensibilities of a more susceptible female, but I think *you* will be quite safe."

I didn't want to go. I was afraid of what might happen—of what he might do, and still more of what I might accidentally reveal. But every rustle and creak in the old house seemed to emanate from beneath my bed. "Scientists promote the notion that their work is dangerous to the female imagination in order to make themselves interesting," I said primly.

Damn her, she snickered!

He was laughing too, and didn't seem to hear it, but after that I did not even want to delay to put on my cap or find my slippers. I tried to brush past him into the passage—but at the last moment, I couldn't bring myself to come so close to his oil lamp.

He saw it, and courteously moved aside. "You had better lock it," he said as I pulled the door shut, and held his lamp where it would light the lock without coming near to me, as though he thought only of my comfort.

How can I describe the anger that rose in me? Can I even justify it? As far as he knew, it made no difference: the door to the nursery was locked, and if I screamed at this very moment, there was no one who could reach us.

But I had given his fears so much tender sympathy, had imagined they were a bond between us. *I* had never used my fear to persecute others. He was afraid of men who came in the night and took what was not theirs, because he *was* one.

I had *never* wanted to burn anyone—had avoided even lighting a candle to read by. When I killed him, it would be because he had left me no choice. He had made his again and again.

Go ahead and ravish me, I thought. *It won't save you.*

"Yes, sir." I whispered it, so he would not hear my thoughts in my voice. I turned the key, ignoring the gleam in his eye, and followed him up the narrow stairs as though I climbed to the gallows.

He left his lamp on the stairs. The stars were bright, the moon a sliver. The last new moon I would ever see without blood on my hands. The last Sir Kit would ever see in life.

He turned away, leaning on the edge of the little roof—the side with the long drop, for it had the view of the sea. The weather had been fair for weeks, but at the horizon the stars were blotted out by gathering clouds, perhaps heavy ones. "What does your and Tabby's little book say? Will it rain before we bring in the last of the corn?"

I wanted to ask how much longer he thought that would be, and did not dare. "It depends on the wind, I think."

"This is the best harvest we've had in years. And what's better is that the northern counties are having a bad one, so the price will be high this winter. But if it all rots in the barns…"

What if I did it now? One neat push, with conviction— I drew a little nearer, eyeing the precipice.

It was not a scruple that stopped me. It was not even fear of falling myself. No, I was afraid of the blind scramble at the edge, afraid of Sir Kit's hands reaching vise-like from the darkness: the same unreasoning physical horror I might feel when a bat tangled in my hair. I felt myself soft and weak, without even the boned armor of my stays.

Then I remembered with a sick relief that Jael was not in her room— that if there was an accident, that fact might somehow become known, and she would be suspected.

Settling against the parapet, I replied to Sir Kit's queries about my week, and Tabby's. Within a few minutes, I had nearly ceased to think of my fear that he would discover his wife. I very nearly enjoyed the conversation.

I had imagined it his own peculiar charm that made me forget over and over that I had meant to dislike him. But I had wounded his feelings too, and he had passed it over. I thought of the maids who could be kind to me, yet leave Jael's basin dusty and dry and her sheets rank.

Perhaps it was a taint in human nature itself, some essential elasticity of mind. English gentlefolk gave it different names in different people, of course: *they* were well-mannered, while servants were two-faced, Italians subtle, and Jews inscrutable. But it all came to this: we set the truth aside when it suited us, as much by instinct as by calculation.

At last he led me again to my bedroom door. I was torn between wanting to shut the door between him and me as soon as I could, and wanting to keep the door shut between him and my bed—not to mention him and his wife. "Sir, you had better—"

He cupped the nape of my neck.

Not yet, I thought, stunned fear freezing my joints. *Not yet, I must hold him off until Harvest-home.* But I could not move.

He brushed our lips together. "Good night, Miss Oliver. Thank you for being my friend."

He let me go. But my grandmother's hand lingered on my shoulder as he walked away, and as I heard his footsteps retreating down the stairs.

I couldn't quite picture vó's face anymore. But my body would always remember that her index finger was weak, while her middle fingertip and the second joint of her ring finger dug in sharply.

I laid my hand atop hers on my shoulder, and squeezed. "Obrigada pelo seu conselho, vó," I whispered. *Thanks for the advice.* "I miss you."

When I did open my door, I was glad I had waited, for Jael was snoring faintly.

I gritted my teeth and looked under the bed. Her head was pillowed awkwardly on my coil of rope. Some of her tangled, straggling curls were in her eyes, and some were pinned between her body and the wall, visibly pulling at her scalp. She snored again—and the sound cut off abruptly as she seemed to gasp and hold her breath, afraid even in sleep. Her pulse fluttered in her neck.

I sighed, my irritation fading a little, and poked her shoulder.

She started up in dismay, cracking her head against a bed slat. "Ow! I don't know what's wrong with me, I slept all day."

I shrugged and held out my hand to help heave her to her feet, having given up (somewhere after the twentieth time she made this remark) on pointing out that she got no exercise, and that her slumber was plainly neither deep nor peaceful.

The imprint of the rope on her neck made me shudder.

"We ought to talk our plan through once more," I said. "Harvest-home can't be far off. Since you insist on signaling me when Sir Kit is awake, there is too much to be lost and too little to be gained by more meetings before then."

Her jaw set mulishly; her hard look, full of stifled recrimination, must have been the mirror of my own. But when I tried to shape soft words, my lips twitched, as if to shake off the memory of Sir Kit's kiss. I pressed my knuckles to my mouth to keep it still.

We should not talk of this here, but where could we go? It was not safe to leave my room until we were sure Sir Kit was in bed. He might return to the roof, and her room was closer to his.

I dragged out the extra blankets I had not used in months and shoved them under each door, listening with my ear to the wood for any sounds of stirring. I shoved tissue-paper in the keyholes, and we huddled in my bed and went over the plan again, in whispers.

We would wait together in his room for him to return from Harvesthome; if he was not drunk enough, I would ply him with more liquor; she would remain hidden until he was in his bed; we would smother him and set the bed on fire.

"We must take his keys," I said shakily. "Without them, we can't get out of the house, or reach the servants' wing to rouse them. I can only open the shutters and interior doors in this one tower."

She stared at me. "Rouse the servants? Are you mad? There are several nearby villages smaller than Goldengrove! They've nothing to fear all the way at the far corner of the house, and if they do, Mrs. Cross can let them out when she wakes. We'll have to break ourselves out. Just hide Kit's keyring somewhere in his room where he might plausibly have dropped it."

"Her room may be far off, but it's still the nearest of any of the servants', and will be the first to fill with smoke, if the fire does spread in that direction," I argued. "What if she doesn't wake?"

My blood ran cold at the thought of all those children—for so half the servants seemed to me—trapped in their rooms, screaming and pounding at the doors, smelling the smoke, with no help coming.

I disliked Mrs. Cross. I liked only a handful of the servants, really, and trusted none of them. But I was not a Christian, and did not believe that people I disliked deserved to burn. Sir Kit was a question of necessity, not *desert*.

"They've never let *me* out," she said cynically. "They must take their chances. You can run round the house and shout at their windows if you like, once we're out. If we use his keys, it will never pass as an accident. Why should he have given them to you, and then gone alone to bed?"

"I could say I smelled the fire and went to his room, but could not wake him—"

She snorted. "So you took his keys and left him to die?"

I thought this would be quite reasonable behavior, and I gave Sir Kit enough credit to think it what he himself would wish, since his daughter slept above him. But Mrs. Cross was unlikely to agree. "Then how do you propose we escape the house?" I asked.

For a moment I was all out of patience with her, that she did not know her own home—and then I remembered the injustice of it, when she had been two years a prisoner, and when I had gone over this exact eventuality a thousand times in my mind before ever I dreamed *I* would be the cause of the fire. "The keep's ground floor has only those impassable arrow slits, remember? The lowest windows I can open are Sir Kit's own, and we cannot use them. I could say he gave me his key-ring to lock up with, because he was too drunk to do it himself."

"Does that seem likely to you?"

"It does not seem *impossible*," I hedged. "Or I could say that I was afraid of a fire, and begged him for them."

"And they won't think it strange, that you were afraid of a fire on the very night one erupted?"

"I am afraid of a fire every night!" I flashed in a furious undertone. "If you have truly not remarked that I am terrified of fires, then you are the only one in the household. They all know I am quite mad on the subject." I dug my fingertips into my aching forehead. "Drunk people do leave candles burning."

She blinked. "You are? Oh…I suppose you are. That explains a great deal. You poor thing, and I threatened to burn you up! Is *that* why Kit gave you that key? I thought it was so you could—" She coughed with belated and superfluous tact. "With that rope under your bed, we can easily climb down from the chapel balcony. One of my windows opens onto it."

"You're going to easily climb down a rope? You couldn't even pull yourself up to sit on the parapet." I was not in the least confident that *any* of us could do it. In my private plans, I had generally sent Clarice down the rope first to catch Tabby, as the youngest and strongest adult. In this scenario, she would also be the least guilty.

"Why on earth do you have a rope under your bed, by the way?"

"Because I am *terrified of fires*."

She yawned again, eyes drifting shut.

"Go to sleep," I said evenly, fetching a chair for myself. Jael slumped readily down and snuggled into my pillow. "I will wake you when it is time to go downstairs." I would have to vigil until very early myself, to be sure of neither meeting Sir Kit in the night, nor the servants in the morning.

She shook her head. "Entirely too virtuous. I don't trust you..." She was already asleep, the rope-mark fading on her neck.

If she hanged...if we both hanged...if Tabby and Clarice made it to the ground, but Jael and I did not...if Mrs. Cross did not wake, and the servants burned...

At least if Jael fell, Tabby would have her money to live on. But who would raise her, if the whole rest of the household perished but Clarice?

I pictured myself trapped on a rooftop, trying to help someone who outweighed me by several stone climb down a rope in the dark.

Again that choked-off snore. Jael held her breath in her sleep, with a frightened whining sound.

We needed Sir Kit's keys. Then we could walk out the door, easy as anything. We could wake the house.

There was no help for it. I would have to find it in myself to set a fire. I would do it without her help, and I would take the keys.

I did think of going together, and then defying her. But I tried to imagine myself, in the middle of a blazing house-fire, desperate to get out, having the energy and will to disobey her if she commanded, *Leave the keys there and come with me.* I couldn't.

I tried to go over the plan again. On my own, unless Sir Kit was *very* drunk, I wasn't strong enough to smother him first. I might try to strangle him—with a guitar string, or piano wire—but if he *woke*—

I could not keep it all straight in my mind. As soon as I went down one path, one eventuality, I forgot the last. What would I tell Clarice? If anyone suspected the truth, it would be her.

All the more reason to save her friends.

Once I sat at my desk and set pencil to paper—but I could not bring myself to write.

I would set the fire. I would lock Sir Kit in. I would hope he did not wake. Those were the chief points.

His wife slept on in my bed until one candle had burned down, and half of another, before I judged it safe to return her to her room.

The clouds stayed over the sea. A fire caught in one of Mr. Abbott's haymows, but was extinguished in time to save the crop. No one would admit to starting it, and perhaps no one had: in this dry, baking heat, fires started on their own.

Jael signaled that night. I did not go down.

On the second night, she signaled again—for an hour, at ten-minute intervals. I could hear Tabby wake, in her little bed. "It isn't safe tonight," I whispered. "I'm sorry." Tabby didn't answer.

On the third night, I sat up—but I remembered Sir Kit's hand on the back of my neck, and stayed on my sofa. She knocked again, harder. I buried my face in my pillow and put my hands over my ears.

Something smashed against the floor between us. I told myself the shattering sound was too dull to be glass, and hoped she had not got pottery shards in her hair.

More thuds, and a sound like furniture overturning. Then she began shouting.

Her voice was thick and so were the floor beams; it took me half a minute to realize she was speaking Portuguese. Even then, I made out one word in ten—and a few insults my mother had refused to translate.

By now I could not go down even had I wished to, for she must have woken Sir Kit. Rubbing my temples, I lit my lantern and went to Tabby, who was certainly awake by now.

For once I didn't step on Adeline, for she was already clutched in the little girl's arms. I wedged myself into the royal little bed, moving Tabby's sad box of treasures aside and pulling her into my lap.

"It's all right." I hesitated, then followed the lie with truth, hoping I wouldn't regret it. "Your mama is angry at me for not letting her come up and see us, only I didn't think it safe tonight—" I broke off abruptly, for I had heard Sir Kit's voice.

So did Tabby, and went rigid—*more* rigid in my lap. But when I covered her ears, she pushed my hands violently away. I could not bring myself to fight her—and it would keep *me* from hearing what went on below.

Clarice crept out of her room and knelt on the floor, trying to stroke Tabby's hair. Tabby pushed her away too. "I'm listening!"

We were all listening.

"*STOP!*" Sir Kit roared.

I nearly went down. Perhaps I could coax him away. But if Jael said something that betrayed our acquaintance... *Stop*, I echoed silently. *Please stop.*

She didn't stop.

"I won't have you frightening Tabby and harassing the governess," he told her.

"That's rich, Kit! *I*, harassing the governess? When she's too afraid of *you* to sleep in her own bed? Why can't you keep your damn hands to yourself—don't touch me! Don't—" She shrieked.

Her voice cut off abruptly, like a muted note.

29

Tabby's fingers dug painfully into my side. Her eyes were wide and white. I wavered, braced myself to stand, changed my mind, changed it again—

The door slammed below, and I heard Sir Kit's footsteps storming off. I did not breathe, listening.

Jael made a wracking sob.

I let all my breath out in a great whoosh. She was alive. She was conscious, even.

There was another crash—only one; and another sob—many more.

I did not dare go to her. Instead, I fetched her guitar and sang to Tabby, drowning out her sounds of distress. I did not understand how my fingers and voice could obey me, when I heard that cut-off scream every time I muted a quivering string.

I sang the Cherry Tree Carol, a favorite with Tabby, and realized too late that it was about a quarrel in the Holy Family.

The sobs faded sooner than I had expected. Had he dosed her with laudanum?

I thought of Jael's blood on the strings. I would lick Sir Kit's blood from my fingers like syrup, before he touched her one more time.

Sir Kit came into the library as we read the barometer, which had not dropped below thirty all week. "Good morning, Tabby-kitten." He tugged her braid.

"Good morning, Papa," she said politely.

I expected him to pretend nothing had happened, but he surprised me. Crouching down to look her in the eye, he said, "I'm afraid your Mama and

I fought like Kilkenny cats last night. I hope we didn't wake you."

Tabby hesitated. "What's a Kilkenny cat?"

He laughed, and carried her over his shoulder to one of the great library tables. "Well, I believe Kilkenny must be a place in Ireland. Shall we see if it's on the map?" He pulled out an atlas. "The origin of the expression is a joke, not about the ferocity of cats, but about the simplicity of Irishmen…"

Carriage wheels crunched on the drive. Tabby flew to the open window, scrambling up onto the seat. I was close behind her—half because I still didn't trust her with windows, half curious myself.

The carriage's door was already open, hiding the crest, and an enormous pink hat hid the face of its occupant. But the tiger wore Tassell green and gold.

I felt a thrill of apprehension. If Iphigenia had written to her—if the countess had seen my letter—if she *showed* it to Sir Kit…

"That's a wonderful hat," Tabby breathed.

Sir Kit peered over my shoulder, throwing me a reproachful, laughing glance when I stepped away. "You and your mother think entirely too much of hats, poppet."

"It's pretty!"

He flicked a finger at her braids. "Your hair is pretty. I'll be sorry when you put on caps."

Tabby, little brows lowering, launched into a description of the splendid caps she would wear.

"That does sound splendid," Sir Kit interrupted as one of his footmen entered. "Yes, Mark, so I see. I had no more notion of her coming than any of you." Was it my imagination that his sharp eyes rested briefly on me? "Convey my sincerest apologies to Mrs. Cross and Mrs. Bishop, but could they contrive something nice for tea?"

He turned back to his daughter with a long-suffering sigh. "I suppose nothing will do but to see the countess's *ensemble* up close," he said with an affected French flourish. Tabby giggled. "Her ladyship is tired from traveling. If you pester her, I'll have the footman carry you from the room."

"I must put on my best dress," Tabby said, endeavoring to tug me bodily from the room myself.

"Miss Oliver," Sir Kit called lightly. "If you neglected to mention her ladyship's intention to visit, Mrs. Bishop will never forgive you."

"I have received no letters from the countess in some weeks." That is, unless he had intercepted them. I watched his face closely, and saw nothing out of the ordinary in it.

We were nearly to the door when he called after me again, "How do I look, Miss Oliver? Ought I to comb my hair before my audience with her ladyship?" He made a show of anxiously straightening his cravat.

I was already laughing when a memory of combing Jael's tangled hair killed my mirth—but I kept laughing after. This sensation was becoming familiar, though never less jarring: my thoughts out of time with my actions, my body dancing by rote while my mind lost the tune. "Perhaps you ought to change into your court dress, sir."

"Put on your blue waistcoat, Papa. The *sky* blue. It will match my ribbons."

I don't know if Tabby was influenced by her father's jokes or the countess's title, but she made a grander toilette than she ever had for the neighbors, of all her favorite things at once. She only agreed to forego hat and gloves when I explained that a hostess in gloves was a sign she was going out and wished to hurry her guests on their way.

The effect was silly and charming. I hated that Jael couldn't see her, and cast wistful glances at the thick oak door as we passed on our way to the parlor.

Sir Kit had obediently donned the sky-blue waistcoat, though the change exposed several inches of crushed cravat, and must have even dropped a word in Lady Tassell's ear, for she exclaimed at once, "Oh, how sweet, you match your Papa!"

I dragged my eyes away from Sir Kit to watch for my own cue to curtsy—and met Lady Tassell's shrewd gaze. Flushing, I dropped my correct obeisance with a correct murmur.

"I do very well, my dear, thank you," Lady Tassell replied. "That is, I've been ill, but I'm mending. The sea air will put me to rights in no time."

"You really had better stay the night, my lady," Sir Kit said, with the air of one resuming an interrupted argument. "Why drive another three miles on narrow, hilly roads, when you might have a good dinner and a good night's sleep here, and be on your way after breakfast with rested horses?"

I was relieved to see that the countess had no intention of agreeing. "You are very kind, sir, but I sent word ahead to ready the house for today. The Toogoods will never forgive me if I don't eat the fatted calf fresh from the spit."

I thought that must be Sukey's mother- and father-in-law, unless there were relatives I'd forgotten; John Toogood's fall from grace had left him the only member of his family *not* in faithful lifelong service to the Tassells.

Her ladyship and Sir Kit went on being cordial at each other while Tabby drank in her fashionable appearance. I sat quietly in the corner, prey to the same kind of morbid premonition I'd felt at that long-ago breakfast at the boarding house, watching the gruel dribble from my spoon.

Even if we got clean away, I would still be the governess, and sit faithfully in a corner while Jael and Tabby entertained.

I reminded myself that I did not believe in premonitions—that I was *not* at Mrs. Humphrey's any longer. But when Sir Kit said, "Well, kitten, you have shirked lessons long enough. You may take her out, Miss Oliver," I rose with intense relief, and was glad when the nursery door was shut upon us.

I knew it would be at least an hour before Tabby would be able to sit still for book learning, but a lesson in serving tea was enthusiastically agreed to. I brought out her little creamware set only rarely, and as a result, Tabby retained for its painted flowers and gilded handles the reverence due a holy mystery, and had refrained from smashing it to bits in a temper.

"Would you care for weak tea or strong tea?" she was reciting earnestly, when Peter came to inform me that Lady Tassell wished to speak with me again.

I cursed the countess in my heart, but I rose with a show of calm. "I shall put your tea set in my room for safekeeping. I'll bring some ginger beer back with me, so you can practice filling the cups."

For once my bribe had the intended effect, and Tabby only grumbled a little as I locked the tea tray in my room. "Ask if she liked my dress."

"She already told you that she did," I reminded her.

She favored me with a look of pitying scorn. "Maybe she was only being polite."

When Sir Kit saw me hovering in the doorway, he broke off a question on whether Parliament might permit the distillers to use wheat this winter, and rose from his chair. I thought it only manners, but he remained on his feet even after I sat at Lady Tassell's invitation.

"Thank you, Palethorp," she told him. "I shall send you my compliments when I go."

"Your ladyship really ought to let me wait and escort you to your carriage. You said yourself you've been ill."

"In the middle of harvest?" Lady Tassell flapped a hand at him. "I've wasted enough of your time already. Yes, yes, you've been very good-natured about it, but you must be dying to get to the home farm."

There was a long pause as Sir Kit sought for a way to deny it without looking idle. Then he grinned at her. "I don't think you've ever wasted a moment in your life, my lady. The men won't ruin the corn in the next quarter of an hour."

"Sir, surely you are aware there are subjects women hesitate to discuss in the presence of men?"

"Oh, I don't…" I protested. If Sir Kit had suspected me of secret dealings with the countess earlier, what must he think now?

"Far too many of them," he said readily.

"Well, I agree with you there." Lady Tassell eyed him. "Is there some reason you don't wish to leave?"

I froze, a squirrel once more caught between two snakes. I wished they would devour each other, and let me go.

"Yes! I wish to offer you my arm back to your carriage, so you don't trip over all that muslin and break your neck on my antiquated stairs."

"Very tactful—rather than calling me old, you insult my dress." She gave him a droll, very motherly look. "You're dismissed, Palethorp."

I went stiller yet, with a confused, apologetic glance at Sir Kit. But after a fraught moment, he let out one of his appreciative barks of laughter and bowed over her hand.

He turned to me and, with a slight hesitation I hoped Lady Tassell did not remark, thought better of bowing over mine, giving me an affable nod instead.

When the door was shut, the countess patted the empty sofa cushion between us. "Sit closer, child. How do you do?"

I changed my seat reluctantly. "Well, my lady, thank you."

She tilted up my chin. "Not with those circles under your eyes," she said quietly.

I stiffened.

"Go and see if he's listening at the door."

Seeing no alternative, I cracked the door. "Oh, Luke, I beg your pardon. Her ladyship wanted…"

"Some water to wash my hands," she said promptly. "Thank you, dear. And could Mrs. Bishop spare a little rosewater for my eyes? The weather's so dry, I think half the road is ascending to Heaven."

Luke went unwillingly, with more than one backward glance. But he went.

Lady Tassell smiled at me and patted the cushion again. "Hurry, child. What is the matter?"

Tears pricked at my eyes as I took my seat. *A month ago, I would have been so glad to see you.* "Nothing, my lady. I don't sleep well in the heat, that's all. Thank you for helping me to my place."

She huffed. "Don't remind me of my culpability. Spit it out. I'll help you."

I hesitated—of course I did. But my decision had been made, and made, and made. "I don't know what you mean, my lady. Did something in my last letter worry you?"

She frowned. "No," she said, rather accusingly. "You told me nothing at all. Iphigenia Lemmon wrote to me."

I suspected my confused blink was unconvincing. "About me, my lady? Whatever for?"

"Enough." She clasped her hands around her knee, leaning in. "How is Lady Palethorp's health?"

"I—I scarcely know, my lady. I never see her."

Her frown deepened. "Do you think it, perhaps, better than is generally believed?"

She understood! The temptation to pour out the whole story nearly overpowered me. But Jael had expressly forbidden it. *The best lawyer in the world wouldn't get me Tabby.* I shook my head mutely.

"Do you think yourself in any danger?"

My heart raced. "My lady, I don't understand."

"Miss Lemmon said you were afraid of inheriting your grandmother's trouble with her hands." She took my hand in both of hers. "My dear, she said your grandmother—she said a young man was unkind to her?"

"My grandmother had arthritis, my lady." But I longed to know what exactly Iffy had said.

"And your hands have been bothering you?"

"A little." I rubbed at my palm with the opposite thumb. Then I thought of Lady Macbeth, and stopped. "In the mornings."

"So do mine. Try camphor liniment." She sat back with a sigh. "I can't help you if you won't let me, Miss Oliver. But if you will, I promise you that I can."

The door-handle turned. I started violently, and wished very much I had not.

Luke arranged a half-full basin, a vial of rosewater, and a neat stack of towels on the table. Lady Tassell smiled at him as she poured the rosewater into the basin. "Thank you, that will be all."

The door shut as she wet her handkerchief. I waited for her to lay it over her own eyes, but instead she tilted up my chin again and wiped mine—first the lid, gently, and then the skin beneath.

My tears rose at the simple, motherly gesture. But this had been my downfall from the start: I could not resist a kind look, a soft chair, a little white bread. *She is not your friend.*

"There's talk about you and Sir Kit." She bathed my other eye. "If it's only talk, never mind it. After all, you may bound over many decorous prejudices following the path of virtue, as Mrs. Godwin says. But he's an extraordinarily prepossessing young man despite that unfortunate forehead. And chin. And…" She shrugged. "In short, he's entirely too prepossessing to be trusted. If you are so much as *tempted*, I shall carry you away with me this instant and find you another place."

God forgive me, I nearly went.

It would take only a small lie, scarcely a lie at all. *Oh, my lady, I do think him handsome, and he—he has said…*, and I would sleep at the Tassells' lodge tonight, snug and sound.

Lady Tassell had said *the path of virtue*, omitting *truth*. As she flicked rose-scented water from her fingers, I could quite imagine her saying with Pontius Pilate, *What is truth?* Yet she had not washed her hands of me; she waited for my answer. And I longed to give her one.

The truth shall make you free, Papa used to tell me. Hypocrite that I was, I'd given Tabby more or less the same advice.

But if I had told my teachers that Iphigenia and I were lovers, I would have been expelled. If I had told my father I was an atheist, I'd have broken his heart. If I had told Sir Kit my mother was a Jewess, I would have been shown the door.

Mrs. Godwin had not been honest, either. It had been her husband who told the world of her married lovers and her attempts at self-violence, when she was dead and could not object. Now only impudent young men and stubborn older women dared to quote her in polite society.

My grandmother had told the truth, and her family had burned.

If I told Lady Tassell the truth, I could not even guess at the consequences. I leaned in. "Please don't repeat this to Sir Kit."

Her fingers tightened on her damp towel. "Upon my honor, child."

"I could not love a man so short."

Lady Tassell let out a startled, dubious laugh. "Truthfully?"

Truthfully, I had rather liked that Sir Kit was short—out of, I think, some obscure feeling that he would be safer. Well, I knew my mistake now. I smiled at the countess. "If you call me a liar, I shall be obliged to demand satisfaction."

"Please don't, dear, I want to sleep in tomorrow."

We giggled together at the folly of men and their decorously bloodthirsty prejudices, and she asked if I thought Tabby would like her sons' old badminton set from the lodge.

"For they don't want it anymore." Her voice grew husky. "Forgive me, I think some of that damned dust has got in my eye after all. And have some cake, you're turning into a shadow."

Sir Kit called me into his study when she was gone. Another interrogation—but strangely I feared this one less. "I'm sorry I left you alone with her. But you saw I couldn't get out of it. I hope she didn't upset you."

"I owe Lady Tassell a great deal," I said mildly. "She helped me to my present place."

Hope flared in his eyes. "I owe her a great deal, too. But I'd like to think she's unaware quite how much."

"She said there was gossip about us," I confessed, chewing at my lip. "Maybe she's right that I ought to go away. For Tabby's sake. If people really think you're keeping your mistress in your own home…"

Sir Kit's jaw set obstinately, as I'd expected. "I won't live my life to please Mrs. Abbott. If she thinks it *respectable* that Mr. Abbott pays the household expenses of a Rye fishwife because he's home in time for dinner, that's her affair."

"Surely it is Mr. Abbott's affair," I said demurely, to make him laugh. But the revelation unsettled me; I was sorry for the sailor's wife. Such arrangements were common enough, for children had to eat while sailors and deep-sea fishermen waited to be paid at voyage's end. In Portsmouth I used to look after our neighbor's baby while her merchant was visiting. Her eyes were always red when she came to fetch him, dropping the penny in my hand as if it burned her fingers.

Sir Kit put his hand over mine. My fingers twitched.

"What I mean is," he said quietly, "that's sordid, and this isn't."

"Perhaps Mr. Abbott doesn't think that's sordid, either." I didn't expect him to understand the edge in my voice.

Sure enough, he said promptly, "Very well, we shall be sentimental. Mrs. Jack Tar has a beautiful soul, and Mr. Abbott kisses the Rye sidewalk after she passes, not minding the taste of fish. Why not?"

My mother was a costermonger, I wanted to spit at him. *That* would end his pursuit and my employment, where my repeated rebuffs had not.

"I had better go, sir. I'm teaching Tabby to pour tea."

"That reminds me. Tomorrow we'll cut the last of the corn."

I froze. Had he really said tomorrow? I had thought I had days before I reached the Rubicon—maybe weeks, if the weather changed—

"There's a ceremony to carting it to the barn—known colloquially, if you can believe, as the Hollerin' Pot. And then next day is Harvest-home. The men will toast the master and dame, so I'd like you to bring Tabby."

30

The day after tomorrow—and he expected me to be there? I hadn't expected to actually *attend* the Harvest-home. "I don't know if a scene of public drunkenness is the place for a gently reared girl."

"Pooh, Tabby will love being fussed over, and Clarice may take her away very early."

I, then, was to stay?

Mixed with my distress was a surprisingly sharp indignation. The head of the Harvest-home table was Jael's place, her *right*, and he handed it to me as cavalierly as the delicate chain around my neck. She was the Dame of Goldengrove, not I, and what's more, she would be *better* at it!

I faltered, thinking of the neighbor ladies' sniping. Perhaps her graces of manner or winning smiles wouldn't matter to the men either; perhaps what would be affable in an Englishwoman was brassy in Jael. "Did your wife ever preside over a Harvest-home?"

He grimaced remorsefully. "I ought to have watched over her better. I'm afraid she got quite drunk."

I hoped he could not see my smile for the fondness it was. "Isn't that the purpose of the evening?"

"Yes, only I was too drunk myself to carry her home! Just between you and me"—he felt his own bicep with a mournful expression—"I'm not sure I could have managed it sober." He looked my narrow figure up and down. "*You* may get as drunk as you like."

"Thank you kindly. But if I may do as I like, I shall leave with the nursery party." I cleared my throat. "Perhaps…perhaps after Harvest-home… How late will *you* stay?"

"Oh, not too late." His eyes sharpened already. "It's good manners for the farmer to leave early, and let the men kick over the traces."

Everything depended on my next few speeches. I was desperate to have it over with, and yet I could not help asking, "Will anyone make sure the lanterns don't get kicked over as well?"

He smiled at me. "Yes."

"Then perhaps..." I took a deep breath. "When you return, we might toast the harvest here, where two flights of stairs is the farthest anyone might be obliged to carry me."

His eyes searched my face. "In the library, do you mean?"

I swallowed hard. "I had thought...perhaps..."

"Yes?"

"In your room," I whispered. My face flamed.

He leaned so far across his desk I thought he would overturn the inkwell at last, his voice low and intent. "Don't say it unless you mean it."

"I do, if—if you will send your valet away. I don't wish him to see me intoxicated. I don't wish him to see me at all, or to know..."

"Of course," he said at once. "You have my word. I'll fetch the champagne from the cellar with my own two hands." His eyes shone with happiness, and in two days he would be—

I asked his leave to go. I scarce knew what I said, and he could not have made much of it either. But he came round his desk and looked into my troubled face. "'They that sow in tears shall reap in joy,'" he said solemnly, and kissed my hands.

I was halfway up the stair—I was passing her door—before I could quite remember that he had sown this unhappy crop with the same two hands whose warm pressure I still felt on mine. It had sprung up rank and thick; I could let it go to seed, or I could reap it, and plant fresh.

Too late, I realized I should have said I would prefer brandy to champagne. Champagne didn't burn well.

The morning of the Hollerin' Pot, the wind was still in the west, and the barometer needle steady. I helped Tabby dress in all her best things once again. "Today I can wear my gloves and my hat *and* carry my parasol!" she said triumphantly.

I put on the plainer of my dresses, and my simplest linen. I wanted to look like a governess.

The nursery party descended the stairs. On Jael's landing, I paused.

It was folly, so close to the end, to risk so much for so little. I had been so firm on that point with Jael, that to be rash myself would be close to losing a quarrel.

But Sir Kit was at the home farm, and most of the servants had already trooped off in their Sunday best, for *this*, not Easter or Christmas, was the greatest holiday of the rural calendar. "Wait at the foot of the stairs," I said to Clarice, "and don't let anyone up. It will only be a moment."

Clarice raised her eyebrows. "Ma'am, I don't know…" But she glanced at Tabby, and her face softened. "Well, I suppose any mama would like to see her little girl so fine. But only a moment, or we'll all regret it, and that's smack."

I regretted it already. "Wait here a moment, Tabby. I must see if your mama is at home to callers."

It was like stepping into an oven—a foul-smelling one. What had I been thinking of? Jael sat stark naked on the bed playing cards with her nurse, who was sober for the first time in my recollection. Her unfamiliar lucidity unnerved me now nearly as much as her intoxication had, especially when she narrowed her eyes at me. "You hadn't ought to be in here, madam."

"Pfft, she's my daughter's governess." Jael unfolded herself from the bed, winking at me. "What's to do, Miss O?"

Her hair was plaited for once, baring the rest of her entirely. Very conscious of the nurse, I looked determinedly into her face—and flinched at the deep purple bruise under her left eye, fading across her cheekbone.

I did look at the rest of her, then: another bruise on her shoulder, not so dark. Had he pushed her? I wished I could see her back.

"Good Lord, m'lady, cover yourself." Mrs. Churchill tossed her a shift.

Jael didn't reach out in time. When she bent to retrieve it from the floor, I did see a bruise near her spine, at about the height—I compared it—of the door-handle. "I'm sure it's nothing Miss Oliver hasn't seen before."

I flushed hot.

The nurse gave me a hard look. "I don't rightly know, m'lady, I'd wager that one bathes in her shift so the Lord don't peek. You really hadn't ought to be in here, madam."

Jael straightened with difficulty, the shift crumpled in her fist. "You don't rightly know your arse from—"

"Tabby is outside," I interrupted at last. "She's dressed to the nines to see the last wheat-sheaf go to the barn, and I thought you might like to see her." How would Tabby take that black eye? I should have just slipped out again.

Jael's wide eyes—the right rather wider than the left—darted around the squalid room in dismay. "Of course, I'll—I'll come out onto the landing."

"It's nothing Miss Palethorp hasn't seen before either, I suppose, at the hour of her birth," the nurse remarked.

"Oh!" Jael rushed to her clothespress. "No, this one has to be pinned…" She tugged out a mass of sprigged muslin. "Help me get into it." But there was no hope of it fastening in the back. She tried to laugh. "Sausage isn't easy on a girl's soul *or* her figure." She turned up the corners of her mouth and set her face to the door. But when I opened it, she hesitated a moment too long about crossing the threshold, and Tabby ran into the room.

To my relief, she wiped off her impatient scowl to make her mother an artful little curtsy, and was delighted by Jael's raptures. Even Mrs. Churchill said, "Aren't you the spitting image of your mama? Look at those dimples!"

I held my breath for fear Tabby would protest, but she only said, "Why is it so dark in here? You can't see how shiny my shoe buttons are."

"Those buttons are her pride and joy, my lady," I said to soften the criticism. "Whenever we see a bit of abalone on the beach, she says, 'This is what my shoe buttons are made of.'"

Jael put a hand to her heart, and I realized suddenly that Tabby had copied the gesture from her. "I have something for you, minha filha."

She took up a dish from her dressing table, and tipped out the contents with a clatter. Wiping away the dust with her bedsheet, she handed it to Tabby: a whole abalone shell, polished inside to expose the mother-of-pearl. "I collected seashells when I was younger. Do you think you might like to start?"

Tabby looked around. "Where are your others?"

Jael tapped her chin, smiling. "I believe there is a basket of shellwork flowers I made in the drawing room. Unless it's been moved, anyway. And an antique nautilus chalice in the music room. The rest…I think they broke."

I wondered if Sir Kit had done that—or if she had decided one day that such fragile beauty had no place in this world, and ground them into the carpet of her prison with her own heel.

"We can't stay," I reminded myself more than her. Strange, how my own bias made pasting little shells into the shape of a lily-of-the-valley seem fussy and small-minded in Sir Kit's mother, and adorably painstaking and whimsical in his wife. The muslin was slipping from her shoulder, the tail of her braid tucked into it. She looked hoydenish and dear, and I would a thousand times rather have stripped and played cards on her bed than gone to the Hollerin' Pot.

"Come along, Tabby. We will set your mama's gift here for safekeeping and fetch it later." I had to pry it from her hands. I hoped she would forget it; it seemed mad to risk Sir Kit remarking it in the nursery, now when we stood on the Rubicon's bank. "Your papa is waiting. You know how he worries when we aren't punctual."

That swayed her, and soon we rejoined Clarice and made our way to the home farm. Even the hot summer breeze was a relief after Jael's room.

Tabby bounced with excitement as the bells were put on the horses who were to cart the ceremonial load. A woman offered Tabby an aster with hands scratched raw and bloody from twisting sheaves.

Tabby tossed her flower with much ceremony and little force; it fluttered to the ground several inches shy of the cart. The women and children who had worked the harvest cheered anyway, and commenced throwing their own armfuls until the sheaf was as overdressed as Tabby, blossoms piled at its feet like—*like kindling at the stake*, I thought, and wished the morbid idea away.

There was a toast to Sir Kit, and then a toast to "the little dame." I was relieved to be ignored, and grateful for the invisibility of a plainly dressed plain woman of middle years.

At last the cart jingled away, and we walked slowly back to the house, Tabby wishing she had thought to wear her second-best dress so she might outdo herself tomorrow. We dined in the kitchen and then, at her insistence, went down to the beach to look for seashells.

If I could have stopped thinking of tomorrow, it would have been an idyllic afternoon, trailing behind Tabby with a basket as she studied tiny crab shells and empty barnacles, passing me the chosen specimens. I found a shard of blue and white china in a pretty fish-scale pattern, myself.

I had been finding sea porcelain for as long I could remember. I'd taken its presence on the beach for granted, half imagining, I suppose, that it came from port-town ash heaps, or that sea captains who had dropped a dish tossed the pieces overboard in a temper.

Today it occurred to me sharply that they might come from shipwrecks. Maybe I'd been a wrecker all my life, callously pocketing dead women's treasures and merchants' ruined hopes.

I pocketed the pretty shard anyway.

31

"I think your eyes are bigger than your stomach, Tabby," I said, but after all, it was a festival—and perhaps her last dinner with her father. I tried to set that thought aside, and piled her plate high with whatever took her fancy: rolls, apple slices baked in a buttered pumpkin, cheese, sweet fresh peas and buttered beans, roasted potato and seedcake. Back at the family's high table, I stole a ripe fig from her plate. But I was used to eating them dried or preserved, and their natural state proved a disappointment, watery and not very sweet.

Sir Kit appeared with mugs of fresh beer. "Made with Goldengrove corn and hops! Now, what shall I serve you, Miss Oliver?"

"Oh, I shall dine on what Tabby can't finish." I lowered my voice. "Did you speak to your…?"

"The servants' hall is feasting at home, and my valet snores terribly when drunk," he said. "In point of fact, he snores terribly all the time, but I was at the farm before dawn today and I need my rest. I told him to bunk with Mr. Christie tonight, and not to wait up for me."

I tried to be glad. But I almost wished he had forgotten, so I might have an excuse not to go through with it after all. I lifted my beer.

He shook his head. "Don't drink it 'til you've eaten! And best to wait between pints. One never knows how strong it will be."

But when he had gone to fill his own plate, I gulped some down, letting the ordinary numbness of liquor briefly replace the icy pins and needles of fear.

I had already examined the lights, relieved to see no oil lamps, only candles in glass chimneys on the tables, and punched-tin lanterns in troughs along the walls. It was bright enough to be cheerful, and dim enough to be cozy. The smell of fresh hay wafted from the bunting-swagged lofts, and the trestle tables groaned with food and late-blooming flowers. Cornucopias overflowed with new-picked fruit, and a man and woman played the oboe and fiddle, skilled and lively; there would be dancing after dinner.

It was all very wholesome, very simple and gay, very *English*, a celebration of honest labor and its rewards. For a moment I allowed myself to be charmed, gazing about me with my elbows propped impolitely on the table and my chin in my hands.

Mr. Kirk stopped by the table. "Congratulations on a fine harvest, sir," he said warmly.

Setting down the pear he was slicing for Tabby, Sir Kit wiped his fingers and gave the farm manager a hearty handshake. "I had rather congratulate *you*, as all the credit is yours. Speaking of credit—shall you need to draw on mine to finish out the season?"

Kirk beamed. "I had thought I might after redeeming the hop tokens, but the London brewers can't buy our crop fast enough, and the barley…"

I took my elbows off the table. *Shall you need to draw on my credit?*

I had almost forgotten that Jael's straw hats paid for this too; her blood watered the pear orchards as freely as the manor's hothouses. If the harvest fell short, credit against her income bought next year's seed corn. While the hops dried in the oast houses, her cash redeemed the migrants' hop-tokens. Sir Kit had told me as much: *My heir will be in the hands of the Jews within five years.*

If I succeeded tonight—

Tonight! My gorge rose. In a few hours I would be a murderess, and in a few years there might be no Harvest-home in this barn.

But I made myself choke down some bread. Starving could not save me from eating blood, any more than suffocation could save me from miasma, or frostbite could save me from fire. No doubt children's fingers had bled plaiting straw for those hats, too, while Jael's grandfather grew rich. *We must act, or atrophy…*

I was going to walk with Jael on the seashore while she exercised her legs, and I must learn to tolerate a murder on my conscience, as I tolerated fires in winter.

But I felt sicker and sicker all through dinner. The toasts rushed past in a blur of nausea. I can only remember Sir Kit telling me to lift Tabby up so they all might see the little dame. He pinched my rear out of sight as they toasted, and I nearly dropped her.

I vomited up my supper on the way back to the house. It smelled like yeast and hops. I wished Peter hadn't seen it, and hoped he wouldn't tell Sir Kit; it was not much of a prelude to seduction.

"Why were you sick?" Tabby asked, as I stood shivering and wiping my mouth.

"Mrs. Thomas's beer," Clarice told her. "It's rather a shock, if you haven't grown up on it."

The last of the light bled from the sky as we came up the drive. Mrs. Cross had locked up early; barely eight o'clock and the house was already dark and shuttered. Peter rapped at the porter's door. "Miss Palethorp and Miss Oliver!"

The lock's tumblers had the effect of a gunshot in the still night. I blinked against the light from the opened door.

Mrs. Cross had been taking sherry with the porter's wife. She lit a candle, and led us up to the nursery. We passed through the little room where I had spent my first night in the house, whose paneled shutters had seemed a blank wall. *A premonition*, I thought suddenly.

Had my lifelong terror of fire been a kind of premonition too? Had I been dreaming of tonight all along?

"Might you send up some tea for Miss Oliver, ma'am?" Clarice asked the housekeeper, surprising me. "She's feeling poorly."

"I'm sorry to hear that, madam," Mrs. Cross said without looking at me. "But I'm afraid I've already locked up."

"I could bring it up, ma'am," Peter offered.

"I'm sure you could," Mrs. Cross said, her contemptuous glance at Clarice implying ulterior motives for Peter's generosity. "But I'm afraid it isn't possible tonight. Come along, Peter." She locked us into the nursery with a decisive *click*.

"What crawled up *her* arse?" Clarice said.

Tabby giggled.

"*Clarice.*"

"Begging your pardon, Miss Oliver, I'd ought to have said, what crawled up her posterior? Does she think we didn't notice she's drunk as a sailor?"

In fact, I hadn't.

Clarice sighed. "Everybody's enjoying themselves belowstairs but me."

"Tabby, such expressions about the body are vulgar, and your Papa would not like you to use them," I said, before I remembered there was no point in warning Tabby not to offend her father. I pressed a fist to my stomach. "I think I will lie down. The tea was a kind thought, Clarice, thank you."

She pulled the rest of yesterday's ginger beer from the cupboard. "This'll settle your stomach, ma'am." Following me into my room, she lit my lantern, helped with my stays, and offered to fetch me water-biscuits from her own stores.

On any other day, I would have appreciated this kindness so much. Tonight I felt like screaming. "It's only an upset stomach. Please, I just want to lie down."

She frowned at me. "I dunno, ma'am, you look feverish."

"I merely had a little too much beer."

"So did I, and I hope I don't look like Death."

I'm sure you will look like a blushing English rose when they lay you in the grave. I bit my tongue, praying my spiteful thoughts would not bring Clarice ill luck.

First I fretted over premonitions, and now the evil eye. These were superstitions, fit for Tabby's old nursemaid. I was an educated woman. I was…

I was Death in a whitework cap.

Clarice shrugged and lifted my ewer out of its bowl, setting the basin by my bed next to the ginger beer.

I will pass over your friends, I promised her silently.

"You wake me if you need anything, ma'am. Don't be afraid to shake me, I reckon I'll sleep like the dead tonight."

Thank God she was not looking at my face. "Thank you. Truly."

When she was gone, I curled up on my bed, pressing my forehead hard into my knees. After a while, I realized I was rocking back and forth like a madwoman.

I must calm myself—must dredge up some English self-restraint. In a few hours it would be over. It had to be. My nerves could not bear a second such vigil.

I dragged myself to the mirror. I did look like Death, feverish, my long face bone-pale even in the warm lantern-glow. I could not go down to Sir Kit like this.

I gagged down sips of ginger beer until my sickness receded a little, and wished I had taken the water-biscuits. Then I scrubbed my face and arms and combed my hair, tying it back with a ribbon.

I must wear my nightgown, so I could claim later to have been roused from sleep by the fire. I hoped against hope the fire would not entirely consume the nursery before it was put out. To lose my stays, and all my gowns!

I must reconcile myself to the prospect. Fires climbed, and the ceilings and floors were wood. Yet I opened the clothespress to stroke my burgundy printed cotton, the prettiest thing I owned. It was a dress for cool weather; I had not worn it since Easter.

Why was it the small griefs that woke us in the night and held us fast? I had never seen vó weep for her brother, though she had loved him more than her guitar.

I pinched the soft sprigged cotton between my fingers, and could not let it go. I would have to speak to people tonight. I didn't want to face the magistrate in my shift.

They had stripped vó, to torture her. The man being pressed in the *Newgate Calendar* was half-naked, too. Why? Vó had been so young—Clarice's age. Would they question Clarice? Would they blame her? What if she slept too soundly, and I could not wake her?

It would be so easy for Sir Kit to undress me, in only my nightgown and wrapper. I did not want him to undress me. Maybe he would be too drunk, and fall asleep directly.

I thought of Jael snoring in my bed. *I don't know what's wrong with me, I slept all day.* It was not too late to take her with me, as I had promised, and let her handle the worst of it.

But she would make me leave the ring of keys, and climb from the chapel roof. I was drunk. So was Clarice. I would fall. We would all fall.

Clarice had been kind to me tonight, and she loved Peter, who would soon be locked in his room for the night.

And what if Jael grew impatient, and came out of her hiding place before Sir Kit was asleep? What if *she* fell asleep, and snored? If I went alone, there could be nothing to make him suspect me until the very moment I set the fire.

If I went alone and failed, no one could say *she* had anything to do with it.

I took down my commonplace book and read it through, perhaps for the last time. I lingered over Iphigenia's comedic poem, which opened: *In early youth's unclouded scene / The brilliant morning of eighteen...* Iffy would think I'd gone mad if she knew what I meant to do.

Had I? Perhaps Goldengrove had darkened my senses and deadened my imagination, until I could not see the true path inches from my feet. Or was it Iphigenia whose imagination could not see beyond its narrow circle of light, to encompass the vast darkness of Goldengrove?

I read Mrs. Dymond's poem: *For Mercy has a human heart, Pity a human face, and Love, the human form divine, and Peace, the human dress.*

I had never quite understood the last line. Now, somehow, I did: violence was naked. It concealed nothing; it was not ashamed.

I ran a hand over Papa's peg leg, and mãe's wedding slipper. I held my bits of sea-glass up to the lantern, as Jael had, and dropped them back into my box one by one. I took the cherry bounce from my trunk. Then I tidied my room for the last time.

I stripped to my shift, like a prisoner. I would have left even my wrapper behind—but then I thought, *It will please Sir Kit to finally remove it, and that will help distract him from any strangeness in my manner.*

I blew out the light, and went downstairs to tear off Goldengrove's respectable veil and destroy its peace forever.

32

I tiptoed past the second-floor landing. I couldn't see Jael's door, but I could feel it in the darkness, malevolent and watchful as I had not felt it in weeks.

I checked for light under Sir Kit's door before I unlocked it. It was a modern door like mine, a few sturdy beams around thin, decoratively beveled panels—new and light enough to swing easily inward on its hinges without a sound. Still I could see no light, but I held my breath, afraid his valet would be sitting up in the dressing room after all.

I heard only the clock's ticking and the last few fingers of brandy sloshing in my bottle. Slipping into the room and shutting the door behind me, I shuffled my way over the smooth floorboards—then carpet—until I came up against the bed. I climbed in, cradling my brandy in my lap.

Now I did hear a sound—a very faint one, come and gone. What was it? A droplet of liquid falling, but muffled. Outside, or onto the carpet, I decided. Could it be raining at last?

But no, it was just the one brief *plip*, at odd intervals. A crack in Sir Kit's basin? An overturned bottle? I could smell nothing but strawberries and starch and, very faintly, fresh wheat.

Was it Jael in the room above? Had she heard me, and understood I had not kept to our plan? Was she trying to frighten me?

A moment's reflection showed me the absurdity of that. If Jael wanted to frighten me, she wouldn't limit herself to dripping tea onto the floor. I *was* frightened, though, and freezing, despite knowing the room must be warm. Maybe I did have a fever. Maybe I would be deathly ill by morning.

So much the better; everyone would think it grief and shock.

I waited. I wished I could pray, and believe that Something in the silent, dead darkness loved me. But I could not even believe anyone would weep if

I died of the fever tomorrow. I *knew* they would—Iphigenia would, if no one else—and still I didn't really believe it. I was alone, entirely alone.

Then I heard Sir Kit singing.

I froze. Would anyone be with him? Mrs. Cross? Should I hide, or stay where I was? But light gleamed below the door, and still no other voice intermingled, nor a second set of footfalls. He was singing one of those mournful field songs. A dirge for his funeral.

He steadied himself against the door. The faint glow along the floor gleamed bright, all of a sudden. The door-knob rattled.

"Dark?" he said to himself. I realized he had set his candle down, and looked through the keyhole for mine.

A long pause ate at my nerves. At last I heard his key scrape across the lock. It took him four tries to get it in. I tried not to think about what else might take him four tries to get in.

His face lit with relief when he saw me. "You're here!" he said loudly.

"So are you," I said weakly, listening for sounds from above as he locked the door behind him. He set his candle on the night table. My voice trembled when I said, "Light the lamp." I hated my own nerves. I wished I could slice them out, like boning a fish.

"I don't know," he teased. "You'd probably find me more attractive in the dark."

"Please."

He looked surprised, and owlishly touched. The polished brass reservoir of his oil lamp shone as he held his light clumsily to the broad wick. The candle guttered and dripped wax onto his hand, and in trying to hold the lamp steady, he nearly tipped it over. For a moment I was sure he would fire his clothes himself, and save me the trouble.

But at last the wick flared and the room brightened, searing my eyes. I shaded them with my hand until he had softened the lamp's harsh glow with a little painted screen. I checked its distance from the flame by habit, and had already raised my hand to increase it when I thought better of it.

"Where are your keys, sir?"

He giggled. "The only thing I'll set ablaze will be your loins, I promise." But he fumbled in his coat pocket, clattering his profusion of keys onto the night table before removing the coat with a glad sigh. "I hope whoever outlawed shirtsleeves in mixed company is burning merrily in Hell."

"Which key opens the outer door at the base of the tower?"

He held them to the light, nearly overturning the screen. "This one. No—this one, with the nick here."

I took the keys gently from his hand, and returned them to the table with that one set apart from the rest. "You've already nearly knocked the lamp over twice."

He laughed. "You have the soul of a grandmother, don't you? Everything's all right. Come here."

I think he meant to pull me into his lap, but he misjudged, and I ended up wedged awkwardly under his arm. I could smell the beer on his breath, stale and pungent.

That was when I noticed the champagne, laid out on a little marble-topped table. A few solitary chips of ice floated on the surface of the elegant bucket, which must have been filled hours ago, and a pool of water spread at its base.

This was the sound I had heard: as I watched, a single glittering drop fell onto the deep-pile carpet I had crept across. Now I could see its rich, vibrant colors, spilling across most of the floor before giving way to oiled wood, smooth and gleaming as though dust had never touched it. What a contrast to the room above!

There was a bowl of strawberries on that shining tabletop, too. The fruit of Venus.

My throat closed. *It will all burn save that patch of wet carpet.* I saw the table's graceful cabriole legs turning black and giving way, the slab of marble crashing to the floor…

Sir Kit stroked my shoulder. His arm dragged at my neck. I stooped, squirmed, and at last simply moved his hand to my waist. "We shall have to share the glass," he murmured, pulling me snug against him. "I brought only one in deference to your modesty." He nuzzled my neck. "You're here."

While his intoxication was unmistakable, he was still far too awake for my liking. I held up my brandy bottle. "I don't know if I should have champagne. I drank some of this cherry bounce while I waited."

He squinted at it, and laughed delightedly. "You drank *most* of that cherry bounce while you waited."

"I only had a finger." I indicated, not the thickness of my index finger, but its full length.

He gave my hip a squeeze. "You'll have another finger soon."

Somehow that seemed worse than his cock—more a part of *him*, more an extension of his will. I handed him the bottle. "You first."

Sir Kit inhaled the liquor's scent. "Mmm." He took too deep a swig and coughed, pounding his chest. "I didn't really think you'd come. You're so proper."

"I'm not so proper."

It was the simple truth, but he laughed in satisfaction as though…I don't know. As though I had unbent for *him*, when my mistrust was the only reason he thought me proper in the first place.

"Is yours a *maidenly* modesty?" He walked his fingers down my hip. "You didn't answer me last time I asked."

No, I hadn't. The question still seemed meaningless and vulgar. "Strange, how the word 'virgin' changes," I said. "When a woman is young, men say it salivating, and when she's old, they sneer. But women aren't grapes; we don't wither on the vine if we're not plucked."

"You're not *old*." There was a smile in his voice. Another swig of brandy, and he set the bottle down to try again to get me in his lap.

"Good to know I have a few years left before my raisinhood."

"So…are you?" His eyes gleamed.

"Yes." If I said no, he would want to discuss my lovers, and I could not take much more conversation. Was Jael listening? How much could she hear through the floor? I had been listening for *her*, and heard nothing yet.

He paused—and to my surprise, he tipped my face towards his and met my eyes. "Are you sure? About tonight?"

I hesitated. But fucking seemed less intimate than any other way to pass the time until he slept. And then—in some perverse way, it seemed the least I could do for him. The *only* thing I could do for him, in his last hour. *Please let it be his last hour.* "Quite sure."

"Thank God," he said in heartfelt tones, pushing me down into the coverlet.

When he leaned over me, he wobbled and nearly slipped off the bed. I moved backward until my feet were on the mattress. My heart raced as he struggled with his boots, then gave up and left them on.

"I can't wait another moment to have you." He covered me eagerly with his body. "But 'had we world enough and time'..." His fingers could not manage the knot of my wrapper, after all, and I had to do it for him. He pulled my shift open to expose my breasts.

To my surprise, I felt no self-consciousness. I felt nothing—until I saw Jael's chain snaking across my breastbone, and my keys dark against my skin. *Then* an icy wave rushed over me. *That*, I clenched my fists to keep from covering up.

"'Two hundred to adore each breast.'" He shaped them with his hands— kissed them. He was growing perceptibly drunker. I could only make out his words because I knew the poem. "'And you should, if you please, refuse / till the conversion of the Jews.'"

I shifted in distaste. My keys slipped over my collarbone and onto the sheet, the chain cutting into my larynx.

He snickered. "I didn't mean it. An angel in the choir couldn't wait *that* long." He put his hands at the neck of my garment, as if to tear it.

I twisted away. "No!"

He stopped in utter confusion. "But...you said..."

"Don't tear my shift. I only have the one."

He giggled at me, but reached for my hem. Relief was an icy wave too.

"You're shaking, love." He eased the nightdress over my head. I felt a sharp ache between my legs. Not *all* unpleasant, but I hoped it wasn't a sign of things to come. "Don't be afraid. I'm not going to hurt you."

"That's not why I'm afraid." But I pretended to take a nervous swallow of brandy, and handed him the bottle. My face felt hot, but the rest of me was so cold, even in the hot room—coldest where his wet mouth had been.

He drank and set the bottle on the floor, blinking as though he couldn't remember what we'd been speaking of. "Don't be afraid," he repeated, unbuttoning his pantaloons.

I would never have done such a thing on any other night, but I moved the bottle carefully to the nightstand, by the lamp. "I'm always afraid."

He shook his head. Dizziness swept across his face; he shut his eyes and pressed his forehead to my shoulder. "Don't be afraid. The doors are locked. We're safe. Do you want me to check the shutters?"

It's not too late to change my mind, I thought. But it had been too late weeks ago. Maybe it had always been too late. "Draw the bed-curtains," I whispered.

"The shutters are closed, and everyone is locked in for the night. No one can see us."

"Please, sir."

The outer bed-curtains were striped and tasseled cotton, tied and swagged at the bedposts. But he yanked at the inner ones of sheer muslin. Could Jael hear the curtain rings shrieking on their rod?

At last they blocked out the room, flat sheets that would burn like paper. He pushed me down again, and climbed on top of me.

I felt his cock at my entrance. Somehow I was wet, but it was barely a mercy. I felt him pushing into me distantly, as one hears music while reading. I watched the shifting patch of muslin where the lamp's glow fell.

He pressed his thumb hard between my brows. I did feel that. "Don't frown," he murmured. "Don't frown, darling." He strained up to kiss my brow, and landed on my cheekbone. He tried again, confused—pulled out of me with drunken persistence and inched up, kissing the lines on my forehead. His hand landed on my key, dragging Jael's gold chain tight across my larynx. "I'm going to marry you."

I gasped. "Your wife is alive!"

"I didn't say tomorrow." His huffs of laughter blew brandy in my face as he crawled back down, only to overshoot his mark and rest his forehead between my breasts while he steeled himself for the task ahead. "Mmm."

Maybe he would fall asleep now. I steeled myself to my own task.

But he startled up, blinking. "Sorry!" A lopsided smile melted across his face. "You shouldn't have given me brandy."

Had Judith borne this too? Or had she better judged her victim's tolerance for wine?

Somehow, as he pushed back into me, I had to know: "Do you still fuck your wife?"

He shook his head. "Don't talk about her. Why do you keep talking about her?"

Did that headshake mean *no*, or just *I won't answer*?

"She isn't here. Look at me." He turned my face to his, and when I dropped my eyes, he shook me. "My darling, *look at me*. Nothing stands between us but dec...decor...dec..."

"Decorous prejudices," I supplied, so he would stop. I wished he would stop, or else *finish*—that he would not be touching me, that no one would be touching me. The feeling from the coffeehouse rose up, that a kind smile was an unbearable demand. That meeting another person's eyes was to open a vein.

I shut my eyes and tried to—to enjoy myself somehow. To *feel* something, so the blood congealing in my heart would rush back into my veins and warm my numb fingertips. I could not smooth out my brow where he had pressed his thumb; my forehead ached.

I went over my plan again. *Set the fire, take the keys, run upstairs—no. Put on my shift and wrapper, search the room for any traces of my presence, then set the fire, take the keys...* I jumped when he grunted in my ear. I jumped each time the lamp flickered. If he noticed, I supposed he thought it pleasure.

At last he sank onto my breast, spent or sleeping.

Something dripped between my legs. His hair tickled my cheek. He did not move when I pushed gently at his shoulder, so I heaved him bodily off me.

"Put out the light," he mumbled. "I promised you no fires."

"I will."

He groped for me; afraid he would wake, I leaned my head on his shoulder. Soon he was snoring.

I lay beside him, and listened. Water dripped from the table. The clock ticked, then chimed eleven. No sound from above, except a creak now and then that might have been the house settling. Sir Kit still snored.

I eased away from him. He did not wake.

I sat up. His hand fell heavily from my hip, and landed on the coverlet. The snoring stopped for a moment—and started again. I let out my breath.

I opened the bed-curtain by a foot, and went to clean myself at the basin. I tilted the towel towards the light: a smear of blood, and a faint slick reflection. Was it seed? How could I tell? I wished I were in Lively St. Lemeston, and knew where to buy pennyroyal.

But that was too distant a calamity to think of now. I dressed swiftly—only realizing I was sweating when the linen stuck to my skin—and peeked between the bed-curtains. Sir Kit was curled towards the depression in the bed where I had lain. I averted my eyes from his cock, still dangling from his unbuttoned pantaloons.

I took up the bottle of cherry bounce. I watched his sleeping face as I poured the last half-inch of brandy onto the muslin. Memories crowded at the smell: Christmas, Iphigenia. A preserved cherry crushed against my tongue.

I set aside the lampshade, the room flaring brighter. Sir Kit turned his face into his pillow, and light glinted off the ring of keys. They would clank when I lifted them; better to wait a little longer.

I took up the lamp. The scarlet brandy stain was still spreading. I had only to move my hand an inch.

Sir Kit rolled onto his back.

I started so violently I managed to spill a drop of hot oil onto my hand, despite the lamp's double spout. At my whimper he opened his eyes, and saw me.

But somehow the flame had not touched the curtain. There was nothing yet to stop him from smiling at me as he pushed himself up on one elbow. "Chamber-pot."

My blood roared in my ears. There was a drop of fire on my hand, at the join of thumb and forefinger.

"Miss Oliver? Are you well? ... What happened to the curtain?"

I did not move. I don't say that to exonerate myself—only to tell you how it happened. But of a sudden, the flame leapt across the inch of air and the brandy caught like a plum pudding, blue and soft and sinuous.

33

Sir Kit's eyes widened.

I let the lamp fall onto the mattress, through the gap in the curtain. It seemed to take an eternity to arc through the air—

—and then pain flared in my hand, a clear bright agony that dispelled my stupor. I sprang back from the flames and snatched up his keys.

"Water," he croaked, half rolling, half staggering off the bed. He dragged himself upright at the opposite bedpost, tangled in muslin. His cock flopped.

A wave of heat drove me further back from the bed. I wished he would do up his buttons.

"Fetch the water."

Water, for an oil fire? But by now I wasn't sure even the bucket of sand at the hearth—if he managed to remember it—could put out the fire. It was spreading impossibly fast. If I had not woken him, he would have caught by now. I could hardly take my eyes off it.

He stumbled towards the champagne bucket.

I ran for the door, feeling for my own key. There was no time for fumbling with the clasp or trying to pull the chain over my head—but I yanked far too timidly, and only wrenched my neck. The breath I drew to steady myself tasted like smoke.

I squeezed my eyes and my fist tight shut, and snapped the chain.

Behind me I heard the splash of water, and a roar from the oil-fire. Then another. I glanced over my shoulder. Sir Kit had the empty ewer in his hands.

"Water doesn't douse oil," I muttered—too quietly for him to hear, but I couldn't help myself. The key clinked against the plate and slipped in, my hands managing better without my conscious direction. My mind had always been my enemy.

I opened the door, and went through it into the corridor, and shut it behind me.

The fire had ruined my eyes for the dark. I could see nothing but the red line beneath Sir Kit's door, and the faint red keyhole—a gift I had not thought to expect. The key rattled as I guided it in with shaking fingers, rattled as I turned it, rattled as I drew it out. But it was in my pocket again by the time he reached the other side of the door.

"Deborah?" he said, confused. "Deborah, I'm still in here."

I pressed myself against the strip of wall between his door and the stairwell, so he could not see me through the keyhole.

"You have my keys, remember?"

What should I do? I couldn't run away and leave him alive. What if he somehow escaped?

"It's hot. Let me out." I heard the first word clearly. The last was nearly lost in a rising crackle. The fire danced faintly through the crack below the door, with two black gaps for his feet. It peered through the keyhole, making a bright spot on the opposite wall—brighter as I watched. I nearly expected the spot to burst into flame.

"Why won't you let me out?" At least, I think that's what he said. His voice was distorted by more than the fire now; there was a sob in it, like a lost child. An answering sob rose in my throat. "Miss Oliver? Are you still there?"

The bright keyhole-spot vanished from the wall, and his shoulder thudded uselessly against the inward-opening door. The handle rattled.

"She couldn't have forgotten me," I think he said to himself. He walked away, the gaps in the light below the door shrinking and vanishing. The wall was growing warmer at my back.

Then I remembered it might only be retaining my own heat as I leaned against it. Yet the keyhole-spot on the opposite wall grew lighter and sharper and brighter every moment.

There was heavy dragging sound, a scrape—and a violent crash. The door shook on its hinges.

I could not make sense of it until a line of light appeared in the door. As I watched, the crack widened and bent. The edges of the lower right panel glowed, and I saw the corner of the marble-topped table break through.

He battered the panel until it fell to the passageway floor, inches from my feet. A bright window opened in the door between the handle and the floor, tall and narrow, framed in black. *Run,* I thought. *Run!*

But his forehead protruded, monstrous and shifting in the fire's glare, and I could not move, except to press myself harder against the wall as his eyes rotated inexorably towards me. Our gazes met.

I nearly screamed. Then his head was withdrawn, and his hand shot out and grabbed my ankle, dragging me towards him.

I let out a desperate sob as the heat from the open rectangle seared my shin. His wild eyes ran over me. "Give me the keys." He held out his other hand. "Don't panic. Breathe, and give me the keys. It's too late to put it out, but we'll save Tabby."

I sobbed again. Tabby! I began to struggle in his grasp.

He held on with both hands. "Deborah! Calm *down.*"

"Let me go! Let me go!" My face was full of smoke. I could not speak for coughing.

I leaned back to get a glimpse of the fire behind him; I could not help myself. I could see little, except that the fire was eating rapidly through the carpet and spreading in a sheet across the rich oiled floors.

He was trying to push himself through the panel, but I could have told him it was far too narrow for anyone but a child. With my ankle in both hands, he could not even get his head through.

I pressed my palms to the door for leverage, trying to tear my leg from his grasp. The wood was warm under my hands, I was sure of it.

"Give me the keys." He let go with one hand to snatch at them. "I'll die!"

Without thinking, I threw the keys towards the stairwell.

The heavy ring clattered on the stone. He stilled for a moment.

Then both hands closed again on my ankle, tightening until the bones ground together. "Did you—did she put you up to this?"

I shook my head. "No, no, no, no…" My eyes were streaming from the smoke.

"What did she tell you? She's a liar, she's mad. Let me out!"

She had no key. Tabby had no key. I had to get away, I had to—

I flailed in his grasp, pushing against the door, but fear dulled the force of my movements. Smoke gave sharp edges to the light spilling into the corridor through the missing panel. I was afraid to reach into that crisp stream of light, to jab at his eyes. He would grab my wrist, he would drag me through. I would die here, I would die, I had lost everything. They would find his skeletal hand clasped around my bony ankle.

I pictured Tabby's little charred skeleton. "I'll fetch the keys for you if you let me go," I bargained with my last scrap of weak cunning.

A door banged open. Jael barreled out of the stairwell and snatched the ring up.

We stared at each other.

Her hair was in a long plait, and her feet were bare. In her simple, square shift, she might have been going to her execution. *Help me*, I wanted to say, and could not.

She sauntered over, and stood just out of range of Sir Kit's grasp. "Hullo, Kit."

He looked up at her, tears streaking his sooty face. "Let me out, Jael."

"That's not how you pronounce my name," she said, and stomped hard on his wrists—*one, two*.

His fingers opened, and I stumbled out of that dreadful sharp-edged box of light.

"For the love of God, Jael," he begged. "I'll give you anything. A divorce—the house—"

She smiled at him. "See you in Hell, Kit."

He glared at her, and retreated into the room. Smoke poured out of the gap.

"I don't believe in Hell," I breathed.

"I hope you're right. Come on, Olivia, let's go."

There was a heavy, rattling crash from within the room. "He's trying to break open the shutters!"

She jerked her head towards the stairwell. "We discussed this. The stone frames won't let them give. I've tried it."

"He's stronger than you are." Was that a shout from within?

"He's drunk."

"He's fighting for his life."

"So was I," she said, almost drowned out by a series of crashing sounds. Sir Kit, or the bed collapsing? Had his clothes caught yet?

There was another bright flash of light. I backed away and looked into the room. In the moment before the heat on my face grew unbearable, I saw the floor was a lake of fire, the dark bedposts rising from it like the masts of a wrecked ship. Could anyone possibly be alive in there?

I pictured Sir Kit's skin blistering, his flesh melting from the bone. He had taken me in his clothes; if I touched his bare body now, my fingers would stick to his ribs. I set a fingertip gingerly to the knob, and snatched it back with a hiss.

That could not be the timbre of his voice any longer. My ears were playing tricks on me. I pulled my key out of my pocket and set it in the lock.

"What are you doing?" She grabbed my wrist, squeezing until my fingers spasmed.

I whimpered in pain and fear. "By now he must be—he's not— If I open it, I can say he gave me his key-ring and stayed to fight the fire."

"That door is going to burn to a cinder, and no one will know whether it was open or not."

The door was already charred around the missing panel. But it was new wood, thickly painted, and would not burn like that ancient oiled floor. The lock and bolt might not burn at all. "You don't *know* that! We can't risk it."

"Can't *risk* it? If you open it, the fire will spread."

"Take his keys and go get them." I turned my own in Sir Kit's lock and pulled it out before it grew too hot to touch.

Jael dropped Sir Kit's ring of keys on the floor. I could barely hear the *clank* over the crackling from the door. Then something dangled near my face.

"What is it?" My watering eyes were useless.

"I have a key," she said, voice dripping with scorn, and dropped my wrist. In another moment she had disappeared into the stairwell and slammed its door behind her, leaving me alone with the fire. I prayed I was alone with the fire.

There was no time to puzzle out Jael's revelation. I scooped up Sir Kit's keys and dropped them in my pocket. Then I wrapped my hand in my robe and turned the knob.

Heat and light burst from the door in a tidal wave, sweeping me into the mouth of the stairwell. I cowered against the door, peering round the jamb at the narrow, blazing gap between the world and the Hell I had made. I did not dare retreat into the stairwell, lest out of my sight Sir Kit's fingers wrap around the edge of his door and pull it open, smearing blood and flesh on the blistering paint.

As I watched, the fire danced out the gap, whirling and writhing. It began to eat the corridor's walls, then the ceiling. *Hell is empty, and all the devils are here.* My face felt dry and tight—I saw spots—

A tongue of flame licked towards me along the wall, and at last I leaned on the door-handle and fell back onto the landing, shutting the door with a bang. False flames danced in my vision, blue and silver and flashing orange like a stormy sea.

A sound solidified in my ringing ears: Tabby, screaming above me. "Hurry," I called. My voice came out soft and weak. My throat spasmed when I tried again. I heard them coming—I sensed their presence on the landing—but I could see nothing but the ghostly echoes of my crime.

Jael grunted with pain. "Grab her legs," she pleaded. "I'm going to drop her."

Tabby kicked at my hand, scratching lines of searing pain across my burned skin. "You're kidnapping me," she shrieked. "I don't want to be kidnapped!"

Grimly, I flailed in the direction of the kick and seized her knee, then her ankle. Her other foot kicked me again, hard, before Clarice wrenched it away. Slowly, agonizingly, we shuffled down the stairs—the air at least a little cooler as we went.

The ring of keys slapped my thigh with each step, heavy and awkward, their weight dragging at my wrapper. I didn't care. I was glad to have confirmation that they hadn't tumbled out of my pocket and onto a stair.

At last I felt for the next step and jarred my ankle, yanking poor Tabby's leg as I overbalanced. "Stop a moment!" I cried in a panic. "We're at the landing."

I knew I must be standing on the double-wide step where the stairs branched. If we continued, we'd reach the passageway. But somewhere a few inches to my right was a narrow, plunging flight of stone steps without a banister.

"You hurt me!" Tabby screamed, thrashing.

My ankle ached, and my head, and my eyes, and my hand. "I'm sorry, baby," I said, not even sure she could hear me over her own voice. "I didn't mean to."

I inched backward, feeling with my feet—trying not to flee recklessly from the faintly warming air of the stairwell. "This way…"

I stumbled over my instructions, words eluding me, but somehow I guided us down onto a broader landing, through a sharp turn, down a few more shallow steps. We were in the passage. We were at the locked, barred door.

"Clarice, can you take this leg? I need to open the door."

The key I had separated out so carefully was mixed with all the rest now. I felt for it, struggling to understand the intelligence forwarded by my fingers, but my thoughts darted and danced and sparked. There was so much noise: voices and wailing and the fire shouting above us. Oh God, *above us*. If the ceiling should fall— There the nick was! I felt for the keyhole and slipped the key in.

It didn't turn.

I used both hands and all my strength, whimpering as my burned fingers slid on the brass. I jiggled the key. I jiggled and pulled at the door. We would die here. Smoke was filling the passage, I thought, unless the fire had damaged my eyes. I had inhaled too much already to tell by the smell or taste. At least we would suffocate before the flames reached us…

"What is it?" Jael demanded.

"It doesn't open." My voice was several octaves too high.

"Let me try."

I refused to move aside for her. I didn't believe she could do it.

I remembered all at once that it was a symmetrical key, with teeth on each side of the stem. I pulled it out, half-spun it, rattled it back into the lock—

The tumblers clicked.

So much for the modern lock. Now for the ancient iron bar. How could it be so dark, when it had been so bright a few minutes ago? If only we had a candle! We could have lit it at the fire… I stifled a giggle, my sweaty fingers wrestling painfully with the iron latch.

"What is taking so long?" Clarice pushed forward, elbowing me. "Are we trapped?"

"Shut your goddamned mouth for once!" I wrenched the bar up at last, jamming my finger between two pieces of iron as I did so. Cursing freely, I felt for the edge of the door.

Clarice was before me, shoving it open. We spilled out onto the lawn in a heap. I cried out as I put my weight on my jarred ankle.

Wrenching free of us, Tabby dove back towards the door.

Instinctively, I gave the door a shove to shut it. Next moment I reached for it again, picturing her soft arm mangled—but my fingertips only brushed the edge—

Jael pulled her back by her collar.

I hurled myself at the door, sagging against it as it clicked shut, gasping like a beached fish. I wished I could lock it, to keep Tabby outside, but how would I explain that later?

I heard a sound of pain from Jael, and then Tabby was upon me, clawing and biting. "We have to find Papa. We have to go back and get Adeline. I hate you, I'll kill you!"

For an instant I shrank back, putting up my hands to shield my face.

But she couldn't reach my face. She was small and under my protection. I seized her hands, letting out another self-pitying whimper as her fingernails dug into my palms.

"You can't go back in." I was surprised at how firm my raw voice sounded. "We don't even know if your Papa is still inside. When you're settled here, I'll look for him." I dragged her away from the house.

Thank God she was as worn out as I was, or I'd never have managed it. My knees threatened to give out with every step, and my hands shook on her arms with each racking cough, my throat itching uncontrollably. "*Christabel.* The sooner I know you're safe…" I gave up, coughing. I would have killed for some tea.

But no, I could never say that again, for I *had* killed— I hoped I had— At last we were a good distance from the house.

"You'd better sit on her, my lady," Clarice said. "I'll stand by and grab her if she gets free."

The moonlit night was tinged with flickering orange, but Jael looked very white as she straddled her daughter's torso, pressing her small arms into the earth. "I'm sorry, *minha filha.* I'm so sorry. I can't let you burn up."

I turned to go back, looking full at the house for the first time.

"You're not really going back for him," she said, behind me.

I was transfixed by the dark hulk against the lightened sky, its tall keep burning. The fire had opened Sir Kit's windows—had burst the glass. Flames twined up the tower like ivy. As I watched, gold spread across Jael's dark window.

Faster than I could have dreamed, the square blazed white, and window panes rained tinkling onto the lawn. How strange, to see that sleeping eye awaken at last, and fix its wide, baleful gaze on me.

"She is going back!" Tabby said. "She is. She's going to rescue Papa."

"I-I'll do my best." How I longed for water. "I'll let the servants out. I..." My coughs turned to retching. I tried to swallow, but there was no moisture in my dry mouth.

"Miss Oliver," Jael said tightly.

Surely she knew Sir Kit could not still be alive. I wondered what would be left when they found him. His boots? His buttons? Some shards of tooth or bone, gleaming white through the ash?

Her eyes were intent, with a look I could not read. Clarice's were hard and suspicious, and Tabby's pleading. I could not stand their eyes on me another moment.

I grimaced reassuringly—if I spoke, I would cough—and loped as best I could towards the servants' quarters. I heard shouts as I neared the corner of the house, and rounded it to see dark figures breaking out of the night and racing towards me across the great gravel drive.

I shrank back like a fox from the hounds. They were coming to arrest me already!

Then I understood a word, repeated. "Fire! Fire!"

A figure reached me, a face I knew. One of the grooms, whose name I could not recall. Of course: the grooms slept in the stables, and as the horses were too valuable to risk losing to fire, they were not locked in.

I held up Sir Kit's keys. "The servants," I forced out. "Let them—let—"

Thank God, one of them had a bucket of water. It was not clean—I could *smell* nothing but smoke and ash, but when I gulped the water gratefully out of my cupped palms, it tasted of horse.

"We need to let the servants out," I said.

Most of them had not even stopped to hear me, but run onward towards the fire. The groom with the bucket lingered, unwilling to be rude to a lady. "Maybe you'd better give me those keys, ma'am."

I clutched them to my chest.

Someone screamed. I turned to see the porter's wife running out of the house in her bare feet, crying fire. Her husband stumbled out after, staring openmouthed at the tower.

Then his gaze fell hungrily on my ring of keys. "You've got—but why have you got those?"

"Sir Kit gave them to me. We need to let the servants out."

"What about the family?" his wife asked.

"The two ladies are safe, and the nursery maid." That was when I realized Jael had left Mrs. Churchill behind. The stable water tried to force its way back up my throat.

"Not the master?" The porter glanced back to the tower.

I breathed through my nose until vomiting seemed slightly less imminent. "I don't know. He gave me his keys..." I knew the spirit of what I wished to convey, but my exhausted mind could not seem to match words to ideas. I gestured helplessly at the vast column of smoke rising from the tower, a signal beacon that surely needed no translation. "If he hasn't yet... He told me to let the servants out."

"Do you know which key it is, ma'am?" the porter's wife asked me.

I shook my head hopelessly.

"I'll go then, and wake Mrs. Cross. Isn't that like the master, to think of others first." She pried the keys from my hands with a sorrowing shake of her head. "You'd better go and open all the entry doors," she told her husband. And off they went, leaving me alone and empty-handed.

They had believed me so easily.

I heard his confused, heartbroken voice: *Deborah, I'm still in here...* Now, now when it was too late, regret swept over me. They would look for him, and he would be *there* all the while, where I had left him. Where I had *put* him. I had not even had the mercy to strangle him first. He had died like vó's brother, awake and in agony.

I was a monster.

What had Sir Kit ever done to me but love me? Out of *that*, I had been led on to kill him?

You're only tired and sick and frightened, I told myself as I hobbled back the way I had come. *You'll remember all your reasons in the morning.* My fire was bright enough now to illumine the drive where I stood, and cast a shadow from the jutting porch—not a crisp, straight, still one, like moonlight, but a shifting, dancing border between light and dark.

No one glanced in my direction as I neared the little group from the nursery. Tabby, finally still, huddled in Jael's lap as though trying to burrow into her mother's flesh. But her tearstained face was turned resolutely towards the house.

"Papa," she hiccuped. "Where is Papa?"

Jael watched her daughter—but now and then she stole wondering glances about her, or shivered and cast a startled, indignant glance at the wind, though it wasn't cold. It was the furthest thing from cold.

The parish fire-bell began to clamor.

I remembered Sir Kit after that last fire. Asleep on his feet, ash in his hair, setting up an infirmary in his hall. *Isn't that like the master, to think of others first?*

Silently, I sank to the ground—a little behind them, farthest from the fire. I put my face in my knees and sobbed.

I wept for the frightened little boy who had been birched at school. I wept for the flashes of kindness, the generosity of spirit that had been corrupted by selfishness and suspicion and prejudice. *Like sweet bells jangled...*

He had meant to be a good father. He had never meant to be a monster, any more than I had.

All my life I had tortured myself, so I would not start a house-fire by accident. *Can't escape fate*, I admonished myself, smothering a hysterical laugh. *You tried, and you made it worse.*

A hand seized my shoulder, shaking me until my teeth snapped together.

I wrenched away, heart pounding, and looked up into the wild face of Mrs. Cross.

34

"Where is he?" I only made out her words over the roar of the fire by watching her lips. "Where's my boy?"

I got carefully to my feet, wiping my nose on my sleeve. "Come, madam, let us—" I took the housekeeper's arm to lead her away from Tabby.

She shook me violently off. "You tell me what's become of our Sir Kit!"

Wordlessly, I walked off without her, and waited for her to catch me up. "I don't know," I said evenly. Strange how resentment could buoy me up even at such a moment, despite my own guilt. "He stayed to fight the fire. He commanded me to get everyone out of the house. I could not make him come away. He said if he couldn't put it out, he would follow me."

I tried to think. What would Clarice say had happened? "I woke her ladyship and went back to find him, but the fire was into the corridor. I hoped he would be waiting downstairs—but we mustn't abandon hope. Did he have a spare key? Or his window is not so very high…"

"Why were you with him?" she demanded. "Why were you in his room?"

"I wasn't," I said, startled to realize I had started my prepared lies halfway through. "That is—not when it started. It was so hot—I opened my window. I heard—I don't know what I heard, exactly."

The grief and condemnation in her face would have made me falter if I had spoken the unvarnished truth. I looked away, and took in the scene on the lawn.

Either I had been weeping longer than I realized, or the fire had been swift indeed. The chapel's enormous two-story window was turned to Popish stained-glass, an exquisite pattern in crimsons and golds.

The servants were carrying furniture and valuables out of every door but the one we'd come out of, piling them on the grass. If you removed the house and added a few old-clothesmen to the scene, the lawn might have been any secondhand market in England.

Mrs. Cross shoved me. "Go on, then!"

I rubbed at my shoulder. "I shall forget that," I said with absurd dignity. "You are overset. At first, I thought the noise was—well, I have heard him and his lady quarreling sometimes. But I had an ill feeling, and I went down. I don't know what had happened before I arrived. The bed-curtains were on fire—"

"You'd ought to have made him go!" She shoved me hard again, both hands right on my heart; it stopped my breath for a moment. "He was drunk, he weren't himself, you'd ought to have—"

"I'm sorry," I whispered. The farm folk were stumbling up from the barn now, the women and children with flowers still in their hair. "I was frightened, and he said—"

"*You* were frightened! What do you suppose *he* was? I see through your lies."

I fell back.

"We all saw how you looked at him. *You* knocked over the lamp, and *he* stayed to put it out like the good, brave gentleman he was, when it should have been you. Yes, you'd ought to be frightened, you Delilah, you Witch of Endor!"

"How I looked at him?" I flared. "You mean how he looked at me! And you penned me up bleating every night at nine-thirty sharp. If you thought I was his mistress, Mrs. Pander, then what does that make you? His procuress?"

Her eyes widened, and I really believed she would fly at me. I felt ready to claw her beady English eyes out myself.

But the cook ran up to drag her away, and my eye was caught by—my mother's guitar case, hurrying past in strange hands. I snatched it violently, snarling, "That's mine!"

It was the fiddler from Harvest-home, her flower crown askew and her apron sooty. "I was just carrying it away from the house, ma'am," she stammered, and fled.

I dragged the instrument from the case and cradled it to my chest. It must have been in the music room, or the study. I had not even thought to do the same with Jael's.

It would have looked awfully convenient, I comforted myself, running my fingers over the wood as one might check a child for injuries.

The crowd grew, until most of the faces on the lawn were unfamiliar. Many of them were drunk and only stared, slack-jawed. But a few women brought up pails of water on milkmaids' yokes, and some men, soberer than their fellows, cut a bare strip into the lawn downwind of the fire with scythes and hoes, wetting the ground and setting the children to stamp it down.

People were still rushing in and out of the house, dropping armloads of possessions and leaving it to others to remove them to a safe distance away. Possibly I'd done the fiddler-woman an injustice. But as I watched, a girl carried a vase straight past the jumble at the edge of the firelight, and into the darkness. I was sure half these things would be spirited away by morning.

The fire streamed from the nursery windows now, turning our little parapet into a golden crown.

Then a twisted chimney crashed down from the tower roof, taking half the turret with it. The crowd on the lawn broke, surging back like water. I thought of Archimedes and his overflowing bath, and pressed my palm over my mouth so I would not cry out, *Not gold after all, the house is a cheat!*— the private jest of the too-long imprisoned.

The footmen had been carrying out the best furniture: yes, there were Peter and Luke setting down the sofa I had shared with Lady Tassell, just a few days ago. As they turned back to the house, the tall panes of the chapel window burst.

The roundels remained intact a moment longer, flames licking at their painted crests. The Tudor lions shattered, then the fleurs-de-lis. I had never looked closely at the Palethorp coat-of-arms; as I squinted, trying to make it out, it vanished too. The empty stone tracery might have been a wrought-iron grill in an enormous hearth.

"Peter!" Clarice's cry broke my fascination. I saw her darting after him, towards the house. Did he mean to go back in?

"Peter, wait," I called. My voice would not go loud, but to my relief she caught him up before he had got far, and hung on his arm expostulating. I gritted my teeth and limped towards them. "Help," I coughed out. "Peter. Help me with…" I gestured at Jael.

Clarice gave me her first really warm look since the fire.

"Don't leave us alone," I added for good measure. "The place is full of"—I choked on Sir Kit's favorite stratagem—"thieves."

It worked. Peter spoke to Luke, and they arrayed the sofa with bizarre care some twenty yards beyond the wet firebreak.

Luke took up a position beside it. Jael would not let Peter pick up Tabby; he had to put his hands under her armpits and heave them both up with a grunt. I trailed after them to the sofa, where Peter took up his own place with a wry nod to Luke.

Jael looked between them, and then sat in the exact center of the sofa, as far as she could get from both. I hovered awkwardly until Clarice pushed me down on the cushion nearest Luke, and took the one near Peter herself.

And there we sat, with the footmen standing impassively at attention in their best livery coats, shirts half-tucked and breeches unbraced. Peter wore stockings but no garters; Luke's hairy calves were bare. Firelight played over the gilt buckles of their shoes. I felt a deep sense of unreality, as though we had been commanded to a faerie ball.

Jael's bruises looked very dark in the dim light. I wondered if they would excite pity or suspicion. None of my own injuries had darkened yet. In the ruddy light, only my pain told me which skin was burned and which was not. To keep myself from pressing and poking, I set mãe's guitar over my knee.

It was out of tune, and Jael winced.

That faint twitch of one eye, that curl at the corner of her mouth had first led me to suspect Sir Kit of lying about those cut strings. They were the first fellowship I had ever felt for her. But I could not tune my strings in this pandemonium. Mozart himself, with his famous ear, could not have confidently named any tone but the panicked, unending fire-bell.

So I played tuneless ballads on my mother's guitar, watching Jael grimace—and then I thought, *They all noticed me looking at Sir Kit*, and cast my eyes down. She was only a sofa cushion away, but it might have been an ocean.

Tabby was drifting asleep at last, and Clarice was telling Peter her account of the fire at the other end of the sofa, too quietly for me to hear. I leaned my head low over the guitar and shut my eyes. My calluses were thick enough that my fingertips themselves were barely burned—or at least if they were, I could not feel them. It hurt more to stretch my hand into the proper position than to touch the strings.

I wished I could have burned down vó's prison too.

"Please—please stop," Jael said suddenly. "I'm sorry, only there is so much noise, and everyone is staring at me."

In fact, nearly everyone was staring at the fire. But she had been two years immured from the world. The handful of curious eyes must feel like a thousand. I turned to Luke—and suddenly remembered him saying, *Lady Palethorp has all that she wants*. I could not ask his aid.

"Clarice, would you find some sort of veil for her ladyship?"

The shawl and bonnet they brought us was rough and humble to my eyes, but Jael ran her fingers over the straw and said, "This is careful work. I hope she took something worth her pains in payment." The glance they exchanged made me think they had traded something valuable for it.

She was tying the bonnet under her chin when Mr. Munk found us.

The magistrate's cravat was tied and his seal dangled from his buttonhole, but he hadn't shaved. I tried to marshal my distracted thoughts, which *would* wonder whether it vexed him that his beard was gray.

"My lady." He bowed stiffly. "I am glad to see you unharmed." His eyes flickered to the bruises on her arms. "Mostly."

She didn't stand, or let go of Tabby, or put up the veil. But there was something at once queenly and candid in the way she held out her hand. "Mr. Munk. I'm glad to see you well, also; it's been far too long."

He nodded jerkily, and turned to me. "Miss Oliver. The housekeeper said you were the last to see Sir Kit?"

"I think so," I said cautiously. "I did see him, at any rate. I've been hoping—" For once I was glad my voice gave out. "That someone might have seen him after."

He glanced at Jael, his manner growing even stiffer. "May I lead you a little ways off, ma'am? I don't wish to distress her ladyship."

I heaved myself once more to my feet. But to my surprise, Jael threw back her veil. Mr. Munk's eyebrows went up as he took in her bruised face. "Sir, you must have seen that Mrs. Cross is quite frantic. Poor thing, she has lived at Goldengrove longer than any of us. She was always quite jealous about Kit. I don't mean to embarrass her, but I saw how she spoke to Miss

Oliver just now, and she will be embarrassed herself tomorrow."

Mr. Munk shifted impatiently. "Yes, my lady, quite."

She stood, cradling Tabby awkwardly on her hip. I didn't see how the magistrate could be unmoved by the sight, though his face did not change. "Can't you speak to Miss Oliver in the morning? She's in a state of exhaustion, and I—I want her by me when Miss Palethorp wakes. You will think me neglectful, I daresay, but in truth she's the only one of us who can do anything with the child when she's upset."

"No, indeed, it is quite natural for children to care for the opinion of a stranger before—" the magistrate began.

I was unbearably grateful for her protection, but I had rather get this interview over. When I tried to interject, however, my throat convulsed, sending me into a paroxysm of coughing.

"Oh, she'll take a chill," Jael exclaimed.

I was doubled over and wheezing helplessly, but at this I pushed myself upright, remembering that she had barely been outside in years. "*She'll* take a chill," I got out. "Sir, please…the air…" I gave up.

So did Mr. Munk. In short order, a bottle of barley water was pressed into my hand, and soon after an outrider in green and gold appeared, to inform us that the Countess of Tassell offered us her hospitality.

Tabby woke as Luke lifted her into the carriage, and wailed for several minutes. But she sank back into a whining, trickling kind of crying; at last she slept again.

I don't think I could have dozed, with my nerves in such a state, but I remember nothing more until the carriage stopped with a jolt. I looked out the window, and nearly burst into tears again when I saw Lady Tassell bustle down the steps of a neat little house.

On her heels came a motherly old woman who wrapped us all in shawls, and a stern old man who took them back again. "Mrs. Toogood, if they perspire, they are more likely to take a chill. Begging your pardons, of course, my lady, madam." My fingers tightened on my guitar case as he took it from me—so weakly, I don't know if he even remarked my reflexive resistance. "How do you take your tea, madam?"

I was given a room to myself, with a change of clothes already laid out on the bed and a pristine wax taper in a candlestick on the night table. A maid lit the taper while I put on a shift that was too short and a man's silk dressing gown that was too big, wishing it hadn't been judged unhealthful to bathe so soon after an exposure to noxious air and extremes of temperature. Then the maid carried away my filthy clothes, leaving me alone.

I sat on the bed and stared at the light, rubbing at the ash and grime coating my skin. Was I still afraid of it? I held my palm over the flame to see.

The pain woke me from my stupor. I blew the candle out, took off the dressing gown, and drew the bed-curtains shut.

I saw Sir Kit's bed blazing.

If I had been less weary, I would have made up a pallet on the floor. Instead I lay in a tense daze until sleep swallowed me.

I awakened to the smell of the smoke, and was out of my bed and searching for the fire when I realized the smell was me, not the room. I put the dressing gown back on, and waited for morning.

It was after nine when I was called to breakfast; the countess and my mistress were at table already. I wondered which of them had remembered at last to send for me.

The only servant was old Mr. Toogood, who at once rinsed a teacup in hot water and offered it to me upside-down in its saucer, warm to the touch. I took it reluctantly. Did the absence of younger, less confidential servants signal that the countess meant to question us?

Spectacles perched on her nose, she was working her way through a small mountain of newspapers and correspondence at the head of the table. "I hope you don't mind serving yourself, Miss Oliver," she said. "I can't abide ceremony at breakfast."

Indeed, she looked terribly comfortable, her morning gown a miracle of whitework and tassels, her easy posture redolent of short stays. It should have set me at ease about my own entire lack of underthings, but I felt a stab of longing for my well-worn stays, that had fit me like a glove. I would have to buy new stiff ones now, and wait for the whalebone to learn my shape, the seams to stop poking, the laces to remember where I knotted them.

Everything from now on would be new and strange and *not mine*. I bore the mark of Cain.

Like me, Jael wore her nightgown, but her shawl was silk and fastened with a silver pin, and her hair was neatly tucked into a lace cap. Lady Tassell had plainly loaned Jael her own things, in keeping with her station.

How would I even *pay* for my new stays? I had no money at all.

I sat staring at the bewildering array of dishes. The food was all fit for invalids: half a dozen jellies, boiled chicken, a covered tureen of gruel—but gruel as far above Mrs. Humphrey's as my dining companions were above me.

"Some hot salep, madam?"

My eyes flew to the butler, suspecting him of mocking my low birth, and absurdly wounded. But he poured a cup of the thick, warm drink from a small silver urn and set it by me, grating nutmeg over it with a rehearsed flourish worthy of Garrick. "It will soothe your throat, I hope, madam."

I raised it to my nose, and could not smell it. I could not smell anything but smoke. My throat closed.

I could feel Jael's eyes on me from across the table. Under such scrutiny, choosing my breakfast seemed impossible. I blew on my cup, counting the seconds until it would be cool enough to drink. I wished I might pour it into the saucer, as I used to do before I cared about being ladylike. Instead I ran out of patience and burned my tongue.

Of course I could barely taste it, so my judgment that it was not as good as mãe's must be taken with a grain of salt. And for all that it used sassafras and lemons, instead of Turkish orchid-root and rosewater, it was sweet and thick and coated my aching throat. My eyes stung.

I had to pull myself together. I had to wake up.

I wrapped my hands around the hot mug, so each little burn would flare. But after the first moment, I scarcely felt it.

In daylight, the hand and forearm that had held the oil lamp looked sunburned beneath its layer of grime. I saw the lamp in my hand—saw the muslin catch—alluring, soft flames and a spicy, spirituous smell, like Christmas pudding.

Mr. Toogood's fresh nutmeg gagged me, all at once. I set my cup down with a clatter.

"Take whatever you like," Lady Tassell said from behind her newspaper.

"I'm not hungry." I wished I could go and sit in the corner. "I should look in on Tabby."

Lady Tassell set her paper and her spectacles down, frowning at me. Then she reached for a tall flask at her elbow, uncorking it with a pop and a hiss. Briskly, she poured me a glass of the contents and set it by my plate.

I stared at it.

"Well, drink it, child."

It was fizzy and sharp, with a sweet orange flavor. My hunger stirred unpleasantly to life, though the idea of actually eating sickened me no less. Reluctantly, I dished up some chicken and jelly.

"If there is anything else that would make you more comfortable, or tempt your appetite, please believe we should all be delighted to know of it. I have asked Dr. Robeson to come up from Hastings and examine both of you a little later. Do you require any particular care, Lady Palethorp? Or would you prefer your own doctor? You have been ill, I believe."

I could hear the searching in her voice. I kept my eyes on my food, chewing and swallowing mechanically.

"No, I—I am quite weak, but perhaps there was—a want of energy, too. If Kit—if Kit really—" I heard her swallow. "If I'm all Tabby has, I'd better not die."

"I am very glad to hear you say so, my dear," Lady Tassell said.

"Y-yes. I think—" She put her face in her hands. "I'm sorry," she said in a choked voice. "It's only that you're being so kind, and this is such a good breakfast. The best I've had in ages."

I wondered if Lady Tassell thought that a mannerly veil thrown over a deeper grief. I knew it was probably the truth. I wished some tender impulse would prompt me to go to her. To comfort her. But I felt nothing.

Surely it was only that Lady Tassell was watching us; Mr. Munk was coming to question me. When matters were settled, my heart would beat again.

What would I do if it didn't?

My body felt dead, as dead as Sir Kit. I barely noticed that my chicken tasted like ashes, or that my hand hurt, or that my ears still rang, or that my lover wept. Even the knot in my chest and the fear stringing my nerves taut felt far away. The only vivid thing was a sudden memory of violets and sugar: *sweet, not lasting.*

Out of the corner of my eye, I saw Lady Tassell lay a hand over Jael's. "It's quite all right, my dear. Who among us hasn't cried at the breakfast table at one time or another? I really am sorry about Palethorp."

I set my knife and fork down—in their proper places, as if it mattered—and fisted my hands in my lap. "Did anyone else die?" Had that been too loud? I could not tell. "The—the staff—" I could not move, or raise my eyes from my plate.

My half-eaten jelly wobbled sickeningly as Lady Tassell folded her hands on the table. "Are you equal to speaking of this, Lady Palethorp?" she asked, kind but businesslike. "There's no hurry."

Jael's fingers tapped the table. "You might as well."

"I gather that your nurse was not found. I'm so sorry."

My nails dug into my thighs through my napkin.

"Your footman Matthew has a bad burn. After the doctor has visited with you, we will send him to see if the poor fellow's arm can be saved. But no one went back into the house after that accident. I believe all your staff is accounted for."

In all honesty, that was better than I had hoped.

"Kit would be glad to hear that," Jael said.

"I'm afraid that was the best of the news," Lady Tassell said with brisk sympathy. "The fire in the tower has not yet burned itself out, and with this west wind, the rest of the house remains at risk." She put on her glasses to consult a note. I wondered who her informant was. "Some very intrepid young men have done their best to water the roof, and have sandbags in the passageways to keep the fire in the oldest part of the house. Fortunately, those walls are very thick."

She slid the glasses down her nose to look at Jael. "If you are lucky, half the house will be saved, though I'm afraid the family rooms will get the worst of it. The Great Hall is so far intact, which I'm sure will be a relief to the antiquarians—but perhaps we should speak of all this later. It was your home, after all."

"No," Jael said sharply. "It wasn't."

I held my breath.

Lady Tassell did not say anything for several moments. "I have sent to Mr. Simeon Benezet. Are you acquainted with him? I was informed he is one of the trustees of your jointure."

Jael looked startled. "Yes, my lady."

"I know him a little, for we have both been active in encouraging subscriptions among our friends to the Naval Asylum. He is on holiday in Brighton just now, so I sent by water to inform him you might need assistance setting up a new household. If we are lucky, we may get a swift answer, but of course there is no hurry. You are welcome here for as long as you like to stay." She laid her hand over Jael's again.

Jael regarded her blankly. "Thank you," she said, too late.

Lady Tassell's smile faded. "I believe Mr. Munk—well. Sometimes there is no kind way to say the truth. I believe Mr. Munk has sent to Sir Kit's solicitors in Rye, to ask them to write to his heir. Of course nothing is yet certain, and cannot be until they are able to go into the house."

What would they find in Sir Kit's room, besides bones?

In dreadful detail, my mind showed me his clothes burning away from his body, his skin cracking open, his hairs blackening and curling. His exposed cock burning down and crumbling like a cigar. I bit the inside of my cheek.

Lady Tassell was still talking. "...But a great deal of the rooms were covered last night while trying to save your belongings, and the grounds have been searched without result. I'm so sorry."

Jael bowed her head gravely. "Your ladyship is very kind."

Resolutely, I picked up my fork and took a bite of jelly, tasting sugar and smoke. Had I inhaled Sir Kit's cooking flesh? Was some of the fine ash coating my throat his?

If I vomited, they would all look at me, and I could not bear that. I took another sip of orange soda-water, and choked. *It tastes like blood!*

Then I felt my cheek throbbing, and realized I had bitten it through. That was all. Of course it was.

"Are you well, Miss Oliver?" Jael asked.

"Yes, thank you," I got out.

Our eyes met. For a brief instant I felt pierced anew by her beauty, the sweet curve of her cheekbones and the angle of her jaw. Her face was shaped like a cell of a honeycomb. It made my teeth ache.

An instant, and the pain faded. I dropped my eyes so Lady Tassell would not see us looking at each other, but perhaps I was overcautious. Perhaps there was nothing left for her to see.

I excused myself soon after, and made my way to Tabby's room. But I found myself stopped before the closed door. She would be frightened and angry and grieving, and it was my doing.

Tabby was frightened and angry and grieving when you came to Goldengrove, I told myself.

Should I go away, and let Tabby have a governess who wasn't lying to her with every breath, every gesture of affection?

Screaming started inside the room. I heard Clarice's weary voice. "Christ, not again. Can't you go five minutes without shrieking your head off?"

I went in.

Tabby sat up in her trundle bed with the covers pulled to her chin, wailing. Had she ever woken anywhere but at Goldengrove?

I sat on the edge of her bed. "Good morning, Tabby. This is Lady Tassell's house. She wore a very beautiful morning gown to breakfast. Would you like some breakfast?"

"No! …Maybe."

I had stood to lay out her clothes for the day before I remembered that there were none. "Are you cold?"

"Where's Papa? I want Papa."

I felt Clarice's eyes on me. "We don't know, sweetheart," I said. "They're still looking for him."

"Is he dead?"

"Witch-child," the nursery maid said under her breath.

"*Clarice,*" I bit out. But I was afraid to chide her any further. Had she been awake and listening when I left my room last night, hours before the fire? I had told Mrs. Cross I heard the fire from my room. Why hadn't I said I couldn't sleep, and was wandering up and down the stairs?

"Tabby, it is a mark of steadfast character to prefer a hard truth to a kind lie. But we *truly* don't know. We must be prepared for bad news, but the fire is still too dangerous for someone to go in and look in his room."

"You could go in," Tabby said. "You could be very careful."

I shook my head. "It's too dangerous." I reached for her.

She jerked away. "You're just scared! You're scared of the fire. You don't care about Papa. You don't care if he's all by himself and hungry and needs a hug!"

"Spare the rod and spoil the child," Clarice muttered.

I gritted my teeth. "I'm sorry that you're scared and hungry. You're right, I *am* scared. This is very scary. Do you want a hug, or some breakfast?"

She looked at me slit-eyed. "I want Mama."

My head felt like lead as I nodded. "Your mama was here with you all night, and only left to eat some breakfast. I'll go and see if she's finished." I stood. At least if Jael came back to watch Tabby, I could have some private conversation with Clarice.

Jael was still toying with the crusts of her toast, but she bolted up from her chair halfway through my first sentence and hurried to her daughter, with me forgotten at her heels. Tabby climbed at once into her lap.

"Clarice, may I speak with you a moment?" I said when I could breathe around the dull ache in my chest. I led her to my room. "I know that we are all overset, but Tabby is a frightened little girl—"

Clarice's fair complexion mottled. "*She* didn't have to watch her friends go in and out of that firepit to save a few sticks of furniture."

"The only person killed was likely Tabby's father. She is a child, and you are behaving like one. Have some damned compassion."

"The same kind of *damned* compassion her ladyship had on Mrs. Churchill?"

I sucked in a breath. "I am sure Lady Palethorp tried to wake her. The woman was probably insensible with opium." Even to myself, I sounded unconvinced. I would have to do better with Mr. Munk.

Clarice eyed me cynically. "You'd ought to stay here with me. Lady Tassell'd give you a job, too. You don't owe that little brat anything."

I felt a pang. I had grown fond of Clarice—and more to the point, she knew enough to do us a great deal of mischief. *You are not Sir Kit, to keep people under lock and key*, I reminded myself. *Tabby deserves a kinder nursemaid, anyway.* "Are you leaving us, then? I'll miss you."

She snorted. "I'm sure you will, in that madhouse."

I screwed up my courage. "Clarice…Mr. Munk will probably want to speak to you about last night."

She looked right at me. "I slept like a top," she said flatly. "First thing I remember is Lady Palethorp waking me up."

I felt cold. Did she mean that as reassurance, or a threat? Was it wise to press her?

She rolled her eyes in exasperation. "As if she'd have bothered to wake me up," she said *sotto voce*. That wasn't true, was it?

If Jael had not brought Clarice down, I would have gone up and fetched her…wouldn't I?

She sighed. "I know you didn't *mean* to hurt anyone, ma'am. You tried to steer clear of him, and he wouldn't have it. Just put it behind you. Go work for a *nice* family. You stay with the Palethorps, and next time there's trouble they'll forget all about *you* in their rush out the door."

Fear had not been burned out of me, but *something* had. I felt hollow. "And you won't—you won't tell Mr. Munk," I whispered.

"Why should I stick my neck out for a dead man? I've got her ladyship's ring, and Lady Tassell gave me a bit of something, too."

I blinked. "You have the ring? Where?" She wore nothing that could possibly have a pocket, and her neck and hands were bare of jewelry.

She slipped one foot from its shoe. The sapphire winked at me from her second toe. "It's torn a hole in my stocking, but what can you do?"

I felt another dull pang for my emeralds, abandoned in their tin. "Good luck to you and Peter, then."

We shook on it.

Neither the dressmaker from Hastings nor the doctor had arrived by late morning, and by then I was nearly ready to beg for a bath. But the magistrate was expected any moment, so Lady Tassell's secretary, Miss Macnamara, loaned me a dress, and her ladyship herself let me borrow a pair of stays, as she was the only person in the house with more than one set. The dress was too broad in the shoulders and too short in the sleeves, and the stays too small everywhere save my bosom, where they gaped.

"You look fetching," Jael said. "Shall Tabby and I arrange your hair?"

"Oh, yes, please, Miss Oliver!"

I hated to disappoint Tabby, but I had just scrubbed my face and hands raw, and did not want my hair pulled, too. My burned skin throbbed, and the tight cuffs rubbed painfully against my protruding wrists. "Thank you, but Mr. Munk is expected very shortly."

Jael frowned at me. "Do you feel equal to speaking with him?"

"I don't see that I have much choice."

"You could always swoon."

I was still considering it when his carriage wheels crunched outside. I examined myself in the mirror. My cap drooped, my dress drooped, my eyelids and my mouth drooped. The skin beneath my bloodshot eyes was dark with sleeplessness. What would Mr. Munk see, besides a Friday-faced spinster? Did I look capable of murder?

Lady Tassell rapped on the door, and poked her head in. "Mr. Munk is here."

That she had come to fetch me herself instead of sending a servant told me how little confidence she placed in my self-reliance now. I nearly swooned after all—would have, if I didn't feel sure it would be even less convincing than my lies. "Very well."

To my surprise, Lady Tassell led me to her own room, not the parlor. She pulled a pair of long gloves from a drawer. "Try these on." She began digging through hatboxes.

The gloves were tight; I got them on, but when I made a fist, the seams dug painfully into my burn. "Won't he think it's strange that I'm wearing gloves?"

She handed me a straw confection festooned with yellow taffeta, a whole robin perched on the brim. "I'm sorry, it's the plainest one I have. Say you were on the point of going for a walk, and that you feel cold."

"But—"

"We don't have time to argue, child," she said with mild finality. "And don't let that glove fall down your arm. Now, can you tell me what happened last night?"

I went into my explanation again, very conscious of her shrewd eyes on me. She must suspect something, for why else conceal my burns? But if she suspected, why help me?

She frowned at my recitation. "Have you already told this to other people?"

I nodded.

She sighed. "All right." She gave me a tired, perfunctory smile. "You'll get through this. Just keep your wits about you and don't answer questions before they're asked."

"Y-yes, my lady. Thank you."

"Take your time, and don't be afraid to say you don't remember. Kindly do not contradict me in any particular. If I interrupt you, stop talking, and if I tell you not to answer a question, don't."

I blinked, confounded. "Are you coming in with me?" I did not want her. I would lie more easily without her knowing presence.

"Of course. What did you think patronesses do? Believe me, your situation is far better than the runaway apprentice I spoke for last week—who had also done nothing wrong, by the by." She swayed a little as she took up her work-box, and I remembered abruptly that she had been ill.

"You should rest, my lady," I said quickly. "You mustn't tire yourself out more than you already have."

Her lips pressed into a thin, tight line. "I told you I would stand your friend, Miss Oliver. I sent you to Goldengrove, and I will bring you safely away again."

My shoulder twinged. *You are not my friend*, I thought. *Then what are you?*

But when vó had been put to the question, they had stripped her naked and broken her fingers, one by one, to make her betray the people she loved. Did I really think she would not have been glad to take an ally into that room with her? *Any* ally? I curtsied. "Thank you, my lady."

Miss Macnamara was waiting in the corridor, a book open on the lap desk cradled in her arms. Dog-earing her page, she slipped the volume inside the desk and fell into step behind us.

The parlor was airy and white, with a view of the cliffs. Today its loveliness was marred by the hazy light coming through the great southern windows. If I looked closely, I could see flakes of ash on the breeze.

Mr. Munk was a dark shape at the center of all that hazy white.

He rose when he saw us, sober as a judge. For a moment I almost laughed, remembering mãe's instructions: *I'm a good Christian girl, sir. It's all my mother's fault. She lives on Albion Street, if you go now you can get her before she leaves for market.* How he would stare if I said that!

Squaring my shoulders, I went in.

35

"What's the joke?" the magistrate demanded as Lady Tassell led me to an armchair nearly as comfortable as Goldengrove's bergères.

"I beg your pardon, sir, I was thinking of my mother. I hope you are well this morning."

"I am tired." He looked it, still unshaven and in last night's clothes. "If you want this room, my lady, we can use a different one," he said pointedly.

The countess had settled herself on a sofa beside Miss Macnamara, who was very busy laying out paper and ink. Her pen did not suit her; she trimmed it with a fastidious air. I smothered a nervous giggle at Mr. Munk's obvious irritation.

Lady Tassell smiled at him. "That is very obliging. But Miss Oliver is a protégée of mine. I couldn't allow her to undergo interrogation without an advocate. I promise we won't be in the way. Shall Miss Macnamara send you a copy of her notes? You may rely on her accuracy; she writes a very good shorthand."

His eyes rested on me with distaste. "This is hardly an interrogation, my lady."

My skin crawled. *And don't you wish it were?*

"Very well, sir," Miss Macnamara said. "If you change your mind, you must let me know." Her pen's officious scritching sound drew my gaze. Under the date and a few other notations, she had headed the page, *Miss Oliver's Interrogation,* and was underlining it neatly.

I stifled another giggle.

Taking a memorandum book and pencil from his pocket, Mr. Munk dragged his chair very close, between me and Lady Tassell's sofa. "If you would tell me everything you remember, Miss Oliver."

I went through the first part of my story. "...I found him fighting the fire—"

"Where did the fire start?"

"It was in the bed. I think it must have started there, but I don't know."

"Was Sir Kit dressed for bed?"

"No."

"Did he seem sober to you?"

I remembered the countess's advice. "I don't know. He was cheerfully intoxicated when I left Harvest-home with Miss Palethorp, but that was hours before." I twisted my hands in my lap. "I'm afraid I had celebrated myself. Sir Kit poured my glass himself; it would have been rude not to toast. I was quite sick on the way back to the house."

"It is fortunate you were awake, then," he said, rather sardonically.

I shuddered. "Yes."

"Why *were* you awake?"

"It was hot, and I couldn't sleep."

"And you are quite certain the bed was already on fire when you came downstairs?"

"Yes, I—I told you that."

"How big was the fire? Did you think there was much chance of putting it out?"

I saw that blaze on the curtains, and the lamp oil spattering across the mattress. "No," I whispered. "But he did. He would not come away."

"Did you attempt to persuade him?"

"Yes."

"Did he give you any account of what had happened?"

"I don't think so. I was only there a few moments. But I was not—not—I don't remember everything. I have a terror of fires. And I wanted to get to Miss Palethorp. She was above us, locked in—"

"In short, you ran away."

The accusation in his tone silenced me. But was it worth my while to contradict him? Running away was not criminal.

"Running away from a fire that could not be put out seems like good sense," Lady Tassell observed, crocheting steadily. "I wish to God Palethorp had done the same."

Mr. Munk shot her a glare.

"I begged him to," I said, finding my footing again. "But he would not. He gave me his keys, and commanded me to wake the household. Indeed I did less than he ordered, for I gave Lady Palethorp the key to the nursery and went back down. But the fire was spreading into the passageway, and I didn't dare leave the stairwell."

"*Was* Lady Palethorp sleeping when you entered her room?"

My heart pounded. "Yes, I woke her."

"Then her candle was not lit."

"No."

"Did you smell one in the room?"

"No, sir."

"She had not heard all this ruckus that woke you."

"You know her ladyship is an invalid. She frequently takes laudanum to help her sleep."

He leaned in, eyes hard. "What aren't you telling me, Miss Oliver?"

"I beg your pardon?"

"Come now, madam. A man takes up with his governess under his wife's nose, and suddenly the house is in flames?"

Lady Tassell set down her needle with a click, and Miss Macnamara's pen paused. The silence was deafening. I felt hot, suffocated by their gazes.

"I beg your pardon, sir," said the secretary. "Could you explain what you mean by that?" Her imperturbable face was still bent over her desk, her hand suspended above the page with cool poise. I felt a sick, gnawing envy for her dispassion, her lack of direct involvement in this little drama.

"You look old enough to take my meaning," Mr. Munk snapped.

She lifted her head in mild surprise, the lenses of her gold-rimmed spectacles flashing orange.

"Mr. Munk, you forget yourself," Lady Tassell said.

He set his back resolutely to them once more. "Mrs. Cross tells me Lady Palethorp was not allowed a key to her room, because she could not be trusted."

I remembered suddenly that she *did* have a key—or had had one. Where was it now? Might it be found? I had not thought her capable of keeping such a secret.

Lady Tassell let out a long breath. "She was not allowed a key to her room."

"You had a key, however, did you not, Miss Oliver?"

A sick, clammy feeling swept over me. Here it was. He suspected—and the countess's face was worse. She looked as though her worst suspicions had already been confirmed.

"I had a key because I have a terror of fires. Sir Kit was kind enough to give me one when I first arrived." My voice cracked.

Mr. Munk's eyebrows rose.

"Well, and if I had been locked in, we would all be dead!"

"Miss Oliver, did you *know* Lady Palethorp did not have a key to her own room?" Lady Tassell asked me.

"My lady, please," said Mr. Munk.

"My good sir, surely you don't think there can be any excuse for such a thing unless Lady Palethorp were a madwoman, which she plainly is not."

"Mrs. Cross seemed to think she might be," he said. "Or subject to fits." His eyes bored into me. "Perhaps she was passionately jealous?"

He doesn't suspect you. *Let her take the blame,* I thought for a wild moment.

Shame flooded me. I did not fault vó, for informing on her family. She had done as her parents instructed her. She had ransomed her life and her freedom, and raised my mother in love and safety.

But I—I had made up my mind a hundred times that for myself, I would prefer to die rather than give up Jael. Mr. Munk had done *nothing* to me, had not broken one finger or touched a single hair on my head, and already I thought of saving myself at my lover's expense? Why was I so weak?

I thought of the man who had tried to eat his confession. He and I, we were weak; still we must set our faces to the path, and go on as best we could. If my muscles of independence and resolution had atrophied, I could only strengthen them through exercise.

"What difference does it make *what* she is, since she had no key?" I asked. "I don't understand what you suspect, sir."

He sighed. "Neither do I, which is why I would like the truth."

"The truth is that I would have died to prevent what has happened. The truth is that when I think of Sir Kit alone in that room, I—"

Deborah, I'm still in here.

I shuddered violently. "But how could she have done it? Sir Kit would have accused her to me, would have *warned* me. I must have heard something—met her on the stairs. She could not have eaten breakfast with us this morning so calmly, knowing—"

"I thought you said you heard him and Lady Palethorp having a row."

The secretary cleared her throat, turning back a page. "I believe she said, 'I heard a faint racket. At first I thought—I had sometimes heard him and his lady quarreling.'"

Mr. Munk shot her a glance of pure dislike. "Thank you."

She nodded placidly.

"Miss Oliver, let us stop beating about the bush," he said. "I am tired, and I would like to go home. You are concealing something, and until I know whether it is a crime, I shall be obliged to stay here and probably waste my time and her ladyship's. If you were carousing with Sir Kit and the lamp overturned, kindly say so. It is a tragic accident, and I cannot say no one would *blame* you. But the days are over in this district when gentlemen and -women were brought before the bench for ungodly behavior."

I hesitated. Should I do it?

"Mr. Munk," Lady Tassell cut in. "You are offensive."

"I've been kinder than the coroner will be."

My head swam. I had not even thought of the inquest. It astonished me, that I had not. To go through all this again, before a jury and spectators...

"He told his valet to sleep elsewhere," Mr. Munk pressed. "Was he expecting you?"

It was over. I would have to go away, and never see Jael or Tabby again. *You chose your course,* I told myself. *You made a vow. Stick to it for once.*

Calm descended, the relief of a decision it was too late to take back. I was in the eye of the hurricane. I *was* the hurricane, surrounded by the destruction I had wrought. I could see it drifting past the window.

I opened my mouth.

36

"I—I beg your pardon again, Mr. Munk," Lady Tassell said. "But I confess I find all this very troubling. Evidently, I placed poor Miss Oliver in a highly irregular household. Did he *often* ask his valet to sleep elsewhere?"

"In fact, the man says not," Mr. Munk said. "But believe me, my lady, I don't like it any more than you do."

Lady Tassell looked at me. "I hope you will forgive my asking, Miss Oliver, but where did *you* sleep, as a rule?"

I hesitated. But all the servants knew, anyway. "Of late, on a couch in Miss Palethorp's room, my lady."

Lady Tassell's hand curled into a fist in her lap. "I see."

"She had been having nightmares." I bit my lip. "They will be worse, now." Now, they would be real. "But last night I was in my own room adjoining the nursery," I admitted. "I felt unwell after my overindulgence."

Mr. Munk raised his eyebrows at Lady Tassell.

The countess fussed with her needlework "I don't quite like to suggest this, sir, but there *is* another explanation for Palethorp's behavior."

With heavy sarcasm, he swept a hand towards an imaginary jury-box. "Pray enlighten us, my lady."

The countess leaned towards us, her face full of regretful sympathy. "Miss Oliver, you did say Sir Kit was insistent that you leave him? You begged him to come away, and he refused. And he did not tell you how the fire started."

"Yes, my lady."

She hesitated for long moments, smoothing her work in her lap. "You did not think the fire could be put out."

I shook my head.

"Do you believe that Sir Kit thought it could be?"

"I suppose he must have," I said slowly, beginning to see what she was getting at.

"So you don't think—well. You *do* think it was entirely an accident?"

"He wouldn't," I said swiftly. "He was a Christian."

Mr. Munk shot to his feet. "Stop writing," he snapped at the secretary, who ignored him.

"Was his door open when you came downstairs?" the countess persisted.

"It was locked," I whispered. "I thought nothing of it. All the doors were kept locked at night."

"Did he seem pleased to see you?"

The magistrate took two strides and ripped the pen from Miss Macnamara's hand. Lady Tassell shot up from the sofa in a flutter of whitework. "Mr. Munk!"

"Nobody would seem pleased with their bed on fire," I protested weakly. It seemed a singularly dreadful method of suicide. Would anyone really believe it?

But it was a splendid out for my reputation, as well. If pressed, I could say I had virtuously refused him, and be full of remorse at driving him to desperation. Probably no one would quite believe *I* had broken a man's heart, but they might believe I thought so myself.

"Your implication is disgusting," the magistrate said harshly. "The man was shouting and fighting the fire. Why would he do that if he intended self-murder?"

"*Was* he fighting the fire?" she countered. "Or was he only not in his bed?"

The magistrate glared down at her.

"I should be sorry to believe it, too," she said gently. "But you cannot deny that he has been a disappointed man. I saw him not three days ago. The harvest was going superbly, yet he did not seem happy. His wife's illness preyed upon his mind."

Lifting the lid of her desk, the secretary brought out another pen and began to trim it. Mr. Munk slapped a hand over her paper.

She gasped—the first break in her composure I had seen. Lady Tassell put a hand on her shoulder, shifting even closer. "*Sir.*"

"A woman may be ill without driving her husband to suicide, I hope! I'm surprised at you, my lady. You haven't been free of family disappointments yourself, I believe. Yet if you lost your footing on the cliffs tomorrow, I would not put it about that you must have jumped."

Lady Tassell's eyes flashed. "Perhaps I should warn my husband that if I fall from the cliffs, it is because you pushed me, is that what you mean to say?"

"I *beg* your pardon?" The magistrate looked genuinely taken aback.

The countess shook herself, her shoulders relaxing with a visible effort. She rubbed at her eyes. "My apologies, Mr. Munk. You have quite proven your point, that my recent illness has left me susceptible to morbid fancies."

She sat, smoothing her skirts with faintly trembling fingers. Miss Macnamara put an arm around her shoulders. "I am ashamed of myself. Please forgive my rash words, and I hope you won't repeat what I said to poor Lady Palethorp." She smiled crookedly at her secretary. "Keep these notes under lock and key, dear, if you please. If anyone does require a copy, you may redact this exchange."

"Of course Sir Kit meant to come away safe," I said in a tone of relief. "I know he did. They might still find him alive."

A muscle jumped in Mr. Munk's jaw as Miss Macnamara's pen began scritching again. "Between the lot of you, I begin to feel sorry for the Jewess. Spare her your morbid fancies *and* your false hope." He slumped back into his chair, a yawn splitting his face. "Your pardon, ladies."

He looked at me, fingers beating a tattoo on his thigh. "Well, I suppose Palethorp wouldn't thank me for dumping his private life onto the lawn with his furniture. The vicar is coming this afternoon to pay his respects to the widow. He's a pietistical jackass like his father and grandfather before him, so I'll thank you to say nothing that might give him *scruples* about putting whatever's left of Palethorp in the family crypt where he belongs."

"Sir, I know you have been much put upon, not least by me, so I will forgive your lapses in manners," her ladyship said mildly. "I cannot speak for my secretary."

The baleful red daylight glinted off Miss Macnamara's spectacles again as she raised her head. "Please don't regard it. I certainly shan't."

Mr. Munk looked discomfited.

Smiling tiredly at her, Lady Tassell stood and crossed to the bell. Poor Mr. Munk heaved himself politely out of his chair.

"Of course you knew Palethorp better than either of us," she said more warmly. "If you think it an accident, I am satisfied, and I'm sure the coroner will be, too. As you very wisely said, why turn a tragedy into a scandal?"

Mr. Toogood appeared in the door. "Shall I fetch your hat and coat, sir?"

"Not just yet," he said. "I'll need to speak with Lady Palethorp and the nursemaid."

That was it? The interview was over? I had answered none of his questions.

"Her ladyship is not well, sir," the butler said. "But if it cannot be put off, I shall go at once."

Mr. Munk rubbed at his forehead. "And she was excitable even before her illness." He sighed. "My lady, would you oblige me by remaining a little longer, to chaperone? *Without* a repeat of your insinuations—I'd rather not cope with hysterics on top of everything. If their statements agree with Miss Oliver's, it shouldn't take more than a few minutes."

All Jael needed to say was that she had been asleep, and I had woken her. Surely she could manage that?

"Of course, Mr. Munk. Won't you take some tea?" The countess smiled ruefully at him. "And a splash of brandy, perhaps. You've had a difficult night."

A splash of brandy. I saw the red stain spreading on the bed-curtain.

He passed a hand over his face. "I wouldn't say no to strong coffee."

"I will inform Mrs. Toogood at once, sir," said the butler. "Shall I ask Lady Palethorp to step in?"

"Yes, thank you." Mr. Munk's eyes rested on me once more. "You may go, madam."

I rose with a shaky curtsy. I could feel their eyes on me—all of them, even Mr. Toogood holding the door. I scurried back to Jael's room, to watch Tabby while she spoke with the magistrate.

Jael was lying on the bed, staring out the window at the trailing tendrils of a clematis vine against the smoky sky. It was a modern sash-window with smooth, unblemished panes, and still everything we saw was blurred.

Tabby was instructing a sullen Clarice on how to take tea in an extremely superior manner, using invisible cups.

Jael's eyes drifted to my face. "Well?"

That did not sound innocent. I wished she would be more careful before Clarice, and I did not dare contrive an excuse to speak to her alone. "He wants to speak to you next, my lady."

Jael rolled to face the wall. "I don't want to speak to him. I don't want to speak to anyone. I can't do it."

My head began to pound. My reprieve was not complete until she and Clarice had confirmed my account. "He said it will only take a few minutes."

"I don't feel well. Where is Mrs. Churchill? I need her."

Panic tickled my throat, and Clarice shot to her feet.

Tabby kicked her ankle. "You spilled your tea!"

"She's dead," I reminded Jael. "God rest her soul."

"Oh," she said in a small voice. "I forgot."

"I'm giving notice. Goodbye, Miss Christabel. Be a good girl for Miss Oliver, if you've got it in you." Clarice stormed through the door, and slammed it.

Tabby began to cry.

My headache blossomed. "It's all right, Tabby. We'll find someone new you'll like just as well."

"I want Rhoda," she wept.

I opened my mouth to say that maybe we could find her and hire her back—and remembered that she had said demons were pulling Jael's father's beard. "We'll find someone you like," I promised her again. "Someone nicer."

Mr. Toogood rapped at the door and, hearing no protest, opened it. "Lady Palethorp, do you feel equal to speaking with Mr. Munk?"

"No," she said. "Thank you."

It was folly to press her. God knew what she would say to the magistrate. God knew what she would *do*. "Perhaps it would be easier to have it over and done," I said tightly anyway.

She sighed and sat up. Her shawl slipped, and the hem of her nightgown rose. Mr. Toogood averted his face as she swung her legs off the bed, entirely exposing herself.

My heart sank. Mr. Munk was a man of decorous prejudices. Probably he believed that any woman capable of such a display must also be capable of murder.

In this instance, of course, he would be right.

"Never mind." I tried to keep my voice steady. "I'm sorry I pressed you. We had better wait."

Jael shrugged, wandering over to press her forehead to the window.

I hurried to Mr. Toogood. "Please excuse her ladyship. She has been confined to her bed for the last two years, and is unaccustomed to society."

He bowed. "I quite understand. If there is anything her ladyship requires for her comfort, she has only to ask."

"I want my tea set," Tabby piped up.

He smiled at her. "Do you think you might like some sandwiches, too, madam?"

"Yes."

"Why don't you come along to the kitchen, and we'll see what Mrs. Toogood can do."

She gazed up at him, calculating. "This house is very small. Is your kitchen small too?"

"*Tabby*," I said in despair.

"Indeed it is," he said. "But I believe our sandwiches are of the usual size. You must inform me if I have mistaken the matter."

I felt that I ought to accompany my charge, but instead I sat in a rocking chair, still wearing my hat and gloves. The only sounds were the ticking of the clock, the clematis tapping at the window, and Jael breathing. I tried to decide which was worse: noise, or silence.

"I'm sorry I couldn't talk to Mr. Munk." When she turned to face me, the imprint of her forehead stood out on the smooth glass. "I haven't spoken to so many people in…how long has it been?"

"Two years," I reminded her a little hopelessly. She had seemed saner at Goldengrove.

"If I died, would you look after Tabby?"

Was fear the only thing that could pierce this haze? It was a stake through my heart. "You said you wouldn't leave her." I tasted copper at the back of my throat. *Don't leave me.*

"I said I wouldn't leave her with Kit."

"They wouldn't let me." My tongue stumbled over the words in my haste. "They think I was Sir Kit's mistress. Her guardian would never let me stay."

She sighed and turned back to the window. Her weight was on one leg, with the other bent so only her toes touched the floor. Her calf was round and perfect, and the back of her knee looked soft.

"Tabby needs you," I said. Why did she watch the ash drifting by our window, when I was crumbling to dust and blowing away this very moment, and she would not look at me?

"Tabby needs a mother."

"You *are* her mother."

"I'm nothing." She began to cry. "I'm nothing! I thought I would feel better when he was dead, but I don't. I want my old room. I don't know anyone here. I don't know how to talk to them. You're ashamed of me, and Tabby will be, too. I should have just stayed in my room."

I shook my head, but she was not looking at me. I could not speak. I was half-surprised to still see my gloved fingers on the arm of my chair, for I could not feel them.

Someone knocked.

Jael didn't move. I pried open my clenched jaw and said, "Come."

It was Lady Tassell. She frowned at Jael's back, and said to me, "Might I trouble you for a moment's conference, Miss Oliver?"

To my surprise, my joints functioned normally as I stood, walked into the corridor, and shut the door. "Thank you for—for standing my friend, my lady. You were—"

I didn't know how to finish the sentence. She had not been an avenging angel, or a Daniel come to judgment. She had been partial and corrupt, in fact. But I thought of Portia's high-flown, hypocritical speech: *In the course of justice, none of us should see salvation; we do pray for mercy.* Lady Tassell had had mercy on me. "You saved me."

Her smile didn't reach her eyes. "That is kind of you to say."

I felt an unexpected pang of sympathy. "*Kind* does not always mean *false.*"

"I suppose not. Clarice's statement accorded with yours. Mr. Munk and I have settled it that you will dress very plainly at the inquest, and stick to the facts."

My head swam. I put a hand on the wall. Of course there was still Jael's testimony to be got over, but—"Thank you." Why could I not say more? But my tongue lay heavy and torpid in my mouth, without the necessity of lying to spur it on.

"One does one's poor best. One's wealthy best, rather. I subscribed a few pounds to parish relief, to help the Goldengrove servants." She fussed with the fall of her lace. "What should you like to do now? Shall I inquire after another place? I would pay your passage home…"

My own hands felt heavy, especially the throbbing left one; I could not raise them to fidget at my own too-tight cuffs. "I don't know. That is, I shall stay with Miss Palethorp if I'm asked. If not—*could* you find me another place? After—after—" I meant to gesture towards the parlor, but my hands only twitched, and fell limply back to my side.

"Certainly," she said. "Though it might take a month or two. In the meantime, you might perhaps condescend to play for Miss Macnamara and me. It makes letter-writing so much less tedious, and we are neither of us musical."

If I spoke, I would cry.

She saw it in my face, and folded her arms around me. "Oh, you poor girl. I'm so sorry. I ought never to have sent you to that house. Why didn't you *tell* me? You promised to write to me. I begged you to write to me."

Yes, she had been very emphatic on that point. Did she mean, *I sent you there on purpose to write to me*? She knew one of Jael's trustees.

I felt that the idea should trouble me more. But sorting out the implications seemed an exhausting task: did it mean I should trust her less? Or did it mean everything might have been averted if I had trusted her more?

She would not protect me, if she knew what I had *really* done. But I rested my head on her shoulder for a moment, and said without elaboration, "My letters went through him."

She let out a shuddering breath. "This is all my fault. I ought to have made you come away with me last week. Did he hurt you?"

I felt his thumb pressing between my brows. Would there come a day when that was all I could clearly remember of him?

"You really don't seem well." she said, letting me go to feel my forehead. "Where is that damned doctor?" Her brows drew together. "You're not with child, are you?"

I drew in a sharp breath. I had been trying not to think of that. I had succeeded in not thinking of it.

She closed her eyes against the look on my face. "That bastard. Oh my dear, I'm so sorry." She pinched the bridge of her nose; the pressure between my brows deepened. "All right, let me think. I wish I knew the doctor better. Perhaps I'd better send for a different one."

I was tempted to deny it all, and hope my courses came. But hope seemed beyond me, somehow. "I don't think so," I said, so quietly I could barely hear myself. "But do you know if your cook grows pennyroyal?"

"I shall find out directly. Oh, poor child, I've got ink on your face." She rubbed at my forehead.

I flinched.

"You must not blame yourself for anything. Whatever may have occurred last night… You are not to blame, if you felt you had no other recourse."

So. She imagined I had fought to defend my virtue, when nothing could be further from the truth. "I didn't…"

"Of course," she said resignedly. "I am sure it happened just as you said. You had better go for that walk, and get some air. I wish it were fresher, but…"

I wanted to tell her that she must not blame herself either. I wanted to say I wasn't sorry I had come to Goldengrove. Who knew how long the house would have stood without me? I would have liked, even, to fuss over *her*—to pour her tea and fetch her a shawl and tell her not to run herself ragged.

But I could not find my tongue, and she did not need me. We were not friends. I went for my solitary walk under the hazy red sun, wishing freedom tasted sweeter.

When I returned, sweating behind my veil, Mrs. Wakefield and Mrs. Abbott were just descending from a carriage with baskets of fresh fruit. As I hurried into the house and past the parlor, determined to avoid them, I heard Mrs. Toogood telling a story about Tabby's ill manners, and the countess laughing.

When I passed Jael's room, I saw, with a shock, Lady Tassell's maid cutting her hair. "No, shorter," she was saying. "As short as it can be, and still be tied up." She didn't notice me.

I went to my empty room, and carefully brushed my borrowed clothes over the grate. It seemed rude to give them back covered in ash.

The doctor came at last, and allowed that we could safely bathe, if we were sure to dry our hair very thoroughly afterwards. So the worst of the grime was gone when the dressmaker arrived with two assistants.

Tabby could not be barred from the room for such a thrilling occurrence, and so I was present too as they took Jael's measurements, averting their eyes from her bruises. Lady Tassell's maid was present; that was good. If the countess thought—*knew,* I corrected myself—Sir Kit a brute, she would protect us the more surely.

At first Jael behaved with a good grace, and the ease of a woman who had been dressed by others all her life. Despite her bruised face, she looked the part too, an embroidered bandeau wound over her newly shorn hair. The slightest pouf peeked out at the crown of her head, and a few thick curls escaped to brush her cheek and fall into her eyes.

But her social muscles would need exercise as surely as her legs. Within half an hour she was silent and sullen again, shifting restlessly and invariably contriving to move her flesh into the path of a pin—and invariably glaring at the hapless woman who had pricked her.

They had not brought black cloth. We were all pretending Sir Kit might yet be found—all of us but Jael, who snapped as they debated which of two sober green cottons better suited her complexion, "Why are you wasting your time and my money? Make it black."

I winced. I could see the dressmaker smile insincerely, her jaw clenched. "God willing you shall wear this many times in joy, my lady, but I won't make it up yet, since you don't wish it." Probably she had never meant to make up any of the colored gowns at all; she spoke with the anger of one who has had a kindness rebuffed. "I brought some plain gowns ready-made, for you to wear until you have settled on a complete new wardrobe."

"Mama will order her complete new wardrobe from London, won't you, Mama?" Tabby piped up with a hard stare at the dressmaker.

Jael broke into a smile at that, and seemed to get some of her patience back. She gave the woman a sidelong, apologetic look: *the things children say!* "I don't know if I'd like to go to London just yet, *minha filha*. I'm sure Mrs.—I'm so sorry, I've forgotten your name."

"Fisher."

"I'm sure Mrs. Fisher can make me up some lovely gowns to wear until I can order better."

Thank God for my sore throat, which turned my laugh into a fit of coughing. Alas, it was my turn next to be poked and prodded and stared at—my unease growing all the while, for no one said a word about who would pay for my new dress, and I knew very well I could not myself.

The worst of it was that *she* stared at me, eyes narrowed, almost as though she was angry. And I could not talk to her. Even if they all left, I wasn't sure I could do it.

"Mrs. Fisher, I only need one, or perhaps two—" I began despairingly.

"Don't put her in tan," Jael burst out. "Look at her complexion. She should wear dark colors."

My stomach roiled.

"Anyone could see *that*," Tabby chimed in.

"Oh, for Heaven's sake, I didn't mean dark brown." Jael jumped up from her seat. "Haven't you got anything wine-colored?"

Mrs. Fisher glared at *me*—most unfairly, when I would have worn the tan without complaint. But I stood like a doll and let Jael hold up fabric to my face, flushing hot whenever she exclaimed in satisfaction and set a bolt of cloth aside, while Mrs. Fisher and her assistants exchanged bemused glances at the idea that any shade or style could flatter *me*.

By the time the dressmaker began to pin me into a claret muslin I could not possibly afford, I felt lightheaded from standing still so long. When there came a clatter of hoofbeats and carriage wheels, I started so violently I nearly overturned my stool, a pin scratching a line of fire along my collarbone.

Sir Kit!

It was the fancy of a moment, and vanished like a dream, leaving only the dull pounding of my heart. To this day I cannot say whether I feared a specter, or had only forgotten he was dead.

"I beg your pardon, ma'am," the seamstress said perfunctorily.

"It was my own fault," I said flatly. "Who is visiting so late?"

"It's only six o'clock, ma'am."

"Oh. Of course," I said. "It's only so dark because…"

I ceased to think of the visitor, who must be a friend of Lady Tassell's—

until a maid poked her head in to say, "Mr. Toogood's compliments, Miss Oliver, and you have a visitor."

I felt lightheaded. Dreadful possibilities swarmed: it was Mr. Munk, with the constable and a warrant. It was Mrs. Cross. It was the mother of poor Matthew, come to reproach me for his burned arm. "Me? Are you certain?"

The seamstresses fell away from me. For a dizzy moment, my stool felt like a scaffold. Then I realized they were only letting the maid through, to hand me a card, and one as familiar to me as my own. Two finely drawn and colored half-slices of lemon bracketed the words *INSTRUCTION for Ladies in* Drawing, *Painting in* Watercolors *and* Oils, *Anatomy, & the Modern Languages by Miss Iphigenia Lemmon.*

37

"Miss Oliver is not at home to callers," Jael said.

I realized I had been staring at the card for several seconds, not breathing. "No! I shall be there directly, tell her I will be there directly." I barely noticed Jael plucking the card from my hands as I looked down at my half-pinned dress in indecision.

"You can wear it if you like," the dressmaker said resignedly. "We'll measure Miss Palethorp while we wait."

For a moment I could see only difficulties. What if the seamstresses wished to leave before Iphigenia, and what if…? But the alternative was to make Iphigenia wait, so I nodded gratefully and hurried down the hallway. With every other step I trod on the unpinned hem, resolved to be more careful, and forgot again at once.

The door I had just shut opened behind me. "Mama!" I heard Tabby protest.

"I'll be right back, minha filha," Jael said in honeyed tones. She was at my elbow, catching her breath, when I entered the airy white parlor for the second time that day.

Iphigenia leapt up from the sofa with a shriek, her smile splitting her face. "Livvy!"

I could not breathe for how familiar she was—and how strange that familiarity felt to me then. I knew her spring-green pelisse, her cap of dotted toile with her hair glowing through it, the deep laugh lines bracketing her mouth, the mole to the left of her nose that she used to try to hide with powder. I knew how she smelled, and how it felt to be wrapped in her long arms.

It had not even been five months since we parted, yet I felt I was seeing a specter after all.

"Look at you! That wine color is marvelous on you."

"You must be Clytemnestra Lime," Jael said behind me. "I've heard so much about you."

I felt sick. Jael had heard far too much.

Goldengrove had felt so secret, so immured from the world. It had seemed impossible they would ever meet. Now it was borne in upon me that Iphigenia lived in the neighborhood, and I had no real measure of Jael's discretion.

Iffy's wide smile turned quizzical, her nose wrinkling. Her eyes flicked to her own card, pinched between two of Jael's fingers. "I beg your pardon?"

"My old schoolfellow Miss Lemmon—Lady Palethorp," I said.

Light dawned in Iphigenia's face. "It's an honor, my lady. I'm so sorry for your recent ordeal."

Jael inclined her head. "You are very kind."

"Can you spare Livvy for an hour or two? I'm afraid I can't stay longer."

Jael considered. She and Tabby had the same weighing stare; my heart thumped in my chest, a sweet, piercing pain.

Then Lady Tassell bustled in. I could not decide whether I was relieved. "Miss Lemmon, what a pleasure."

Iffy curtsied with graceful informality, not nearly low enough. "How do you do, Lady Tassell?"

Lady Tassell eyed her indulgently. "Tired, mostly. I would ask you the same if you were not the picture of good health. I am so glad Mrs. Musgrave could spare you. I thought of sending the cart—I did not know she kept a carriage."

A strange expression flickered over Iphigenia's face. "Her mother has just come for a visit, and insisted on loaning me hers."

"How kind of her."

"Ye-es," Iphigenia said doubtfully. "I can't stay long. I wish I could, but… Is there somewhere Livvy and I could sit, out of everyone's way?"

"You must stay right where you are," the countess said. "You shall have your supper on a tray. Are you sure you can't stay the night? If the only difficulty is the carriage—"

Iphigenia shook her head swiftly. "But thank you."

Jael hesitated, but at last she swept out in Lady Tassell's wake.

"Is she *jealous* of me?" Iffy murmured delightedly.

... *Was* she? I should be pleased by the idea, shouldn't I? Instead I only felt tired. Iffy glowed as much as she had in the brilliant morning of eighteen, and I would never be well again, or whole.

"Oh, poor Livvy." She hugged me again. I could feel myself atrophying. "I'm so sorry. What happened?"

"I can't speak of it. I—I can't. I'm sorry."

She frowned. "If Sir Kit weren't already dead, I think I'd have to murder him."

The ugly sound I made was half a laugh—half worse things.

"Was that awful of me to say?" She bent to unlace her boots. "I'm sorry, I just can't wear these another moment. Maybe you'd better sit farther away."

"I can't smell anything but smoke."

"Are you sure you don't want to talk about it? For *you*, of all people, to be in a house-fire! I wish so much I could stay longer."

"How is Mrs. Musgrave's?" I had some vague idea of being polite, and not monopolizing the conversation. But there was a little silence, and I realized it had sounded like a set-down, to turn the subject so abruptly.

"It's odd," she said at last. "Mrs. Musgrave..." She shook her head with a little laugh. "Well. I suppose she has reason to be unhappy."

"Odd in what way?"

Iphigenia pressed her lips together and didn't answer.

I felt dull and hopeless. She was severed from me now. She had been for years. I had pulled away from her, little by little, had made myself narrower and smaller. *They are not your friends.*

But vó had not meant the whole human race. Iphigenia *had* been my friend—still was my friend, when I had stopped being hers. For years now, she had tried to have enough heart for both of us. *Darling Livvy*, she had written, and I had sent back, *Dear Iphigenia*.

"I'm sorry, Iffy. I don't know what happened to me."

"What do you mean?"

My throat hurt. "I—I got old, I suppose. I dried out."

She laughed. "Livia Drusilla! Women aren't *grapes*."

Which of us had been the originator of that phrase? I couldn't remember; we had been so young. "I feel like a raisin."

She glanced outside. "Do you think it's warm enough for sea bathing?"

"The air is awful."

"You were going to walk all the way to Rye to meet me, and now you won't go swimming?"

"It's a mile to the nearest beach, and the soldiers in the Martello tower…."

"Oh, they won't glance twice at two old ladies like us."

I opened my mouth, meaning to protest again. But my misery was a harsh red light sweeping across my mind: it sought an argument, and found nothing. Was I only protesting out of habit, then?

"They won't glance twice at *me*, anyway," I said. "That's a comfort." My lips twitched when she elbowed me.

My turned ankle flared up as we trudged along the cliff, and sweat coated my skin. But I was absorbed by the great plume of smoke rising in the distance, though Goldengrove itself was out of sight. The sun was smudged, as though I had made a pastel drawing and rubbed my thumb across it.

"I've really missed you," Iffy said.

I glanced at her in surprise. "I missed you, too," I said much too late. "More than you can imagine."

She frowned. "Why wouldn't I be able to imagine it? Honestly, Livvy, I don't know why I bother paying you compliments, when you never believe them."

I was still turning that over in my mind when we reached the shore. I turned it over as I undressed mechanically, barely managing to care that I was probably already ruining my new dress, or to be nervous about the whistles from the nearest Martello tower. I waded into the sea, still distracted.

Iffy closed her eyes and dropped underwater, and I mimicked her. The saltwater stung my burns, and everywhere I had scrubbed raw to get the ash off, but I felt cool for the first time in days.

When I came up, wiping my eyes, the air was still hazy, the sun wavering, the ocean too fiery to look directly at. But I felt somehow that my eyes had not been focusing, and now they were. The world was blurry, not my own vision. I felt that my legs were solid under me, and would hold me up.

"I should paint the sea like this," Iffy said. "I wish I had more carmine in my paint box. But I suppose a little will do, when there are so many shades."

I had been spending too much time indoors, where everything was still, the colors even. I picked out shades of red, floating, rocked in the sea's arms. Archimedes's principle explained buoyancy, too: it was not only for appraising crowns. I must explain that again to Tabby, in case she had not understood it.

The water moved against my skin, and the wind. Iphigenia was beautiful and smiled at me.

I did not feel clean, or whole, or even happy. Maybe I would never feel clean or whole again. But I could still *feel*.

We must act, or atrophy and perish.

"Thank you," I said quietly to Iphigenia as we walked back to the house. More time had passed than I realized. The smudged sun was halfway to the horizon, and blood-red.

"What are friends for?"

My shoulder twinged. I was relieved to feel it so sharply.

We were nearly dry again by the time we reached the house, but they scolded us anyway, and made us drink hot tea and spread out our hair by the fire—already lit for Lady Tassell, who felt the cold keenly after her illness.

I could feel Jael watching me.

I just want to touch your hair, Euphemia, she had said. I wished I could believe that was why she watched me. Did I imagine something darker in her gaze?

When the clock chimed, Iphigenia set down her half-emptied cup. "Lady Tassell, might I take some of that supper with me? I'm so sorry to be a bother."

"Miss Li—emmon, could I have a word with you?" Jael said.

My heart sank, but I could find no good reason to object, so I let Iphigenia hug me one last time and scold, "Write more often."

I wrote you every week, I wanted to say, but the words died in my throat. And what if she said, *Yes, I know, more often than that*? I was afraid to find that I had wronged Sir Kit, about anything.

I sat in the window and watched the three ladies conferring with each other. About me? But why? At last Iffy climbed into the carriage, and was borne away.

If I had been at Goldengrove, I could have watched the road for miles. Here her carriage curved left after five minutes, and was out of sight. I should go and find Tabby. But I stayed at the window, watching the burning sea.

Someone cleared their throat.

I jumped, and turned to see Mr. Toogood proffering a crisp, starched bundle of clean clothes.

I lifted Tabby's nightdress, astonishingly white again, free of any trace of grass or dirt or smoke. Beneath it lay my wrapper. Clean, folded flat and square, there was nothing to distract the eye from a smattering of stubborn yellow spots.

I could not breathe: drops of lamp oil. The matching red circles on my hand stood out starkly as I took the garment from him, fighting the impulse to hurl it into the hearth before it condemned me. Had it already? Did he know? *Out, out, damned spot!*

Mr. Toogood launched into an abject apology, voice stiff with shame. "…Stains that have been exposed to heat are always difficult, but that's no excuse."

"It doesn't matter," I forced out at last, hoarse. "Thank you."

I avoided the breakfast room the next morning. Jael appeared in my doorway as I was finishing my rack of toast, a silent, accusing apparition in hat and gloves and new gray summer pelisse.

"Did you want company on your walk?" I asked finally.

She raised her eyebrows as if to say, *Obviously*.

I put on my own new clothes. The navy-blue gown felt stiff and tight across my shoulders, and I held myself stiffly in it. I was still wearing Lady Tassell's stays. Maybe that was why my head began to ache as I followed Jael towards the cliffs. Certainly the sun was not bright enough to hurt my eyes.

She was winded by the time we reached the sea, less than a hundred yards distant. She put her head down and her fists on her thighs, gasping for breath.

I saw the plume of smoke had stopped rising from Goldengrove at last. A low brown cloud hovered instead.

Jael put back her veil. Her eyes were cold. "I'll have to talk to Mr. Munk soon."

She didn't mean to sound so harsh, I told myself. *She's only out of breath.* But my heart pounded as I lifted my own veil. "It shouldn't take more than a few minutes. You have only to tell him that I came and woke you—"

"But you didn't."

My heart beat faster. "I know."

I had been trying not to think of it. Tabby could have died. I tried to shake off the phantom pressure of Sir Kit's fingers on my ankle. Why hadn't I stomped on them, as she had? Why hadn't I—

"Were you ever planning to?"

"When we made the plan, yes. But then I thought—I wanted his keys. I wanted to free the servants. If Peter had died, Clarice would have—"

"You thought if both the Palethorps burned together, you would have Tabby all to yourself?"

38

"*What?*" I could not breathe.

Were you ever planning to? She had meant—she thought—

"Of course I was planning to let you out! I didn't mean I didn't plan to let you out at *all*. I meant I would do it after I had already— How could you think that?" My borrowed stays dug into my ribs as I gasped for air. "I did it for *you*. I thought it would be surer if I went alone, and if it didn't come off, no one could suspect you, if you were locked in your room all the time—"

She frowned at me, as though she could have no way to measure the truth of my words. As though I were a stranger of whose character she knew nothing. "So it was only that you thought I was too reckless to be trusted."

"I'm sorry. I'm so sorry. Tabby could have died." My ankle flexed restlessly, a petty little stab of pain. So much less than I deserved.

"You had an extra key, and you kept it from me. Just like him."

I wanted yesterday's dull distance back. "How did you know?"

"I searched your room that night you left me under your bed. A stale Christ bun weighs about one twentieth what a brass key does." Her eyes were too bright. "I should push you over right now. Give me one good reason why I shouldn't."

I didn't step back from the edge. I didn't step away from her. I shut my eyes, and remembered the cool seawater closing over my head yesterday. "It would look awfully suspicious."

"Is that the best you've got?"

I opened my eyes. I saw her very clearly: pale in the sunlight, face puffy, eyes red and swollen, her bruise yellowing. Her beauty was a sharpened knife, cutting out my heart. I had been afraid nothing would ever be so sharp again.

What could she take, that I didn't owe her?

I felt myself smile. "The quality of mercy is not strained; it droppeth as the gentle rain from heaven, upon the place beneath."

She narrowed her eyes at me. "I can't remember the last time it rained here."

I stepped closer to the edge of the cliff. I could not wipe the smile from my face. Why? What was funny? *Maybe I'll jump*, I thought dreamily. That seemed funny, too.

The murky sea was beautiful, its comforting susurration like a shell held to my ear. I counted shades of red and orange. My eyes were caught by the smoke hovering over Goldengrove.

I, Deborah Oliver, had brought those walls tumbling down with my bare hands.

Jael was reaching towards me. To pull me back? To push me over?

I lifted my hands over my head, reaching for the sky. I remembered that night on the roof, the wind catching my hair. Now my clothes weighed me down, but I still felt light enough to catch the wind and float away—the god going back into the machine—

Then I saw someone coming from the house. Running, in fact, a swift figure in gold and green. I dropped my arms hastily and stepped away from the cliff's edge, solid again, and embarrassed by my theatrics.

"Do you think the wind is turning seaward, Hal?" I asked Lady Tassell's footman as he dashed up, putting out my hand as though that was what I had been doing all along—as though the direction of the wind was not plain in the drifting ash. "None of the neighboring houses have caught, have they?"

"They've dampened all the nearby roofs." Hal looked between us. "A young gentleman is here to see you on business, my lady. A Mr. Eleazar Benezet?"

I could not read the penciled note on the calling card he gave her unless I stepped closer, and I did not dare.

I didn't even catch a glimpse of Mr. Benezet that day. At the house, Jael asked me to keep Tabby company, and went into the parlor where he was waiting with Lady Tassell. Poor Tabby was fretful and subdued, so I dined with her in the kitchen while the servants rushed in and out with chafing dishes, the least of them better informed than I was about my employer's doings. As I watched Mrs. Toogood arrange fresh fruit in a porcelain basket, careful not to brush the bloom from the grapes, she told me Mr. Eleazar was a nephew of Jael's trustee, and her old friend, and seemed very desirous of helping her and hers—indeed, if I wished him to perform any little errand for me, she was sure he would be glad to do it, and I must just give Mr. Toogood a note.

This last was added in such a way, and after such a pause, as made me very certain it was her own kind notion, and no one else's.

"*I* want grapes," Tabby said stridently, and I was shamed to hear my own thoughts in a child's mouth. How could I blame Jael for thinking me jealous and spiteful enough to leave her to burn?

Mrs. Toogood seemed glad to give her a bunch of grapes, and bore it philosophically when Tabby then refused to eat them, for "I only like the *green* ones," as though their color was a surprise. So I had my grapes after all. They tasted sour.

After supper, I tried to entertain Tabby with books and objects I had found around the house, but she only demanded *The Wise and Witty Governess.*

"It's not here," I told her. "It's at Goldengrove. It might be a few days before we can get another copy."

"Ask Lady Tassell for her copy."

"I don't think she has one."

"But Mrs. Dymond is married to her son. I'll ask her if you don't want to."

"Tabby, you must not mention Mrs. Dymond to her ladyship. They don't get on." I felt a little sad when Tabby subsided without protest. One more secret for her to keep.

At last Jael appeared, eyes bright with drink, to rip all the pins from her hair with a groan of relief and chase Tabby about the room, giggling and shrieking.

"It's almost time for bed," I said wearily.

Tabby came to a screeching halt. "I can't go to bed without Adeline."

"Adeline isn't here, sweetheart. You know that." I reached for the buttons of the old-fashioned little dress she wore—one of Mr. Anthony Dymond's from before he was breeched.

She clenched her fists and pressed her arms against her side. "I want Adeline."

"I know. I'm sorry. I wish she were here, too."

She narrowed her eyes at me. "You left her to die."

A chill struck my heart. Behind her, Jael drew back.

Tabby knows, I thought. *She knows, and she will hate me.*

"I know you miss your doll," I said again, gently. "I know you loved her. I'm sorry."

"*I* left Adeline to die," Jael said unexpectedly. "Not Miss Oliver. I did. Because you are my little girl and I only care about you."

Tabby's scowl relaxed into a mere frown. "And Clarice and Miss Oliver." She did not include her papa.

Jael's lips curved. "And Miss Oliver. Clarice...well, I know *you* like her, minha filha, and that is what matters."

I tried not to read too much into this very minor admission.

"I don't like her that much," Tabby said. Thinking her distracted, I reached again for her buttons, but she drew away. "I want to wear mourning for Adeline."

Jael and I glanced at each other. "All right," I said, voice not quite steady. "We will tell the seamstress to make your new clothes black."

"Can I have a veil like yours, Mama?"

I shivered at a memory of my first sight of Jael, in the chapel—her hands like a waxwork, and the faint stench of laudanum. *Can you hold him down while I smother him?* she had said. Was that the method they had used to drug her?

But Jael laughed. "You can wear mine, how's that?"

Tabby gave her mother a weighing look. "I want my new doll to be blond. With curly hair. She should wear black, too. Adeline was her sister."

"Very well," I said, resolving to make the new doll soft enough to sleep with. "I'm sure the dressmaker will have scraps for us. We can look through fashion plates tomorrow. What will you name her?"

She gave this some thought. "Kitty." Jael and I both flinched. "*Lady* Kitty."

"A very elegant name," I said after a moment. "But you must not make up your mind until you see her face. Perhaps she will not look like a Kitty."

Again I felt a flash of dread at her shrewd look—*she knows.*

I was afraid to sleep in my own room that night. I wanted to hear Jael and Tabby breathing. I took Clarice's abandoned pallet, my hip-bone scraping against the floor through the thin straw.

I dreamed I was being crushed by Sir Kit's body. He was on fire above me and I could not get free, couldn't move my limbs. My sleeve caught, then my hand. Soft, languid plum-pudding flames. I was numb. The fire merely tickled as it spread.

I opened my mouth, and could not scream. Sir Kit's blood soaked my nightgown, pooling between my legs. I could hear the rising rush of the fire…

I woke tangled in my sheet, my burned arm trapped beneath my body. Rain pattered on the roof, a sweet rushing sound, and moonlight meandered through the open shutters.

I dipped a hand between my legs and held it towards the window. I did not imagine the faint dark smears of blood on my fingertips, did I?

But no, my courses had come, though not heavily enough yet that I need worry about staining the sheets. My belly ached sharply, and my despair felt less thick. I wished I had not said anything to Lady Tassell.

There was a slight chill in the air, finally. Why did I still have bad dreams?

I wished I had the right to crawl into bed with Jael. Should I wake her anyway? *We must act, or atrophy and perish.*

My mother's guitar case leaned against the wall. Feeling very foolish, I laid it down and cradled it against me, my arm curled over its neck. The clasp dug into my forehead, like Sir Kit's thumb.

I flipped it open and slipped my fingers inside to feel the threadbare velvet lining. I didn't let myself cry. I didn't think I could do it quietly.

Tabby woke me. I blinked, groggy. What time was it? The shutters were closed, but enough light came through to glint off Tabby's eyes and hair and make her nightdress seem faintly luminous. Near dawn, perhaps. The rain had stopped. I wondered if Goldengrove was still burning.

"What's the matter?" I croaked.

"I had a bad dream about smugglers."

I blinked at her, trying to puzzle out the truth. At last I gave up, pushing the guitar out of the way and patting the pallet beside me.

She curled up against me, warm and pointy. I drew in a deep breath for the first time all night. "What was your dream really about?"

Silence.

Wearily, I kissed her head. "If you change your mind, I'm here." I hesitated. "I have bad dreams too sometimes, especially when the weather is warm. Wake me up if I push you or make strange noises."

"What are your dreams about?"

I knew there was a reason to lie. I couldn't remember whether it was a good one. I couldn't manage to care. "Fire. I'm half-Jewish, like you. My grandmother's family lived in Portugal. The people there didn't like Jews very much, so they burned them sometimes." Then I remembered the reason: she was too young. She would be frightened. Her courage would atrophy, like mine had.

"Do people like Jews anywhere?"

"I don't know." Her braided hair smelled so sweet. Well, perhaps *sweet* was the wrong word. And why was it sticky? I kissed her again. "I like Jews, though."

"Is Mama a Jew?"

"You must ask her."

"But you like her," she pointed out, as though it were evidence in favor. Maybe I should prepare a lesson or two on logic, if Jael decided to let me stay.

"I do, yes. But I don't *only* like Jews. I like some Christians, too."

"Like me."

I sighed, fully awake now. Would I have to keep on with catechism lessons? "I do like you, very much. But it's up to you if you want to be a Christian or not."

"I want to be a Christian like Papa."

No, I thought. *If you are a Christian, you will be a different sort than your Papa.* "All right."

"Is Papa in Heaven?"

Tabby deserved honesty, and I only had so much of it to give her. "I don't know if I believe in Heaven. What do you think?"

"I think he is," she said decisively. "He's looking down at me. He misses me."

I snuggled close. I had no right; I should have felt guilty and ashamed. "Of course he misses you. You're the best little girl in the world."

"Mr. Benezet is taking me to Rye to buy a new guitar," Jael announced at breakfast. "Miss Oliver, you must come and help me choose it."

We would have to pass Goldengrove to get to Rye. Would people stare? What if we met a friend of Sir Kit's? "But Tabby…" I protested weakly.

"Don't worry about that," Lady Tassell said kindly. "One of my housemaids has a cousin who would love to fill Clarice's position, and I asked her to come up this morning to see if she would suit. By all accounts she is a good-hearted, sensible girl. Between her and Mrs. Toogood, Miss Palethorp will be quite well looked after."

So I grimly buttoned myself into my stiff new dress and let Mr. Toogood assist me into my stiff new pelisse. Eleazar Benezet handed us into his rented carriage, and off we went.

Jael was still inquiring eagerly after old acquaintances and family connections, for she and Mr. Eleazar had evidently been thrown so much together before her marriage, that all of yesterday afternoon and evening had not been sufficient to bring her up to date. I felt very middle-aged, pressed into my corner watching the stubbled fields go by.

The landscape was strange without being picturesque: dusty roads over marshy flats, chopped up by straggling, slatternly rivers and the crisp military canal. At last Rye rose up ahead, perched atop its hill.

It had been a prosperous port when the Yorks and Lancasters ruled England, but the harbor had been slowly silting in ever since. Now the town resembled the last Stuart at the end of her reign—elevated only to be gawked at, turning her throne into a nest of mustard plasters and crumpled handkerchiefs. But I had always nursed a secret fondness for splotchy Queen Anne, and as we crossed the River Brede and bumped up a steep cobbled street, I discovered a senseless partiality for Rye as well.

As we rose, the horizon dipped out of sight until the town seemed to float in the sky: a few streets lined with a jumble of bleached stone, faded brick, plaster and peeling timbers. Everything was scoured by sun and wind and salt water, and gray-green moss crept over the roof tiles.

It felt like home—even the faint but pervasive smell of drying fish. Quieter, of course, but I had grown older and less fond of bustle since my Portsmouth days. Rarely, in the gap between houses or down a narrow side street, I glimpsed ships in the quay and silver flashes of marsh, tidal beach, or the flat Rother snaking its brief way to the sea.

The music shop was in a ramshackle little townhouse, with an overhanging upper story of Tudor plaster. SHRIVER'S MUSIC WAREHOUSE, it said above the double windows displaying violins, flutes, and a harp. Jael ignored Mr. Benezet's proffered arm, and rushed in.

Mr. Benezet, nothing daunted, offered the arm to me. We followed her at a snail's pace, for he seemed to think my ankle nearly broken. As we minced past a myriad of notes and placards advertising concert tickets, music lessons, and dancing masters, a small sign caught my eye, in a spidery, old-fashioned hand.

Miss J. A. Chapel, guittar lessons.

Those few words were a whole tale to me. I could imagine Miss Chapel clearly: a frail, shabby-genteel lady with hunger pangs scored into her face. She lived alone, and wished she could afford an extra ha'pennyworth of milk for the kittens in the mews.

Would I starve when I was old?

"Oh, I meant to ask you," Mr. Benezet said. "You must have lost some money in the fire." He hesitated, a hand going into his pocket. "Shall I give you cash, or would you rather I pay for your purchases today?"

Jael had entirely forgotten me, rooting through the sheet music piled on the counter.

"Do you mean to stay until Michaelmas? I could advance you this quarter's wages." He grimaced at my expression. "Forgive me if my questions have somehow insulted you. I never quite understand genteel etiquette about money."

"It isn't that."

"Look at this, Calpurnia!" Jael waved a sheet at me. "You should choose some music for yourself. Is Mr. Shriver in? I seem to remember him always somewhere about the place."

"He's out tuning a piano, but I can assist you with whatever you might need," said the apprentice. He nodded to me without a flicker of recognition.

She held out her hand to him. "I'm Jael Palethorp. I need to replace my guitar."

He changed color, and stammered. I wished we had not come—or at least, that I had not.

But Jael followed him eagerly to the back of the shop, where the pianos were displayed, and tried guitars, one after the other. For the most part they were beautiful, warm-sounding instruments, finely ornamented—and plainly she was not satisfied with any of them. Probably it was only that she missed her own, but I felt poorer and poorer.

She smiled at my expression. "You don't like them either, do you? Which is the best of the lot, do you think?" But she shook her head at the one I indicated. "I shall take the plainest, for now, until I find something better— Why do you make that face? What did I say?"

I shook my head mutely.

"Sophronia—"

"Call me Miss Oliver," I hissed.

She frowned. "Why? No one can think anything of it. You are my daughter's governess, and my—my friend—"

I felt a crushing sense of familiarity. "A governess and her employer cannot be friends."

Her cheeks flushed. "I beg your pardon?"

"Let's go for ices," Mr. Benezet said, too cheerfully. "This heat's enough to wear on anyone's nerves."

"First I think *Miss Oliver* should say what she means for once," said Jael in a hard voice.

"You know very well what I mean," I snapped. "You pay my salary.

Without it, I would be—I would be Miss J. A. Chapel."

"Who?"

"I mean that you cannot pretend us into equality. You may take the plainest, for now, until you find something better. But when you do, *I* shall have nowhere to go but the workhouse." That was enough of an exaggeration to reduce my whole argument to absurdity—Lady Tassell had already offered to find me another job—but I did not care.

Her sweet mouth compressed in a hard line. "I have done nothing to deserve this."

"It is not a question of desert. It is a question of facts."

"Is pistachio ice still your favorite, Jael?" poor Mr. Benezet tried again.

Jael and I stared at each other, unyielding.

39

Jael avoided me after that.

During the day, Mr. Benezet squired her about on errands and walks. At dinner he rhapsodized about the scenery with the enthusiasm of the inveterate guidebook reader, and in the evening he energetically filed away all her bills in a fine leather portfolio.

Perhaps they will make a match of it, I thought, not even truly believing it. No, I said it to punish myself, for I had refused to sit by the fire, and now I must bear the cold.

I had felt so light, so peaceful at the cliff's edge. I had wanted the dreadful choice to be hers—for her to answer the question *To be or not to be?* in my stead.

I had betrayed her the night of the fire, because I hadn't been sure I could trust her. I still wanted to be sure now. But there was no surety in this world, and no safety. It was time to put that by.

There was no path of truth or virtue. There was only choosing a direction to walk, or standing still. Act, or atrophy.

Jael was exercising her legs. What was I doing?

And so, alone with Tabby, I stretched my muscles of courage as much as I could bear—in other words, not much. But I came as close to the fire as I dared, then advanced another inch. I borrowed a novel from Lady Tassell and stayed up late reading by the light of an oil lamp.

I even replied *My mother was Jewish herself* to an uncharitable comment from the new nursery maid. And though my heart pounded and the girl grimaced, nothing momentous occurred.

After a week, the fire at Goldengrove had mostly burned out, though there were still smoldering places. We were informed that nothing could be retrieved from the keep—that we must not hope even for a body to bury.

The thick-walled tower had operated like a furnace, or a chimney, drawing air from the shattered lower windows and incinerating everything above, floor by floor. The walls themselves might yet fall if something disturbed them. At the first hard frost, perhaps.

I asked Hal, who had been to look, if *nothing* could truly be found within. I don't know whether he thought I regretted Sir Kit or my lost belongings, but his face was full of pity as he said, "I peeked in at the bottom, ma'am, and I could see all the way up to the sky."

Sir Kit's heir had come. Out of delicacy, no one said outright that it was to take possession. He was putting up in Rye, still calling himself Mr. Palethorp and still unable to venture inside his new property, for fear an apparently intact stair or floor or wall might crumble at a touch.

Though he had promised that if the house proved livable, he would retain as many of the staff as possible, most were already looking for new work. Mrs. Cross, determined to retain her post, was lodging with her sister in Rye. We heard she had taken to wandering the countryside, to spy out Goldengrove's purloined treasures gleaming in a workman's hut. Those who had not already pawned their prizes took fright and began bringing them to us, in hope of a reward.

Properly, most of the things belonged to the new baronet, but everyone had quickly learned he had no ready money. In fact, he had already arranged a loan from young Mr. Benezet—on such generous terms that he came to thank Jael for her part in it, and to meet his young cousin.

I was afraid to take Tabby in to meet him. He might resemble Sir Kit. He might be *like* Sir Kit. He might be miserable. He might be angry. He had no doubt built castles in Spain about the riches that might one day fall into his lap. Instead he had inherited an unprofitable farm, and a house-fire.

What had he been told about how the fire started?

What if Jael did something to give us away?

Courage, I told myself, and in I went. I chose my seat in the corner nearest the fire, and sat sewing a dress for Tabby's new doll.

Jael seemed entirely unself-conscious through the visit, as though there had been no reason for awkwardness at all. I think, even, she took a liking to him. I could not decide if that was a mark of perversity, or kindness.

At any rate, she agreed to pay the servants back-wages through

Michaelmas, and after he had gone, she gave Mr. Toogood *carte blanche to* buy back Goldengrove's spoils at any price he thought fair, and return them to the new baronet with her compliments. I comforted myself with the reflection that the butler's idea of a fair price was likely narrower than her own.

One day, when she had gone into Hastings on some business, I happened to pass the open kitchen door and catch sight of the butler frowning at something on the table, hidden from my view by a chair-back. I took another step, and recognized Jael's shellwork flowers.

I was no hard-nosed bargainer myself, for I let out an involuntary cry and rushed into the kitchen.

Mr. Toogood gave a resigned sigh and pushed a shilling across the table to the woman, before taking out his handkerchief to remove her fingerprints from the glass dome. I saw that a spray of bubble-snail willow catkins had broken off at some point in its ordeal, and lay crushed at the bottom of the dome.

"It's worth more than that," the woman said mutinously.

He raised his heavy brows. "I am not purchasing it. That is a reward for its safe return. Miss Oliver, you do recognize this item as rightfully belonging to Goldengrove, do you not?"

I nodded. "That is—no, it belongs to Lady Palethorp. It is her own handiwork."

The butler immediately wiped the disdain from his face. "Very lovely. Her ladyship has an artist's eye." And he set one of the maids to cleaning every last speck of dust from it.

"Will you send it to my room?" I asked, flushing. "I don't want Tabby to break it."

It was delivered to me in due time, the glass gleaming, the wooden base waxed, and the shells improbably clean. The broken catkins had vanished, and no trace remained of the thick clump of glue where they had been.

Jael came by as I was setting it on the window-sill. She stood quietly in the doorway, a stack of bandboxes in her hands, and my hands shook so badly I nearly knocked it to the floor.

"A new hatstand." A thread of amusement was in her voice.

I felt a pang for my father's wooden leg. "Would you like—that is, of course it is already yours—"

She laughed at me. "*You* must have salvaged it from Mr. Toogood."

"I am not a privateer. I do not expect to keep my prizes."

She shrugged. "Maybe you should."

So simply the longing started up in me, the desperate covetousness. She was beautiful, even dusty from the carriage, even when she dropped her packages helter-skelter on *my* bed and took off her new snail-shell chip straw hat and dropped it on top of them. She pulled the tortoiseshell comb out of her hair and balled up her fine veil, two yards of the best black lace I'd ever seen, crumpling it into the bonnet's crown.

I killed for her! I won her. She is mine to keep now—she said so herself—take her!

I was not a privateer, and I did not reach for her. But I had been giving my heart exercise, and I smiled shyly. "Then perhaps I should keep your new clothes, since you have put them on my bed." For once I almost managed to be arch.

She looked surprised. "Oh, those are for you."

I blinked.

"I haven't looked through them yet, but it should be some of your things from Lively St. Lemeston. When your friend Melpomene was here, she suggested I see if any could be found, and Lady Tassell gave me her daughter-in-law's direction." She surveyed the pile with satisfaction. "Mrs. Dymond succeeded better than I would have expected. Here, she sent you a letter. I asked for another copy of that dreadful book for Tabby, too. I hope to God it's in here somewhere."

Speechless, I picked up a box and tried to pry off the twine. It was knotted tightly and my hands were shaking, but I kept on yanking at it, as though somehow perseverance would make me look less foolish.

She laughed and began cutting all the strings with her new penknife (which had a mother-of-pearl handle and a chased silver blade, and which she insisted on letting Tabby hold, saying, *She can't open it*).

The first box I opened held Papa's recorder, mãe's paste hairpins, and one of the corset busks he had carved for her. I could not seem to think what to do.

Finally, I unfolded the scrap of paper clipped into one of the hairpins. *I'm so sorry, your mother's wedding ring was sold already*, it said in Mrs.

Dymond's handwriting. *It seemed indelicate to ask the bride to return it.* A fat tear fell on the paper, smearing the ink.

I set the things back in the box and stared at them.

Jael, pleased at the effect on me and impatient as ever, began opening boxes herself and piling things on the bed. A small pile, no doubt, to her, but I could not stop the tears trickling down my face. Two old dresses—vó's ragged scarf—a jumble of books, which Jael did not bother to shut when they flopped open—a hand-me-down spencer that had always dragged at my neck—Papa's medals—a pair of pattens.

Half of it I did not even want, but my heart beat nearly as fast at *Explanatory Notes Upon the New Testament, by John Wesley, M.A.* in yellowing paper covers as it did at the medals, for it meant someone had troubled to remember it was mine.

The pile was all scattered through with notes: *You liked this one, didn't you? I really don't know why, but one man's meat, &c.* tucked into a book; *Toogood promised to pack this safely, but if it breaks I'm sorry* rolled inside an ugly glass inkwell; and *Helen insists this was yours, but I never saw you in it* pinned to a wool muffler.

Mrs. Dymond must have seen me in it a hundred times. That made my heart fuller, somehow. Some things we forgot, some we couldn't understand; yet love remained.

Helen also insisted on retrimming your bonnet for you, I hope you don't mind. I set my old straw hat atop Jael's shellwork, brushing the little paper bluebells with my fingertips. I didn't love the giant blue satin rosettes she'd added at each ear, but Tabby would.

No one loves me, I had told myself all this time. Why had it felt so true? Vó had warned me against Sir Kit, and mãe had told me it was wrong to eat blood. Iphigenia had sent Lady Tassell to help me, and rushed to see me after the fire. My committee-minded friends had bustled about rescuing my odds and ends.

Honestly, Livvy, I don't know why I bother paying you compliments, when you never believe them.

"Oh, I forgot." Jael grinned ear to ear in a way that made me think she had not forgotten at all. She reached out into the hallway and produced my best guitar, which I'd left behind in Lively St. Lemeston. "I tuned it for you."

I burst into sobs, groping on the bed for one of Papa's handkerchiefs.

"Don't *cry*," she mimicked Tabby.

I laughed and blew my nose. When I emerged from the handkerchief, she was staring at me with a face of hard resolve. I faltered. "What is it?"

"There's one more thing." She rushed off, and returned with her arms wrapped around a shining leather album.

"That isn't mine." But she thrust it at me, and when I opened it to a strong smell of paste, *Commonplace Book of Deborah Oliver* looped across the title page in beautiful round-hand. Two scraps of paper fluttered out, pinned together. *Mrs. Peachey* **would** *send this wretched Anne Bradstreet poem about a house-fire, but she'll never know if you don't paste it in.*

I made a watery sound and traced the loops of the intricate *D* with my fingertip.

"Miss Macnamara's writing-mistress must have adored her," Jael said.

There wasn't much in it yet: a few pasted-in sheets of carefully copied verses and passages from the boardinghouse ladies, a handful of other acquaintances, and some officious people I didn't really know, but who wanted a part in my drama.

I would write to Iphigenia, and ask her for a new poem.

"Turn the page."

Had she written in it? My heart leapt—but it was not her handwriting on the loose sheet of paper tucked firmly into the binding. It was a smooth clerk's hand, small, the lines narrowly spaced. My eyes jumped down and down, uncomprehending. *Deborah Oliver…a sum of three thousand pounds, to be invested in the five percents…*

That was her handwriting at the bottom—her signature, anyway. *Jael Palethorp.* And there was Eleazar Benezet's next to hers. *Authorized agent of Benezet & Sons.*

"What would you write in my commonplace book?" she asked me.

Courage. I looked her in the face. "Is this a gift, or a bribe?" I asked quietly. "You don't have to buy my silence. I already said—"

She narrowed her eyes at me. "Yes, Artemisia, *you said.* You said twenty or thirty pounds a year was not enough to live on. You said I could not pretend us into equality. You said a governess and her employer could not be friends." She tapped a finger on the paper. "This is an annuity for life.

Now you are an independent woman, and may speak to me as freely as Elizabeth to Lady Catherine de Bourgh."

I stared at her.

She sighed. "I don't know why I'd buy your silence when the supply always so far outstrips demand. I wish Mr. Munk joy of you."

Independent. The word seemed to have nothing to do with me, any more than *self-reliant*—certainly nothing to do with how I felt about *her*. But I had not been through these last months to go a lamb to the slaughter now. I moved my fingertip, then wiggled my right hand. "Take a walk with me, then."

She chewed her lip, frowning. "Fine, put on your sloppily made hat and let's go."

"A little apprentice from the workhouse made that hat!" It *was* badly made, but it had been cheap and the girl had been proud to see me wear it.

"And now you can afford a better one."

I didn't want a better one. I wanted *mine*. I settled it over my cap, humming with contentment as it fitted perfectly to my head, and examined myself in the glass.

Damn Mrs. Dymond's sister anyway—she'd managed to arrange the flowers so the asymmetrical brim looked almost intentional, and those wretched puffs of blue satin *suited* me. It was less obvious that my face was too long, my jaw too wide, and my forehead too high and narrow.

It didn't hide the circles under my eyes, but after all one could not expect miracles. I tilted my mirror to see the rest of me.

I disliked my new dress. The sea-green printed cotton was too stiff and new, its white flowers too stark. My eye snagged on it, and so did my attention, especially when I moved and met unexpected resistance.

And yet—it would not resist me forever. The thought struck me sharply—*I* was like the sea. I would wear away this dress's rough edges, and make it submit to my swells and dips. Now my new shoes gave me blisters, but soon they would mold themselves to my feet.

I flexed my fingers in my stiff new gloves, and picked up the guitar Jael had redeemed for me. She tilted her head in surprise, but did not comment.

We turned towards the cliffs, towards the sight of the faint brown cloud still hanging in the air above Goldengrove. The sun was crisper today, but still smudged. It was easier to smear things than to make them clean again.

"Remind me to thank the servants for cleaning your shellwork," I said, knowing she would forget. I liked that, somehow. It felt so ordinary.

Despite the lingering haze the day was fine, very warm but not oppressive. The sails in the bay were round and smooth as pregnant bellies. The brisk wind pressed Jael's veil flat against her face until I could *almost* make out an expression—and then she huffed and put it back, picking a thread from her tongue. "Elie took me to see Mr. Munk today."

I felt a flash of jealousy at *Elie*, and a flash of nerves at *Mr. Munk*—the stronger because I had not been thinking of it. Because I had dared to hope, for a moment. "What did he ask you?"

"Oh, nothing much repeated several times over. I wept all over his blotter about how I'll never love another man, and how only my assurance that Kit's whole heart was mine bears me up in my grief. He won't dare ask you anything improper at the inquest. I'll faint dead away if he tries it."

I blinked. "And he believed you?"

She shrugged. "He twitched a great deal and said 'Just so' about six dozen times. Then I said I'd write to the coroner and offer to pay the expenses of the inquest instead of the county, so he ought not to hesitate in calling witnesses, for I would be glad to put them up overnight if necessary, and the jurors too. Of course, Mr. Munk positively forbade me to do any such thing." She laughed. "You know how much he hates the coroner."

"No," I said slowly. "I didn't know that."

She waved a hand. "Oh, I forgot, you're new to the neighborhood. Ask Lady Tassell if you don't believe me. The Rye jurats are solidly Tory so she hasn't much real influence here, but she keeps informed for the fun of it. The county gentlemen think the jurats make too much of themselves, you see, and Mr. Munk is always refusing to pay inquest costs. He thinks the coroner convenes juries on natural deaths so he can collect fees, and take bribes from the burghers to keep them off the jury rolls...."

I could feel my tiny store of courage leaching out of me. Why could I only be strong when she was weak? Would I let my moment pass by, and my fate be sealed?

But that was nonsense, too. My fate could not be decided in a moment.

I must decide again and again and again, every moment until my death. "I don't know what I would write in your commonplace book," I interrupted. "Something boring, probably. May I sing you a song?"

She raised her eyebrows. She looked unspeakably fine and rich, with her black dress perfectly fitted to her perfect bosom, her skirts draping like a fashion plate. Far above me.

Yes, I realized, ashamed. Her weakness had given me strength; her degradation had given me confidence. She would not need me anymore when the inquest was over. She could decide freely to take me or leave me, just as I could. I could not even marry her.

Would I wait to reach for happiness until I was sure of hearing good news—of only ever hearing good news again? I might as well wait until the sea was still.

I settled myself on a rock and peeled off my gloves.

Jael had replaced one of my guitar strings with a new one, which already needed tightening. I tuned it carefully, so I wouldn't make her wince.

In the sun, the mottling on my burned hand stood out starkly. But summer was nearly over. Soon I could wear mitts, and by next year it would have faded.

The memories—searing points of pain, Sir Kit's startled, unsuspecting eyes meeting mine—those would not fade so quickly. Could they be broken in, like a guitar string or a new boot? Or would they be as fresh in thirty years, like my grandmother's hand on my shoulder?

I had been so angry to think of her treacherous lover sleeping peacefully in the shade. Did I even want to wear my murder as comfortably as an old pair of boots?

Vó had done what I was doing now, hadn't she? What I hoped to do? She had been betrayed by a man she trusted. She had burned her own home to the ground and come away with only the clothes on her back. And then— she had loved her husband with her broken heart, and held her child in her broken hands. She had loved me, and I had loved her.

I shut my eyes, and felt her hand on my shoulder.

I wasn't sure, even as I opened my mouth, that any sound would come out. But my voice knew its cue and came in—weakly, for I had forgotten to fill my lungs. I paused for breath, and sang.

"I wish I was a red rosey bush
On the banks of the sea
And every time my true love would pass
She would pluck a rose out of me…"

The song was a drawn-out sort of thing, not designed to end either of our suspenses quickly. Meant to spin wool to, maybe, the foot slow on the pedal, the thread dribbling between the spinster's fingers.

I didn't look at Jael. I didn't need to. I could rarely say what I felt; I didn't like to be seen. I was not passionate in the ordinary way of things. But I knew how to make a sound box of my hollow chest. I knew Jael could hear my heart weeping.

"I wish I had a golden box
To put my true love in
I'd take her out, and I'd kiss her twice
Then I'd put her back again…"

I hoped she understood that was an apology, an acknowledgment of a wrong. I would explain it after, if I had to.

Of course I had started to cry. My voice grew high and nasal. I was mortified. I was afraid. I was miserable and ashamed. But I pried open my own chest, rib by rib, and let the air rush in.

Some decisions couldn't be taken back. Some things never quite mended. That wasn't injustice, but a simple law of physics: time did not flow backward. Sometimes we railed drunkenly against our pain, and sometimes we laughed and forgot it. Sometimes we remembered, and laughed anyway.

Better to suffer and lose sleep, than for the heart to atrophy.

"…And every time my true love would pass
She would pluck a rose out of me."

I set my palm over the strings, to still them. I couldn't speak. I couldn't look at her. I couldn't move to wipe away my tears. If she didn't love me, I would be pitiable and grotesque to her.

For this single moment, I believed the risk was worth the reward. Then she kissed me, and it *was*.

Author's Note

Thank you for reading The Wife in the Attic! I hope you enjoyed Miss Oliver's story.

You've just finished Book 1 in my Rye Bay series. Book 2 will follow Iphigenia Lemmon in her job as lady's companion to Mrs. Musgrave.

Would you like to know when my next book is available? Sign up for updates at RoseLerner.com or follow me on twitter at @RoseLerner. You can also support me on Patreon, and receive weekly sneak peeks at what I'm working on!

Reviews help other readers find books. I appreciate all reviews, positive and negative.

Did you know that I've written a series of historical romance novels about Lively St. Lemeston, Miss Oliver's home at the beginning of the story? *Sweet Disorder* is the full story of Phoebe Dymond's whirlwind courtship by Lady Tassell's son. *True Pretenses* is a marriage of convenience story about Ash and Lydia Cahill, who you saw playing marbles in the first chapter of this book—Ash is really a con artist named Asher Cohen, and Lydia isn't as decorous as she appears!

Listen to the Moon is about Sukey and John Toogood (who marry to get a plum job), and "A Taste of Honey" is a sexy novella set in a bakery (you didn't meet Robert and Betsy in this book, but they did make the hot cross bun!).

Visit my website for *The Wife in the Attic* extras, including deleted scenes (eleven of them!), podcast and video interviews, music, a bibliography, historical research, and maps.

Turn the page to learn more about my other romances.

MORE BOOKS BY
Rose Lerner

LIVELY ST. LEMESTON
Sweet Disorder
True Pretenses
Listen to the Moon
A Taste of Honey (novella)

To find out when new Lively St. Lemeston books release,
sign up at RoseLerner.com!

RYE BAY
The Wife in the Attic (audiobook)
The Girl in the Cellar (working title, forthcoming)

To find out when new Rye Bay books release,
sign up at RoseLerner.com!

NOT IN ANY SERIES
In for a Penny
A Lily Among Thorns
All or Nothing
(novella, first published in the *Gambled Away* anthology)
Promised Land
(novella, first published in the *Hamilton's Battalion* anthology)

TURN THE PAGE for an excerpt from *Sweet Disorder*,
in which a wounded officer tries to find a husband for a prickly widow to
help win a local election.

Sweet Disorder

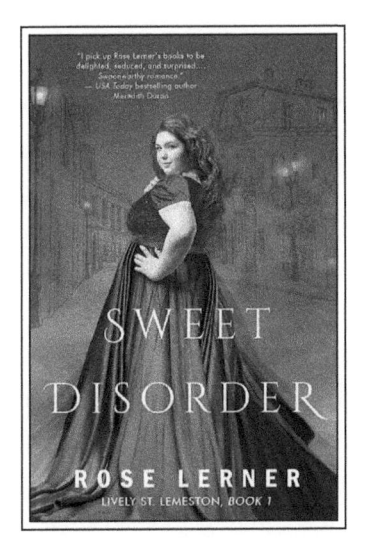

Campaigning has never been sweeter...

Prickly newspaperman's widow Phoebe Sparks has vowed never to marry again. Unfortunately, the election in Lively St. Lemeston is hotly contested, and the little town's charter gives Phoebe the right to make her husband a voter—if she had one.

The Honorable Nicholas Dymond has vowed never to get involved in his family's aristocratic politicking. But now his army career is over for good, his leg and his self-confidence both shattered in the war against Napoleon. Helping his little brother win an election could be just what the doctor ordered.

So Nick decamps to the country, under strict orders to marry Phoebe off to *somebody* before the polls open. He's intrigued by the lovely widow from the moment she shuts the door in his face.

Phoebe is determined not to be persuaded by the handsome earl's son, no matter how charming he is. But when disaster strikes her young sister, she is forced to consider selling her vote—and her hand—to the highest bidder.

As election intrigue thickens, bringing them face to face with their own deepest desires, Phoebe and Nick must decide which vows are worth keeping, and which must be broken...

Contains elections, confections, and a number of erections.

EXCERPT: *SWEET DISORDER*

Chapter 1

Phoebe sat at the foot of her bed, her elbows propped on the deal table she'd placed under the window. She was supposed to be writing her next Improving Tale for Young People. But the shingled wall and gabled roof of Mrs. Humphrey's boarding house across the way were so much more absorbing than the tragic tale of poor Ann, who had been got with child by a faithless young laird and was now starving in a ditch.

If Phoebe strained, she could even see a sliver of street two stories below.

The problem was that she couldn't quite decide what would happen to Ann next. Tradition dictated that either the girl die there, or that her patient suffering inspire the young laird to reform and carry her off to a church, but…that was so *boring*. Every Improving Tale-teller in England had already written it. It had been old when Richardson did it seventy years ago.

But she couldn't afford to waste this precious time in daydreams. It was washing day, and Sukey, the maid she and her landlady shared with Mrs. Humphrey, would soon be back from her shopping to help. Then tomorrow Phoebe had to piece her quilt for the Society for Bettering the Condition of the Poor's auction in December, and what with one thing and another, she wouldn't have any more time to write until Tuesday. She had promised this story to the editor of the *Girl's Companion* in time for typesetting three weeks from now.

There were footsteps on the stairs and a knock at her door. *I do not feel relieved*, she thought firmly. Standing and crossing into her sitting room, she opened the door to discover—

"Mr. Gilchrist." She felt much less relieved.

The dapper Tory election agent stood at the top of the narrow spiral of stairs leading to her attic. A few drops of rain glistened in his sleek brown hair, on his broadcloth shoulders, and on the petals of the pink-and-white carnation—the colors of the local Tory party—in his buttonhole.

Drat. If it was raining, washing would have to be put off until she had Sukey again next Friday. And she'd have to keep a careful eye on the bucket under the leak in her roof to make sure it didn't overflow.

"Ah, you know of me," he said with an oily smile. "Pleased to make your acquaintance, Mrs. Sparks."

Oh, his smile is not *oily. Prejudice combined with the urge to narrate is a terrible thing.* She smiled back. "And I'm pleased to make yours. But I should warn you, I'm Orange-and-Purple, and so are my voting friends." There was a general election on in England to choose a new Parliament. While many districts could go decades with the same old MPs, the Lively St. Lemeston seats always seemed to be hotly contested.

He tilted his head. "Your father and your husband were Whigs. But from what I hear, you're an independent woman. Decide for yourself." His expression turned rueful. He couldn't be more than twenty. "Besides, it's starting to rain and I'd rather not go outside again just yet."

She sighed. He was good at this. "May I offer you some tea?"

"I'd love some."

Maybe his smile was oily after all. Phoebe went to take the kettle from the fire, but she didn't bring out the cheese rolls from the cupboard. They cost a penny each, and she wanted them for herself.

Mr. Gilchrist waited patiently while she topped off the teapot with hot water. She didn't add any tea. A second steeping was good enough for him.

"I know you're a busy and practical woman, so I'll come straight to the point," he said as she poured. "Thank you, I take it black." A politic choice, visiting a poor widow. "Under the Lively St. Lemeston charter, every freeman of the town has the right to vote for up to two candidates in an election."

"I know that, Mr. Gilchrist." Men always wanted to explain things, didn't they?

"Also under the Lively St. Lemeston charter," he continued, clearly having no intention of modifying his planned oration, "the eldest daughter of a freeman who died without sons can make her husband a freeman."

Phoebe tapped her foot on the floor. "My husband is dead," she pointed out, since apparently they were telling each other things they both already knew.

The young man took a sip of tea. He had an eye for a dramatic pause, anyway; she had to give him credit for that. "You could marry again."

She blinked. "What?"

"Mr. Dromgoole, our candidate, would be happy to assist in finding any prospective spouse a lucrative place in his chosen profession." His smile didn't falter. Definitely oily.

"You think I'm going to get *married* just to get you extra *votes*? The polls are in a month!" She set her still-empty teacup back on the table with a rattle.

"Allow me." He put a small lump of sugar into the cup, poured it half full of tea, and then filled it almost to the brim with milk.

"You found out how I like my tea?" she asked incredulously.

There was a hint of boyish smugness in his smile now. "I know how you like your men too. If you'll just meet my nominee—"

She stood. "How dare you? Get out of my house."

It wasn't her house, though. It was her two cramped attic rooms. His eyes drifted for a moment, letting that sink in, reminding her of how much more she could have if she married.

He might know how she liked her tea, but he didn't know a thing about her if he thought she'd be happier in a fine house that belonged to her husband. These two rooms were *hers*.

He rose. "I'll give you a few days to think it over. A message at the Drunk St. Leonard will always reach me."

She went to the door and jerked it open. "Even love wouldn't convince me to marry again. An election certainly won't." She'd always had a tendency to bend the truth in favor of a neat bit of dialogue. But *love wouldn't convince me to marry again unless I were sure it wouldn't become a bickering, resentful mess like the first time* just didn't sound the same.

Mr. Gilchrist shook his head mournfully and bounded down the stairs. He passed out of sight—and there was a squawk and the sound of bouncing fruit. "I'm dreadfully sorry," he said, not sounding very sorry.

Phoebe started down to help Sukey collect the groceries, turning the corner just in time to see the girl pocket something. "Pardon me, did you just bribe my maid?"

"It's not a bribe." Mr. Gilchrist tossed a couple of apples back in the basket with unerring aim. "It's damages for the fruit."

She considered throwing an apple at him as he disappeared around the next bend, but even in October the fruit wasn't cheap enough to justify it. "The Orange-and-Purples would never stoop this low," she shouted after him instead.

"Don't count on it," Mr. Gilchrist called back.

"I hope he's right," Sukey said cheerily. "I could use another shilling."

Read the rest of Chapter One and buy the book at
smarturl.it/SweetDisorder